THE ART
FALLIN

Also by Deborah Lawrenson

Hot Gossip
Idol Chatter
The Moonbathers

DEBORAH LAWRENSON

THE ART OF FALLING

arrow books

Published by Arrow Books in 2005

1 3 5 7 9 10 8 6 4 2

Copyright © Deborah Lawrenson 2003

Deborah Lawrenson has asserted her right under the Copyright,
Designs and Patents Act 1988 to be identified as the author of this work

First published in the United Kingdom in 2003 by Stamp Publishing

Arrow Books
The Random House Group Limited
20 Vauxhall Bridge Road, London, SW1V 2SA

Random House Australia (Pty) Limited
20 Alfred Street, Milsons Point, Sydney,
New South Wales 2061, Australia

Random House New Zealand Limited
18 Poland Road, Glenfield
Auckland 10, New Zealand

Random House (Pty) Limited
Endulini, 5a Jubilee Road, Parktown 2193, South Africa

The Random House Group Limited Reg. No. 954009

www.randomhouse.co.uk

A CIP catalogue record for this book
is available from the British Library

Papers used by Random House
are natural, recyclable products made from wood grown in
sustainable forests. The manufacturing processes conform to
the environmental regulations of the country of origin

ISBN 0 09 948189 8

Typeset by
Palimpsest Book Production Limited, Polmont, Stirlingshire

Printed and bound in Great Britain by
Bookmarque Ltd, Croydon, Surrey

Acknowledgements

This story is based on several real events, but the characters are completely fictitious. Any errors in fact or misinterpretations are mine alone.

I am immensely grateful to ex-Lance Corporal Norman Yates of 503 Field Company, Royal Engineers, for long conversations and for permission to draw on his wonderfully anecdotal article *Lighter Moments of Service*. I was also privileged to meet Colonel Dillon Snell, US Army (retired) who kindly sent me a copy of his memoirs *My First War – Italy 1944-45*.

Hall's antiquarian bookshop in Tunbridge Wells kept me in ample supplies of research material. I am particularly indebted to Leonard Melling's *With The Eighth In Italy* (Torch Publishing, 1955); *Italian Art, Life and Landscape* by Bernard Wall (William Heinemann, 1956); *Tuscan Retreat* by Vernon Bartlett (Chatto and Windus, 1965); and Richard Lamb's authoritative *War in Italy 1943-1945, A Brutal Story* (John Murray, 1993).

I also thank the authors of the many articles which have appeared in the national press and New Civil Engineer magazine for vital information about the projects to stabilise the Leaning Tower of Pisa and the work of Professor John Burland of Imperial College, London.

Heartfelt thanks to the following people for their invaluable help and support in bringing this book to its present form: Joy, Stan and Helen Lawrenson; Robert Rees and Phil Rees, who published the first edition through Stamp Publishing; Richard Cook, Sonia Ribeiro; Jeremy Thompson at Troubador; and my wonderful friends who did so much to help it along the way, especially Bernard Behrens, Lucy and Jonathan Hills, Helen Minsky, Felicia Mockett, Sue Percival, Louise Piper and Josine Thanou Kamerling.

Of all the many booksellers whose support was so crucial, I am particularly grateful to Nina Woods at Ottakar's in Bromley; Venetia Vyvyan at G Heywood Hill; Leila Gilholy at Ottakar's, Tunbridge Wells; Polly Gurdon at Waterstone's, Tunbridge Wells; Angela Porritt and Freddie Barnes at John Adams Books in Tonbridge; and Sheila O'Reilly at The Beckenham Bookshop.

Huge thanks too to Stephanie Cabot, Jamison Stoltz (and his train journey to Cambridge), Kate Elton and Justine Taylor.

And never overlooking the contribution made by Madeleine Rees, especially during our trips to Italy.

I

1

Isabel Wainwright was six when she saw a picture of the Leaning Tower of Pisa for the first time.

Any moment now and she will finally see it in life. The decision to come has not been easy. So far, she has no regrets. It is a delicate balance, though: travelling both hopefully and with defences intact from the past to whatever lies ahead; her heart pounding in the hard pinch of the present.

In the taxi from the airport, Isabel stares intently out of the window at the streets and buildings, as if she can make herself familiar with them by sheer force of will.

The evening is silky warm. A sensuous light drapes the palazzos lining the Lung'Arno, the colours apricot and umber beneath the indigo mountain backdrop. The city seems empty and shuttered. At the top of one of these elegant, aristocratic buildings, a line of washing is strung between two tiny windows.

'You have come to Pisa before?' The driver cuts across her thoughts.

'No, never. I've always wanted to . . . but, no.'

'You have holiday? Business?'

'I . . . well . . . ' It is a good question. How should she think of this trip? 'A little of both, I suppose,' says Isabel. 'I've come for a ceremony.'

'Aah!' The driver grins, a leer in the rear-view mirror, confident that he knows exactly what she is saying.

Isabel lets him think what he likes.

He drops her at a hotel on the Via Santa Maria. It seems comfortable – elegant even – although the prices are reasonable. It seems she has struck lucky.

Her room on the second floor looks out on a bustling street. She cranes to see the end of it as she dials the telephone number she has been given for the Criachi family. She has promised she will let them know she has arrived safely. But, even after several attempts, the number is engaged.

Isabel can wait no longer.

The light is fading rapidly as she hurries towards the Piazza dei Miracoli where the great marble cathedral stands with its pepperpot baptistry and failed bell tower. There are thick steel cables wrapped around the tower. No visitors are allowed to climb up; it has been closed to the public for more than a decade. The tower bends towards her, straining in its harness.

She has a picture on a wall of her office: a framed print of a drawing of the Leaning Tower of Pisa by Edward Cresy and G. L. Taylor, a pair of early nineteenth-century English architects who had made a survey of the famous bell tower. Their obscure names have been a part of her life for so long that it seems the most natural thing in the world for her to have a print of their drawing on the wall. Most people – if they notice it at all – take it to be a grand visual joke in the same way that others pin up newspaper cartoons that encapsulate the particular humour and despair of their working hours, for Isabel works as a chartered surveyor in a medium-sized firm in the south of England. She ensures that houses are safe: inspecting foundations and damp courses, assessing cracks in walls, making judgements about the true solidity of what appears to be whole.

She feels a tremor in her legs as she walks closer.

Her father showed her the picture of it in a large red book. It appealed to her sense of drama; even at that early age her practical tendencies were already in place. How long would it be before the tower fell? Surely – a delicious thrill – it would be soon. Naturally the expectation faded, as she enquired periodically of its tantalising progress towards destruction only to be told that – somehow – it had failed to topple. She was given renewed hope when she discovered, in another book, that in 1902 the campanile in Venice had crashed spectacularly into a pile of red rubble. It was promptly rebuilt, which had seemed pointless to her, given that the lucky Venetians had had their fun and it was unlikely to fall twice.

Her father Tom was obsessed with the leaning tower, although she has never been sure exactly why that should be, only that it became one of his defining quirks of character.

As a buildings surveyor, Isabel is naturally interested in (and more than a little appalled by) the fact that the foundations of such an ambitious project were set at the ridiculously shallow depth of less than three metres, and then on a pile of dry masonry. This rested on alluvial subsoil, which, although it was relatively cohesive on the surface, tended to

give way at any depth. The miscalculations were fundamental, right at the start. The first stone was laid on 9 August
1173; in this place of uncertainties, the date is confirmed by
an inscription to the right of the entrance door. By the time
the third ring of pillars was completed, the slide had begun.
The soil beneath it was subsiding.

Tom Wainwright had been missing for twenty years when
the letter came.

The envelope was thin with an indecipherable postmark
over an odd speckle of stamps.

'Italy,' said Patricia through tight lips, as she allowed Isabel
to take it.

After Tom went away, Isabel's mother Pat became a reader
of detective stories and solver of crossword puzzles, unwilling
to speak of him. It was her way, Isabel rationalised, of
reassuring herself that there was order in the wild uproar
of life, and that she was able to sit in her armchair and find
answers. The police told them that people who went missing
could be found, but only if they wanted to be.

But two months ago it was Patricia and Isabel who were
found.

Pat broke the news.

'Your Aunt Margaret has rung. She said she was going to
get in touch with you.'

This was rare, now, and Isabel acknowledged as much.
Contact with her father's sister had never been easy.

'She's had a phone call from someone at the district council.'
A sharp exhalation of breath from Patricia proclaimed the
difficulty she had with the crux of this information. 'Whoever

it was – they were trying to find your father. Something to do with . . . Italy.'

'I see.' A lump formed in Isabel's throat. 'Go on.'

'It seems there's a village where they want to . . . honour him.' Pat pursed her lips tight with the irony of that. 'For what he did in the war.'

'What was that? I mean, I know he fought there – but what in particular?'

'I'm not sure.'

'He never mentioned anything that might – ?'

'No.'

'Does Margaret know?'

'I've no idea.'

Over the following weeks they received a series of telephone calls. An official letter arrived at Patricia's house, expressing heartfelt gratitude for her husband's brave actions. Gradually it transpired that, after all these years, a group of village elders in northern Italy intended to name a small piazza in honour of ex-army Corporal Tom Wainwright, for services rendered above and beyond the call of duty.

They were delighted – more than delighted – to have made contact with his family. The chances of doing so had been slim. More than one stroke of luck had been involved.

After much discussion between Margaret and Pat – the first time in many years the two women had spoken – it was decided that an honest reply was required. The request could not be ignored and neither could Tom Wainwright's brave actions – Margaret was firm on that.

So the three women wrote back to the Italians, hoping for a fair translation by the bureaucrats of Perugia, that they felt he would be delighted to accept the accolade but they were unable to verify this, for they had had no contact with him for some twenty years.

A letter was dispatched in return. The villagers of Petriano were keen to press ahead with their naming ceremony and could see no reason why, in the end, they should not name their new small piazza after whomsoever they pleased, and would be glad to accept the surviving womenfolk's acquiescence as sufficient.

So an invitation was issued and Isabel has travelled to Italy to witness the auspicious occasion on behalf of her father. Her mother has declined the invitation.

There has already been a misunderstanding, however. Somewhere, lost in translation, a crucial but mistaken impression has been given. The heroic Tom Wainwright may or may not be dead. His family simply does not know.

The women of his family – including Patricia, who calls herself his widow these days – have constructed their lives on not knowing. Isabel, in particular, knows that it is not only possible to live with uncertainty, but that possessing the skill to do so is essential.

Next morning Isabel takes the autostrada east towards Florence, then hives off south towards Arezzo. The white Fiat car she has hired at the airport goes surprisingly fast. The road is smooth. She is glad to clear her mind of everything but the road and its dangerous swooping bends.

Umbria. Now she is impatient to see signs for Assisi and Perugia. She opens the windows and lets the breeze whip her face.

At Petriano, she comes down a steep bend and sees a restaurant-bar. She swings the car sharply into a small square and parks. Her heart is beating fast from the wild drive and, she has to admit, a degree of nervous anticipation. She takes a deep breath and forces herself to walk slowly, calmly, to the small terrace where a waitress is clearing tables.

At the bar Isabel orders a beer and takes it outside to study her surroundings. The main part of the village appears to be nestling in a large shallow hollow near the top of a hill. There are houses perched higher up, and there are cascades of roofs down among the trees. It is a place that seems to be built on the vertical.

The waitress delivers a large slice of pizza. On the plate is a picture of a man serving spaghetti, the colours and outlines scraped off by years of use. Isabel forces herself to eat most of it, used to days out on site when lunch is whatever chance decides. After ordering coffee, she wanders back to the car and, with deliberate casualness, returns with the road map.

'*Scusi, signora? Le Macchie?*' she asks the middle-aged waitress as she sets down the cup.

'*Sì?*' It is a question.

'Ah . . .' Isabel points at the open map.

'*Turista?*' The waitress smiles.

Isabel hesitates, unsure whether to try to explain.

The woman tries again. '*Tedesca?*' she asks, hand open towards Isabel.

'No . . . *Inglese.*'

'Aaah.' She is nodding. There is a tiny shift in her face, a subtle warming. It is not that she was unfriendly when she thought Isabel was probably German, but now Isabel senses that she is being offered, very subtly, helpfulness of a higher gear.

'*Ca Lo Spelli? Famiglia Criachi?*'

'*Sì, sì.*'

With a mixture of nods and smiles and pointing – and then a tracing of fingers on the wiggling lines of the map – the woman tells her what she needs to know.

Isabel leaves a good tip on the saucer.

Petriano is larger than she had expected, which is good. She wants to be able to ask questions with some degree of discretion. This may be impossible, of course. In a place where families have been interwoven for centuries, and talk is the currency of day-to-day life, news blows and swirls around the café, the shops and the bar like a soft breeze, freshening and invigorating all social contact. This is a place where the women gather to exchange gossip at the delicatessen counter in the tiny supermarket, where Signora Monti holds sway over the parmesan and the conversation in equal measure, and where a growing line of customers is regarded not as cause to hasten the service but as a pleasing addition to the party.

On a quiet day early in April, Isabel reasons, a lone female stranger in a white rental car, who produces a map and asks for Ca Lo Spelli and Le Macchie will be good for at least ten minutes of speculation.

Up the hairpin-bend climb away from the main square, Isabel catches up with a wheezing three-wheeler Piaggio, a tiny truck fashioned from an ancient motorcycle. It grinds pigeon-toed up the arduous slope emitting noxious black puffs. Away from the sleepy dustiness of the hollow there are grand houses thrusting square towers into the fresh hilltop air.

The first time she goes too far and turns back at a sign for Faustino. Retracing her tracks on the right side of the road, she finds the turning easily. Round an inauspicious bend she is suddenly in an avenue of gnarled cypress trees, which frame a sumptuous villa with such perfection that the effect is of driving towards an illusion in sepia. She cannot see the extent of the villa, nor begin to imagine the treasures stored inside.

Close by, behind a wall, is a honey stone house, grand on a domestic, country scale and fringed on either side by sentinel cypress trees, which are young and straight-backed compared with those of the avenue. This could be it.

Isabel parks the car on the road, not sure enough that she has come to the right place to surge straight into the driveway. Nor to overlay these first impressions with thoughts of her father, that this might have been somewhere he knew, where he returned on a summer's evening to drink on the terrace, where he strode around to survey the land and helped to build cosy fires in the depths of winter. She cannot allow herself to do that. So she walks to the doorstep, knocks and waits.

A youngish woman comes to the door.

'Fabrizia?' asks Isabel.

'Isabel Wainwright?'

She nods.

'At last!' cries Fabrizia, leading the way inside.

In a long room that is part kitchen part day room, with an atmosphere like the snug of a country pub, an elderly man is sitting at the head of a table. Sunshine haloes him from a window behind.

'Pappi,' begins the woman and continues in rapid sparks of an Italian dialect Isabel cannot follow. Isabel studies her as she speaks. She has sharply cut short hair, plummy with henna. Her nose is long and straight, an Etruscan nose in profile. She is wearing a rough sweater and long linen skirt, but no country apron of a garment; these are well-cut, urban clothes.

Isabel stands expectantly as a smile begins to reveal the old man's tobacco-stained teeth. The sun makes chasms of the deep lines radiating from his eyes.

'Signorina Wainwright, this is my father, Signor Criachi.'

At this, he begins, with some effort, to lever himself from his chair. Isabel takes a step forward, her hand outstretched. He takes it, but then pulls her towards him in an awkward hug that threatens to topple them both. His grip is surprisingly strong. When he releases her he says, still grinning and pointing to himself, 'Massimo.'

'Isabel,' she replies.

Isabel is unsure how to proceed. They are both looking at her and nodding. There is affection in this, a softness to their stares that seems to hint that she is no ordinary stranger but some kind of lost member of the family. Appearances are being assessed for a resemblance. Her person in the flesh is being weighed against their expectations.

'We are so pleased you are here at last,' says Fabrizia.

'I am very happy too.'

The brown skin on the old man's face is pitted and wrinkled as a walnut when he smiles, which is often. She cannot read the expression in his slack lips when they relax. She is invited to sit at the table, and Fabrizia busies herself with glasses and a jug of peach juice.

The door to a rear terrace is open and Isabel can see newly chopped wood stacked neatly, its splinters and offcuts still on the concrete to be cleared. There are a couple of cats dozing in the sun. Herbs are planted within a cook's stride of the doorstep. Beyond is a small but vigorous kitchen garden.

Massimo is still appraising her. 'So . . . Tom Wainwright's daughter . . .' he says in an Italian she can follow. 'So young – as young as my daughter. And beautiful . . . *bella*.'

Isabel smiles and shakes her head at the overgenerosity of the compliment.

Probably it is the habit of a lifetime, but there is genuine warmth here, as if he feels he already knows her.

'I can see him in your face – not too much, but he is there,' Massimo is saying. His eyes glitter. He is flirting with her, just a little. It is so gentle, so ingrained and practised that he seems to do it automatically. He must be in his nineties, she thinks; of course I seem young, to him. And he knew Tom as I never did, when he was young.

'We must drink wine together, on the terrace, Isabella. The beautiful daughter of Tom Wainwright! And we will talk, too – of wonderful times, of music and romance . . .'

'Pappi!' Fabrizia sighs.

As Isabel leaves he pops her a huge wink. She smiles back at the indomitability of his spirit.

'The next farm, it is the place where we think it will be nice for you to stay,' Fabrizia says. 'It is not like a hotel, but in summer they have visitors – tourists. There are nice apartments, and you can be very comfortable and a little bit private.'

'That sounds lovely. Thank you.' Isabel is pleased; more than that, she is delighted by their thoughtfulness.

'If you want to go there to see – I will take you when you are ready?'

A sign at the turning off the road reads: Agriturismo. Isabel and Fabrizia are in the hire car, which is lurching alarmingly. The dusty path is a shifting pattern of bumps and ruts, already set hard after the spring rains. It seems to go on for a couple of kilometres, past several unsigned turnings. Isabel wonders how any but the most intrepid tourists ever made their way to the beds at the farms without losing heart and turning back.

At last they come to what looks at first glance to be only a small house. But as they get out of the car and approach, Isabel sees that this is only the end of a long, low, two-storey building, a farmhouse of peachy-coloured plaster. Vigorous climbing plants scramble here and there up the walls as if to anchor it to the hilltop. It is a large house with no grand design; a building that has evolved to suit its use over several centuries. Doors and windows and outside staircases occur along its length apparently at random, giving the impression of a row of labourers' cottages making up the whole.

At the far end, making the building a long L shape, a tiny chapel is attached. At the apex of its shallow-pitched roof a bell hangs, silhouetted against the sky.

The house points along a spur of the hill; on either side the land tumbles away, in terraces of kitchen garden planting to the east and in steep woodland to the west. A gravel path leads along the sunny side, and at the end of the house there is a loggia of three impressive arches and an area of gravel where two cars are parked. A breeze catches the plants in pots by a doorway and ruffles the leaves. A dog barks, then another. They approach the door that looks to Isabel as if it might be a side entrance to the kitchen. Fabrizia does not need to ring the bell.

Across the grass to greet them come pigs and an inquisitive flock of geese.

Elsa and Bruno Sarna are a couple in their early forties. They appear from different directions, but with the same shout and hiss at the geese, shooing them away. The pigs they leave to their own devices.

Fabrizia performs the introductions. Like Massimo Criachi, they embrace Isabel when she holds out her hand.

Elsa is slight but strong, her face is tanned and creased with chronic tiredness and laughter lines. Her brown hair is caught back in a ponytail. There is an earthiness about her that is reassuring.

Bruno is stocky, slightly bow-legged in his determined, efficient trotting about the farm. His manner is relaxed, the twinkling chocolate eyes promising fun. Yet, when he sees Isabel for the first time, he is earnest, reverential almost, although clearly this is not for her but for Tom. Both he and Elsa speak excellent English. They are parents to four boys.

'Each one worse than the other,' explains Elsa cheerfully.

Elsa shows Isabel to her apartment. It is on the first floor, reached by a flight of outside stairs. It is the conversion of what might once have been a granary or hayloft. Now it is a comfortable holiday let: a sitting room with stone-flagged floor, beams made of whole tree trunks stained dark brown and varnished, a fully equipped kitchen, cupboards set roughly into the walls. A wood-burning stove stands in the corner, with a basket of logs. To the side of this room is a large bedroom with a pretty wrought-iron bedstead and whitewashed walls. In addition there is a modern bathroom. Every surface is spotlessly clean.

'It's lovely!' says Isabel. 'Thank you so much.'

'It's very little, that we can do, to say thank you,' says Elsa. 'You know, this is the place where we found the old book, with your father's initials in it.'

'I still can't quite believe it.'

'It was good luck.'

'The house – that address – was knocked down in the nineteen sixties. It just happened that the official letter from Italy landed on the desk of a council worker whose father had once been a postman. The retired postman remembered the condemned row of cottages, and the name. That's how they managed to find my Aunt Margaret – Tom's sister.'

'She did not want to come?' asks Elsa.

'She's old now, and . . . she thought it best not to.' Isabel hesitates. 'Tell me about you – how long have you lived here? It looks wonderful . . .'

'It is wonderful. We've lived here since Bruno's father died ten years ago, but Bruno has known it all his life. He knows all its corners and awkward steps, all its strangeness and shifts in temperature. Don't get him started on the stories of his family!'

Elsa gives Isabel some keys. 'Bruno and I will be somewhere around when you want to find us,' she says and leaves her to her thoughts.

Isabel puts her travel bag on the bed, but does not unpack it. Instead she goes into the large room and sits for a while on a window seat. Below her she has the top of a vine-covered pergola, under which a courtyard holds chairs and an iron table. There are the geese wandering around the grass, honking their superiority over the jumpy, scurrying hens. Beyond, where the land slips away into wilderness, there are tall pines and limes and ilexes. Down below are scrubby olive trees, but above, between the outlines of the sentry pines, is the cloudy blue of distant hills. The sunlight is intensifying behind them now, burning their fringes as the long afternoon dies.

It is evening when Isabel descends to look for her hosts. She feels relaxed, optimistic; simply pleased to be in this place and curious about what she will see of their lives. She is taking one moment at a time.

The outside stairs lead down to the rear of the farmhouse, where the practical business of running the small estate is more in evidence. The other holiday apartments are empty, for it is not yet the tourist season and there is no reason for the rabbit hutches, and snaking hosepipes, and machinery awaiting repair, and the rusting motorcycle to be crammed away behind picturesque outhouse doors. A lolloping rabbit makes its way down to the vegetable patch. Pine cones have rolled on to the path.

She knocks at various doors at the back of the house and gently pulls open one or two of them, but she does not see Elsa or Bruno. At one point she hears shouts that she takes to be from their boys, the eldest of whom is eleven.

The door of the chapel is open and she goes in. It is larger inside than it appeared outside; part of it, she works out, has been set into the house. The walls are a worn whitewash. The splintered chapel artefacts exhale a dusty Catholic scent. There is a single small window at the far end.

A rough red carpet runs up to a wooden platform, which in turn abuts a stone altar on which is placed a statue of the Virgin Mary, worried-looking, hands together in prayer. Two triple candlesticks stand guard over her. Above her, centred over the altar, is a carving of Christ on the cross, which sends a shiver down her spine. It is a rough carving, stained with dark varnish, but in its simplicity there is something achingly familiar, something modern perhaps, which disturbs her. On the wall to one side hangs a tide-marked print of La Madonna Addolorata.

It occurs to Isabel for a fleeting second that she could add her own pleas to those already whispered into this still air, but she does not. It is the tug of yearning, not of belief.

There are two wooden pews facing the altar, with kneeling steps in front. And, as Isabel turns round slowly to take in the full picture, she sees that, to the right of the entrance, there is a shack of a confession box, its mystery cracking apart with dryness and worms tunnelling.

There is a stone bowl set into the door frame. She guesses it has not seen holy water for many years; but it is used as a shelf for a large box of matches. She slips out, feeling suddenly intrusive.

In the gathering darkness Isabel makes her way further into the gardens, then the small orchard of apple and plum trees. There is a large swimming pool to the side of the orchard. She can see enough to make out that she has come to the end of the high spit of land and that the hill she stands on tumbles away beyond a wire fence. The north star is out, brighter than she has ever seen it.

As she retraces her steps, she can hear the pigs snorting

and carousing from their shady dell. And there are suddenly footsteps to her right.

'Isabel?' It is Elsa. She comes alongside. 'I have been feeding the pigs. So greedy!' One small boy is with her. 'This is Alessandro, our youngest.'

'Hello, Alessandro. I've been looking at the sky. It's so clear here. Just beautiful.'

Elsa laughs, although Isabel does not understand precisely why.

'He loved it here. He was so happy,' she says. 'That's what they all say.'

Isabel does not realise immediately that Elsa is talking about Tom.

She is intrigued by the way that Elsa has spoken of a man she cannot have known personally but who has clearly become real – or rather, familiar – to her through repeated stories of him. What is also disconcerting is the casual, affectionate tone of her words; it is a way of speaking about Tom that has not been used for decades by his own family.

2

'I have invited some people to have dinner with us tonight,' says Elsa. 'Some of the members of the committee. They are all so happy you have come. I thought it would be nice for you to meet them before the ceremony tomorrow.'

Elsa does not even begin cooking until just before nine. Then the telephone shrills and a lengthy, excitable conversation ensues. A dog's cut paw is attended to. The chickens are fed. The boys are still running around shouting as she orders them – yet again – to get ready for bed. A farmhand arrives to detail the events of his day.

The cooker is an old-fashioned monstrosity, blackened with age and heat. The wooden cupboards are overflowing. But Elsa is imperturbable. There is a quality in her deft movements through the chaos that makes Isabel think she will nonetheless produce a feast.

Isabel offers to help and is politely waved away. She slinks off, happy to find her own sanctuary for a while. The house, she realises now, is built on rock like a medieval fortification. It is not impossible that that is exactly what it once was. A third of the way along the building is a deep arch into the heart of it, dark and cool. Isabel peers inside. Various agricultural implements line its vaulted walls, a tapering wooden ladder and an ancient wheelbarrow.

In the little apartment, she sits for a while at the open window. Outside in the courtyard a mountainous clump of rosemary sends rich waves of scent into the night air. Among rolls of hills there are other houses perched alone on their promontories, their lights blinking across the infinite replication of tiny valleys.

Down below, Elsa is bringing out guttering candles set in jam jars to the courtyard. Isabel sees now that she has hardly registered the laying of the long table and the lighting of the tall lamps by the iron railings. The flutter of moths blurs their outlines.

Then the guests are arriving. The gravel crunches under car tyres and doors slam.

Isabel goes down the steps to the courtyard. She is weighed down by the feeling that she is about to do something that will change the way she thinks and the things she has always thought. This is the moment. If she did not want it, she should not have come.

There is a blur of introductions.

The Criachis are there, Massimo and Fabrizia. Massimo's son Gianni is expected.

The mayor and his wife are present, Vittorio and Lucia Rossi, an amiable couple in their sixties, he an ironmonger by profession, now the proud owner of a builders' merchant yard and several stores. Then there are neighbouring families – all except the occupants of the vast villa at the head of the dust road: they are wealthy Swiss and come to live in their palace only in the summer months.

And, most movingly, there is Annunziata Coia, a woman in her late fifties, who clutches Isabel's hands and tells her with tears in her drooping eyes that she would not be here today if it were not for her father Tom. 'He pulled me and my mother from the house after the bomb hit. It was collapsing all around us and still he went in. He was a brave man and a good one. And so you can see, there are still people here who remember him.'

Annunziata Coia is small – she has to look up to Isabel. But she is portly now. Isabel tries to imagine her as she must have been that day Tom Wainwright performed his heroic deed, but Signora Coia has retained no childish characteristics.

Isabel hesitates, unwilling to admit how little she knows about this, feeling adrift and unprepared. These are the first details she has been told.

Signora Coia has a stout woman's stance, with the air of ease at having used it so long to make her presence felt at the head of the classroom. For generations of children in Petriano, she has been the school's most rigorous and, according to Elsa, its most loved teacher. And she is adept at reading the signals.

'Did he never say?' Her face is stern.

'No. He didn't.'

'Oh, my . . .'

'He was a good man,' says Isabel at last, smiling in an awkward attempt to reassure them both.

It is true. She does think he always tried to do the right thing, even when he got it wrong. Even now, despite what happened in the end, despite the years of confusion and resentment, she remembers him as a kind father.

She accepts a slim glass of prosecco and raises it shyly to the assembled company.

Conversation is stilted. Her grasp of Italian is not good enough to unscramble the tumult of words being shouted from all sides. Apart from Annunziata, hardly any of the older guests speak reasonable English. But Isabel is able to piece together the basics of the story which has brought her here: the bomb dropped from the winter skies; the family running towards the supposed safety of their house; the direct hit on the corner of the piazza; the English soldier who risked his life to save the mother and the daughter but tragically, not the son. It has passed into village history and her appreciation of the honour they are bestowing on Tom, and on her, grows along with the pain of realising how much she has never known.

Massimo is determined that she will understand the words he speaks to her in Italian above the babble if he delivers them slowly and loudly enough.

'Here, your father,' he blares.

'*Sì*,' says Isabel.

'No, Tom was here in this house – his Italian home.'

This is news. It has not occurred to her that this was the actual house he had stayed in.

Feeling stupid, she reaches for Elsa's arm as she passes and asks for confirmation that she has understood correctly.

'*Sì*,' Elsa nods. 'This is the house where he stayed. Massimo was there – just like now, he was always around the house to make sure the wine was maturing all right and the cooking was as good as it should be,' she adds, teasing the old boy.

Isabel is struck once again by how thoughtful these strangers are in bringing her here and how they have taken for granted that she has the background knowledge to be able to understand the subtleties of their kindness.

It is warm enough to eat outside. The spring heatwave is heaven sent for the occasion, although no one has forgotten to bring a jacket and woollen sweater. From the open kitchen they can feel the warmth of the vast oven. Voices rise as they shout across the table in both languages, Fabrizia, Elsa and Bruno translating when they can. It does not matter that Isabel misses most of it. She knows what they are saying. They all want to make her understand how much her father's actions meant to them. Again, a sharp fear strikes that she never knew the man they did.

Elsa brings the food. First there are huge platters of home-reared and home-cured prosciutto and salami, which shine darkly under the candlelight. Then Elsa's pride: her own foie gras and smoked goose. The guests applaud her. They drink Bruno's brother's red wine, made a few hills away.

Gianni Criachi arrives. His lateness is accepted by the company as inevitable; it is clearly a personality trait. He is greeted with friendly jeers and joshing from Bruno. He shrugs good-naturedly.

'My brother,' says Fabrizia, introducing him. 'He does his best . . .'

Gianni is older than Fabrizia, short and powerfully built. With a relaxed economy of movement, he sits down next to her and begins to help himself to food, olives and bread, pouring himself a glass of wine from a carafe. He also speaks excellent English. He works for a computer company, he tells her, travelling all around Europe; in the course of his work, English is essential. Isabel begins to relax.

'Is this your first visit to this part of Italy?' he asks.

'Yes, it is.'

'How do you find it?'

'Very beautiful. Especially this place. It feels different from the pictures I've always seen of Tuscany and Umbria, with the rolling hills and plains. This seems more . . . enclosed, secret, almost.'

This pleases him, she can see. 'It is the trees and the shape of the hill spurs. It is a special place.'

'Yes, I can see that,' she says. Now that she knows that this is the place, she is beginning to see. All around her she is overwriting the outlines of the land and buildings with her imagination of the past. Tom's descriptions of the place, long ago, before he stopped speaking of his past to her, are coming to life breath by breath.

Elsa brings spaghetti tossed in oil with tiny snippets of smoked eel and tarragon.

'You stayed in Pisa, then, last night?' asks Gianni, filling her glass with red wine.

'Yes. I was pleased I did, in the end. I – I have always wanted to see the leaning tower.'

'Ah, the *torre pendente*!'

'I've been reading about it in the newspapers back home – the engineering project to stabilise it. I find it fascinating. I spent quite a long time yesterday just standing and looking.'

'Yes, and the fraction they are pulling it back is just millimetres, all that steel and tension for a tiny distance that the eye would never notice. Twenty-seven millimetres, at the last estimate, is all that it will be.' He rolls his eyes and approximates the tiny distance between a thumb and finger.

Isabel laughs, then says, 'How do you know all this – does everyone in Italy take this much interest?'

'We live with it, we expect it to be there . . . No, I have a friend who is at the university – he's working on the latest project. I hear a lot about it. And you? How is it that you have this interest?' It is not the usual kind of diversion that English ladies look for in Italy, he implies.

'I'm a buildings surveyor. And – my father was always interested. He used to show me pictures. He even once sent a plan in with his idea to stabilise it!'

'Ah.' Gianni nods sagely as he assimilates this.

Massimo has latched on to the conversation from across the table. 'It is not possible to walk up the tower any longer,' he says.

She understands and nods.

'Not for ten years!' adds Massimo. So he does understand English when he wants to.

'What was it like, to walk up?' she asks.

'A little odd,' says Gianni. 'There are strange tilts to the marble floor and changes of angle.'

Isabel, as she pictures the tower, cannot visualise any metal railings for safety. A surge of adrenalin shoots through her. For a long time now Isabel has been wary of heights, afraid of falling.

She forces herself not to think of it.

'The tower is falling and we are trying to stop it, to go

against the forces of nature,' says Bruno, hoisting his bull's shoulders in a shrug. He is a practical man, through and through, decides Isabel.

'Or to hold on to something beautiful,' says Elsa.

The atmosphere alters subtly as the candles burn lower. 'Tell us about him,' says Annunziata.

Everyone is listening. Of course she has known that sooner or later she will have to say something. But Isabel still does not know how she will tell them that she has no answer to the question they will all ask. She thought she had prepared herself for this and she realises now that she has scarcely begun to acknowledge how much she does not know.

It is hard to know where to start. She clasps her shaking hands under the table.

'When he came back to England after the war, he became a builder. But he was always very ambitious, always trying to improve his education. He took courses in bookkeeping and quantity surveying, and when he had learned enough to set up his own building company he would still take courses, but in subjects he enjoyed, like astronomy, and philosophy. He was very well read. And his business was successful.'

They are silent around the table as Gianni, with a brotherly gesture, nominates himself her translator.

'Then, when he was over forty, he married my mother, Patricia. She was twenty years younger and worked as his secretary at the firm. I was born a year later. When I was a little girl he used to talk about Italy. It was he who first told me about the leaning tower, and showed me books of the stars, and mythology, and science, and encouraged me to read.'

She would like to stop here, on this note. She does not know how to put the next part of the story into the right words. These people are waiting. As she hesitates longer, she can see that they realise somehow that she has told them the happy part and that now they must hear bad news.

In the end she says, 'When I grew older he didn't talk as much about Italy. He was quieter. He used to take trips away by himself. Then, when I was seventeen, there was one night when he did not come home.'

The night everything changed: an evening in March, when the fact that he was unaccountably late home was absurdly counterpointed by a meteor shower lighting up the skies above southern England. Across three counties, alarms were raised as flashes and smoke trails, shooting stars and rumbling explosions raked across the dark. Coastguards and police and fire stations, she learned later, were besieged with calls from an anxious public convinced they were witnessing distress flares from ships in trouble, or missiles from behind the Iron Curtain, or aliens preparing to land.

Isabel remembers watching these pyrotechnics from an upstairs window. She had looked out when she heard what she thought was the sound of her father, expected hours before, turning his car into the driveway. The display was spellbinding. The lights seemed to draw her up and into the velvety depths of the universe until, mesmerised, she seemed to be falling towards them, her perspective oddly distorted.

She did not know what it was she had been watching in the sky until the next morning. According to the newspaper, it was the annual arrival of a group of meteoroids called the Virginids that visited the earth every spring. They stayed for a few weeks, then whirled on and away to play around in other, blacker, colder skies. This time the display had been particularly entrancing due to the full moon and perfectly clear night as the earth passed through orbiting clusters of rock and iron.

It was also apparent that Tom had failed to return home all night. After a barren, tear-stained day, the police were called.

Even now, Isabel trembles at the memory. 'They took notes and statements, and gave what assurance they could. Which was not much. They never found a body. They opened a missing file, but there was never any information about him.'

She looks down as Gianni translates.

Then she resumes. 'We thought he would come back – but after a week, and then another week . . . and then when the months turned into years, we knew he wouldn't.' She has told versions of this story for so many years, but she is close to breaking down this time. Her voice is scarcely louder than a whisper as she says, 'We don't know what happened to him. We don't even know if he is still alive.'

There is a shocked silence after Gianni has relayed this to the party.

'We had no idea . . .' he says.

Isabel gathers her courage. 'For a long time I thought that if there had not been . . . an accident, if he was not dead in some circumstances we knew nothing about, he might have come back to Italy. There was never any indication that he was in England. The police never believed that he was dead and we never found any trace of him through the national missing persons organisations. It was just something . . . I had a feeling about. But I had no idea where to start looking.'

'And you came because you thought, after all these years,

that we might know something?' Annunziata is astute. She is nodding at Isabel, not taking her eyes away.

Isabel nods too. 'He used to talk about this place with such . . . warmth, when I was a child. In a way he never did about anywhere else – and yet his experience of it, during the war, was also' – she is struggling to find the right words – 'must have been dangerous and . . . difficult.'

The friends and neighbours are visibly perturbed. This is not what they expected to hear, by no means the sad yet tender conclusion to a long ago story they had imagined. Isabel is suddenly ashamed: she has come here under false pretences and has spoiled what should have been a joyful occasion. Worse, she has shocked them.

Some of these people actually knew him. They knew him as he had been and they wanted a triumphant end to the story, not this inconclusive, cowardly diminishment of their heroic young soldier.

She puts her head down. 'I'm sorry.'

She will not cry. She senses the embarrassment around the table, hears the rustle of napkins and the muffled sounds of glasses replaced on the cloth.

Then Massimo is speaking. 'He was here.'

Isabel has to look to Gianni for confirmation that he is saying what she thinks he is saying. That he has not misunderstood the chronology of her story.

'But he was here!' insists Massimo, pointing to the ground. 'Where?'

'At this house!'

'But when was that, Pappi?' asks Gianni carefully.

Massimo pulls down his rubber lips and shakes his head slowly. 'A time ago.'

Isabel shivers. He has misunderstood. He must have done. But Massimo is hitting the table with a club-like fist.

Gianni translates so she can be certain of what he is saying. 'It could have been twenty years. He doesn't know any more the exact times. The years all go into each other as he gets older.'

Isabel is numb, staring at him, as if trying to drag the information out of his head.

'It didn't seem so strange,' insists Massimo. 'He came back to see the village. We had dinner together.'

'And then?' Isabel's voice cracks.

A tense silence sits over the party for a moment, as the guests realise what is being said.

'And then . . . he went.'

'Did he . . . did he come back – did he say where he was going?'

Massimo shakes his head. 'He might have come back. I only saw him once.'

Isabel struggles and fails to find words. Her throat feels strangulated.

'I'm sorry. It didn't seem so important at the time,' reiterates Massimo. And then to Isabel, 'How could I have known that his family did not know he was here? He was on a tour, seeing old places, that's what he said.'

Isabel presses her eyes tightly closed.

But Massimo is upset now too, on the defensive. 'I did not know you were looking for him! Could I have stopped him going any more than I brought him back here?'

Fabrizia has her hand on his forearm.

The silence settles again as Isabel shakes her head.

'*La poverina!*' whispers someone.

When she does look up, she finds she is the only one who has fought back tears. And then she is being hugged this way and that, her hands held in theirs, her hair stroked, as the hot tears course down her face as they have not been allowed to for years.

It is midnight. The table has been cleared and it is too cold to continue sitting outside. Elsa and Bruno, Isabel and Gianni are drinking tisane in the volcanic warmth of the kitchen.

'When I was very young,' says Isabel, 'he used to tell me stories about a family he knew here. A family of daughters. As I grew older, he wouldn't talk about that any more. My mother told me once that my father had fallen in love with an Italian woman. A woman in Italy, that was how she put it. But I don't know . . .'

Isabel sees her mother, her taut cheekbones and groomed exterior, a woman who has given her strength to maintaining the illusion that she is strong, a circular notion that is as sapping as it is self-deluding.

'A family of daughters?' muses Elsa.

'That could have been the Parinis,' suggests Gianni.

'Tell me . . .'

'This was my aunt's and uncle's house,' says Bruno. 'My father's aunt, I should say. They had three daughters and a son – but the son was away during the war. But it has been a long time since any of the three girls has lived here. I think one of them tried to run the estate for a bit, after their parents died, but things did not work out. There was a caretaker here for a while. So my father Raffaelo – their cousin – took over the running of the house. Then we bought them out – what? Ten years ago?' He looks to Elsa and she nods.

'What happened to the girls?' asks Isabel.

Bruno exhales softly. He shrugs to show that he is not absolutely sure. 'One went to America quite soon after the war. Another to Brindisi, I think it was, in the south with her husband. And another is an artist, a specialist in botanical art. She travels all over the world. I never heard that any of the girls was involved with an Englishman, but then, in our family we are talking about two generations away.'

Isabel strains to recall her father's face and voice, but still the exact characteristics elude her. The emptiness she has felt for months only grows larger.

'You have never asked your mother?' asks Elsa gently, 'If he had stayed . . . friends with anyone from here?'

Isabel bites her lip. 'It was difficult. She is still bitter . . . She has never been able to understand how he could simply walk away like that. We stopped talking about it for a long time. It seemed better that way.'

They do not ask her about her own hurt and she is grateful. It is understood and therefore it stands with its own grace.

'It doesn't seem likely,' says Elsa after a while. 'If he was in touch all this time with someone – a woman – in the village, then surely it would be known by at least a few of the people who were here tonight.'

'You're right. I'm being silly,' admits Isabel. 'Of course it doesn't make any sense.'

'No, but you need to make sense of it. That's understandable,' says Elsa kindly.

'I have spent the last twenty years trying to pretend that I don't,' admits Isabel.

Elsa nods.

'But now I know,' says Isabel. 'I know that what I have wondered about for all that time was not just in my imagination. My instincts were right. When he left us, he did come back here.'

3

The ceremony in the piazza – the newly named Piazza Tom Wainwright – takes place at six in the evening. It is not the small almost private affair that Isabel had envisaged, imagining that most people have forgotten and younger generations do not want to know that a long time ago a British soldier saved the life of a small girl when a bomb fell on the village.

A sizeable crowd has gathered in this little enclave. It is no ancient terracotta-bricked square, but rather a pleasant modern open space off the main road that leads into a couple of the old streets.

Next to the proud new street sign set into the wall in the corner there is a café-bar and it is here that an Italian and a British flag have been hung down from two upstairs windows. A long table is laid out, strung with bright pennants. Rows of sparkling wine and fluted glasses stand to attention on the white cloth.

Isabel is raw; the protective shell on which she has relied for so long seems to have slipped from her in the past days. She cannot stem her thoughts and tears are not far from the surface of her eyes. What would Tom have felt, had he been here? Pride, modesty, sadness for those who did not survive those times? Would she have been here with him, and her mother, and Margaret too?

There is something else. Before she came out, Isabel saw her father's face. She looked into a mirror and saw that her own features were superimposed on his bone structure. Contours once hidden by youthful plumpness are now exposed and familiar. Isabel finds this disconcerting. It is not unattractive; if anything the shape gives added depth to her strong lines. She is amazed that she has never seen it before.

Her Aunt Margaret should have come. It was she who always wanted to talk about Tom, was astute enough to realise that they all needed to talk about him. It was to her that Isabel would go at first to sit and then to look at dog-eared photographs. These photographs would come out of a biscuit tin, rusting at the corners. Margaret's eyes would grow moist as she recalled events from the past and they would both sit, misty with memories and incomprehension.

Isabel is grateful to Margaret. From her mother, Pat, Isabel knows little of him. Her mother does not speak of these matters.

There were no birthday cards, or Christmas post, from Tom. There was nothing to suggest he was either dead or alive; he had merely gone. Margaret heard nothing from him either. Isabel defied her mother and did not break off contact with her aunt. The two women had ceased to be on friendly terms due to their radically different approaches to dealing with what had happened. There was resentment that Isabel was more inclined to Margaret's point of view. But after years of visiting her occasionally, illicitly, after school, there was less that could be said and less that had not been exchanged.

Isabel was left with the books and maps. There were some photographs, nothing unusual, to supplement her increasingly elusive memories of him. There was no address book, nothing personal from more recent times, which might have led her into his secret life.

After a while, for a long time, she shut even these away. With an effort, she shakes herself back into the present.

The ceremony is about to begin. A school band marches in, beefed up by a few enthusiastic elders. All are in their Sunday best. Isabel is nervous, steeling herself. But she is strangely happy to be here, with these people she is already beginning to think of as new friends. Annunziata Coia hugs her again. Massimo makes her laugh with an obscene wink. A flashbulb pops as a photographer records the occasion.

The shops are open. Signora Monti has left the sociable queue of shoppers in her little supermarket to their own devices and come out for the spectacle. Women carrying fresh bread and ham stop on their rounds and are called over to join in the party. The waitress from the café shakes Isabel's hand solemnly.

Gianni and Elsa are never far away. They are looking out for her and she allows herself to enjoy the feeling. This is new. She has made herself so independent that it is hard to let others glimpse her true emotions. Is it the physical distance between this Italian village and her normal life or something more profound that has made the difference?

'It's a shame about the rockets,' says Alessandro, shrugging thin shoulders in his stiffly ironed clothes. His brother Carlo concurs morosely.

There has been an argument among the committee, along with much impassioned shouting and gesticulation, over whether to have fireworks at the ceremony. After fierce debate, explosions have been overruled on the grounds of taste.

'You know, it would have been nice to see the Parini girls again,' says Lucia Rossi. 'But I suppose it was not possible.'

'The Parini girls – the family who lived at Le Macchie?' asks Isabel.

'I say "girls"! They are older than I am by now! But it brings it all back . . .' She wipes away a tear. 'So many years ago. My poor mamma . . .'

Isabel takes her hand and squeezes it. She cannot say anything.

'I think they were invited – I know they were,' goes on Lucia. 'But then, when people leave the village and go to a new life, maybe sometimes they do not want to go back into the past.'

Gianni is at her side again. Without preamble he tells her, 'We will look for your father. If it is true that he came back to Italy then we will find him.'

She is overwhelmed, again, by this gesture of kindness. The 'we'. 'I'm going back to England tomorrow,' says Isabel instinctively. She means, in the moment she says it, that she wants to cut herself off now, to retreat into that zone of scepticism about other people and their professed commitment which until now has seemed more comfortable.

'When are you coming back, then?' Gianni persists. In his mind, it seems, there is no obstacle that can prevent them from achieving their aim.

Isabel hesitates. 'I could . . .' What would she be signing up to here? Then she is angry with herself. If she had not wanted this, why had she come in the first place? 'In the summer. I could come back – take a couple of weeks, maybe even three . . .'

'Then that is what we will do. Meanwhile – here, we can start. I think there may be a photograph in the newspaper, a story about the piazza and this evening. People will hear about what has taken place. We can talk to anyone who remembers him, we can put an advertisement in the other newspapers, to say that we are looking for him, if that is what you want.'

'Yes,' she hears herself saying. 'That is what I want.'

On the dot of six, after the tinny bells have rung out from the church, Vittorio Rossi says a few words in his capacity as mayor and a toast is drunk to Tom Wainwright and the newly named piazza. It is simple in the extreme. Isabel has been dreading a long drawn-out, emotional event, but abruptly the burden is gone. At the end everyone turns to Isabel and claps her, in his place, and she accepts their good wishes with gratitude.

She smiles and holds the hurt deep inside her.

There is no option but to continue what she has begun.

But she has known that since she made the decision to come to Petriano. It has taken too long already, thinks Isabel.

There comes a point when we all have to admit it: the way we live is founded on small deceptions and superficialities and fear, and what some of us are most afraid of is letting ourselves be seen in our true colours, or maybe even of knowing the truth about ourselves. It is hard. But what is far harder, Isabel is realising, is ploughing on through life never knowing that this is the secret wound that will not heal.

II

4

I t was the worst weather southern Italy had seen for years
when they landed, two maybe three years out from
home. Tom, like most of the men, was resigned now to
foreignness, to sleeplessness, to brutality and death. He was
exhausted by alternate terror and boredom. He had embarked
on the troopship at Tripoli knowing only that it would be
somewhere in Italy. Nearer home than the desert campaign;
a little less hot, a little less dry.

The first winter in Italy was mudbound. From September
onwards in 1943 there was no relief from the rain and slime
and swollen rivers and slippery slopes. The men longed now
for a sighting of a strong sun through the oppressive water.
They pushed against wind and water and fire as the grim
manoeuvrings of the Eighth Army took them slowly north
from Calabria. Their feet slithered for weeks on end. The
cold and wet seeped through flesh to bone, until finally it
touched the spirit.

Tom was a mechanic; he and his unit were a support group
to the fighting men, repairing the vehicles, keeping them
grinding along the sodden roads north into the fire of the

front. Tom, afterwards, rarely spoke of these months and, when he did so, would recount only the rivers of mud, the trucks wheel-deep in sludge, of blizzards and balls of ice from the sky, the convoys bogged down and stalemated in the quagmires of the Abruzzi. There were short rations due to the same mud. Their stomachs tight, the lads lay under sodden bivouacs and smoked tea leaves. 'So this is sunny Italy!' they joked bleakly.

The drowned earth dissolved under his boots and the foundations of his world shifted. He was twenty-one years old.

Near the River Sangro a heavy battery position sat in cold brown water backed by bare knobbed trees which seemed to grow in the flood pools. Serpent trails of wetness stretched towards distant hills as far as he could see.

It was a desperate landscape, walls of brown and grey closing in on them speared by strange stripped trees pointing upwards. In front of them the engineers – the sappers – worked feverishly, wading through minefields, swimming in dangerous desolation.

Behind them now were the bridgeheads across the Trine; the battle to construct them and capture the town of Petacciato had cost more than a thousand casualties. Mud and blood; Tom saw them mingle on every side. He went on because he decided the past no longer existed, not even the past that could be measured in days. Only the present and the very near future were worth thought.

The heavily defended approaches to the Sangro were obscene villages of pillboxes and other fortifications on the morass. And all the while the great swollen river swirled, out of man's control. The sappers worked thirty-six-hour stretches, wet to the bone after a few minutes, to construct the first bridge over the watery fury and into enemy fire.

Tom was one of the first men to cross the bridge. Three of them had to carry parts to coax a vital engine back to life. The operation to hold the bridgehead was still going on. The lorry he was in was pitched against the roaring wind, its own motor grinding. Raindrops slapped his face, the vibrations from the engine took over from the shivering of his body. Still the rain did not cease. He and his comrades had been battling for an hour to repair the stricken crane when a spectacular cloudburst swelled the river where no more water could be held, and the hard-won bridge was swept away. It took with it two men Tom had come to regard as friends.

There was nothing to be done but to turn away and point his weapons outwards. For two days and nights, under remorseless fire, a detachment ferried ammunition and supplies across the perilous waters. Tom stood his ground, on this precarious outpost, but felt he did little more than that. It was only later that he discovered that standing still could also be the preserve of the hardest and the bravest men.

But then, he saw only the strain of the boatmen heaving across the churning river with their precious cargo, heard only the noise of bombardment. These were the men who would win the war, while he, Tom, was cowering where he had been sent, dazed with fear and self-reproach.

Until then, war had been a glorious adventure. Even when they risked their lives and buried those less lucky, he and his mates were too young to die. They knew that it must happen to someone else because there was no other way forward for them. Survival was a matter of luck and of detaching oneself from the truth.

How did they keep going? 'Backbone,' said Tom and his friends agreed.

When the worst of the first phase was over, he was shipped out of Italy on leave. Tom, along with two other jacks of all trades in the support unit, found themselves back in the searing sun of North Africa. He, Frank Bates and Jonno Martin, with pay newly in their pockets and the opportunity to blot out what they could, did their damnedest in the cabaret bars of Mena, near Cairo.

When they returned to Italy it was high summer. Tom's regained strength was most apparent in his eyesight when the troopship landed at Taranto on the heel of the boot. Under the fierce sun, Tom could see so clearly it almost hurt. The precision of every line, every plane and colour dazzled and disorientated him as if he had woken after a long, long sleep.

What he saw was squalor: on the dockside, in the wretched graffiti on almost every building, in the clothes of the urchins who followed their single-file march through cobbled streets. There was desperation on the faces of the starving children and women, disease on their bare legs and feet. They begged for food, for cigarettes.

Sometimes the Germans had retreated only days before, leaving monstrously distorted roads and buildings behind them. The locals had not yet returned to reclaim their land and its ruins. Corn was rotting in the sodden fields and grapes shrivelled on the vines. Apples and plums lay bruised and oozing beneath the trees in orchards, fallen ripe at picking time. Parched from hours in a jolting convoy on the road, Tom and the lads snatched handfuls of whatever fruit they could find, from back gardens as well as farms.

His division was loaded on to a train bound north, packed like cattle in the stifling wagons that stopped and started interminably in long tunnels. It stopped eventually at some godforsaken halt in sizzling sunshine. On the platform was an astute boy with a barrow of ripe apricots. Groans of thirst and greed raked the van.

'I've a throat like an ancient bloody chimney!' rasped Jonno, scrabbling over bodies to the open side. He was small and simian, and his tough bandy legs were always the first to jump or scamper or scuttle towards an objective. Sitting still seemed physically painful for him. He led the leap towards the pile of apricots.

The barrow overturned. Haggling was intense, the price fixed in cigarettes.

Jonno returned with a handkerchief full of fruit and lobbed them towards his immediate cohorts. They sank aching teeth into the velvety skin and aromatic flesh of the apricots, and sighed. It was a tiny resuscitation of pleasure.

'Scratch game of football, anyone?' Jonno was straight up on his feet again. He could dribble a ball or a melon or a bundle of rags until everyone else was dizzy. He was a flame-haired monkey on the ball, the best football player Tom had ever seen. Even with six apricot stones bound in a scrap of material.

Frank waved him away. 'Too bloody hot.'

But Tom joined in the dusty scuffle, glad to feel his limbs moving, although thirst was already pulling at the back of his mouth. The boy leaned on his empty barrow and observed them dispassionately through his cigarette smoke.

The support unit was bigger now. They were a travelling band of craftsmen: menders and botchers of the machinery of war, patchers-up of equipment and shelter. Frank was only a month or two older than Tom. He had been an apprentice electrician. He had a reputation for being able to fix anything – for solving problems by the way he saw them, which was not the way the others did. He would bend his head – tufted with blond hair like a boy's under the tin helmet – over the pieces of metal or broken frame and think, quite absorbed in the puzzle, whatever the chaos around him. Tom admired this talent greatly.

'No leadership,' Frank had taken to saying. 'Your average Italian soldier isn't that bad. With decent officers and free of a madman at the helm, they'd do all right.' He was reiterating this, stabbing a forefinger in the direction of the fruit seller, while the men swayed together as the train wheezed forward once more, fresh sweat adding pungency to their closeness.

'That's what they say,' concurred Tom, eager to seem well informed, in agreement. 'And they seem to know how to make others do the right thing too. I heard one good story . . .'

His source was another mate, Titch Carter. Titch was a signalman and information was his stock in trade. He was a great storyteller. All part of being a communications man. To the ordinary soldier who only ever saw part of the picture, it was strange and yet vital to hear news of the other theatres of war, to find a way of discovering his position in the vast pattern, to make sense of what he had achieved and of what might face him in the short-term future.

As for Tom, he was ordinary. That was how he thought of himself. There were thousands like him, tall, lanky lads with no particular distinguishing features. He was here and he was doing his best. Although he never seemed to get any further into the battered copy of *Paradise Lost* he had carried since embarkation. That was defeating him.

He liked stories spoken aloud, stories of men in other armies and dangers. Like the one he was told one night in Cairo, and was now passing on, of a Yugoslav officer allied to the partisans in Naples.

'There was a disagreement which had led to some local difficulty between him and the partisan cause – no one could explain exactly what the problem was, but that's not the point. The Yugoslav was requested to meet the partisan leaders. He did so. Across the table, one of them drew out a revolver and placed it in front of the Yugoslav.'

Tom watched the faces of his audience carefully as he retold the tale: Jonno was smirking, one knee jiggling up and down; Frank's face was furrowing as he thought around the equation.

'He was told to shoot himself,' said Tom. He savoured his moment as storyteller. 'And he did.'

Tom's days in the transit camp south of Naples, during which he and the lads took possession of their lorry and equipment, put their kit in order, arranged for their clothes to be washed by local women, bought fruit and drank wine, prepared him for a pattern which would recur. Survival of body and spirit would be a matter of barter.

Tom had a tommy-gun. It was a dull black brute with a

large drum on it. It made him feel like Al Capone. He had used it, too, and that knowledge still had the power to shock him.

They slept outside, in the ground. They made slit trenches, eight feet by three or as near as they had energy to dig: shallow graves, by any other name. In orchards they put fruit boughs over the top, or sandbags if available, then camouflage nets. They would lie in their resting places at night listening to machine-gun fire cutting through trees, tearing through the leaves with a sinister rustle.

In the opera house at Salerno, they watched a grainy film while fighter aircraft droned overhead, and heard the crash of battle over the dialogue. A comic called Leslie Sarony, out with ENSA – the Entertainments National Service Association ('otherwise known as Every Night Something Awful,' quipped Titch) – gave a show in a bombed-out theatre. Sarony brought what was left of the house down with a rendition of a song he had recorded before the war, 'Ain't it Grand to be Blooming Well Dead'.

Their staple entertainment was the Vino Hunt. Groups of soldiers would set off into the dusty countryside to some likely farmhouse or cottage and introduce themselves to the inhabitants. Cigarettes would be offered and conversation initiated – invariably concerning the futility of war, the harshness of life. In some cases wine would be produced straight away; if not, then one of the lads would ask. The importuned local would duly produce a bottle, all the while emphasising how little was in the house and how short of any comforts all inside were.

One evening while drinking wine the lads shared some rough bread with the father of the family. They had drawn the line at the rock-hard crusts and left them on the table. There were three small children playing listlessly in the kitchen, hardly saying a word. Occasionally their wide dark eyes would appear at the edge of the table and then they would slide away. As Tom was leaving, his stomach full of warm acid, he turned back and saw — before the goodbyes had been said — the children gnawing like rodents at the abandoned crusts. He cursed himself, all the stumbled way back to the camp, for his stupidity and selfishness.

It was a slow progress north. Then, near the town of Perugia in Umbria, the long convoy halted. The front was around Urbino, thirty miles up. They dug in and waited. There were route marches and inspections. But still they did not receive orders to advance.

Over the hedge of the field where they were encamped, they bartered cigarettes for eggs, fruit and wine, and learned to speak Italian as the locals did. Tom, keen to acquire this new skill, spent every chance he had in halting conversation with the farmers whose produce he acquired. It helped to lessen in some tiny way the disadvantage he was at, in these strange places. Helped to pass the hours, the days of waiting.

Women came to the camp. In the main, they came to take away washing, to earn a few meagre lire, or preferably cigarettes or bully beef. There was a river nearby and the enterprise was a communal affair. They talked as they beat the clothes on flat white stones. Shouts and occasional laughter rang out from the bowl of the half-moon beach. The washerwomen returned the next day, with the laundry clean and pressed. Some of the married women, whose husbands were in the forces, were beautiful and intent on proving that they were.

Tom did not see his washerwoman for some weeks. His kit was collected and delivered by two young girls, urchin-faced sisters of eight and ten. They asked, one day, if he would care to visit their house and he accepted. They led him up a steep hill, silvered on either side of the track with olive groves. They scampered ahead, their bony knees visible from behind as they kicked out for home and out of sight in the trees. He ambled along in their wake, hoping he was on the right path, glad to be away from the camp, happy to be lost in the warm countryside. The early summer sun pierced into the pink skin of his bare forearms.

The dusty path was a shifting pattern of bumps and ruts, already set hard after the spring rains. Some way along he came to a long, low, two-storey building, a farmhouse of pitted plaster. Plants scrambled up its walls. At one end was a small chapel surmounted by a bell arch. A gravel path led along the sunny side until, at the end of the house, there was an arched loggia. It was a beautiful place, but crumbling.

A man and a woman were sitting outside the meanest part of the house. They stood up as Tom approached. They were shelling beans. The man was considerably older than the wife, gnarled by the wind and hard toil. His twig fingers worked over the pods. The beans were small, the creamy white of bones and already almost as hard. It was a poor crop. But they were thinking ahead, preparing for the months when the soil would have shrunk into itself and nothing would grow in the claws of old roots and frozen ruts. These beans would be the family's winter staple.

Tom was invited to sit down. He wondered vaguely

whether this might prove an unusually profitable vino session. This was not the stony crumbles of the other poor small-holdings they had been frequenting. This house seemed to promise old, rich wines long stored in a once venerable cellar. There was a dignity and bearing about the family that transcended the pitiful food.

Then the man stood up and rasped out a greeting, an offensive, 'What do you want?'

Tom was taken aback. 'Lance Corporal Tom Wainwright. From the camp.' He held out a hand.

'British.'

'Yes.'

The man took his hand. He was a small, wiry individual, wearing what appeared to be a formal black suit of ancient vintage, shredded and darned over and over again so that it was held together by the threads of repair. 'Giuseppe Parini,' he said. 'My wife Anna.'

The woman nodded. She too was diminutive. Harsh lines were etched into her face, but then she smiled and her expression transformed her into a merry apple-cheeked elf. There were footsteps behind him. Giuseppe barely turned round to see who it was. 'Daughter Giuliana and the two little ones, Maddalena and Natalina, you know.'

'My kit's never looked better,' said Tom, turning to smile at the wife but speaking respectfully to Giuseppe.

There were smiles and nods all round.

Tom had never met a woman who could be so still. That was what he noticed first about Giuliana. She was seventeen. She could run with her young sisters and she danced, but when she walked she glided, and when she sat it was with a stillness that was a revelation to him. Other women, his mother, his sister Margaret, were constantly moving as if to sit still were a crime; even if they were seated calmly, their hands darted and pulled at their knitting, or crochet work, or the mending over wooden toadstools. Giuliana's calmness seemed to radiate from her, like coolness from stones in high summer. She did not need to speak constantly, to fill up silence. He thought at first that this was due to his difficulties with the language, but he soon realised that she was the same with her family. She spoke, but she did not prattle about inconsequentialities.

Giuseppe had offered some thin wine, watered to stretch further.

'The farmer has the advantage,' he was saying. 'He knows how to scrape food from the land. He will survive when the city man will not.'

Tom thought, with some shame, of the ruined crops of the south the previous year, the rotting plenty in the fields, overseen only by the murderous salvos exchanged by two warring armies while those who would have tended them to feed the desperate were cowering out of range.

No one mentioned the pitiful beans.

'This farm has been in Anna's family for generations. Once it was part of a grand estate. There is a Renaissance villa, still beautiful on the outside – have you seen it yet?'

Tom shook his head.

'Beautiful, but black and wrecked inside. The Germans – pigs.' This was clearly a great sorrow to Giuseppe. 'It is a few kilometres up the road towards the village. Luckily for us, they found that more to their taste than a farmhouse.'

Giuseppe was warming up as the wine's gentle effects dampened his reserve.

On the family's smallholding were olives, naturally, but also, in tiny, barely sustainable quantities, figs, apples, pears, grapes, lemons, walnuts, cherries, pomegranates, greengages and persimmons. Giuseppe and Anna kept pigs and geese. A cow had recently died and a beehive on the far side of the orchard had performed a heroic feat.

Giuseppe nodded vigorously as he explained. 'My bees are loyal fighters! They protected us from the Germans!' he cried. The skin around his eyes crinkled.

Tom looked about at the women of the family, but they were fondly deferential to the tale and its teller.

'A party of German soldiers had come up the path. Their big cruel boots trampled on our wild flowers. We heard them coming and hid what we could in the minutes we had. Then – a miracle! The bees swarmed! They were like a black cloud, humming with anger. They set their course like dogs. Like guard dogs! The advance came – and these were our defenders!'

Giuseppe's eyes spilled over with mirth. He slapped the table and roared. 'My heroic bees! What patriots!' he said, shaking his head at their excellent nerve and timing.

He was sanguine at the loss of a good part of his hive – for after routing the Germans the bees had continued their maddened path north and never returned – and consoled himself by wrapping the hive in wire to keep safe the remainder, all the while imagining ever more daring exploits by the swarm battalion.

'Ah!' he said. 'I would say to myself, "Where are they now? They are doing their bit for Italy – they will have taken back Milan by Christmas!"'

The laughter was superseded by silence.

'*Eh, Milano* . . .' Giuseppe sighed.

Tom nodded, wanting to know more, unsure of how to proceed.

But his host poured a little more wine and obliged without prompting. 'It's madness! The Italian people have been bartered – *bartered!* – by Mussolini and the King for hope of a seat at the side of the Nazi victors in Europe. *Ha!* They have overthrown Il Duce and now our country is a battleground between two invading armies at war with each other.

'In the north, the Germans have a regime of terror. Innocent civilians are randomly arrested and executed. But for the lucky ones who keep their heads down and survive, it's possible to eat and there is work in the towns. In the south, where you have liberated, there is freedom but no food, so more are dying!'

Tom swallowed hard.

'Don't look so worried,' said Giuseppe. 'What can you do? What can any of us do? Most Italians want only to keep their families in safety and health. But they don't know which way to turn! By the time we had seen the Nazis close up, most of us were not Fascists. The Communists seem to be fighting for the right cause, but there is much tension between the partisan factions. With them in the partisans are the Action Party, the Socialists, the Christian Democrats and the Liberals. A fine mix!'

Fascinated, Tom ignored the mounting alarm on the wife's face and urged his informant on. 'There must be partisan units nearby?'

He felt the eyes of the eldest daughter on him, shyly.

Dark-brown eyes that looked down when he tried to meet them.

He wanted to hear the tales of these bands of adventurers: the men attacking the Germans from forested hillsides; the Poles, Slavs and Russians who had allegedly deserted from the German army to join them; the Allied soldiers and airmen who had escaped from prisoner of war camps and found themselves fighting the war on their terms; the thugs and criminals who masqueraded under the guise of partisanship for more dubious ends.

But Giuseppe seemed to catch himself. He cast down his glance and spread his palms. 'We have all been betrayed.'

In time Tom came to learn that the tale of the heroic bees was an unfailing method of restoring Giuseppe to good humour when the vicissitudes of wartime and his depleted life threatened to overcome him. He and Tom would sit over jugs of bitter red wine and drink until the world was no longer mad.

Back at camp that night after their first meeting, all Tom could think of was when he could return to Le Macchie and on what pretext.

It was food that sealed the friendship in the end. Walking up to the house early one morning, Tom picked a mushroom. It was yellow, unblemished, cool and smooth. He put it gently in his pocket and looked for more. He arrived with twelve, although none of the same velvet purity. For half an hour or so of innocent pleasure he had been back in his boyhood fields as he searched.

He presented them to the mother, Anna. She stepped

back, aghast. 'Drop them from your hands!' she cried.

'It's a field mushroom,' said Tom, holding out the perfect specimen. 'Just an ordinary field mushroom.'

This provoked another outburst. They were the most noxious fungi, puffed full of evil juices!

'We eat them back home,' he insisted. 'We've always eaten them. Look —'

'No, no, no!' cried Giuseppe.

'Look . . . I will show you.' Tom began to slice it with his penknife. 'Get me a frying pan.'

A look of horror spread over Anna's round face.

'It will poison my pan!' she gasped. 'It's too old — your mushrooms have gone off!'

'I will eat them. I want to show you.'

Reluctantly she disappeared into the kitchen. An old tin can was produced for the Englishman to perform his amazing feat. Tom shrugged and followed her inside to the range. A dash of olive oil was proffered with absolute scepticism. Tom fried the mushrooms and ate them at the table, to silence and an intensity of gaze that seemed to suggest he might falter and fall at any moment. Tom smiled and sat back in his chair, exaggerating his satisfaction by leaning against the wall.

There was awkward shuffling and no conversation. Giuliana's eyes filled with tears.

How long? the family's expressions seemed to ask.

When he was still alive two hours later they had a sing-song.

When, the next morning, he was able to walk unaided up the hill, he gave a bellowing rendition of 'They'll Be Coming Round the Mountain'. 'See?' he called to Giuseppe, feet planted apart on the track, arms wide to show the extent of the pinkness of his health.

The Italian solemnly noted the evidence. 'You are fine,' he said. Then he added, 'But you are an Englishman. An Italian could never have eaten those mushrooms and survived.'

5

I n defiance of the orders in a fusty booklet widely distrib-
uted to warn of the dangers of fraternisation, groups of
men were soon wandering daily into the village and the
neighbouring small town of Bastia to hang around in the hope
of meeting girls and tasting the wine. Jonno and Vince, in
particular, were all for these trips, having struck lucky one
afternoon with a group of giggling farm girls.

Tom always went back to Le Macchie. It was an act of
faith that he would be welcome. Anna mothered him: washed
his clothes and fed him what she could. Giuseppe loved to
talk and seemed to relish the new audience. He felt calm and
safe with them. But he knew he was going in the hope of
seeing Giuliana.

On the woodland path he strolled over tufts of tough
vegetation growing down the centre of the path, suggest-
ing long use by farm vehicles. A cyclamen, wild and pale
pink, had managed to grow in the middle of the dust. He
stepped aside to avoid crushing it. Pine cones crunched
under his boots. Simply to be able to walk alone at an
unforced pace was bliss.

In the tiny vineyard at Le Macchie the grapes were dense clusters of dusty blue beads. Tom made his way through, towards the orchard of apple and plum trees. A flash of bright colour caught his eye. There she was – among the fruit trees.

She came towards him, carrying a willow basket.

As she came closer, he felt awkward. But she did not seem surprised to see him. Without a hint of curiosity about his reasons for being there, she smiled and showed him the contents of her basket. In it were dandelion leaves and dark-green courgettes complete with yellow tulipped flowers. He had never seen courgette flowers before.

'They're pretty,' he said.

'You have to pick them at exactly the right time,' said Giuliana.

'What do you do with the flowers?' He was wondering if perhaps they were put into a vase on their sturdy stalks.

Giuliana laughed. 'You eat them, of course!'

'Are you serious?' He gave her a quizzical look. After the fuss over the mushrooms, he feared he was to be the butt of some family joke in return.

'We do!' she said merrily.

'Well I never.'

'I have to take them to my mother straight away. Do you want to come?'

'Yes, please,' he replied, even more gauchely.

Anna sat at a rickety table outside the kitchen where the terrace was shaded. She had collected a basket of pine cones and was in the process of extracting the small sweet kernels, those that the birds had not already stolen. These, she explained patiently, for she was clearly concerned by his lack of knowledge of the ways of the world, she would use to sprinkle on their rare cakes, or alternatively, if she could collect enough, she would pound them with a pestle and mortar, and use this delicious and nutritious dust as the basis for a pie that was the stuff of life itself.

Tom asked if he could help, but she waved his request away. 'Sit and talk to us,' she said. 'Your Italian's getting better.' She indicated a chair, so he pulled it up closer.

Giuliana emerged from the kitchen with a bowl and some other mysterious ingredients that she proceeded to stir and pulp to her mother's instructions. She bowed her head intently over the bowl and he was able to study her face covertly: her smooth forehead, the long neck round which she was wearing a rough necklace of seashells, mainly the whorls of tiny sea snails and cockle fans.

'I like your necklace,' he told her.

She blushed. 'I made it myself.'

'Very pretty.'

Giuliana continued to pound the contents of her bowl, but the blush spread down her throat.

Casting around for a neutral topic, Tom asked, '"Le Macchie". What does that mean?'

'It means "the shrubs, the bushes",' said Anna. 'So . . . the house with shrubs.' She brushed stubborn flakes of cone to the ground and straightened up. 'But it is also – a *gioco di parole* – a play on words. *La macchia* is a stain or dark spot.'

Tom was intrigued. 'So . . . does that refer to anything?'

'No one knows. It is simply the name the estate has always been known by.'

They went inside, bearing their preparations.

That evening Tom ate a flower for the first time in his life. In fact, he ate two: spicy yellow courgettes on their thick green stems, stuffed with bread and nuts and diced peppers. Then Giuliana brought him a dish of the dandelion leaves mixed with nasturtium leaves, garnished with the bright nasturtium flowers.

He stared at her in disbelief. Now he was sure this was retribution. The family watched his expression. Then Natalina reached across and plucked up a flower, and crunched it in her smiling sharp little teeth.

He followed suit. It was strange and peppery.

He was about to make a face when he heard footsteps on the gravel and tensed automatically.

Maddalena slithered from her seat and ran off in the direction of the sound. She returned seconds later holding the hand of a laughing man, clearly at ease with him. The man's strut was confident, arrogant in Tom's estimation.

'Massimo – sit!' commanded Giuseppe. 'We have another guest you see,' he said, indicating Tom. 'Tom Wainwright, our English soldier.' To Tom he said, 'Massimo Criachi, my very good friend.'

The two of them shook hands.

Massimo was a short bulky individual, about the same age as Giuseppe, Tom guessed. Luxuriant dark hair sprouted and dived excitedly from his parting. He hitched his belt up over his belly – the appalling food shortages were clearly not making much of an impact on his fine figure.

'Massimo is a great connoisseur of Giuseppe's wines,' said Anna drily. 'And of my cooking, it seems, he is so often at our table.'

'But he is the brewer of a grappa which commands a proper respect,' added Giuseppe with proud reverence which overrode his wife's sarcasm. 'Massimo', he informed Tom, putting a finger to his nose, 'has an outhouse on his property which is something of a . . . centre of excellence in the field of fine liquor.' He licked his lips luxuriantly and rolled his eyes.

'And which is banned to many of the men, such are its effects,' said Anna. 'Massimo's grappa is notorious.'

'Banned by the authorities?' asked Tom, with new respect.

'No!' said Anna. 'The authorities know nothing about it. By their wives.'

Massimo laughed good-naturedly. 'And how is my beautiful Giuliana this evening?' he asked, turning his attention to her.

A knife twisted in Tom's gut.

Giuliana smiled calmly. 'Well, thank you.'

'Bring him a plate for some food. I don't suppose we'll get away with not feeding the old rogue,' said Anna, but fondly.

Giuliana did as she was asked.

'Now,' Massimo turned his full attention to Tom. His eyes flickered down the sleeve of his uniform. 'Corporal . . . Wainwright?' He pronounced it well.

Tom nodded.

'What is your part in the glorious British army?'

Tom was unsure whether it was intended he should take

offence. He played it straight, sitting as he was at the table of his new friends. 'I'm a member of a support group. Mainly I do mechanical repairs, but I'm a carpenter too. I do whatever I have to do.'

Massimo digested this, along with a large forkful of food. 'Not a fighting man, then.'

'I've had my moments.'

'I'll bet you have,' said Massimo, deadpan.

Tom acknowledged the fact.

'A mechanic,' said Massimo. 'I have a beautiful car. It is twenty years old – a Bugatti – and it is locked in a lonely shed backing on to a large rocky cave beneath . . . well, I shall not tell you where it is beneath! It is a great shame for it to be so far out of sight, although naturally I did not think so when the Germans were playing their thieving games around here. Besides, it is now illegal to have kept a car that should have been turned over to the Fascists. But this is no longer a car, it is a prize, a gift from the gods, an object of such beauty that it has no place in these terrible times. But now – the war is almost over and perhaps I have found my man, eh?'

Tom said nothing.

'I always say – do I not Giuseppe? – when the war is over, my car will rule the road again. And now, are we close to that, are we?'

Tom hoped his scepticism showed.

'I need some parts, you see – and perhaps the British can help me . . . in return for other favours, of course. There must be services that we, impoverished though we are, can provide, no?'

'Perhaps,' said Tom with extreme caution. He had a feeling that this man was very confidently being rude to him.

It was Anna who noticed his discomfiture. 'Take no notice, Tom. You' – she gestured at Massimo – 'get on with that, for no doubt you'll want to fill your face with my special courgettes.'

Massimo flapped a hand at her with high good humour and ate up.

'Would you help me, Tom?' Anna was on her feet clearing empty dishes.

Tom sprang up.

'He's not as bad as he makes out. He is teasing you,' said Anna when they were out of earshot in the cavernous kitchen. 'In fact, our Massimo has made it his business to keep morale high in the village.'

'They must share his sense of humour,' said Tom.

'Times have been hard,' she said sternly.

Tom was crestfallen, aghast at his own lack of thought.

'I didn't mean –'

'Let me tell you a story,' said Anna, as she put a few nuts on a plate. 'We have a very kind padre in our church here in Petriano. A very nice man, who has been here man and boy, but a man who gives terrible sermons. Where we needed hope and inspiration, we often got irritation, and worse, boredom. But it was Massimo, when times were very bad, who took matters into his own hands. From somewhere – God knows where, but Massimo can often find things that no one else can – he got a large bag of gilt dust, shiny gold powder as might have been used once in a show at a theatre.

'Then, before the congregation came in on Sunday morning, carrying this bag he climbed to the roof where there is a ledge above the altar. At the right moment there was a sprinkling of gold dust from the heavens. To give the congregation hope, you understand. They were beginning to lose heart – and the ability to believe in miracles. But after that . . .'

Tom shook his head in amazement. 'So it worked?' He found it incredible.

'Oh, yes,' said Anna. 'It was a very moving display. Sometimes even I am able to believe that the Hand of God had a part in it.'

Massimo was a wheeler-dealer, she told Tom. Before the war he had been an entrepreneur, and would be again. He had been a successful dealer in piano accordions for many years, with a renowned factory near Rimini. The factory had now closed down, of course. 'He is always looking for the next . . . opportunity.' She smiled.

'This time not a fast buck, my friend – a fast horse!' he was announcing to the table as they returned bearing clean dishes and utensils. Massimo was fully animated. An idea was boiling behind his forehead, as evidenced by a dewdrop effect beneath his hairline. 'We will breed horses – no, we will build a racecourse!' The schemes were coming thick and fast as usual. 'We can't lose: we will charge fees for the races to be run, we'll take advertising, we'll take bets. Everyone knows bookmakers are rich. While you are looking up at the stars like dreamers, I am looking at the ground and planning the way to a heaven on earth!'

Tom thought that was a little unfair, since Giuseppe was working the land and tending his animals every day of the year, but he thought better of interjecting.

'That is what the future is: thinking big and thinking modern. Everything shiny new, not the dusty rusty lives we have now. Bright new tall buildings, optimism, gleaming new cars for all who have come through these terrible times.'

'And what of your Bugatti?' Giuseppe raised an objection.

'Apart from the Bugatti, naturally. That is a king among motors.'

'Mmm-hmmm,' mumbled Giuseppe amiably. It occurred to Tom that his host had heard it a thousand times before.

Massimo asked Tom outright whether he could help him with parts for his car.

'You'll be lucky.' Tom grinned. 'I'm the one who's going to be asking you that.'

'Ah! So perhaps I can be of service, then?'

Tom conceded as much. 'We're looking for some radiators and a gearbox for a truck,' he explained.

'You come and see what I have. All kinds of things I have that you need. You bring your comrades. We look, we drink a little grappa, we negotiate, eh?'

'Sounds all right.'

So it was that a session was arranged to talk shop with Massimo in his outhouse.

The next evening at six they gathered: Tom, Jonno, Vince and young Barnes, another mechanic and eager recruit to any sport that Jonno proposed. The session duly began with the opening of a bottle of clear alcohol and the arrangement of five tiny tumblers on a workbench. Massimo led the first toast to friendly co-operation.

They put their heads back and shot themselves down the throat with liquid fire.

'We are men of the world,' said Massimo expansively, generously including young Barnes in this proclamation. 'To *Italia* and *Inghilterra!*'

'Italy and England!' they roared back.

A small amount of business was conducted. Massimo was as good as his word; he had been busy since the previous night. Stacked in the outhouse was a selection of elderly motor radiators, some rusting irredeemably, but others apparently convertible to their requirements. A hulking gearbox dominated one side of the shack, a little oily, a little foreign, but unmistakably what it was. Jonno and Vince joined Tom in looking over the merchandise.

More grappa was drunk. Money changed hands and there was another toast, down in one.

As they were all getting on so well, the men took the opportunity to pick Massimo's brains about the village girls. It transpired that he was the undisputed expert in this field.

'What's the etiquette here, about going out with a girl?' asked Jonno. Rather sheepishly, Tom thought. Jonno's scrambler's knees were bobbing up and down, fidgeting, never still, and an indication that he needed to know the answer so he could hare off and put his new-found knowledge to good use.

Massimo laughed. 'You can ask – but if she says yes, you must be prepared to spend as much time talking to her mother as to her. She will be chaperoned.'

'That still happens here?' Jonno was suddenly downcast.

'Oh yes. Things are very strict where the family is involved.'

Tom thought grimly of the women by the sides of the roads around Naples and in Rome. That was not quite right, he mused.

As if by telepathy Massimo caught his eye. 'There is desperation, of course, but that is something else. There is no etiquette for the starving.'

'No,' said Tom quietly. The man was playing with him again and he was not sure how to react.

'Why have you never settled down, Massimo?' asked Tom.

'Doubt,' said Massimo squarely. 'Is this one really the one? How can I be sure?'

Another round of drinks was dispatched.

'What about Pia?' Jonno asked Massimo, affecting nonchalance.

'Pia? Is that her name?' asked Barnes. He made a face. 'Unfortunate.'

Jonno shrugged.

There were whistles and catcalls from Vince and young Barnes. Clearly they were party to some development on the social front that had so far passed Tom by.

Massimo puffed out his chest. 'Lovely girl. Lovely. But –' He paused for effect. 'That one, she has a mother – oh, what a mother! Mothers are like magnifying glasses: they show all the less good things in store very clearly. From the bad-temperedness, to the terrible effects of gravity –' Here he pantomimed first the droop of a smiling face, then the terrifying plummet of once-pert breasts.

They all contemplated this. Another drink was called for.

'Enough of such matters,' said Massimo. 'What are you men going to do with yourselves after the war? Have any of you thought about the racehorse business?'

Tom found his head was spinning.

Frank, ever the one with sense, as well as the fiancée back home, had volunteered to collect them and any equipment they had managed to purchase. By eight o'clock, when he arrived in the small truck, he heard fits of helpless laughter, singing and raucous catcalls from inside the outhouse.

He was duly invited in for a small one, then two for the road. There were toasts to friendly co-operation, beautiful women and the evasion of stern mothers. He then staggered, on account of a very light head for drink, to the truck, swung himself up into the back and demanded to know what the men had done with his steering wheel.

He was redirected to his rightful seat after some confusion and debate. The gearbox and the radiators were loaded with much shouting and choice British oaths. Then there were the five of them to fit into the front. It would be a tight squeeze, thought Tom. He was the last in, but when he opened the door and peered in to find a spot, there were only two bodies on it, Vince and young Barnes. This puzzled him. He stared and thought for quite a while.

He worked it out, eventually. The far door of the cab had opened. On the ground below was a mound, which was snoring. Tom peered closer. It was Frank and Jonno.

The journey back was a blank. It was a hands and knees job after that, followed by sitting up all night in the tent to defeat the dreaded tent spin.

Next morning the outhouse drinkers could hardly move, let alone clean their rifles. Dishevelled wrecks, they cursed their own stupidity and were cursed in turn by the brigadier. To add insult to injurious poisoning, on the truck was a pile of mechanical junk, for which they had apparently paid, an impression reinforced by the lightness of their wallets. Massimo Criachi's prime merchandise was every bit as useless as they had begun to fear by the time their hangovers took hold.

6

The next day when he walked up to Le Macchie, unco-ordinated as well as responsible for the parts debacle, Tom felt deflated. Their time in Petriano was almost up; he could sense it in the air. The cycle which kept them advancing and stopping was turning. It was in the tone of voice when orders were given, the fraying of the makeshift shelters, the degree of familiarity with their surroundings: these were the twitches on the line by which the message was being sent, reeling them northwards in the vast machinery of war.

A cut lemon lay open in front of Giuliana on the table on the terrace outside the kitchen. By it was a branch of white scented blossom. She smiled up at him as he arrived and stood over her. She was working on a drawing of the still life she had arranged. Reaching down, he picked off a moist curl of lemon segment from her cheek. Slowly, he examined the teardrop sac of juice, he put it in his mouth and crushed the tiny shot of bitter sweetness with his tongue.

'How was your meeting with Massimo?' she asked slyly.

'Not so good.'

'Ah.'

'I suppose I should have been warned.'

'Well . . .'

He sat down thankfully, looking around for Giuseppe or Anna but neither was in sight.

Tom had learned to whittle sticks of wood as a boy. Needing some occupation for his hands, which had been subject to bouts of shaking since his hangover had gripped, he picked up an odd piece of olive branch and took out his knife. While she sat drawing, he worked away at the tinder.

She stared for long periods into the heart of flowers, then made precise replicas of stamens and curling petals with her pencil. It was a gesture of intimacy when she handed Tom the pencil and he sharpened it to a point.

'Is there something between you and Massimo?' he asked.

'No! What an idea! What makes you say that?'

'Just . . .'

'He is my father's oldest friend. Practically part of the family.'

'It's just that . . .'

'Massimo flirts with every woman he speaks to,' said Giuliana firmly. 'It doesn't mean a thing.'

There was a cracking behind them in the dry ground. Tom tensed automatically, but it was Maddalena running up to them, waving a large piece of fallen branch. It was curiously cross-shaped. 'Look! Look what I found!' she panted. Her bare arms and legs were encrusted with bark where she had been climbing.

He took it to examine.

'It's for you,' said Maddalena shyly. She had been watching them, he surmised. There had been a chaperone after all.

73

'I want you to make something. For Mamma's birthday.'

Giuliana was smiling at him.

'It can be our secret,' implored Maddalena. 'What I want is a Christ figure that I can fix to the cross. Could you make one for me, could you?'

'For the chapel,' said Giuliana. 'She prays for Emilio there.'

'Who is Emilio?' asked Tom.

Maddalena looked at him scornfully. 'He's our brother, of course!'

Emilio, the only son of the family, was in a partisan unit somewhere to the north. Giuseppe and Anna, naturally, did not impart this information in so many words. They were careful what they said. But Tom gathered that their son had not been back to Le Macchie for many months.

'Such a good boy,' said Anna, when he asked her directly. 'Now Emilio, he has a feeling for the land. The pigs have better litters when he is here, the grapes are rounder and juicier, the geese make more succulent pâtés . . .'

'All by themselves . . .' teased Giuseppe fondly. He ran a finger gently down his wife's cheek and a private look passed between them.

There was a photograph of Emilio on the wall in the drawing room. It showed a boy-man's face, with the fore-shadowing of Giuseppe's beetle brows, and Anna's straight jaw. When Tom asked Giuliana about her brother she said, 'This will all be his, one day. He is passionate about the estate. I like it but he really loves it.'

'Mamma is right. Everyone loves Emilio. He has many friends. The looks on the girls' faces when we arrive some-where – in town for the *festa*, perhaps – and he is with us! He is brave and kind and . . . he understands things. What can I say? He is my big brother. Do you have a big brother?'

'No. I have a little sister. Her name is Margaret.'

'Oh.' She thought for a minute. 'Then we are reversed.'

'Is Emilio like you?'

'No!'

'Why do you laugh?'

'He is ruled by his instincts – perhaps that is what makes him such a good farmer. That is why he –' She hesitated, unsure how much to divulge, whether she could trust him completely.

'That's why he is with the partisans?' guessed Tom.

A downward glance answered his question.

'I'm sure I would do the same, in his position.'

Tom knew little about the situation. What he did know came second-hand from Titch the signals man: that the fighting on the ground had effectively been handed over to the partisans now in the stalemate situation of the Gothic Line in the mountains north of Lucca.

'Mamma . . . she is so worried. And Pappi too. If anything happened to him – but then it is stupid to think that. It is to be expected that something will happen. A soldier must expect to be hurt – it's just that whenever there is no word . . .'

Tom was suddenly much older. In her eyes, and maybe even in his own, he was a seasoned soldier, a man of the world. 'It's almost over. If we've got this far . . .' And he knew he was lying, that this was not how it was.

But she brightened. 'You're right. Of course you're right.' She gathered herself, visibly. 'Come on, I want to show you something. A poppy has seeded in a crack at the bottom of the wall by the sty. The most beautiful dark-red colour, almost black except when the sun shines straight at the middle of the petal.'

But Anna had seen her and come out to chivvy her into getting on with her chores.

Tom watched her go, then hunted around for a suitable piece of wood. When he found it, he held it in his hands for a while, feeling its weight and density, then he pulled out his knife and began to carve.

Later he asked Giuliana again about her brother – his character and beliefs – to which she replied, 'He is an idealist. If he fights, it is for his land, not his country.'

Tom was perplexed.

'Oh, yes, there is a difference,' she assured him.

He was only twenty. He loved sport and chasing the village girls. 'They stand still for him, too,' said Giuliana coyly. 'Mamma cries about him, but she does not want us to know. We all cry about him, but on our own, so that we can seem strong for the others.'

Tom did not know what to say.

All he could tell her, and he prayed it was true, was that the Allies were looking after the partisans: making air drops of weapons and ammunition for their war of attrition, sending survival kits and money. He stopped short of saying that soldiers of other nationalities were fighting alongside them, for there was a pride in the partisan activities that was desperately lacking in other areas of the country's military endeavour. He looked away to see that Anna had glided up and had heard at least part of the conversation.

Without a word, she put her arms round him.

*

He returned again that night, at Anna's invitation. 'A luvverly village girl,' joshed Jonno, miming a voluptuous figure in the air as Tom went off.

'Send 'em on . . .' Tom laughed.

But he already felt he was beyond all that; there was a seriousness to his intent that it suited him to mask by joining in with the barrack room jibes. This was something quite different from the silly fumbling with girls at dances and cinema shows, all forgotten like dreams in the morning as he walked away.

At Le Macchie they had eaten and were sitting out in the still night heat. Candles guttered in jars on the table. The dishes still lay on the table, while they were all staring up into the velvet blackness, staring up at the stars.

'Orion,' said Tom one time, pointing.

'*La costellazione di Orione*,' Giuseppe agreed. An easy one. And so it started. Tom began to learn and his command of Italian swelled with the names of constellations and the words to discuss them. He and Giuseppe discovered a mutual interest in astronomy, of the most basic variety.

'We say that the moon rises,' said Tom. He was sitting next to Giuliana, wondering if he dared to reach out and take her hand in his in the shadow under the table. Her fingers would feel so soft in his, there would be a warm answering pressure in his palm. 'And that the stars fall — even nowadays when we know that isn't the case. It's only how it seems to us, when we are on the part that is moving the most.'

The child Maddalena frowned. 'But . . . how?'

Tom considered for a moment. He settled deeper into the

languid evening and took a draught of his wine. 'Have you ever been sitting on a train –' he began.

She shook her head, eyes vast with attention.

'All right. What about . . . a cart?' He waited for her to nod. 'You are sitting on a cart, which has come to a halt. Then, another cart draws up alongside you, maybe so that a neighbour can speak to your father. You are sitting on the cart and looking at the load in your neighbour's cart. Then it pulls away without warning and you – on the cart which is not moving – have the sensation that you are in fact going backwards suddenly.'

'Suddenly backwards!'

'Does that make sense now?'

'It hasn't happened,' said Maddalena sadly. 'But you say it might happen?'

'It might,' said Tom. 'And what's more, when it does, you will know with great satisfaction what has just happened, and that now you can begin to understand that the moon and the stars do not rise and that the sun does not go down.'

'And that's scientific?' She glanced for confirmation at her father and his benign acceptance of this curious order of things.

'It is,' he said.

'Then I am learning,' said the child.

Under the table, there was a warm squeeze on Tom's hand. It was as if Giuliana had been thinking the same thoughts as he and had had the same longing. This simple act was one of the purest moments of joy that he would remember his whole life.

To be permitted to sit with Giuliana outside the house in

the gathering darkness. That was his reward at the end of it all. Under the stone table under the pine trees, they held hands until their palms were damp.

Not that they were ever alone for long, only when Giuseppe went off to release another jug full of wine from the barrel in the cellar. The wine tasted wonderful – much less weak now that Tom had gained in status as an acquaintance. This time he was chuckling merrily to himself when he returned and handed Tom a book with his free hand. It was battered, a relic from the previous century and borrowed – once upon a long time ago – from a public library in Livorno. It was a Life of Galileo Galilei. 'This is wonderful,' said Tom, caressing the leather spine.

He flipped over some pages. It smelled faintly of mould and mothballs, as if it had been unearthed from some ancient armoire. 'You know . . . I won't understand it. The language is difficult for me . . .'

Giuseppe nodded sagely. 'Then we make sense of it together,' he said. And he put on the reading glasses he appeared to share with Anna. Wire-framed circles, they were too small for him and too large for her.

He took the book. 'I like the science bit – but I like the stories of human nature best,' he said. 'Now listen, this is one of my favourites.'

He began to read, following the text with a finger. The chapter dealt with Galileo's contemporary, the Danish astronomer Tycho Brahe. 'The best thing he did', said Giuseppe, breaking off, 'was to wear a false nose made of silver! Look, it says here: "his own nose having been lost in a duel over an arithmetical theorem".

'What would this have looked like? How would it have been fitted?' Giuseppe demanded, shaking his head and whistling gently in admiration.

'I'm also very fond of the descriptions of Brahe's assistant Johannes Kepler, who, it says, suffered from the mange, intestinal worms and the occasional delusion that he was a dog.'

Tom found himself entranced by Giuseppe's concern for Galileo.

'A man who was *consumed* by the need to prove himself and his ideas!' enthused Giuseppe. 'He knew he was different and he was determined that he was right. But he was also dependent on patronage – and he often came unstuck.'

When they had read several chapters in this way they found they understood each other better. By the end of the book they were little the wiser about the movements of the heavens yet they felt they were the same men under the stars.

S till and contented, they watched a heavy yellow moon break slowly free from its moorings and float above the orchard.

Then there was an explosion – of a recognisably human kind.

Massimo was skittering along the gravel towards them. He was beaming in the candlelight. The announcement burst out of his puffing cheeks: 'I have bought our first horse!'

Giuseppe positively goggled at him.

'She's a beauty – young and fit and nimble! Say something!'

'Ours?'

'That's right.'

'Oh yes?' Giuseppe was playing along. 'Where is she?'

'At this very moment, on a farm not far from Siena. Just wait until you see her!'

'A beauty, you say.'

'A chestnut mare. With a gleaming coat, soft nose and chocolate eyes like a lover.'

'And this vision . . . can she run?'

'Like the wind, my friend – like the wind.'

'So tell me. How much?'

'That, my friend, is the stroke of genius which I have brought to bear on the project. I did some dealing for a friend of my cousin and the man with the horses is a neighbour of his brother. He has a stud farm, or it will be a stud when the war is over. Anyhow, I explained my plans and he was most interested. The upshot is that, for a small stake in the action, the horse is ours.'

'Free?' Giuseppe was incredulous.

'Free . . . except for the cost of her keep. Imagine that, he will keep the horse for us until we are up and running.'

Giuseppe cast mournful eyes to his shoes. 'Imagine . . .'

'Brilliant, eh?'

'Massimo . . . have you any idea what it costs to feed and train and doctor a racehorse when she is sick?'

Massimo waved away these clearly piffling considerations. 'We'll be in on the ground floor, don't you see.'

'I can see all right.'

'Do you think they would rook me?'

'I think that it is a possibility it would be unwise to overlook. And it worries me when you keep saying *we* and *our* . . .'

'Oh, now . . .'

'Massimo, my friend, where dealing in scrap metal, bricks and wire and food is concerned . . . you are my man. But horses . . . no.'

Massimo was unabashed. 'I have brought some grappa to celebrate.'

'That grappa has affected your brain already.'

'Enough! Now drink – to the beautiful darling who will make our entrance into the wonderful world of the turf, the sport of kings!'

'The wonderful world of your imagination, you mean. But, cheers!' Giuseppe pulled down the corners of his rubber lips. 'Good luck, my friend. You will be needing it.'

'I can feel it. This is the beginning of a remarkable turn-about in fortune,' Massimo said and tossed down the hellfire liquid.

And Massimo – glorious, mad, friendly Massimo as he was to Tom in that one instant – bore Giuseppe away, an arm round his shoulder, explaining to his old friend exactly how the great equine plan would work.

It was several minutes before they were sure they were quite alone. Anna's voice floated from a first-floor window, talking to the girls. She was telling them a bedtime story, with many interruptions. There was a low bubbling sound from the kitchen and the sudden swish of wind in the vine canopy above.

The thought of what he wanted to do made his chest contract with longing. He reached out for her hand and then did not take it. She looked at him, a little confused. Her eyes were poppy dark, her lips were slightly open, plump and smooth. He put one raw hand clumsily on her collarbone and with the other he smoothed back her dark hair from her forehead. He had never touched such hair, so thick and velvety. Neither said a word, only dared to hold each other's gaze.

The breeze whispered in the pines. Somewhere across the still valley of heavy sunset a flock of birds wheeled in the sky. Red geraniums nodded in their pots.

Go on, go on.

There was a giggle from upstairs, but the murmur of Anna's narrative continued.

He brushed her cheek – oh, so gently – with the tip of a finger.

'Oh,' she gasped. She cast her great dark eyes down again. He kissed her.

He closed his eyes and felt the hot wet softness of her mouth with every nerve. He could hear nothing now except a pounding like the sea in his ears. He could smell the faint sharpness of lemons, and wild rosemary and the cool of a long day pulverised by the sun.

When they pulled apart, she stared at him again – what had he done? Had he gone too far, had he broken the spell? Her hand shot to her moist lips.

And then she smiled and he could not help himself. He felt the muscles around his mouth aching and pulling – and he was grinning ear to ear like an idiot. And he was laughing! What was he doing? He had to pull himself back from the brink of this insanity before he ruined everything! This would not do. He was not that kind of soldier. Of course there were men who took advantage of the women, but he was not one of them. But – now, she was laughing too.

He pulled her to him in an embrace of pure clumsy relief, as he lost the battle with his own conscience. Then he was kissing her again, playful butterfly kisses all over her forehead, her cheeks, the end of her nose. And passing on his overwhelming joy until she was suffused with the same happiness. She was laughing, softly as music, and they were kissing, and then it was serious again, as it had always been.

When Giuseppe returned, Tom was glad of the darkness to hide his euphoria – and his embarrassment that he had abused the trust of this most generous of hosts. Giuliana, he could feel, had stiffened with awkwardness.

It was clear that Giuseppe had resumed his father's duty as a chaperon. So they opened the book again, and sat side by side looking at pictures in which medieval faces shone from frescos.

'Look at the front,' said Giuseppe. It was an engraved illustration of the Leaning Tower of Pisa. 'My family was once from Pisa. I know all the stories about the tower.'

And so he told them. He held forth with the tale of the medieval builder whose payment was never forthcoming. When he failed to receive all the money owing, this apocryphal mason flew into a rage and ordered the straight completed tower to follow him away from it – and the curse was so powerful that the stones strained after him. It was a fairy tale tower and always had been. 'Then there are stories of hunchbacks and monstrous campanologists . . .'

In the herb-scented darkness, under the table, Tom held Giuliana's hand, stroking her soft skin, barely listening.

'Can you not imagine the great red-haired figure of Galileo

galloping helter-skelter down the galleries, after he has dropped his stones from the seventh tier, appearing six times to his audience, cloak flying, soles flapping on the white stones, crying out, 'Did you see? Did you see!'

And Giuliana's soft hand clasped in his.

They let Giuseppe talk of the tower until he was slumped in his chair, exhausted by an excess of scientific understanding and the liberal quantities of wine which so oiled the requisite part of his brain for the effort. He began to snore.

'Have you seen the tower?' Giuliana asked softly.

'No. But I will now,' Tom assured her.

'Maybe when the war is really over,' she said, allowing the unspoken invitation to float between them.

'Yes,' said Tom.

7

They moved on to Tolentino, the massive convoy grinding through the night up the Umbrian hills towards the front.

Through the stifling heat of the summer the Eighth Army crawled on its belly up the Adriatic flank of Italy. They captured Florence; the Fifth Army – mainly American – to their left, surged up to Livorno and Pisa, then on to Viareggio, the ports and beaches of the Ligurian Sea. Tom and the lads were towards the rear of this huge orchestration of men preparing to force their way through the infamous Gothic Line.

It had fallen to the Allies by the first day of September. Then Rimini, on the coast, was taken and autumn took a grip. Whenever the weather allowed, the advance troops fought forward, up to Ravenna by the beginning of December. Then came a lull. It was a period of regrouping and preparations for the last big push in the springtime. The winter months saw the two foreign forces facing each other in bleak exhaustion on either side of the River Senio.

Tom found that he thought constantly of Giuliana. In the

hours of lying sleepless in his holes in the sodden ground, when he was coaxing shattered engines back to life, when he was supposed to be concentrating on learning the preliminaries of radio operating on the course he had jumped at taking, there was always in his mind the interlude in Petriano.

Then came his chance. It was the first week of 1945, after they had spent Christmas at Castelfidardo, south of the coastal town of Ancona. Tom had leave owing and was ordered to take it. He had no hesitation in deciding what to do. He and Jonno bummed a lift inland on a supply truck, Jonno fidgeting and jiggling his legs all the way in anticipation of meeting up with his girl. By afternoon they were in Petriano.

In the square they separated. Jonno set off, after much adjustment of his collar, for Pia's house; Tom swung his bag over his shoulder and took the path to Le Macchie, nervous but relieved to be on his own. It was muddy going. Dead twigs, too wet to be burned on a range, split and slimed under his boots. A dank walk, the light flat after the bright exuberance of its summer guise.

He pressed on enthusiastically.

He expected to find the house looking battened down against the winter, that he would have to punch his fists hard against the great doors to gain admittance, but they saw him coming. Giuseppe opened the door as he approached and let out a roar of recognition. Anna waved from an upstairs window and the younger girls charged out to meet him, pulling him in by the hands like boisterous tugboats. And then Giuliana appeared behind them. Her face lit up as she smiled.

'So – we had not seen the last of you, after all,' said Giuseppe, clapping him on the back.

Tom felt himself grinning sheepishly. 'I had leave – just for three days.' His heart was hammering.

'You picked a good time, then.'

Natalina and Maddalena shrieked in agreement.

'Tomorrow is the *festa*,' explained Giuliana.

'It is the first week in January, and the *festa* of Santa Antonia will be held in Petriano, war or no war,' boasted Giuseppe.

'The patron saint of animals,' said Natalina sagely. 'So all the animals join in.' She gave a snort like a pig, then she ran round him, butting his legs in play.

Tom made as if to give chase and she ran off, squealing. He moved over to Giuliana. 'How are you?' he asked.

'Well, thank you.' She had two glowing pink spots at the top of her cheeks. She looked away. 'It's cold. Come inside.'

'I've missed you,' he whispered as they passed into the dark interior.

Massimo was ensconced in his usual chair in the kitchen. He stood up and launched himself at Tom. 'Still no parts for my beautiful car?'

Tom shook his head.

'Any chance of a horsebox, then, or even a simple truck and trailer?'

'A horsebox? This wouldn't be anything to do with a certain grand scheme, would it?'

Massimo rolled his eyes, mischief glittering from their blackness.

'No chance,' said Tom. 'I thought you were leaving your horse where she is.'

'She's hungry,' said Massimo morosely. 'Very, very hungry. I was sent a bill this week for her food. It is not possible that one single small horse could eat that much! Something must be wrong with her. I need to get her here, to look after her myself.' He paused. 'I was thinking maybe . . .' He composed a pleading look at Giuseppe and Anna.

'No,' said Giuseppe. 'Don't think.'

'Not in that way please,' Anna chided him.

'Let me talk to you', said Massimo, mustering all his powers of persuasion, 'of elegant ladies, of rich gentlemen, of silk hats, of steam from the flanks of winning runners.' He was addressing them each in turn. 'After the war, the return of gaiety and laughter, of social events, of beautiful clothes, of the excitement of flying hooves at the race-track . . .'

'Shall we start', said Giuseppe, 'with the price of hay?'

'Then', said Massimo, mopping his forehead with as much dignity as he could muster, 'I shall have to redouble my efforts to find a rich wife, even though this may mean a compromise in the department of youth and beauty.'

'It's a hard life for a rogue,' said Anna.

Tom delved into his bag, bringing out a couple of tins of bully beef for Anna and chocolate for the girls. They thanked him profusely. He wished fervently he had managed to bring more.

'Look, look!' cried Maddalena, pulling at his arm. 'I've got something to show you.' She held a strip of well-creased brown paper. Then, her small pink tongue visible between her lips, she put one end of the paper over the other very carefully until it formed a simple knot.

'Are you watching?' she demanded. Then she flattened it with great deliberation in front of him on the table and stood back for Tom's reaction. 'It's a pentagon!' she said crossly when he was too slow with praise.

Tom looked more closely. 'You're right,' he said. 'I've never seen that before. How clever! Well done!'

'Pappi showed me,' said Maddalena. 'It was in one of his books.'

'I'd like to see it,' said Tom seriously. He caught Giuliana's eye. 'You never know when you might need to know how to do that.'

Giuseppe was occupied with his olive groves. The seasons had turned and no human hardship would stop the olives appearing on the gnarled branches of the guardian trees of the small estate.

On the next farm was a mill where the olives were crushed under stone wheels. Giuseppe insisted Tom join him. Tom watched as the oil dribbled from the press.

The miller, whose hands were as soft as those of a wealthy woman, was paid with the thin compacted cake of brown skin left when the process was complete.

'He will sell it on to a firm which can extract more oil with machines,' explained Giuseppe. 'The final dregs are made into fertiliser to be returned to the land.'

His precious oil in casks, Giuseppe turned his attention to the pruning of the olives, a task he regarded with the seriousness of a medical surgeon sizing up the best way to perform an operation. He would walk round each tree, humming and nodding to himself, then double back. 'The olive grower must *feel*' – he patted his chest – 'before he can cut.'

It was a moment of mysticism, in Giuseppe's hands, when he reached out and made his incisions.

But he seemed preoccupied by more than the olive crop, heavier in mood than when Tom had last seen him.

Some instinct, some clue in the way Giuseppe had welcomed him back, dared Tom to ask, 'Have you heard from your son?'

Giuseppe stared at him for a good while. Then he shook his head and looked away. 'The partisans have been told to stand down, return home and conserve their arms. But Emilio has not returned. He did not come home for Christmas.'

That evening Massimo enlisted Giuseppe's help to transport some equipment to the community hall in preparation for the *festa*. While Anna cooked, Tom joined in games with Natalina and Maddalena which left them flushed and shrieking. He had no opportunity to be alone with Giuliana, but the way she smiled at him told him all he needed to know.

She was sewing in the kitchen, where it was warm. Her glossy dark head was bent over a cascade of yellow material, its brightness in faintly ridiculous contrast to the tattered browns and blacks worn by everyone else who came into the room. She was working a seam by hand with quick neat stitches. Tiny glints of the needle in the light of the oil lamp kept catching his eye, even had he not wanted constantly to steal glances in her direction.

'What are you making?' he asked.

'A dress.'

'I like the colour – nice and cheerful.'

She smiled at that. 'I couldn't bear any more drabness. It's for the spring, but until then, it's cheering me up to sew it and think about when I can wear it.'

'You'll stand out in a crowd. Where did you get the material?'

Giuliana blushed slightly. 'It's an old curtain I found upstairs. Hasn't been used for years. I cut out the lining and made a pattern with that. There didn't seem any harm in it. Mamma did not mind.'

'I think it's lovely,' said Tom. He reached out to feel the aged primrose cotton. It was soft and worn under his fingertips. 'No one would ever know it used to be a curtain.'

'Oh, yeah . . .' Maddalena rolled her eyes.

'It will be beautiful, darling,' cut in Anna, a warning edge in her tone.

They ate a bean stew for dinner when Giuseppe and Massimo returned. But then, instead of the long evening's conversation Tom had been anticipating, the family turned in swiftly afterwards. It was no longer summer, with its natural heat. In winter they had to conserve what they could, and sleep under what blankets they had, when it was dark and cold.

Giuliana kissed him goodnight on the stairway up to the attic room where he was to sleep. He spent the night under the eaves in a farmhand's wooden cot. He lay awake for a long time reliving the soft damp warmth of her mouth on his, imagining her lying beside him in the narrow bed. The blankets he burrowed into were rough but it was the best night's sleep he had had for months.

Early the next morning they walked to the main square. Tom watched as neighbours across the streets of the village exchanged the tails of bunting and hung them from bedroom windows above the road. Soon flags were fluttering defiantly, as if to signal that the events of the recent past would change nothing for this one day. The garlanded streets rang with the laughter of children as they chased dogs and cats, waving pink and red ribbons at them to be tied in bows on their tails, and the tinkle of small bells which were to be hung round the animals' necks.

They joined the stream of people converging on the piazza.

From a distance, they saw Jonno with Pia, her formidable mother an outrider on their expedition, her gaze swivelling like a gun turret on his every move.

Tom waved at them jauntily. A watery smile was telegraphed in return.

Giuliana and her mother walked on to the church for mass; Tom and Giuseppe were soon part of the gathering of men in the square to discuss the latest events. There was no official procession through the town, which in summer would be led by the local dignitaries of the church. This was a cold midwinter morning, not warm enough to enjoy a parade. The children wore bright knitted sweaters over their Sunday finery. Groups of older girls and young women made the most of the milling audience, lingering coquettishly at the most attractive knots of young men, then making their way back, and then past again until they were finally called into the church.

The bell began to toll, monotone, and the congregation emerged. Tom found himself buffeted in the crowds, flowing with them, until he felt anchored suddenly. Giuliana's hand had caught his, secretly in the depths of the throng, and pulled him to her side. 'Come,' she whispered. His heart leaped. Then she said mysteriously, 'It's safer here.'

Tom shook his head questioningly.

'The animals,' said Giuliana.

And there they were. From all sides, butting villagers out of the way, were coming cows and bulls, farm horses, sheep and goats and pigs. Behind them were the peasants, prodding them forward with sticks and pulling them on ropes. There was a noisy altercation in one cramped corner of the square when a pregnant cow threatened to pin a child to the wall, and the shouts and cries and snorts and grunts rose from all the men and the beasts of the surrounding countryside.

'What are they doing?' asked Tom, snug now against a doorway with Giuliana pulled into the contours of his body, safely shielded by the jostling crowd.

'The priest will come on the balcony.' She pointed up to the town hall. 'He will bless the animals, to keep them safe and healthy for another year. Not that there are so many now.'

'Will he take long?'

'Long? No, not really.'

'That', said Tom, 'is a great shame.'

In the community hall the village band had struck up. The musicians positively attacked the roar of conversation all around as they squeezed and blew and plucked the tunes from their instruments. Louder and faster they played. Soon the floor was filled with dancers, whirling round and round, faster and faster as the band accelerated. Whoops and laughter rose above the frenzy. A reckless rhythm pushed them all to their limits.

Tom and Giuliana took to the floor and came off giggling and panting. The smell of sweat rose in a pungent cloud. At the side, Tom saw Giuseppe was crying with laughter at the spectacle. Anna, beside him, was holding a handkerchief to her eyes.

'Can't you keep up?' he asked Tom as they admitted defeat.

'Young people!' said Anna.

'Is this some kind of village tradition?' asked Tom, feeling as if the joke was somehow on him.

The madness of the music intensified. The conductor was flailing around, stabbing the hot gusts of pungent air to the beat.

'He's going to fall over any moment now!' spluttered Giuseppe. 'Just you watch – there . . . oh, almost!'

Tom turned to Giuliana. 'What's going on?'

'It's probably something to do with Massimo.'

'How do you mean?'

'The band have been drinking Massimo's grappa since eight o'clock this morning. He's installed a barrel of it under the stage.'

'They're all having a high old time,' agreed Tom. 'But blimey, I wouldn't want their heads tomorrow. Once tried, never forgotten . . . I can tell you.'

There was an almighty crash from the stage as the percussionist fell backwards, taking the cymbals with him. A great cheer went up from the audience, followed by wild applause.

They went outside for air, still laughing. The crowds had thinned. Tom, holding Giuliana's hand, felt he had never been happier. The next moment the woman came at them like a snarling vixen. She spat at their feet. '*Puttana!*' she curled the expletive at Giuliana. Tom tightened his grip on her hand.

'Hey! What the –'

But Giuliana pulled him away, saying nothing.

'What – ?' Tom was outraged.

The woman was jabbing her finger towards them and sobbing. A man had come to restrain and calm her down.

'Who was that? What was she saying?' Tom was shaken, more so than Giuliana, it seemed.

'Nothing. It is nothing.'

'It is not nothing. Tell me.'

'She is Nunzia. She thinks – she is wrong – but she thinks that her brother loves me and that he wants to marry me.'

Tom stared in surprise, thought for a moment, and then chose his words carefully. His heart was ready to leap out of his chest. 'Why does she think that?'

Giuliana shook her head. 'I knew him, no better than any other of the friends I knew in the village. He . . . always he liked me, but as for me . . . no. He was disappointed. What else can I say?'

'But –' Tom was shaken by the sharpness of his emotions – part jealousy, part fear. This was a twist that had not occurred to him, that she already had a suitor in the village, and he cursed himself for his stupidity.

Giuliana was pulling him away. 'Forget about it. Forget about her. She misses him. He has gone off to fight and they have had no word of him for many, many months. Forget about her. Come, there's Pappi. We're dining with the Sarnas.' She tugged at his sleeve and he allowed himself to be led.

Signora Sarna had produced a feast that would have been stunning under any circumstances. First there was pasta served with crushed chicken livers and preserved tomatoes, then fried chicken, then rabbit and cauliflower fritters. Then, for dessert, she served walnuts with small glasses of *vin santo*.

'To our sons! May they be safe in these terrible times.' Giuseppe was the first to raise his glass.

'Has there been any news?' asked Signor Sarna.

'No news.'

'Nor any news from Aldo Mori, his father tells me.'

'No.'

'His mother has prayed in the church every day for him since the middle of December.'

'I know,' said Anna.

'Worse for the boys on the Russian front, you know. So many lost there. Their parents have all but lost hope now.'

For the second time that day the sudden sadness was a slap in the face after the wine and the carnival in the stinging cold.

The next day Tom was happy to avoid the villagers en masse. Especially, he had no wish to see Nunzia again after her outburst. He wondered how many people she had on her side – even if she was wrong about her brother and Giuliana.

Jonno called round briefly, looking glum. His reunion with

Pia had not been a grand success. Mamma had stuck like she was welded on.

'As I tried to tell her, there was nothing to worry about. A mild interest, that's what Englishmen do best. Where matters of the heart are concerned, it's a slight tingle, not a raging torrent of animal passion. I tried to explain that over-heated blood is for other races – English veins aren't built for it, I said, but she was having none of it.'

The Parinis roared with laughter.

'It wasn't funny for me. Every time I asked Pia a simple question, Mamma would answer. She had this look of stone on her face as we sailed through the crowd and sat down for a glass of lemonade. What a day!'

'Are you going to say goodbye?' asked Tom.

Jonno nodded. 'Not hanging around, though. I'll be in the bar till we have to go.'

'I'll see you there,' said Tom.

Tom prepared for departure with a heavy heart. He put what few spare items he had brought back into his kit bag and went downstairs to where Giuliana was sitting on a monk's seat in the hall. She had been quiet all day.

'We're being picked up at half past twelve – our lift back to Castelfidaro.'

She continued pleating the material of her skirt.

Did he dare to kiss her properly where they might be seen? He reached out and pulled her into his arms.

'I'll send word,' whispered Tom. 'We'll meet just where we said we would, in Pisa.'

'By the tower,' she said.

'As soon as we can, I'll come to you in Pisa.'

'By the tower, like we always said we would,' said Giuliana.

'And you'll wear the yellow dress.'

'Oh, yes, I'll walk towards you, dressed in gold like a dandelion.'

'I'll write to you,' said Tom. 'It's almost over now, you'll see.'

She kissed his cheek.

Then Anna and Giuseppe materialised from the kitchen. They said their goodbyes and wished him luck.

Giuliana went outside with him. Behind her on the wall of the house there was passion flower, bereft of its fantastical summer blooms, winding naked up and along the building, dark leaves nodding in the breeze. He kissed her lingeringly, then reluctantly took his leave. Behind him the landscape rolled back around the family, enclosing the farmhouse, folding them in the only comfort they would take. This was not the time. They had all been unlucky.

Down the track, under the tunnel made by the cypresses interlocking overhead, the road was leopard speckled under a sudden burst of wintry sun. The countryside was full of strangeness as he was detaching himself from it.

It was a bitter afternoon. The hard frost had dissolved into patches of occasional iridescence on the path in front of him as heavy cloud forms shifted above. He saw her before she noticed him and his heart sank at the utter predictability of it all: Nunzia was in front of him on the rubbly mud making her way into the village. She was wrapped in a coarse baggy coat, a child hanging on each hand. She had no large basket, in any case it was too late for shopping. What little had come into the shops would long have been snapped up.

Tom kept up a steady pace, distracted by his thoughts. At one point he stared up at the billowing stacks of clouds, imagining that he heard engine noise, but he could see nothing. The wind was rustling the branches and bushes all around. It was hard to make out higher-pitched sounds.

The Allies, it seemed, were maintaining their campaign of attrition against the Gothic Line, softening up the enemy troops dug in for the winter. They flew reconnaissance missions. That made Tom feel better. At least some small progress was being made in this second stalemate of a winter. But they also made surprise air raids, then withdrew into weeks of inactivity. The bombing runs were a necessary evil, liberation bringing destruction. In the previous year Pisa had sustained areas of serious fire damage from the Allies' aerial bombardment. There was much resentment and sadness when a shell exploded in the south gallery of the Camposanto Monumentale, gravely damaging the fourteenth-century frescos.

Tom followed Nunzia and the children into the tired and cracked alley leading into the square. He had the conviction, unfinished but insistent in his brain, that he should explain his position. He increased his pace, wondering whether he might possibly catch up with her, make her listen to him. Would she listen to him? Then she turned round, hearing his footfall. When she saw who it was, she scowled furiously. She bustled on faster, gathering the small girl closer and muttering something to the boy. Tom was debating his next move when he heard the noise again, this time unmistakably. They were all in the square now and Nunzia had set her shoulders square with determination, heading for her own house just beyond the corner.

Then it happened. Tom felt his body tense as his subconscious registered what the slight change in the compression of the air around them and the particular combination of sounds signified.

'Nunzia! Stop! Come back!' he shouted.

She began to trot towards the door to her home in a cracked sandy building, pushing her son in front of her. Obligingly, the boy scampered ahead. He was a good child. But the little girl dug her heels in and began to complain like all toddlers do when they are shunted in a direction they do not want to take. Perhaps she had seen something in a window that she wanted to examine, or an animal, or maybe she was tired and had had enough orders that day. Whatever the cause, she stopped dead. It all happened in seconds. Nunzia was narrowing her eyes, staring at Tom as if to curse him while shouting at the girl and coming back to drag her into obedience. Petulantly, the girl was backing away.

Tom was running now towards them. The boy had gone on, out of sight.

Nunzia pulled the child violently into the house just as the pressure and the sound intensified. Without thinking, Tom threw himself after them at the moment of the explosion. The noise made the blood beat in his ears. His veins were on fire.

'Come out!' he shouted helplessly.

Nunzia and the little girl were at the end of the hall, the sound of masonry cracking overhead. Tom lunged forward and tried to grab them both. Nunzia kicked him viciously in the shin. She shouted something he did not understand.

He had scooped up the child and was running out with her pressed to his chest before he even knew he had made the decision. The roar of walls collapsing was all around them. The way out was already partially block by rubble he had to stumble over. Smoky flames howled to his left, so he ran right and set the child down, yelling to a horrorstruck passer-by to take her.

Then he ran in again. Nunzia, screaming hysterically, was trapped under stones and a wooden beam, covered in grey dust. She looked like a furious stiff statue, still cursing him as he scrabbled to release her and drag her back down the hall. As they fell through the doorway, they were caught by a rush of plummeting heaviness and sharpness. They lay back winded and bloody. Other hands pulled them away.

The boy's body was found a day later, when the stones of the ruined house had settled. Nunzia's legs were shattered. Tom suffered a dislocated shoulder and deep cuts to his arms. The three-year-old girl, who was howling the loudest with confusion and having the breath knocked out of her as she was felled by her rescuer, emerged with no visible wounds. Her name was Annunziata Coia.

It was known in military parlance as 'wanton jettisoning'. Outside the military it was kept quiet. There had been trouble before – clusters of Allied bombs falling miles from strategic targets – or even on main roads on which the local inhabitants were going about their peaceful business. Just as the population was gladder about the Allied advance the closer it was to the front line, so they were alternately scathing and scared of the occasional careless arrogance of the foreign air forces.

It was the worst moment of Tom Wainwright's war.

For although he was not responsible for the bomb falling, it was he who drove the woman and her children towards it, his selfish concerns which had made her hurry away from him and towards the explosion.

He saw the glass like lethal raindrops in her hair. She was convulsed with pain and grief and hatred. She was entitled and he was full of shame.

And so the balance between saviour and aggressor tipped once again, in a tiny dusty corner of a village which was of no interest to anyone but those who lived and loved and died there.

III.

8

The plane lands. Isabel trudges her way through the hot crowds at Gatwick, waits an age feeling displaced in a clammy hall full of people for the monorail link from the satellite lounges to the main terminal, then hefts her bag on to a trolley with ideas of its own. She fights its runaway wheel through the throng, detaching herself with every step from Italy. She waits in a long untidy line for a taxi, then at last she is speeding along the motorway, through the neat greenness of the countryside. Compared with the exuberant disorder of the Italian roads, all is orderly and clearly marked in fat toytown letters.

At her own front door, she fumbles for the keys to her flat – a practical two-bedroom apartment on the first floor of a block purpose built – and has to push hard at the door. Behind it is a pile of mail on the mat. None of the envelopes looks interesting; none is handwritten. The place smells closed up. She dumps her bags in the small hall, then moves into the sitting room. She throws open a window, then another.

It is past ten o'clock before she thinks of telephoning her mother to let her know she is back. Too late to call. Isabel is relieved. She is not in the mood to recount the events of the past week, has not yet decided how to frame her thoughts.

She has brought back two bottles of good red wine. She opens the Barolo now, pours herself a glass and lies back in her favourite chair, in silence apart from the heartbeat sound of the music system from the flat upstairs.

She has a hot bath and sleeps like the dead in her own firm bed.

Next morning Isabel is energised by the comparative chill in the air, after Italy. She is keen to begin, to tackle the uneasy void.

She picks up the telephone early. 'How are you, Mum?'

'So-so. I've had the most awful cold. Been very down with it. In my throat as well as the head.' Pat does not sound well.

Isabel waits for her to ask how her trip has gone. She does not.

'I had a very interesting time,' says Isabel. 'The ceremony was . . . simple but quite touching.'

Pat does not respond.

'Thought you were fine about me going.'

A pause. It is so protracted that Isabel wonders if the telephone line has gone dead.

Then Pat says, 'I was.'

'Meaning what? That you're not now, after the fact?'

There is a sniff at the end of the line, that might have been to do with the cold, and might not. 'I've had time to think.'

'You've had years to think. We both have,' says Isabel, her anger nearer the surface now.

'It would have been best left alone, after all these years.' Pat has hardened her position, it seems.

But Isabel feels new steel in herself. 'As far as I'm concerned,' she says, 'it's better to know.'

'Better for whom, would that be?'

'For God's sake, Mum, for all of us – can't you see that? We can't go on for ever hoping our imaginations will prop us up!'

There is silence.

'He has been in Italy.' There, it is said. 'One of the people I met in Petriano says that he came back. There was no doubt it was him.'

Nothing.

What kind of reaction is she expecting from Patricia?

'Mum? You still there?'

'I'm here.'

It is hopeless. Pat simply does not want to know.

'I'm going to ring Aunt Margaret and tell her.'

'Fine,' says Pat in a tone that lets her daughter know it is not.

'I think I should. It's the right thing to do.'

'Fine.'

Isabel puts down the receiver and sits back, exasperated. Of course she had known that Pat would find this hard, but she was not prepared for this stonewalling.

Somehow, she had hoped that her own courage would be matched by her mother's.

'Margaret? It's Isabel.'
      'Oh – hello.' A pause. 'Safely back, then?'

'Yes. Last night.'

'How was it?'

'Well, I'd like to tell you about it. Can I come and see you?'

'Of course you can, Isabel. Whenever you want. I don't get out too much these days, so it's up to you.'

'I could come today if you like.' Suddenly Isabel is desperate to tell while it is still occupying the greater part of her thoughts.

'Why don't you come at teatime, then.'

'Just a cup of tea. Don't go to any trouble. That would be lovely.'

The Victorian terraced cottage where Margaret has lived for some forty years is neat and well maintained. A blue-budded ceanothus bush is so well established in the few feet of garden in front of the house that it has been clipped into a small tree to allow light into the bay window. Isabel remembers it well. If anything, at four o'clock on a spring afternoon the house has grown in desirability since she was here last. Gentrification of the quiet street has sprouted merry window boxes here and there along its length; the paint on these small but solid residences is mostly slick and shiny. Isabel taps on the brass lion's head knocker and Margaret answers almost immediately.

Inside it is the home of an elderly magpie, a comfortable nest woven with loose photographs of long-grown children, jewelled with personal treasures and mementoes, every surface cluttered. Isabel remembers her Uncle Larry there, how he and Margaret would sit either side of the fireplace,

THE ART OF FALLING

clucking their long-held annoyances: roof leaking again, tatty
paintwork on the skirting boards, minor domestic details that
had to be discussed and attended to. The patchwork of rugs,
the patterns in the wallpaper and on the tea service are part
of the garlands and swirls of Isabel's girlhood, held in some
forgotten area of her brain.

It has been a long time since she last visited.

Margaret has probably been thinking that too, but she keeps
it to herself. This is not the time for any kind of recriminations.

She serves tea and Isabel tells her about the ceremony in
Petriano and what she has discovered.

Margaret's eyes spill over when Isabel describes the piazza,
the flags on the table and the bunting. 'It would have meant
a lot to him,' she says.

'Yes.'

'It makes sense, I suppose, that he's been back.'

'I think so.'

'Twenty years ago, though. A long time. He might not still
be there.'

'I know.'

It is Margaret's way of warning her not to raise her hopes.
But she also wants to find answers to long-posed questions.
'I've been thinking a great deal, too, since you went,' says
Margaret. Her bright dark eyes are still bird beady. 'One night
I just couldn't sleep, and the thinking drove me out of bed
to the big cupboard on the landing. There I was, in the early
hours, rummaging around in boxes and drawers! Some of
them were mine, some were full of things my mother stored.
I couldn't throw them away and I never did know what to
do with them. Anyway, I found these,' she says triumphantly.

She leans over and extracts something from the shelf of a table by her chair. She holds out a small bundle of papers. 'You can have them.'

Isabel reaches out to take them.

They are friable, brown around the edges, held together by a thick brown elastic band. A lire note. There are two letters and a larger thick brown envelope.

'The letters are from Tom to our mum,' explained Margaret. 'And as for the other thing – either he sent that to her as well, or he left it with her when he moved out. They were down the side of a box full of all sorts: buttons and tins of old photographs and scraps of material.

'I was also trying to remember the names of his old army pals, but do you know, I can't. It was all so long ago. John and Frank, that's all I can come up with. And I can't think that he ever kept up with them much after the war. As for their surnames – did I ever know their surnames? I can't think that I did.'

Isabel is fingering the letters, but she is not hopeful.

'And anything he left at home with Mum would have been thrown out a long time ago,' she says, finding it hard to keep a level voice. As ever, she is torn between pity for Patricia and resentment.

Margaret diplomatically says nothing.

Downstairs, they spread out the letters on the dining-room table. There are photographs, too, many of which Isabel does not recall seeing before.

'You can take some, if you want to,' says Margaret.

'Could I?'

It has not escaped Isabel that she has had to go to Margaret to receive them. It is unsaid that she should have come before. She does not know any longer why she did not.

'I'll borrow some – it's so easy to make copies now. I'll get the originals back to you as soon as I can, then we'll both have them.'

The letters do not give away much, only the date, one of which is February and the other July of 1945. They were written in Italy, but no one would have expected an address. The first is full of bland greetings. He has injured his arm, it seems, although he does not explain how. The second is more interesting.

Dear Mum,

I am well. It is all over bar the shouting now, as you will know. A great relief all round, but there is still a lot to be done. I have a car! I 'requisitioned' an old truck and Frank and I drove back south with some of the others. Have seen the people I wrote about before. A very sad business. It makes you very grateful to be still here in one piece – apart from gouged arm (not serious). I am going to stay here for a while to help clear up the mess.

It is important to me to do what I can. I hope you under-stand, that I will not be back with you right away. I am still thinking of you and Margaret always.

Your loving son,

Tom

'Is this all there were?' asks Isabel.

'All there were in the tin. Of course there must have been letters earlier on, but as to where those have gone to . . . He would always write when he could. I remember Mum reading them out loud to me. I'd be knitting – we were always knitting in those days – and she would read out what he'd written. He'd always try to cheer us up, make us laugh about something, even if the letters didn't tell us much about what was really going on.'

The thick envelope, which is not addressed, contains a crude copy of what seems to be a military document.

'Sergeant Tom Wainwright,' says Isabel, reading a little.

'He was promoted, before he came back home.' There is no disguising the pride in Margaret's tone.

Isabel replaces it carefully. 'I'll look at this later, if I may,' she says.

'As I said, you can have them.'

'Why didn't we try to do this before?' Isabel says sadly.

'Perhaps it wasn't the time, dear.'

'No. Perhaps not.'

But that is not all.

Margaret has also been hurt. It has been easy to overlook the fact that Tom simply disappeared from her life too.

'I think that I might go back – to finish what I've started,' Isabel told her. 'How would you feel about that?'

Margaret folds her hands in her lap. 'I think that would be a very good idea.'

'So I have your blessing for this?'

Margaret does not hesitate. 'Yes, of course you do.'

'It's raking up the past.'

Margaret gives her a shrewd look. 'That's Patricia talking,' she says.

Isabel considers carefully. 'Yes,' she says, 'it is.'

She puts the small bundle of papers together carefully. 'Thank you for these.'

'They don't seem much. I don't know why I never thought to look before.'

'Because we never actually did anything about it before – until something happened to make us do this.'

'They don't really say much, though.'

'Maybe not. We don't know yet.'

As Isabel leaves they hug with a sense of mutual understanding that has not existed between them for many years. Isabel wonders whether to attempt an explanation but decides against it. It is enough that they have come this far.

This is not something she feels she can explain yet to her mother. So when she goes to see Pat that evening she simply says, 'I'm going back to Italy, Mum.'

A deep sigh. 'Whatever for?'

'Because I have to.'

Outside the house when she arrived the air felt autumnal, cold despite the bright sunshine of the day. The dying light held a sweet tang of smoke. This is the house where she grew up, a spacious Edwardian villa in a pleasant tree-lined street with its solid, familiar rooms.

'And can you take another holiday so soon?' Pat is not going to make this easy.

Isabel takes a deep breath. 'I'm not going on holiday. I'm going to resign from Farrers and go for a couple of months . . . maybe longer.'

'What? Oh, no, Isabel – not on a wild-goose chase. You can't!'

'I can. I want to.'

'But your career?'

'What about it? I've been thinking about moving on for a while. If it means I take a break from work, that's not the end of the world. Plenty of people do it – take some extended time off to travel or just do something different. Then . . . I come back, and apply for other jobs. I'm well qualified, experienced, I'll get another job. I have money in the bank, no dependants –'

Her mother sniffs loudly.

'How's your cold today?' asks Isabel.

'I'm all right I suppose.' It is true that her voice is no longer thick with it. But Pat does not look well. Her eyes are red-rimmed and there is a heaviness in her face, its folds pulled down by more than the cold.

'Look,' Isabel continues, 'I'm lucky to be in a position to be able to do this. It's an opportunity – to take time off, sort my life out.'

'A mid-life crisis, that's what this is.' Pat imbues the diagnosis with the sour implication that this could be a hereditary trait.

'You know,' says Isabel, changing the tone of her voice, 'what I'd really like is to have a look through his things, to show you some photographs I took while I was there and for us to talk about it all. I don't see what can be gained otherwise.'

'Well, there you have it, Isabel. Because I don't see what can be gained at all by doing what you want to do.'

Isabel stands up and goes to the door. 'If that's the way you feel, fine.' She glares at her mother. 'But you can't stop me looking through Dad's stuff.'

Pat gives her a strange look.

'What?' Isabel demands to know. She is impatient to go

upstairs and pull out the old books, go through the old trunk of her father's effects she has not examined since she was a girl. She is already moving away, going through the door to the hall.

'You can't go through all that old rubbish.'

'Well, I'm sorry, but that's what I'm going to do.'

Pat shakes her head. 'You won't find anything up there.'

'What?'

'It's not there. I got rid of it.'

'What?' Isabel stops, stupid with disbelief. 'You did what?'

'Everything's gone. Even the books.' Pat is defiant. She is holding her head high in the way Isabel knows well.

But this time Isabel is standing up to her. Wherever the stuff has gone — to a charity shop, to the antiquarian book-seller on the high street — Isabel will retrieve it. 'I want it back,' she says.

'No,' says Pat.

'No?' Anger is surging through Isabel's veins.

'I had a bonfire. I should have done it a long time ago.'

Isabel sinks down on the arm of the sofa nearest the door. 'But why? *Why?*'

'Because I had to. It was for the best.'

'When then? When did you do this?'

Pat does not reply.

Isabel stares at her, this woman who burns books and papers. She doesn't recognise her. 'You did it because I went to Italy, is that it?'

Pat averts her eyes, sniffs and blows her nose. There are smudges of grey on the handkerchief, Isabel notices. This is her mother, who has always been so particular. Then in the very moment of realisation, Isabel lunges towards the doorway, runs through the kitchen, fumbles with the key in the lock of the back door, manages to open it and stumbles up the path to the end of the twilit garden.

The scent is stronger here. Isabel can taste the bitter residue of smoke above the ash, smell that homely autumn bonfire tang she has always loved.

It is simplicity itself to organise her departure.

At Farrers, the surveying firm where she has worked for eight years, the senior partner does not want her to resign. There is a little negotiation. He agrees with her that a period of time off is desirable – he calls it a sabbatical, although she will be unpaid during the three months she has requested.

She does not tell him what her plans are.

After that it is just a matter of honouring the commitments she already has on her desk. As Isabel has always been a conscientious worker, this takes more than a month. She decides against letting her flat. She does not want to be caught out with tenants if she returns sooner than expected.

A neighbour who has become a friend agrees to use the spare key she holds to check the flat at intervals and send on any bills.

By the time Isabel calls two of her oldest friends to catch up with their news and tell them hers, she is no longer in any danger of changing her mind. She has extended unpaid leave from work. It was so easy to arrange she cannot think why she never asked before.

But if she had expected cautionary advice, none is forthcoming. Both of them, married with children, sound delighted for her, as if they have long known this was what she needed to do, but had given up hoping she would realise.

'If I don't do this now, I might regret it for ever,' she tells each of them in turn, as a coda to the main story. 'I may turn out to have something, I may not . . .'

Their answers are the same.

'Italy's no distance,' they both say.

'You don't think I'm – ?'

'Go on. Do it. What's the worst that can happen?'

'I can come back,' says Isabel. 'None the wiser.'

'There you are, then.'

And Isabel thinks of Pat, running harder and harder to escape the strange blow fate has dealt her, and by doing so running herself to a standstill, never moving on, never allowing herself to understand the cause of the impulse, feeling only the bitterness.

Pat has become a woman who burns books, and worse. The terrible knowledge crystallises Isabel's resolve.

When Isabel returns to Italy it is early summer. The heat is intense compared with England.

She has nothing useful to help her, just a meaningless letter, a few old photographs and a military document she will have to think very carefully about before showing it to anyone. Reading its stark words on flimsy wartime paper turned her blood to ice. It concerns a part of her father's life that was always closed to her and she can only speculate what its long-term effects were. Is it a foretaste of what she might find now? What else has she never known about him?

It takes her the best part of a day to reach Le Macchie. She flies to Pisa again but avoids the manic autostrada, its

concrete tentacles and whirling interchanges. She drives the
old roads through a rolling heat haze as hill after hill unfolds.
Past the rickety vertebrae of terracotta tiles on country roofs.
Past vineyards on rounded slopes that are almost vertical in
places. Past fields of sunflowers, through scented clouds of
rosemary, the sounds of cicadas, hill towns perched on
promontories, their stones the same sun-baked brown.

She stops for a break in a roadside café north of Arezzo
and takes a newspaper from the bar to read with her coffee.

Earthquakes have shuddered across the region. The frescos
of the great cathedral at Assisi have gone.

It is a time of instability. The earth's plates are groaning
and wrenching under the hills. The violence far, far beneath
the soil is resulting in tiny movements putting pressure on
the foundations of ancient stones. Cracks are widened, at first
minutely, then with growing force. The frescos by Giotto
which adorned the vast domed ceiling of the cathedral fell
in a cloud of billowing dust, sending priceless fragments floating in the atmosphere like a dirty star shower.

The cupola on the thirteenth-century bell tower in Foligno
has snapped off. It hangs cock-eyed to the left, as if in the
act of toppling. A photograph shows a group of firemen in
the cradle of a hydraulic platform suspended as near to it as
they dare, assessing the risk.

At Le Macchie, Isabel is welcomed like a member of the
family. Indeed, she is now a member of the larger family
of the village. Her father's name is on the plaque in the
piazza. It is still shiny new, but it is part of the fabric of their
stones.

The four Sarna sons shout and wave as the car draws up, and Elsa runs out of the house drying her hands.

'I've saved your apartment for you,' says Elsa, clasping her warmly.

It is ready for her, scrubbed and tangy with cleaning agents. There are families here on holiday in the other apartments now – Belgian and German, a Dutch couple – but the Sarnas will not hear of Isabel paying a weekly rate for hers.

Elsa takes one of her bags and they walk up together. The floor is cool and dark in the familiar sitting room. It seems a long time since she was here that first evening in the spring, uncertain and among strangers.

'How are you all?' asks Isabel. 'I've missed you.'

Elsa beams. 'Alessandro has broken his wrist falling from a horse he had no business trying to mount, but apart from that, everything is good. Bruno says there are all the signs of a huge sunflower harvest. We have plenty of tourist bookings and it will be a good year for wine, too. Oh, and there's water in the swimming pool, so you can swim whenever you want.'

'That's wonderful. Thank you.'

'And . . . Gianni has some news for you.'

Her heart lurches.

'He will be waiting at Sophia's café at seven o'clock,' says Elsa.

9

Gianni Criachi is waiting for her as arranged, in the café where Isabel asked for directions when she first arrived in Petriano. He gives her an unselfconscious hug. Sophia scuttles out, smoothing her apron, to kiss her on both cheeks and summon her son to present Isabel with a glass of chilled prosecco.

'It's lovely to be back,' says Isabel, and she means it.

'I have arranged it all,' says Gianni proudly. They have settled at a table and he is sitting as men here do: over-powering a rickety chair, at ease in his body, effortless in his movements. Isabel sees herself, pale and squinting, reflected in his sunglasses.

'We will go to Pisa tomorrow. Matteo can see us,' he continues. 'He knows someone who may be able to help. You know there have been some quite interesting developments?'

For a lurching moment Isabel imagines he means he has unearthed a lead on Tom. The notion is like a cold touch to her bones. But she is mistaken.

'My friend Matteo di Castagno is working on the latest commission to save the leaning tower. They have built a test tower on the same ground and they are putting the soil extraction theory to the test. They will dig out the earth on the opposite side to the lean to get a realignment. It is exciting, because it seems to be working. It is one of the oldest theories, which has been used successfully in other countries. A British professor is involved, you know.'

Isabel has been following developments, of course, and this is new information to her, yet her mind wanders as Gianni talks. He has begun to tell her of the difficulties the tower engineers are experiencing due to inconsistencies in the distressed foundations.

'You know that I can't even be certain he is here,' she interrupts. Part of her wants to blurt out her misgivings, to tell someone about her mother's enraged attempts to dissuade her from this fool's errand. She wants to explain that the tower has only ever been a means to an end: the only, faintly ridiculous, clue that she has.

'But if he is here,' says Gianni, 'then how will we find him if we don't look? We must do everything we can to find him.'

'Yes, but –'

'I believe in fate,' says Gianni simply. 'If it is meant to be . . .'

Isabel cannot help herself. She laughs. At heart he is a countryman, this man; the sophistication of his well-cut clothes and the trappings of his well-paid job in complex computers is a veneer.

He shrugs good-humouredly, as if to say, you don't have to believe it too, but wait and see.

'Did the newspaper print a report about the ceremony?' asks Isabel.

'Oh, yes. The week after.'

'So . . . I take it that no one came forward with any information.'

'No, I'm sorry.'

Meanwhile there are more prosaic matters, such as: where would records of foreign citizens be kept? This is what Isabel needs to find out first. Perhaps she should begin by asking at the police station. Are the registers of hotel visitors returned there?

Gianni nods. 'In the late seventies, when there was a considerable threat of terrorist activity, the law was made that visitors from another country had to register with the police within three days of arrival. If he had come here in 1980, when there were some serious attacks, he would almost certainly have had to register.'

'So it would be possible to trace those records.'

'In theory, yes.'

'But in practice, maybe not.'

Gianni looks resigned to the probability. 'Perhaps if I could find a friend who might know someone, but . . . ' He is not optimistic.

'Have you any more information now, from your family?' he asks.

Isabel shakes her head. 'Not really. My Aunt Margaret – my father's sister – found a letter and an army document she has given to me. Quite honestly, the letter does not say very much, only that he is planning to stay in Italy for a while longer.'

'And the document?'

'Well, that is more interesting –' She hesitates. Interesting? What is she saying? It is horrific. It is best left unread, undiscussed. Its images disturb her quiet moments. What would they do to those who would have been more closely involved, on whose land they occurred? 'But I don't understand how it relates exactly to my father's story.'

'What is it about?' Gianni is pressing her, cannot understand why she does not simply tell him the contents of the papers.

It is hard and, for now, she fudges. 'It's . . . army stuff. Administration,' she says. She should not have mentioned it in the first place, is regretting her impetuosity. 'Gianni, I need to approach this logically. Is there a British consulate in Pisa?'

'Not in Pisa. But in Firenze there might be . . . It is easy to find out. I can do that at work tomorrow.'

'That would be very kind. There must be records held there of British nationals resident in the country, I would have thought.'

'You could be right. I'm sorry, I don't know for certain.'

Neither do I, thinks Isabel, I am only guessing, as I have guessed at so much.

'Did you put an advertisement in the newspapers, in the end?' she asks, although she is well aware that he would have told her had he gained any kind of result.

'Yes.' He pauses. 'There was no response.'

'Ah, well . . .' She is disappointed. Of course she is disappointed, although – did she really expect anything else?

'It's not the end,' he says firmly.

'No.'

'Sometimes, it takes longer.'

They consider this for a while in the silky evening light. 'I am taking you to Pisa, though,' he says.

*

In his office in the Department of Soil Mechanics at the University of Pisa, Matteo di Castagno has a model of the tower on a side desk. There are papers and books overhanging every surface and shelf. He is a strong, powerful man, who takes up a lot of space in the room, as he stands and strides around and flings out his arms to illustrate a point. Brown stains on the carpet seem to indicate that these expansive gestures of his have caught too many precariously balanced coffee cups and tipped them into flight. A red sheen to his luxuriant dark hair suggests he loves the sun.

'Gianni helped me set up a computer programme such as an architect would use, where every piece of work, every join can be simulated and seen from all angles.'

'My masterwork!' says Gianni happily.

'The greatest problem is the question of judgement,' says Matteo. 'We have to stop the tower leaning any further if it is to survive, but we still want it to lean. If it does not lean, then it is not itself. It will lose its character. It is a very delicate balance because leaning is to do with motion. How do we freeze a pile of stones in the act of falling? But that is what we must do.'

'And the stones have acquired their own stress patterns. To be pulled against that . . .'

'That's right.'

It is clear that Matteo is passionate about his work. His intensity is tangible in the atmosphere of the small office. He leans forward in his chair to emphasise his points, looks from one to the other of them to make sure they have understood the import of what he is telling them. Behind the gold-rimmed glasses he wears, his eyes shine.

'Without intervention, it will collapse. The tower in Pavia

collapsed in 1989 and that wasn't even leaning. Four bystanders were killed. Disaster could be triggered by an earthquake as happened in Assisi. Or even a storm. There is heavy rainfall in Pisa – you would not believe how heavily it can rain! And the tower is fragile. The water table is high, higher than the level of the exposed base columns in the *cantina*, and when the water rises it lifts the tower on the south side. When the sun comes out again it dries the soil and it settles back.

'But it does not react in a predictable way – it is prone to sudden lurches when its foundations are disturbed in order to attempt another rescue.'

'Did you know it was a cylinder?' interjects Gianni, turning to Isabel. 'You should see what they have inside now! Monitoring equipment and sensors that can detect a footstep. Amazing!'

'Is there any chance at all that I might be allowed to see inside it?' asks Isabel. She is careful not to request permission actually to climb it.

'The critical point is at a doorway on the second storey,' says Matteo, equally careful to avoid a question he does not want to answer. 'If the marble which is bearing the load cracks and wrenches apart, then tensions accumulated over centuries will be released. The tower will not simply fall over, it will explode!

'We've built a test tower,' he goes on. 'It's crude, but the soil extraction theory is being put to the test. It seems to be working, but the battle is on to persuade the committee to allow the huge bores to tunnel under the tower itself. The only way is to take out the soil where the tower's foundations are lifting. A ten per cent reduction in the lean, and the attendant stress on the masonry, is all that is envisaged. A minor adjustment which will give it another three hundred years of existence.'

'It is being called mad by experts who hold opposing views, as you can imagine,' says Gianni.

'Who is in charge, ultimately?' asks Isabel.

'The Committee,' says Matteo. 'Although agreements even there are difficult to reach.'

'And what keeps them going?' asks Gianni with a smile. 'You can be sure that no one wants to be the President of the Opera at the time the tower collapses!'

'The Opera?' asks Isabel, confused.

'The Works Committee,' explains Matteo. 'They have had responsibility for buildings since the eleventh century. You have seen the low yellow building behind the cathedral and tower? That's the committee building.'

'And in the archives of the Opera there are thousands and thousands of schemes submitted to save the tower, from historical blueprints to suggestions by schoolchildren,' says Gianni. 'Everything has been kept.'

Isabel is beginning to see the relevance of this.

'You would not believe the papers in the Opera building. Ideas and suggestions from all over the world. Files that are centuries old. Everything is kept – everything!'

So this is why they are here.

'You mean, if ever my father had written to one of the commissions, the letter would have been kept?' Isabel ventures.

'I think . . . yes. If he is as interested as you say he is. Perhaps, yes, we would be able to find it. Although . . .' It is an impressive shrug which hints at the infinite possibilities for administrative chaos behind closed doors.

'Perhaps he did,' says Isabel. 'But . . . realistically, would it be possible to find?'

'I can ask,' says Matteo.

Something unforeseen has happened. Matteo has felt her looking at him. It is clear that he has, for he holds the glance she gives him after she has dropped her long gaze. He knows that she is attracted to him and that this is the beginning of the game.

'We should have lunch – and talk some more,' says Matteo. He makes the suggestion implicitly first, by standing up and lightly touching Isabel's arm.

The three of them walk to a small restaurant in a back street.

Gianni and Matteo engage in a discussion about the steel cables being used. They are careful not to exclude Isabel, but she has plenty of opportunity to look at Matteo across the table. It is unsettling, this instinctive reaction she has had to Matteo, and not to Gianni who is attractive too and kind to her.

Matteo has dark wavy hair, which he wears slightly too long, olive skin and carved cheekbones; a beautiful face, she decides. His gestures as he folds away the menu after only seconds of perusal, as he picks up his glass for a sip and sets it down, imply that this is a man who is supremely sure of himself. His posture is relaxed but alert. He does not fidget with the items on the table; he gives Gianni his full attention.

Isabel explores his high forehead, the slightly hooked nose and full lips. He is a very attractive man. He is most likely married. If he is not then he must be involved in a relation-ship of some kind. She rearranges her own fixed, listening expression and continues to stare as the conversation moves on to relative tensions.

Matteo has dark shadows under his eyes. His irises are a deep purplish brown, which seems to soften when he meets her gaze and she does not look away.

She feels a rush of heat. Inexplicably, this is guilt. She feels guilty for thinking in this way. And a part of her is afraid. This is not what she has come here for.

'Wait!' says Matteo as they are about to say goodbye. 'There's something else I need to get from my office. You might be interested.' He says this directly to Isabel.

'I'll go to get my car,' says Gianni. 'I can bring it to the entrance.'

'OK,' says Isabel smartly.

Gianni walks off in the direction of his car.

Matteo smiles. 'Would you like to come up with me for a moment?'

Isabel smiles too and follows him into the building. She is certain she knows what he is going to say. She is disappointed almost immediately, though.

'I remembered, there was an old librarian at the Opera archive. He retired last year. It was like a labour of love for him. He might remember anyone who seemed to take more than the normal interest, especially if they were English.'

They reach his office and Matteo begins rummaging through an untidy desk drawer. Eventually he finds a tatty copybook, on the cover of which are scrawled some numbers.

'Well . . . that's very good of you. It's very kind of you to take such trouble.'

'It is nothing.'

He writes the old librarian's details – his name, which is Mauro Arinci, and a telephone number – on the back of one of his own cards and hands it to her.

She is surprised to find, when they stand close together for the first time, that he is not very much taller than she is. She hardly has to raise her face to look into his eyes. Isabel is the first to look away.

'I will do some research too. When I have some information I shall tell you over dinner,' says Matteo. He does not ask her. He is sure as anything of her and he is right.

On the way back to Petriano, Gianni tunes the radio to a sports station and listens for some minutes to the football results. After a while he switches it off in disgust. The car seems too silent after the excitable babble. Gianni drives with purpose, dominating every curve in the road as if he were leading a woman in some complicated swooping dance.

'How long have you known Matteo?' she asks casually.

Gianni accelerates smoothly again. 'A long time.' He laughs. 'We were at the university together.'

'Did you do the same course?'

'No! We play on the same football team.'

'And – does it surprise you that he's a *dottore* now?'

Gianni turns to look at her. 'Only in that I always thought he'd make a better defender. He was a good football player.'

Isabel laughs lightly. She does not know how to continue

talking about Matteo without giving herself away. But she has already done so, it seems.

Gianni shakes his head and smiles. 'He is not married,' he says.

A couple of days later one of the Sarna boys comes running out to find her. She is wanted on the telephone. Isabel's first reaction is to reach for her notebook and pen, then to follow at a trot.

The boy runs off before she can ask him who it is.

She has been expecting some calls. Her dogged enquiries, submitted to the police, made to local hotels and banks, have all resulted in promises that she will be contacted if any useful information can be found. Everyone she has spoken to has been polite, but their reactions have not been encouraging.

It is Matteo.

Isabel is absurdly pleased. Even more so when he says, 'Can you come to Pisa? I have found someone who remembers something very interesting. It may be a connection with your father. He is old now, but his memory is still very good.'

'Who is he?'

'He used to work in the botanical garden here – it's part of the university. He's another one who has always had an interest in the works on the tower. Everyone at the department knows him. He stops to ask us in the street what the latest developments are. So, you will come?'

She will, of course.

'Oh,' says Elsa with a grin, 'so you have met Matteo, then?'

'Yes,' says Isabel. 'I thought he was very nice.'

'Very nice,' says Elsa. She is smiling broadly.

*

Isabel has come properly prepared this time. In her bag she has various photographs of Tom and copies to give out. There he is a serious youth in his army uniform, then much older and serious still in a beach snap taken by Isabel the last summer holiday he took with her in 1979. There he is on the south Devon coast. At fifty-seven he is heavier and less clear-sighted. His shirt is open at the neck, but his expression, she sees now, is anxious. Does it presage what is to come, or had it become by then the habitual set of his face?

She meets Matteo at the entrance to the building where she said goodbye. It is a Monday night and the streets are deserted. She could have parked the car within fifty yards of the Piazza dei Miracoli if she had known how clear the roads were. Throughout the drive, she has been wondering whether the attraction she felt for this man was an aberration, whether she was reading too much into the brief exchanges of their first meeting. She is too old for these silly games. By which she means that she is exasperated with herself for feeling nervous, fluttery even, in his presence.

They set off, walking purposefully. He leads her to the botanical garden on the Via Luca Ghini. The shadows are lengthening and for a moment Isabel thinks they have left it too late to get in. But Matteo is a member of the university – he is not bound by visiting times.

They wander in and he greets a man bent over by a maple tree. But then Matteo gives a small grunt of recognition and steers her round to the northern path where the lotuses grow.

'Salvatore!' he calls. A man looks up from his ruminations.

'*Salvatore – questa e una mia amica, Signorina Wainwright.* Isabel, may I introduce Salvatore Olvari.'

He is a man between middle and old age, surely nearing retirement. He has a thin bony face like a deer's, his skin burned almost black by his outdoor life. He has been making notes, but now that they have approached he puts the stub of a pencil behind his ear.

They shake hands.

'*Posso farti una domanda importante? Spero che ci puoi aiutare.*' Matteo has something important to ask him, he says. 'No one knows this garden better than Salvatore does,' says Matteo turning to Isabel. 'He has worked here for years and years – and his father before him.'

Isabel listens while Matteo talks to him for a while. She cannot understand it all. Perhaps Matteo is gently reminding him of an earlier conversation and does not want to invest the occasion with so much significance that the old man veers from the essential truth of his previous story.

'Do you have your father's photograph?' asks Matteo.

Isabel excavates the 1979 version of Tom from her bag.

Salvatore Olvari reaches out for it; his withered hands are shaking. He is considering it intently. Matteo tries gently to coax some recollection from him.

Then, on the turn of a thought, Salvatore is emphatic. '*Sì!*' he says. '*Inglese?*'

His eyes meet Isabel's. She nods.

Salvatore is speaking rapidly to Matteo, but glancing all the time at her as she strains to make out the sense. At last, Matteo turns to her, putting a hand lightly on hers. 'It was a long time ago, but it is possible it was him. He cannot be sure and he does not want to say definitely yes, in case he is wrong.'

Matteo is asking another question. Salvatore has to think hard before answering.

'If he is right,' Matteo says, 'it was possibly fifteen years – something of that order.'

Isabel bites back the questions that surge into her mouth.

'He remembers because it was the year he had a breakthrough with the cinnamon camphora. He could look up the records for that, but it must have been around fifteen years ago, probably more. They talked about the tower and the latest repairs.'

Matteo continues. 'Salvatore remembers that he was very well informed about the methods then in currency to stop the tilt. They had an interesting discussion. He was surprised that an Englishman knew so much.'

'And then what? He went off alone again?' Isabel cannot help blurting this out.

A rapid exchange between the two men.

Matteo shakes his head. 'He was not alone. He was with a woman.'

'With a woman!' says Isabel. Her head is full of fact and imagination, the undertow of put-aside emotion. 'Is he sure?'

There is a brief consultation.

'It was a long time ago,' reiterates Matteo in translation. 'He does not recall everything.'

'No,' says Isabel, embarrassed suddenly. 'Why should he?'

'He knows the woman was Italian – it was she who helped translate, as I am doing. They spoke of complex engineering.'

'When he left England he hadn't spoken Italian for years,' says Isabel softly.

The two men confer.

'In fact, he spoke quite good Italian. He remembers the woman because she loved flowers, was very knowledgeable.'

'Did he see either of them again?'

A further quite lengthy exchange ensues.

'He can't recall seeing the man again.'

At this Salvatore interrupts, as if a shaft of forgotten explanation has illuminated the story.

'Apparently, he did see the woman again. But the man was not with her.'

Isabel thanks him. It is all she can say.

Matteo insists on taking her out to dinner. He leads her to the eastern side of the city, away from the tourist stops and into the warrens of neighbourhood shops. On the way he makes a brief detour to show her the Piazza dei Cavalieri with its magnificent palazzo and distinctive double staircase. It is strangely forlorn, though. There is graffiti on the building that houses the city's department of public works.

'This is where there was once another tower, the Torre della Fame – a terrible place where the Count Ugolino della Gherardesca was imprisoned and starved to death,' says Matteo. He shakes his head, then grins. 'Nice stories, hey?'

From inside a church a choir can be heard singing – practising, it seems, for they stop and repeat a phrase, then reprise the whole piece.

'This is the place,' says Matteo.

There are tables set outside a small restaurant on the corner of a park. They go in and sit under a deep awning. It is perfect, like sitting in a garden surrounded by a hedge of bay trees lined up in pots. Isabel is glad there is space to breathe; suddenly she is feeling nervous in his company.

They order pasta and chicken and house wine. He too seems intent on keeping the atmosphere as light as possible. Perhaps he has picked up her tension.

'So now I know –' She wants to talk, inconsequential though her observations might be. 'My father has been here. At least – if Signor Olvari is right. And I know that my instinct was right, and that's something, you know. When all you've had for years is this . . . imagination. Actually to discover some piece of evidence that makes it more real . . .'

There is a running track in the middle of the park. In the gathering night, men and women take a turn round, some with dogs, pumping their silhouettes past yellow ochre buildings on the far side of the gardens. Other people pass by more closely, the other side of the potted bays, their faces thrown into green relief from the decorative lights underneath.

'Why did you never do this before?' he asks. This is not an idle question. His tone and his eyes are serious.

'I think . . . because I didn't realise that I had to,' she says. 'I thought that I could just go on as normal and that one day I would forget about it. But now I know that it doesn't work like that. The more I refused to think about it, the more it affected me. Not in ways that I could automatically say I'm unhappy because of this, I think about it all the time. It was much more subtle than that. For years and years I felt resentful and angry towards him, but I didn't necessarily equate that with being unhappy. I didn't think I was particularly unhappy.'

Matteo is nodding. He says nothing.

Isabel gets a grip on herself. What is she doing, talking to him like this? He does not want to hear about these things. 'What about you – tell me a little about your family,' she says.

'My family are farmers. I have a brother and a sister. Now, we are talking about you. Have you ever been married?'

His directness takes her breath away. For several seconds she does not reply. Then she gives in to his perspicacity. 'No,' she says.

'I don't think that was because you were never asked.'

'No,' she says again. She thinks of the times when she has shut down her feelings and with them the relationships that might have developed. 'I became pretty cynical.'

'Difficult for you to trust.'

'Yes.'

He is attentive to her needs, pouring a little more wine, more water.

When they leave the restaurant Matteo offers her his arm and she takes it, feels the warm weight beneath the slightly crumpled tan linen suit and tries to ground herself in the present.

10

They are walking back down the Lung'Arno, this time on the south side of the river. It is almost midnight and the stroll that was to have taken her back to her parked car has lengthened indeterminately. Their fingers are lightly entwined. Isabel can scarcely believe what this signifies, what may be about to happen. But for now they are in no hurry. It is a clear, close night. Any wind coming off the slow river is like warm breath. Isabel looks up into the sky as she has always done.

'What are you thinking?' he asks.

It sounds like a lovers' question. But she must not think that, not yet at least. 'I was looking at the stars,' she says.

'And thinking?'

'Thinking about the way they explode into life and fade. Their light takes so long to travel here, by the time we can see them in our sky they might not even exist any longer. What we can see is what once was, not what is now.'

Matteo gives her one of his little wry smiles, as if to say, are you going to surprise me again? He has already told her she is the only woman he has ever met who knows that

Edward Cresy and G. L. Taylor made a survey of the leaning tower in the early nineteenth century.

'Are you an observer or a theorist?' he asks.

'What do you mean?'

'When scientists study the universe they have to be one or the other. The observers look and note and try to make connections. The theorists imagine and calculate, and then try to find a proof by looking.'

'It seems to me that you would have to be a bit of both.'

Matteo smiles. 'I am not convinced this is possible, from an academic standpoint.'

They stroll a little further, in a comfortable rhythm.

'My friend is a cosmologist,' he continues. 'He says that to discover how the universe will end we must go back to see how it began. The bad news is it began with nothing – then an explosion.'

'So it ends with an explosion, then nothing.'

'No . . . not necessarily. But can the universe go on expanding for ever? Will it collapse in on itself at the stage when it cannot? This is what he is working on. I find it fascinating.'

'It is.'

'You see, again there are two choices; forwards or backwards. If there is enough matter in the universe, then gravity will override the expansion. And this will cause another big bang. Or if there is not enough matter for gravity to hold the universe together, then it will get thinner and darker and colder until everything has drifted away and there is nothing.'

'Very dark and very lonely.'

They wonder about this for a moment.

'He's an observer – your friend?'

Matteo nods.

'And what is he seeing?'

'Supernovae. They are watching the stars explode. When that happens – he tells me – they can measure the speed that the universe is moving. They wanted to measure the slowdown in their speed. At least, that is what the cosmologists expected – but something unexpected has happened. They have discovered that gravity is not slowing down the stars – the universe is moving away faster and faster. What the observers have seen and recorded is defying all the known laws of physics.'

'That's . . . amazing.'

'It is very, very exciting. It could change everything. If they are right, it could mean the discovery of new laws of nature.'

'And the old will have to be reassessed . . . so it looks like it'll be the sad dark place, then.'

They walk on for a while in silence. There is a faint slap or ripple from the river, then the sound is lost to an accelerating car on the opposite bank. The brightest lights in the black sky are the blinking wing and tail lights of aeroplanes descending and rising above the airport to the south.

'You only move on in science by proving someone else wrong. Even here – Galileo was trying to prove Aristotle was wrong about gravity.'

'By dropping his weights from the top of the leaning tower, right?' says Isabel.

'You know about that? I'm impressed.' He is teasing, slightly. 'Well, you know – the Galileo legend is disputed. They say now that he proved his theory – that all objects, heavy and light, fall equally fast – by thought experiment.'

'*Thought* experiment? So he never actually did it?'

'Probably not. At least not from the tower itself. He did not need to. He had set up the paradox, you see.'

'Explain,' says Isabel.

Matteo strokes her fingers. 'The accepted belief, advanced by Aristotle, was that heavy bodies fell faster than light ones. But Galileo's thought experiment went as follows: imagine that a light object is attached by a thin string to a heavy object and dropped from a tower.'

'OK,' says Isabel.

'The question is then: does the heavy object pull the light object down faster, or does the light object slow the fall of the heavy one?'

Isabel's answer is immediate. 'Neither. They fall at the same rate because they have become one object.'

'Well – almost right – but you have the benefit of modern scientific understanding. Galileo did not. His brilliance was in asserting that if Aristotle was right, then the light object would trail behind the heavy, and the string would become taut, meaning that the light object was holding back the heavy one.

'On the other hand, as you say, the two objects together have effectively become one slightly heavier piece and so, according to Aristotle, should fall faster than the heavy one by itself. And if that is so, then the lighter object would be speeding up the fall of the heavy one.

'So that is the contradictory conclusion: that the light object would both be slowing down and speeding up the heavy one's rate of descent.'

'Which is nonsensical,' says Isabel, absorbing this.

'Exactly. The only consistent explanation is that both weights fall at the same rate,' says Matteo. 'Simple – and all done by logical thought without actually having to climb to a height with weights and strings.'

They walk on in silence for a while.

'My father told me about Galileo dropping the weights,' she concedes sadly.

'How old were you when your father left?' asks Matteo.

'I was seventeen.'

'Not a child, then.'

'Not really.'

'What did you do?'

What did they do, she and her mother? They worried; they were frightened. Then, when the days turned into weeks and the police remained unmoved by their concerns, they were angry in their abandonment. And they carried on living, doing what they had to do until such time as they had another option. 'After a day or so my mother called the police, and we waited,' says Isabel.

'And there was only waiting?' he asks.

'Well, we – my mother, rather – telephoned everyone we knew who might have known where he had gone. Obviously we tried to find out for ourselves – but there was nothing, no one knew anything. It was a blank wall. We – my mother – contacted the missing persons bureaux and we waited. For a long time we used to talk about what we'd say to him when he came back, whether we'd be shouting and furious, or compassionate and understanding about whatever it was that sent him off like that. But then, as the weeks turned into months, then into years, we stopped talking like that, stopped talking about him.'

'You were very hurt and unable to understand,' says Matteo.

'Of course.' Isabel does not quite know how to react to his attempt at empathy. How to explain the searing pain, the lack of comprehension, the slow coming to terms with the knowledge that however she had imagined her relationship with her father, and had built her understanding of herself so far on that, she had been mistaken? The long years of blocking out and starting again.

'Is this why you have never married?'

She is taken aback again by his directness. She can feel the hairs on her arms standing on end despite the warmth all around her. Her answer is as honest as it can be. 'I don't know. Perhaps, but not consciously.'

Their bodies are lightly touching. Her shoulder brushes constantly against his arm. The first few times this happens she moves away slightly, deliberately putting a little more space between them. But subtly he has moved towards her again.

'Will you let me help you?' he asks.

Isabel hesitates. There is an ambiguity in his question, and equally, more bound into her answer than the acceptance of his assistance in the solving of a twenty-year-old puzzle.

'Yes,' she says.

'Don't go back to Petriano tonight. Stay here with me,' he says.

She wants to, but she says, 'No, I can't.'

'I didn't mean . . . I have a spare room. It is late.'

'No . . . thank you, but I won't, because –' Because it is too soon. Because she has the strongest sense that this – this intangible, fragile link they feel between them – could be important. Because she cannot yet abandon all the ingrained caution.

They walk on side by side in silence a few paces.

'That is not to say I don't want to,' says Isabel awkwardly.

'It's OK.'

She has rebuffed him. Perhaps he is not such a man of the world as he appears.

They are nearly at the spot where she left the car. They turn the corner and it is there. That is it, then. There will be a stilted goodnight and she will drive away. She aches at the thought.

He looks down at his feet.

Any minute now and she will put the car key in the door and it will all be over. 'I would like so much to see you again,' says Isabel. Can he hear the desperation in her voice? 'I've loved being with you tonight.'

A light gleams from a house over the way. He is in outline. She turns in to the black of his shadow. And then he is holding her, his mouth finding hers tentatively in the darkness. His kiss is warm and moist. She is shivering as they pull apart. It is later than she ever intended, she thinks. She must be getting cold.

'Tomorrow, tell Elsa that you are staying in Pisa after you have dinner with me,' says Matteo.

He must have any number of joyful, uncomplicated beautiful Italian women. As Gianni does. Gianni, she has discovered, leads quite a life, romantically.

She knows so little about Matteo. All she knows is that there has been a connection between them. Something indefinable and quite possibly delusory.

They have talked about hers, but what is his history? He is not married – those were the words Gianni used. But do they mean that he was once? Or is he one of those men who have become a new stereotype for the family-orientated Italians: the man who can hardly bear to tear himself away from his mother, who lives at home or close by until he finds a woman who will tolerate Mamma's opinion on all matters? Somehow she doubts that one, but how is she to know?

'You are asking me to come back tomorrow evening?'

'If you would like to,' he says.

'I'm going to Florence tomorrow to visit the British consulate. I have an appointment at four o'clock.'

'Then you can come here afterwards.'

'Yes,' she says, 'I can.'

The British consulate in Florence occupies the prestigious floor known as the *piano nobile* of a stately building on the Lung'Arno Corsini. Inside it is furnished simply in the drably everlasting style of a local government office. Standing in the reception area, having been allowed past the security door, Isabel might be in the planning department of some district council offices in England rather than a sun-baked southern place of world-renowned beauty.

She is shown into a small impersonal office and given a seat. The other side of a large desk, the consular official is a youngish woman with bad skin. To give herself gravitas she is wearing fashionably framed glasses. Her greeting is friendly but perfunctory.

Isabel reiterates the request she has already made by phone.

The consular official introduces herself as Annette Barclay. She places her fingertips together in a steeple and says she is sorry. She has checked as thoroughly as she could, although there have been a few problems with the new computerised system. There are no current records of a Tom Wainwright resident in northern Italy.

'Current records,' says Isabel carefully. 'Does that mean that it is possible he might have been resident here at some time, but not at present?'

Ms Barclay considers this. 'Yes,' she says. 'I suppose so.'

'So,' Isabel says, trying to damp down her irritation, 'Do you keep the records when they are no longer current?'

There is a pause, which threatens to lengthen embarrassingly.

'It's difficult to say,' says Ms Barclay eventually. Then, leaning forward slightly, she admits, 'I'm afraid I'm just on secondment out here due to staff illness. I've only been here since last week and frankly, things are a bit of a mess.'

'I see,' says Isabel. 'So the old records are not on a computer system?'

'You said 1980? Unlikely. Probably would have been on some index file. The point is that registration with the British consulate is entirely voluntary,' says Ms Barclay, clearly feeling on safer ground with this pronouncement. 'In some far-flung parts of the world it is recommended that British citizens register, but there is no obligation to do so. Somewhere like Tuscany, eight out of ten expats wouldn't bother.'

Isabel thinks quickly. 'But you would certainly have contact with a British citizen here if they got into any kind of trouble?' She can hardly bear to say the next part, but she does, 'Or in the event of a death, perhaps.'

'Then, yes, almost certainly. In the event of one of our nationals being arrested for any reason it is courtesy for the foreign government to notify the consulate. Well, in the case of death, I suppose, that would only be if no family were here and immediately contactable.'

'And there is no record of Tom Wainwright in that category?'

'Not that I have been able to find.'

'Not to hand, anyway.'

'No,' says Ms Barclay.

'So, what? Should I try again in a while?' prompts Isabel, her patience evaporating.

'Well, that might be an idea. Although, if I do find a record which includes an address, I would still not be able to give that to you.'

'I'm sorry – you wouldn't?'

'Oh no, all I could do then would be to contact the subject myself and pass on your request. Our records are strictly confidential. Do you want to give me a contact address so that I can do that if it is possible?'

'It's all I can do, isn't it?' says Isabel.

'I'm afraid so. I'm sorry.'

Isabel considers for a moment, then writes down her address in Guildford on the notepad she is offered. Then, to be sure, although she is not keen on impulsive optimism as a rule, she adds another option, care of the Sarna family at Le Macchie.

She takes her leave feeling flat and unsatisfied, though. She goes straight to the underground car park where she has left the car and within minutes she is back on the road heading west. She does not have the heart to spend a moment longer in Florence. Not this time. She does not want to infuse its beauties with disappointment.

*

Matteo's apartment is on the top floor of a modern block on the outskirts of Pisa. It is functional and surprisingly sparse. There are outbreaks of untidiness but these are contained behind screens in the living room.

A large plain mirror hangs over a fake fireplace. A group of brightly coloured obelisks and spheres have been placed in front of it on the mantelpiece. A few large modern paintings hang on the white walls. Mounted black and white photographs of water and rocks hang in the lobby and corridor – one can be seen through the open door.

Isabel picks up a sense that this is a place without history for him.

There is a small balcony facing north. From it Pisa is huddled higgledy-piggledy beneath the folds of indigo hills. She can just make out the tower. It is a tiny white anomaly in the darkening distance. They stand together and admire the view.

'This is the reason I took it,' he says. 'I can stand back and see the big picture.' The way he says it – with resignation – implies he may not mean this geographically.

They must be two hundred feet up in the evening sky, Isabel estimates. She feels a little light-headed.

Isabel has not always been afraid of falling; she hopes this mild vertigo, this irrational fear, will go as abruptly as it arrived. She is not in thrall to the fear. It is more like an awareness, a low-grade hum in the background when she has ascended to the top floors of a tall building, or sees the stately complex engineering of a giant bridge. She wonders sometimes where it came from, this odd disorientation. But she can think of no trauma that has metamorphosed and lodged in the dark reaches of her mind.

She thinks again of the way she loved climbing as a child, whether it was trees, playground frames, hills. And the cliffs, of course, with her hand in Tom's. The edges of the cliffs are white and roaring in her mind. She can smell the tang of the chalk and sea, hear the gulls as they wheel overhead as they would stride across the rolling green grass towards Beachy Head and the Seven Sisters to the point where they could see the sheer drops. Fear tempered with self-preservation. What if they saw someone jump? What would they do? What would they *see*?

Her hand in Tom's, safe.

Why does it make her so sad to think back to that time? Surely she has rationalised her responses to what happened years ago. She was happy, then, and safe, no matter what was to happen in the future. That should not detract from the days which were as they were. Or does the knowledge of what came next poison that happiness?

She will not think of that now, not here.

'Come on,' says Matteo. 'We're going out to dinner.'

She smiles at his directness, wondering whether it is a facet of the way he translates his thoughts into English, or whether he always likes to be in charge. 'I'm not used to taking orders,' she says, teasing.

He pauses in the act of pulling on his jacket. 'You don't want to?' He looks puzzled.

'Yes! Of course I do! I was just –' How could she explain? It was a flip remark. 'I was thinking how nice it is sometimes to be told what to do.'

Matteo grins.

'Where are we going?' asks Isabel, as they leave the apartment.

He offers her his arm with a gallant gesture. 'To Lucca.'

She has seen the name on maps but has only a hazy idea of its location. 'Lucca? Is it far?'

'Fifteen minutes, maybe.'

Isabel winks at him. 'Italian driving, I assume.'

'I can see we will soon understand each other very well.'

'I think you're right.'

Through the dusk to the north-west of Pisa, Matteo takes a little less than a quarter of an hour to reach the city walls of Lucca. He drives fast, but smoothly.

'Not so bad, eh?' he says, as he parks the powerful car expertly.

'I felt quite safe most of the time.' Isabel cocks her head, making sure he knows she is not serious. The banter that is developing between them is precious, too fragile yet to take chances on misinterpretation.

He laughs and shakes his head. 'This way.'

They start to walk into the central maze of streets. 'You haven't said – is there some reason you wanted to bring me here?'

'This is where I come from. Well, my family has a farm just outside.'

'Oh!' She is touched.

'You don't mind coming this far?'

'No! I – I think it's wonderful.'

'It is a very lovely place.'

That wasn't what I meant, thinks Isabel. But she keeps it to herself.

'There is a very tall thin tower here – with trees growing

from the top,' says Matteo. 'In the daytime you can climb up, but we are too late today.'

'Just as well,' Isabel assures him. 'I'm not too good with heights.'

'Why is that?'

'I don't know. It's just something I noticed one day. And once I had noticed it, it never went away.'

He does not pursue the issue and she is grateful. They stroll companionably into the Piazza San Michele. The tiers of delicate white columns on the church are lit like a stage set.

'It's beautiful,' whispers Isabel.

'This is the place.' He leads her into a restaurant.

They are shown to a table in an upstairs room. The interior is modern and minimalist in counterpoint to the crumbling stucco of the building's façade. She is getting used to this contrast, wherever she goes in this part of Italy.

'This piazza used to be the forum in Roman times,' says Matteo, as if reading her mind. 'Imagine – for two thousand years people have been coming here to meet and talk and eat. They have markets here, just the same as then. I used to come as a child, with my family.'

'To sell produce?'

'Sometimes. Honey and almonds, when they were in season. But usually just to meet the other farmers and talk. In July and August we would rush to get a place in the shade of the church. It's the only place that's cool.'

As he talks of past summers, Isabel cannot help but be reminded of the families in Petriano. Were these the kind of scenes her father saw when he was welcomed to Le Macchie? Did the same seductive images of blue hills and slanting sun forming in her mind surround him?

Matteo reaches across the table to take her hand. His touch is warm and strong.

As they leave the restaurant hours later, Isabel feels a sharp tingle on her bare arm. In her state of happy wine-cushioned tiredness she takes a moment to register what the feeling is. It is rain.

Matteo grimaces up at the sky and takes off his jacket to give to her. 'I'm sorry,' he says in the manner of one whose expectations have been unpleasantly let down. 'It hardly ever rains on a night like this. Now . . . we might get a bit wet.'

'No, we won't,' says Isabel automatically and delves into her bag. She has produced a telescopic umbrella and has it waving above them before she realises that Matteo is staring at her incredulously.

'What is *that*?'

'What does it look like?'

But he is laughing at her – he has never seen anything as funny.

'What?' asks Isabel.

He puts an arm round her and they huddle under the umbrella as best they can. 'You could not be anything else but an Englishwoman,' he says and kisses her gently on the lips.

He is still chuckling as they reach the car.

That night she accepts his invitation to stay in his flat, in the spare bedroom.

*

'Yore like him, don't you?' says Elsa archly.

Isabel is sitting with her at the kitchen table at Le Macchie helping to shell peas. Being allowed to join in even this tiny task is a mark of her acceptance, Isabel realises.

'Mmm. Yes, I do. Don't you?'

They exchange smiles.

'That wasn't how I meant –'

'I know what you meant,' says Isabel.

'He likes you. Very much.'

Isabel resists the impulse to say that this all seems very juvenile. Besides, it is what she wants to hear.

'He told Gianni,' says Elsa, neatly pre-empting any need to ask the question.

'Well, then . . . '

'Are you going to see him again?'

Isabel nods. 'I have to go to Pisa anyway on Thursday. I'm going to meet one of the archivists at the Opera to see whether I might be allowed some special access. Matteo has organised it all.'

'I hope it leads somewhere,' says Elsa. 'On both counts.'

Mauro Arinci, the elderly librarian, receives her graciously in a dusty corner of the Opera but does not want to raise her hopes. 'So many papers are stored here, some have been unopened for years – for decades,' he says sadly, raking long thin fingers through his white hair.

'You have never had a visit from an Englishman named Tom Wainwright? He might have come in person if he had been here.'

Mauro Arinci shakes his head. 'Not many visitors like that.

I'm sorry. I don't know of anyone who remembers him coming here.' He looks carefully again at the photograph in front of him. 'You can come in one day and look through some files if you want. You may find someone else you can ask.' But he does not hold out much hope.

'It was always a rather optimistic idea,' admits Isabel.

She leaves feeling chastened, as if she has wildly over-reached herself in this. Is it even possible to unravel the past? Has she left it too late? *Why* has she left it so late?

She spends the rest of the afternoon walking slowly through the great cathedral, then sitting in a wooden prayer seat oblivious to the shuffling parties of tourists being guided all around her.

Matteo is making dinner. At his apartment, Isabel has a sense she had before, that this is a stop-gap living space. It is curiously impersonal compared with his office at the university. There are certainly no signs of a woman's presence here.

'How long have you lived here?' asks Isabel.

Matteo hesitates. He is unwrapping stuffed peppers from a delicatessen bag. His hands are large and square. They are tanned. Above them there are black hairs on his wrists that curl from beneath blue shirt cuffs. He is not cooking dinner, exactly, but assembling it. Either way, Isabel appreciates the significance of the gesture. 'A couple of years,' he says.

'That's not long.' What is she trying to say?

'No,' he says.

He hands her a glass of white wine and their fingers brush.

Isabel allows herself to imagine for a moment his hands on her body.

Matteo arranges fruit in a bowl. He is waiting for her to probe further and Isabel thinks she detects a hint of amusement in his expression.

She does not ask. It is pure arrogance at this stage to assume that any current or recently past relationship of his has a bearing on her. They are grown-ups in a grown-up situation. There is only the present to concern them. That is why she is here. She raises her glass and drinks.

'Let us eat,' says Matteo. He leads her to a perspex table on which several large candles are burning.

'You will stay tonight, won't you?' Matteo's eyes seem to soften as he holds her gaze, inviting as melted chocolate.

Isabel smiles but she is nervous. It is more than a year, she realises, since she was last with a man. She has experience, but that experience has never – all right, rarely – included casual sex. Anticipation makes her heart pound. She suspects her cheeks are flushed.

She excuses herself and goes to the bathroom. It is a small flat and she cannot avoid the open door of the bedroom. A lamp burns on a table and the covers of the bed look clean and crisp. The stage is set, she thinks and she laughs self-consciously to herself.

Why not?

This is what she needs. For lately she has been feeling that she can no longer see things simply, that every article, every view, every sound in this country is freighted with associations. Associations with the past. She needs this small but exciting impetuosity now, here, in the present.

She examines her face in the bathroom mirror, adjusts her hair and adds a little more lipstick. She is wearing a long soft button-through dress which clings to her hips and breasts. Its rich creamy colour makes her look and feel voluptuous. She smoothes it and returns to the sitting room.

Matteo has put some soft jazz on the CD player. He is standing by the open doors to the balcony.

As she walks towards him, her body is loose and free. The curving lines of it feel alive and seductive. It is a powerful feeling.

She comes up close to him and reaches out for him. She has another pang of anxiety: that although she has taken the initiative she will not be able to please him, that she might not be as alluring or skilled as the other women who have seduced him. Then he lays his full soft lips on hers and draws her body close into his. There is a moment of strangeness, which she contains in the darkness behind closed eyes, and then his scent, and the touch and the warmth and the strength of him wrap her in sudden happiness.

Then there is a moment when it seems impossible to tell where the boundaries of her body are and where his begins. They are part of some new force, neither him nor her but made of both.

Still standing, they each feel the recesses of the other's body, pushing deeper into hot wet mouths. One hand is in her dress now, and its exploration is smooth and powerful. She can feel the hardness of his body and is excited, partly by her own daring.

He leads her into the bedroom and pulls her half-open dress back over her shoulders so that it drops to the floor.

He moves back a little. Now he is really looking at her. She can feel the sweep of his eyes over her skin as if it were a physical touch.

They then come together again.

Afterwards he says, 'Stay.'

'I will stay. It's very late. Besides . . .' She teases him with a finger on his thigh. 'I told Elsa . . .'

'No. Stay – for a long time,' says Matteo. His hair is curled damply on his forehead. He is wearing an intense expression, like a child wanting assurance. She is amazed.

Isabel breaks the intensity with a butterfly kiss. This is the last thing she expected.

She feels that he is the one who wants to say too much while she will not stray out of the present. She has asked no questions and elicited no promises. 'Don't make any promises,' she whispers. 'Please don't promise.'

The next morning the matter is decided for her.

As Isabel arrives back at Le Macchie, two couples on German-registered motorbikes are leaving, looking around at the mellow beauty of the farmhouse as they sit two by two astride the gleaming BMWs. They are preparing to leave, but clearly they are going reluctantly. Elsa is pointing across the valley, indicating the place on the map that one of the men is holding out.

Isabel turns her car in nearby. As she climbs out, she hears Elsa telling them, in English, that they will find the other place very comfortable. They are sure to find a place to stay somewhere in that village or the next.

The Germans roar off down the dust track.

Isabel is appalled. Elsa turns to greet her warmly, but Isabel brushes aside her teasing questions about Matteo. 'Elsa, did you turn them away on my account? I can't let you do that, turn away good business because of me!'

Elsa shrugs. 'It is nothing.'

'It is not. Please! You've been so generous, but –' Isabel is embarrassed as she can see immediately her own ulterior motive behind the decision, 'I've been here a week now and this is high season for the tourists. It is time that I moved on.'

'Not exactly a week,' says Elsa.

'Five days, but you won't let me pay anything, not even a token amount.'

'How can we take your money after what your father did for us?'

'And I can't let you lose business because of me.'

'We like having you here.'

'Elsa, I wanted to spend some more time in Pisa anyway.'

Elsa cocks her head. 'Ah,' she says knowingly.

'Yes,' says Isabel. 'I'll go back to that hotel I stayed in before.'

And she will tell Matteo the same. That will be the best solution by far. All the journey back to Le Macchie she replayed his words in her head, hearing them, turning them over this way and that, mining them for sincerity.

She realises, too, that this is quite ridiculous. She knows nothing about him; nor he about her. She has never done anything like this before. But it is wonderful. *He* is wonderful.

Elsa is reluctant. 'The hotel? No, you can't go –'

'If I am going to find my father, it will be easier from

there.' She cannot mention Matteo. It is too fast. It is unseemly. What would they think of her? 'You've been so kind. I've loved staying here, feeling part of the family. But I want to do this. I'll keep in touch, telephone you to tell you where I am.'

'But –'

Isabel smiles as she realises only the truth will do. 'I think – that I want to spend some more time with Matteo.'

'Oh, yes?' Elsa grins.

'I like him very much.'

They exchange glances and laugh.

Now she is talking a language Elsa can understand. The brown pools of her eyes are alive with romance. 'You English . . . so reserved.'

'You Italians . . . so excitable,' says Isabel, touching Elsa's arm lightly.

So she returns to Pisa that evening, but she does not go to the hotel; she returns to Matteo's high apartment with its view over the river and the crooked tower in the distance on its northern field.

They make love slowly. They are both somnolent. He pulls away from her body and then back again, strongly, smoothly. At one point it feels to Isabel almost as if she is lying on a beach at the water's edge with the waves rolling over her. She is lulled to a climax.

That night in his bed she sleeps curled up, half on top of him, her cheek on his stomach. She feels the warmth of his skin and the rise and fall of his breathing. Their feet are tangled in a sheet. It is too hot to pull it over.

Now she is here, she wants to stay here.

She may never find what she started looking for, but she has found something else.

She spends the morning in the low ochre building of the Opera.

In a ground-floor room at the back, she sits at a long wooden table that serves as a desk. She is surrounded by wire baskets of papers.

Somewhere here is the possibility – it is no stronger than that – that Tom Wainwright has, like countless other enthusiasts, contacted the keepers of the tower with his carefully formulated idea to save it.

The archive is labyrinthine. She is rapidly concluding that finding his name in it is an impossible task. There are no computer records of this kind of correspondence, merely the bolts of papers lashed together with rough string and marked with the year of their receipt: curios for the guardians of the records, the full records, which will include the outpourings in green ink of the mentally unstable alongside the serious amateur propositions.

She continues to sift through. Her neck is starting to ache.

Isabel thinks now that it is strange she never had any inkling that her father might have kept things from her. Beyond his work, his office where the mysteries of his day-to-day occupation played out, she had never considered that he was a man of secrets.

There was the inexplicable fascination with towers, of course, and the years which he preferred not to discuss, when he had served abroad during the war. The time in the army she had discovered for herself at the age of about ten from a letter she found in a drawer when she had been searching for something else. It had been a circular letter, like the kind she brought home from school informing parents of dates and meetings, building appeals and bazaars. Only this was about an army reunion. Scrawled across the top was a message from someone who signed himself Jonno: 'Would you come for once, or have you forgotten us?'

She had been curious and had asked him what it meant. He had reacted angrily, knocked her off balance with the sudden gust of fury that greeted her innocent question. He so rarely showed anger, either to her or her mother. That was why it stuck in her memory. Then he had been – what? – sad, she supposed, then sorry for having shouted at her.

'It was an accident, just an accident!' she screamed back.

'What?' His face was pinched.

'I wasn't sneaking through your things, it was just in the drawer in the dining room!'

When they both calmed down, it was the relief that he had not remained cross with her that she remembered. It was only now, so many years later, that the incident seemed to gain in significance.

Was it odd that she had not asked more? In retrospect, yes. Of course. But then, he had liked to tell her things, other things: how machines worked, why the weather systems of the world had discernible patterns, how great discoveries had been made . . . she had never felt that he did not talk to her.

Sometimes he would even talk about his family's house in the countryside and she had assumed that he meant the house where he had been brought up. It always seemed larger in the telling, further into the hills and fields than the little house in Uckfield where he had lived with his mother and Margaret. It is only now that she wonders whether he had intended her to understand when this was not the truth of the matter.

Isabel has assumed a great deal.

Her eyes have grown accustomed to the dazzle of stone under blue skies when she emerges from the archive. Surer now in herself and her own needs, she walks streets and squares and bridges, and finds they have become familiar. She no longer needs to pull the map out of her pocket so often and feels a developing sense of certainty in the probable patterns of the city.

There is something else, something Matteo has told her. The thought experiment. She knows that if she can only find the logical contradiction, by sifting through her memories, she may come closer to an answer.

IV

11

By the end of April 1945 the war was over. Not officially, of course, but in the wooded valleys of Tuscany it had fizzled out. The Allies had crossed the Po, the German armies in Italy had surrendered, and Mussolini had been shot by partisans and strung up by his ankles from the roof of a garage in Milan.

Days at the camp were slack; nights a free-for-all. Men lazed around, chased the local girls, commandeered jeeps and lorries – occasionally even requisitioned farm vehicles – and took to the roads which had been swept of mines to see something of this country they had been fighting to regain.

Exuberant drunkenness was the order of the hour, relief and celebration of survival and youth, drowning of frustrations and homesickness.

It was a time of indecision, of halt and rumour. First they were going up to Pisa to await repatriation, then they were not. Then they were near enough to stay where they were. Then it was Leghorn, but that was overrun by the Americans; the same at La Spezia. Men with wives and families were to be given priority passage back home and there could be no arguing with that. But still they did not move.

All this suited Tom. First he had been moved up to Bologna on the heels of the Americans and the Poles. He and the boys were billeted in a building on the outskirts of the city. It was still warm from the Germans who had only just vacated it. Then they received orders to go to Florence.

Swaying across the bumps and ruts of the Highway 65, Tom was thinking only of how close he was creeping to the place where he had agreed he would meet her one day, his Giuliana. Then beyond Florence, the driver took the Pisa road for Moschiana. He laughed out loud when he saw where he would be staying. It was an extraordinary palace of a building, a villa surrounded by pine forest. His first act was to send a telegram to Giuliana telling her of his proximity.

He was slumbering, early one morning, warm in the womb of a blanket. There was a shot outside.

Tom froze. For a brief moment he burrowed into the protective skin of the rough bedcovering; then he was awake and himself, the soldier. All his sinews were alert; he swung out of the bed and flattened his back by the window, craning his neck to look out. His arm was throbbing as if it had been hit.

There were more shots.

Then he saw, in the pale sky, a blur of tousled wings. The men were out shooting songbirds. Skylarks were falling from the air. The ways of the countryside were reasserting themselves. There were few thrushes to be had, but sparrows were being hunted in the copses of cypresses. Blackbirds were hiding in the undergrowth rather than singing their hearts out from a proud branch.

He cupped a hand over his wounded arm. It was healed but still tender after the bomb blast. He must have hit it when he started. Tentatively he sat up and moved his shoulder. It felt fine, if stiff. He cursed himself for his jumpiness after all that he had endured. The last thing he needed was to dislocate it again. Six weeks wearing a sling and splint while living in an army camp had been enough pain and frustration, even if it had begun with Anna's and Giuliana's gentle care at Le Macchie for five days before he was transferred back north and the not so tender mercies of the camp hospital. He passed through there quickly enough and rejoined his company.

In the gardens of the villa butterflies abounded. The men sat in deckchairs on the lawns, or under the rose-covered pergola, and talked – sometimes to small children who had come to the villa hoping for chocolate or other gifts. They brought flowers with them and were willing to run errands to buy cherries from a nearby estate: fat, luscious cherries that burst with juice the colour of blood in a medieval painting.

All the time Tom was waiting, waiting. Unable to relax in his new and sumptuous surroundings, he took a car the few miles into Florence. The Ponte Vecchio was the only bridge not blown up. In the cathedral, he stared up at the ceiling of the cupola with its gigantic picture of Christ seated inside a rainbow. It was the most beautiful city he had ever seen, but it was not here that he wished to be; not yet, not alone.

All the way back, he was in a state of nervous anticipation. Would there be a reply to his message?

There was none.

During the daytime the hornets and wasps whined constantly, and then at night the mosquitoes came and took over the attack. Tom lay awake.

Nights were sweltering. The air was clammy and still. Sweat soaked the pillow under his neck. His sheets were sodden. The distant sound of artillery had been replaced by the cracks and booms of thunderstorms. They crashed at the roof, rolling round and round the valley, coming back for a new assault time and again.

Snores and grunts issued from other rooms, reminding him how sick he was now of the company of men, their smells and sinews, sweat and noise and lack of privacy.

And then, when he had all but given up hope, one morning her reply was waiting for him. She would come to him – he had only to tell her when. She would stay with her Pisan cousins, she wrote, it would be easy to arrange.

At last, he felt, this was their time, his and Giuliana's.

Tom made his arrangements quickly and wrote back. She wrote him another letter a couple of days later. She was excited. She would wear the yellow dress. He would know her from that, from a distance. She was to stay the night with her cousins. A large party at the home of a sensible friend was the key to their evening trip to the centre of town. The girl cousin was in on the plan; she was keen to meet a young man of her own. It was settled. She was counting the days.

Events were beginning to turn in his favour. Tom propped himself up on his soaking pillow, switched on the light by his bed and unfolded the letter once again.

*

At last the day came.

Tom had read the morning away beneath a slapping fan on the ceiling, although the ancient magazines left behind in the villa were no more comprehensible to him than hieroglyphics. In the slugs of warm damp air he had hunched over photographs of unknown people dancing in a long-ago era before the war and wondered only what had become of them. All the time he was urging the hands of the clock onwards, imagining the smells and brightness of Le Macchie.

He was due to meet her at six o'clock. Straight after lunch, he went to find her. He hitched a lift on a supply truck he knew would be coming through, taking no chances that he might not arrive in good time.

It was a fast truck and the highway was clear. By two thirty Tom had been dropped off by the wide embankment of the river in Pisa. He stood for a while looking into the sparkling water and all around at the buildings. Bombing raids and artillery bombardment had made a gap-toothed beauty of the city.

The sun's heat was intense. Tom walked towards the narrow shady streets on the north side of the river, unwilling to ask directions of any of the few locals who were not behind cooling shutters, making a maze of his way to the Piazza dei Miracoli, conscious that in doing so he was heightening the romance of the moment.

There was still damage in the streets, piles of rubble, gaps in the terraces where nothingness hung suspended between wallpapered walls high above. In others, where there were still floors clinging to the structure, ceilings had landed on them. Slumped piles of rubble and broken possessions collected at the foot. Who knew where the owners were now.

Hours passed as he wandered, lost in his own thoughts, alternately exhilarated and nervous.

At approximately twenty to six Tom turned into one street of once-elegant sandstone houses. On the street corner was a shrine set in the wall of the first house, high enough for an elderly lady to need a ladder to reach the shelf at the feet of the Virgin, on which she was placing a jar of flowers. She was five or six rungs up, but steady on her thick varicosed legs. He wondered whether she would spring down the ladder again and swing it jauntily over her shoulder, or whether she would be forced to drag it back into whichever door it had come from. He hesitated a moment, curious, but she proceeded to take a duster from her pocket and began to buff up the holy figure. He was aware of the time ticking past. So he went on.

He was taking in everything, fixing the moment deliberately in his senses, unfurling his steps so lightly he could feel every faint breeze and hear every beat of the city around him. He was going to meet her!

Over his head were jutting poles of washing which protruded from the many windows. As he was looking up with this thought, a woman appeared on a balcony. There was no washing there, he noticed idly, only pots of leaves – herbs, he guessed, with Giuliana on his mind. In the still, warm evening air, the woman leaned momentarily on the balcony rail. She was voluptuous, he could not help but see the swell of her breasts above the apron, and he looked away, rather ashamed of himself for even beginning to compare her body with Giuliana's.

But in that second there was a sudden snap – and there was silence.

The woman was in the air.

Tom could see everything: the red rust of the balustrade which had given way; the eerie billow of the woman's flowered dress; she was held up by invisible strings, flying above a theatre stage.

For a second or two Tom watched in a trance, his imagination holding her there. A current of air rushed a net under her and she might defy the laws of gravity and float gently down to safety. But this was the horror of the moment and what the imagination will do sometimes to avoid the brain having to register reality.

The woman cried out. It was a brief cry of surprise. Then gravity sucked her down. For a stopped heartbeat she seemed to fly, belly down, arms spread. But in reality she dropped like a large soft doll on to the hard road beneath. Then she lay inert, strangely humped and crumpled. One leg was at odds with her body. Her torso was compressed. Pots had smashed beside her, scattering earth and herbs.

Above, the red-rusted balustrade hung open.

Then the seconds passed and actuality intruded. Tom had the use of his feet again and ran towards her instinctively. Had he been too far away? Could he have reached her to break her fall? Had he imagined that he was nearer than he was? The survival reflexes which had brought him so far had deserted him already. The months of inertia had dulled his physical abilities. All these thoughts clamoured for attention in his head as he rushed forward, shouting for someone to fetch help.

The woman lay in heartbreaking silence.

Tom shouted up at the building again. There came a scurry of feet on stone. Tom looked up to see another man was crouching down beside them.

'It's Luisa!' he cried. 'Oh no! Luisa Olvari!'

Tom was feeling for a pulse, aghast at the whiteness of her face and the welling of blood in ghastly patches underneath the skin. She was only a young woman.

'Are you . . . her . . . ?'

'A neighbour,' the man said. He was shaking his head and sobbing. '*La povera . . . la povera . . .*'

By the time he ran to get her husband Paolo from his work-place in the botanical garden, four streets away, it was too late. The smack of impact on the stone road, which her ample softness had seemed to absorb so easily after her flight, had killed her.

And so Tom was late. It was he who ordered another passer-by to call for an ambulance and who sent the teenager who said he knew the family to run for her husband in case the neighbour was not quick enough.

A boy of around eight arrived and Tom sent him away, told him not to look. The boy cried out, 'Mamma!' Someone else stepped forward and held him, sobbing.

Tom could not leave the scene and the notion did not occur to him. It was only after he had seen Luisa Olvari covered over on a makeshift stretcher and carried into the entrance of the building, and left his name as a witness, that he resumed his way into the heart of the city, shaken and more than an hour late for his assignation with Giuliana.

When he arrived at the place where they had agreed to meet, she was not there. He stood still, looking all about him. Then, after some time, he sat down on the grassy expanse linking the great cathedral and the baptistry and the famous bell tower. Still Giuliana did not come. He imagined at first that she had grown tired of waiting for him and had taken herself off to any one of dozens of little cafés in the vicinity where she could have a drink and powder her nose, maybe. He was sure for a while that was what had happened – she would not hurry because she wanted him to feel a little of the bewilderment with which she had waited, alone and feeling the time drain away into disappointment.

But after he had waited an hour, she had not appeared. He began to worry then. What if some accident had befallen her, just as tragedy had overtaken his journey? He realised that he did not know whether she had come to the Piazza dei Miracoli and had wandered off, hurt that he had not kept their date – or whether she had never even come to Pisa as arranged.

There was a café on the corner. Outside, the owner stood at the door, or served his few customers. Tom went over to him. '*Scusi, signor.* Have you seen a young woman this evening?'

He received a look of misplaced lechery.

'No,' said Tom. 'I was supposed to meet a friend here. Was there a young woman here – she would probably have been wearing a yellow dress, very pretty, hair down to . . . here. She would have been waiting out there by the tower.'

The man shook his head slowly, with obvious amusement.

Tom looked around at the customers, knowing they had all heard. No one came forward to put him out of his misery. He went back to his place on the green. In the hours that followed, he sat under warm air that was heavy with secrets. His expectations were exposed as empty vanities, just he clung to the possibility that his Giuliana would turn the corner and come running towards him.

The sky changed. The temperature dropped.

Still he waited, the fool by the tower, looking all around him.

And so it began, in the long hours after the event: the acknowledgement that a flaw the size of a handful of red rust is sometimes enough to tip the balance.

He stayed in the villa outside Florence until the beginning of June. He wrote a letter to Giuliana and then another. He received no reply to either.

What had happened to her?

He sat and brooded.

Many of the men he had served with were on their way north, to use their skills supporting the main army as it pushed into Germany, across the Rhine. The rest, including him, were due to be repatriated. For days he went through the motions. He was wreckage on the great tides of men, waiting, in transit, floating light and broken, as orders were given and obeyed. Eventually he and the lads were put on the convoy back to Castelfidaro and, unbearably, the route took them through Bastia, so near to where she was. Then, further on in one of the small towns a procession was in progress: the children carrying silk banners; the church elders bearing maces and ornamental staffs. He thought of the day of the *festa* and he wanted to leap out of his confinement on the truck. He wanted to run in her direction. He wanted to punch someone, anyone, to settle the score of unfairness.

Instead, he reached Castelfidaro by nightfall. And he knew that he could not leave Italy without going to Petriano again.

'You not coming, then?' asked Titch.

Tom started. He was bleary-eyed from squinting at a crumpled map after a scratch supper. 'Coming where?'

'We're off to a dance. There's one on in Recanati tonight.'

'What d'ja reckon-ati?' Jonno strode up. 'Find a nice signorina before it's too late?'

'No,' said Tom.

'Suit yourself.'

'You OK?' asked Titch.

'Fine. Hang on a mo – any spare cars?'

'Might be. Why, you thinking of coming later?'

'No. I just need to get somewhere, now. It's my last chance.'

There was something wrong the moment he arrived at the great door of Le Macchie. It was high summer, a replica of the joyous time he had spent there the previous year, yet the doors were shut. The atmosphere under the still bright sun was altered, deadened and flat.

The door creaked. Giuseppe let him in, barely able to manage a smile in greeting.

'What has happened?' cried Tom. 'What's wrong?' But he knew.

'Emilio is dead.'

'Oh, no.'

Giuseppe nodded. His face was deeply lined. Black holes had appeared under his eyes. He seemed shrunken into himself, this wiry man who had always moved with such jauntiness. The spryness was gone, along with the sense of mischief.

'I'm so sorry.' Tom hung his head, embarrassed by the triteness of his own words.

Giuseppe led him along the corridor to the kitchen where Anna was sitting at the table. She looked up with a distant expression when Tom entered the room. He went over and kissed her cheek. It was sunken. She had lost weight dramatically.

'I'm so sorry,' said Tom again. He turned back to Giuseppe. 'When did you hear?'

'Three weeks ago.'

'And how – ?' Was it wrong of him to ask? But there, he had done it now.

It was Anna who replied, with a pained vehemence, 'A friend brings back some of his belongings – and there is no doubt any more. As one day followed the next, it was growing more evident. But we were stupid. No word had been received and so we allowed ourselves to hope.'

'Aldo returned,' said Giuseppe. 'The Moris' boy, you remember?'

Tom nodded.

'He knocked on the kitchen door during the mid-morning break from cleaning the water cistern. We were filling buckets with muddy filth and he came to tell us he was back but his comrade in arms, our Emilio, was not with him.'

'Where had they been?'

'In the hills to the north of Pisa. Aldo had not been able to send word of his whereabouts. He survived for months in the hills. Then slowly he made his way south on foot – alone.' Giuseppe's face too seemed to sink into itself, his skin stretched tight around his eyes.

And when Aldo did return to Petriano, it was with news so horrifying that at first they did not believe him.

'Aldo was always a one for exaggeration, just like Emilio

– always excitable in conversation. And now it gave us cause to doubt what he was telling us.'

'Yet there he was,' said Anna remotely, 'standing there, where you are, sticking to his tale. They had been in a place called Bardine. There had been much killing by the Germans – hundreds of women, children and old people, such as no good person could believe. And it was partly his fault, he told us. They had been killed in reprisal for partisan activities.'

Giuseppe wiped his shirtsleeve across his eyes. 'He and Emilio had been part of a group, which also included Tonio and Guido, who had attacked a party of SS troops who were returning from a requisitioning raid near Bardine San Terenzo. This is what Aldo told us. They killed the entire party of German soldiers in the ensuing skirmish. Later the same day, in different part of the area, another band of partisans scored a direct hit on a German staff car, killing a colonel.

'In return, the Germans reacted so brutally that it could scarcely be imagined. Whole villages were looted and searched, men from an SS detention centre were summarily marched to the colonel's burned-out vehicle and shot, then all the inhabitants of Bardine San Terenzo – innocent people! – were rounded up and the terrible retribution continued. It took two days to complete.

'They pushed them into a small place, like a crevasse in the valley, and then Aldo said they could not see them any more. Then they heard the shots. It went on for ten minutes non-stop. There were no cries. Then all was silent.'

As Giuseppe was speaking, Tom became aware that Giuliana had slipped into the room behind him.

'So Emilio was part of a group that scattered after the reprisals?' Tom wanted to know.

'He was with Aldo. They hid out in the hills, but they were betrayed, for now they were responsible for the killings in the villages. Aldo managed to run, to escape when the Germans came. He was lucky, but Emilio was not.'

Giuseppe wanted to talk now and Tom could do nothing but listen.

Other similar stories were filtered down into the villages, stories of reprisals of such horror that those who were left standing in this broken place felt sickened and useless. In Rome, where the partisans had been ordered to strike German lines of communication and wherever else they could prior to the Allied landing at Anzio, a group managed to detonate several large bombs in the Via Rasella. Their target was a daily parade of German might – an arrogant display of troops whose aim was to police the Romans. The partisans killed thirty-two Germans in one strike. In reprisal, three hundred and thirty-five Italians were taken to the Ardeatine caves to the south of the city, within hours of the attack. It was said that Hitler had demanded the ratio of death to be fifty Italians for one German life, but that even the monstrous Kesselring baulked at that, settling for a mere ten.

It was more than an hour before Tom was able to speak a single word to Giuliana alone.

He blurted it out in the first moment of distraction, caused outside the back door by a cat and two playful dogs baited by Maddalena and Natalina. 'What happened?'

She did not look at him. 'I did come.'

'No one saw a girl in a yellow dress,' he said stupidly.

'There wasn't one. I was in black. I waited for an hour,

and then I had to return to my aunt's house. How could I have seemed to go to a party at such a time? I had come to tell the family what had happened to Emilio. I felt enough guilt running off to meet you when I should not have.'

'But you did come?'

'Yes, I came. I wanted to tell you why we could not do what we wanted.'

They were both helpless in the ensuing silence.

'And you thought I did not — because I was late. There was an accident. I had to help.'

'It doesn't matter now.'

'No, it doesn't.' He was about to sweep her up, to hold her close to him and breathe in the scent of her cheeks. But she held up a hand to stop him.

'I mean, there is nothing to matter. You should go.'

'No! I want to help you — all of you!'

'I'm sorry. There's nothing you can do.'

Tom, who until recently had believed in an ordered surface of the world, felt shame at the sheer impudence of luck: which luck held and which did not, and of knowing that timing was all, fortunate or disastrous.

After all he had seen, he had the sense that an important event was unfolding in his life, but that circumstances had conspired to rob him of its fruition. Like the years of his carefree youth the war had snatched away.

His convictions were fully formed in an instant.

'I won't go back to England,' he said at last. 'There must be something I can do.' He could not see Giuliana's reaction, he only sensed her nervousness from somewhere to his side.

'What can you do? You can't bring him back,' said Anna, coming up on them.

Giuseppe said nothing.

It was clear that they wanted him to go. Anna clasped his hand as he took his leave. They gathered disconsolately by the great door and at last he looked at Giuliana's face. He searched her pallor for a hint of her thoughts, but she was closed to him.

'I'm sorry, so sorry. This is not the time. This is a terrible time,' he mumbled to the utter blankness between them. The people they had been only a few months previously, and the hopes they had had, already seemed part of a lost place with no more substance than a dream, like the vacant faces of the party-goers in the pre-war magazines he had read to pass the time.

12

The countryside outside Pisa was a great brown flatness, the mountains rising to the north, into the clouds. Across the plains, they gave the impression they had ice on their jagged peaks, but no. This was their shape; the crevasses and hollows were drawing the clouds to their summits. Further along, Tom could see what was surely snow — but again, no. It was marble, he discovered, mined out of the stony mounds above Carrara in great white scars.

In the city the bombardment of the great boulevards along the Arno had left holes like missing teeth. The frescos in the Camposanto had been destroyed by fire — except for *The Triumph of Death*, which survived the conflagration.

He was billeted in a damp tenement south of the river, a draft of one, and walked every day to the mess hall at the hospital, and then on to the temporary HQ where his fellow communications specialists pored over maps and reconnaissance photographs taken before the German retreat to determine the areas most in need of further investigation.

*

'You're mad,' Jonno told him, jiggling the keys in his pocket – the keys Tom wanted for his own transport. 'All anyone else wants to do is get home.'

'I know.'

Jonno had been itching to get going for weeks. Not even football was taking the edge off his frustration.

'It . . . it's not over yet for me here,' said Tom.

Jonno shook his head. 'Stark bloody staring . . .'

But he tossed him the precious keys to an abandoned Fiat they had coaxed into life.

As Tom expected, Frank came closest to understanding. He was desperate for his reunion with Irene.

'I can't just pack up and go home,' Tom said. 'I can't stop thinking about *her* and the family. I can't stop thinking about Nunzia Coia and her children. My mind reruns the pictures as they run away from me and the bomb goes off.'

'You can't feel guilty,' said Frank.

'Guilty . . . ashamed . . . angry that it was one of ours . . . I can't stop *feeling*. And I can't stop feeling about her, about Giuliana, when I've no right to mix all that up in it!'

'You can't help it . . .'

'Can't I?'

'Are you thinking you can right wrongs – or are you staying because of her?' Frank stared owlishly at him. Tom was aware for the first time how much older his friend looked.

'It has to be both, doesn't it?'

Giuliana was part of it, of course, but it was something more, too. It was his sense of the balance of justice and prescience that somehow if he did not, now, while it was still possible, he would regret it.

'My Italian is really quite good now. I've got to know these people; they can introduce me to others who can help,' said Tom.

'In love, eh, Corporal Wainwright?'

'Not exactly.'

'What then?'

Tom went to his commanding officer. His request to be allowed to join the war crimes investigations was accepted.

I t was not what he imagined, being assigned to a dull office in Pisa, surrounded by bulging envelopes and files of reports. In their dry leaves lay what was left – officially – of blood in the dust.

One evening he fell in with a rowdy group of Americans. They were GIs, stationed outside the town at the mouth of the Arno at Marina di Pisa. Three of them, around his age, all desperate to get home, weary of the long clearing operations, nerves permanently strung for booby traps and landmines. They were standing near the bar when he went into a watering hole on the Via Oberdan. Servicemen of various nationalities gathered there, to drink under the colonnades and whistle at the pretty girls.

One of them was drunk, telling a loud story, arms flailing. The other two were on their way, too slow to stop their friend backing puppyishly into Tom, sending his glass of beer spuming in a trajectory to the floor.

'Hey, buddy –'

'Get ya nother one. Line 'em up, barman!'

Tom accepted stoically. He was grateful for some undemanding company.

'Excuse our friend here,' said one of the Americans. He

had a broken nose and expressive rubbery features. 'He's gotten a little stir crazy, we been in this place so long.'

'No harm done.' Tom forbore to dab at the streaks of wetness on his chest. He felt the coldness next to his skin warming to stickiness.

'At least he didn't hit ya. That right hook's a legend and we ain't had a KO for a while.'

'He makes a habit of it, does he?'

'Nah – boxing team. Now that's an idea, we should get a fight up, pass some time.'

'I suppose it would,' Tom conceded drily.

'You been here long?'

'Not long enough to get sick of it,' said Tom.

'Ah, you'll learn!' chipped in another, a skinny guy with a savage crew cut. 'We got stuck at Marina under fire and this is as far as we got home.'

'Hey, barman, another round of drinks for the guys who saved the leaning fuckin' tower!' crowed Tom's assailant. The others laughed heartily.

'Steady boy,' urged the skinny one amiably.

The beaming drunk, blond and beefy, was taking a bow.

Tom was intrigued. 'What's all that about?' he asked. 'Saved the tower?'

'S'true, as a matter of fact,' pantomimed the one with the broken nose, puffing out his chest. 'Like Joe says, our detachment got pinned down by enemy fire. The Germans may be running backwards, but they sure are still giving it everything they've got. And accurate, you know. Things are looking bad for us. We're losing too many men. So the commander looks at it all ways and comes to the conclusion they got an observation post on the top of the leaning tower. That's from where they're directing the artillery!

'One night he calls us in – me and Joe here – and he says, take a radio operator and go in close. See what you can find. If you see any sign of Germans up the tower, we open fire. We blow it up!'

'An' this is serious,' interjected Joe. 'There's two of our batteries with their guns trained on the tower and a cruiser lying off the Marina. ' "If you have the slightest suspicion, just the slightest notion that we got enemy observation up there – it goes up." That's what the commander said.'

Tom whistled. In truth, under his bar room bravado, he was appalled.

'So we go. It's dark. There's gunfire, the full works all the way in. We get there and we're staring, staring, but it's hard to see. At one point I think I see German helmets and the points of rifles, but I can't be sure. The tower's lit up by gunfire and it's just this incredible sight.'

'We were looking at each other as if to say – how can we possibly take the decision to destroy this?' explained Joe.

'Naah! Should've done it. What a fireworks that would have been!' The blond GI was crossing the line now between merry and out of control.

Tom ignored him, despite getting another splash of beer from the expansive hand gestures the man used to illustrate his point.

The other man resumed. 'We stayed there a coupla hours. Staring, trying to decide. In the end we reported we couldn't see anything up there. The attack was called off.' He shook his head at the floor. 'Wouldn't have liked to be the person who said "Go! Go!" on that one, no Sirree . . .'

Their drunken friend chose that moment to cannon into

another group of servicemen. The sound of a chair splintering and angry remonstrations sent Joe and the other whose name he had not learned to the aid of their fallen comrade. Puddles of beer formed; there was more shouting.

What a mess, thought Tom. And what chance it all comes down to in the end. A person either cares or they don't. Pure chance.

Then, during August, a year almost to the day after the church and the houses had burned, according to Aldo Mori, Tom succeeded in being sent to Bardine San Terenzo. Little by little he had brought it to the attention of his commanding officer, had pointed out the places of rough burial in the folds of its hills, had made excellent contacts with ex-partisans who had been there. In short, he had made this place important in the files.

So he was allowed to go there. It was a large village, silent in places and defiant, in the mountains north of Pisa. His uniform, his Italian and his contacts within the former partisans: all these ensured he was spared no detail. His senior officer noted his diligence and drew copiously on his efforts.

Tom was getting closer to what he had stayed for.

In intense quiet among the ruins, Tom visited the priest's house.

The doors and windows were open to the still, heavy air. There was no traffic, no birds, no life in the streets. He and the priest, Don Dante Quiriconi, sat opposite each other on wooden chairs.

'I am forty-three years old. I have held this position for seven years,' said Don Dante Quiriconi in answer to Tom's question, having written his name in block capitals in Tom's notebook. 'On 24 August last year I had just taken mass at about nine o'clock in the morning when I heard shooting. I wanted to go out to see what was happening, but I knew that could be dangerous, so I remained at the church. Soon there were people running into the church for safety. An old man ran in and I saw that he had pissed himself. I was disgusted, but I know now what he had seen.'

Tom's pen scratched across the paper.

The priest was a big man. It was not hard to imagine how the village would turn to him and the church for protection. But his voice was frail. His eyes were dead as he told what he had witnessed.

'The sound of shooting continued intermittently throughout the morning. There were about twenty of us inside the church. At around noon a farmer rushed in, battered and bruised, and told us that many people had been killed. Houses were burning. Later that day I learned of the deaths of twenty-eight people and that the bodies had been taken to the cemetery at Valla.

'I went there and saw the bodies of a number of people who were inhabitants of this district. I could see that they had bullet wounds. They were caked in blood and covered with flies. I performed the benediction on these bodies.' At this, the priest drew several sheets of paper out of his robe and handed them to Tom. 'The names,' he said. 'All the while the relatives were bringing more victims to the cemetery. The stench was horrible. There was no question what had happened. They had been killed and their homes destroyed by German soldiers. That is what I understood.

'At about noon the following day, I was back at the cemetery when some German soldiers brought more bodies in a truck. I and my assistant priest and a few elderly men prepared more graves. The earth was hard like stone. We dug with picks. It was difficult to know whether what was stinging our eyes was sweat or tears.

'I officiated at the burial service of fifty-two men, women and children. There were more dead than alive at the service. It was the worst day of my life.'

'Did the German soldiers say why they had done this?' asked Tom, straining to keep his voice even.

'In reprisal for partisan activity.'

'Do you know anything about that?'

'Only that a partisan brigade was captured at Valla after German SS troops were attacked and killed. The same day a German staff car was ambushed and a colonel killed. According to what I was told, two of the young partisans were taken to a tree at the edge of the village and strung up by the neck with rusty barbed wire. The wire was pulled tighter. The German soldiers said that unless one talked, the other would hang. They both were hanged. But not before one of the boys had told the Germans where they could find a larger group of partisans.'

'Do you have any idea of their names?'

'They were not from this area. I will tell you who to speak to.'

When they had finished, neither had energy for a normal conversation.

'Stay for a while. Rest,' said the priest.

Tom nodded. When Quiriconi got up and began moving

around the adjoining room, he closed his eyes, but failed to blot out any of the horror.

Darkness came down and they sat together again, wordless.

With this and other accounts he helped to draft a report. It included the verbatim accounts from the survivors who had seen the weakest in their families cut down so cruelly and their homes decimated in flames. Then he crumpled the papers he had used to compile it, pushed his emotions into some deep place inside him and wrote again, this time his affidavit telling only the unembellished facts, terrible in their starkness.

Occasionally, a vision of houses with square corner towers and wooded slopes in a hot place would steal up on his consciousness, and he would linger there, in that almost mythical place, until he pulled himself together and told himself to forget all that.

He did not feel better when the report was filed; he knew only that it was important to him that many others should feel worse, that no one should shut their eyes and refuse to believe. And yet, and yet – what of the people the truth could still destroy? Tom shut his eyes tight and tried to reason with himself. What devastation might it not unleash even now on the Parini family, who had never shown anything but kindness to him?

The knowledge ran through and past and in him that Giuseppe and his books were wrong about one thing. There were no laws which governed the universe: the minutes of time and the inches of distance were all man-made and make-believe, man's way of imagining he could find order. This was the artificial world of the map makers, of the calendar inventors, of the horologists, the damned weather forecasters and even, perhaps, the historians.

He spent one more anguished night of indecision.

The next day he wrote to Giuliana. He waited a month for a reply that never came. He would have visited her, but the requisitioned car had been re-requisitioned by someone more senior, and in any case his pride burned fiercely. In some respects he was still very young. If she had wanted to come, she would have done, he reasoned. If she had wanted to reply to his letter, she would have done. In any case his bags would soon be packed for England. His job done, his orders were to return.

Then, the day before his boat was due to sail, he found he could not go without trying once more. He could not sit drinking in the bars of Pisa while his bags sat lumpen in the billet.

As he left the dull office for the last time, he went to the cardboard filing system and found the document he had made was still where he had put it. He plucked it from its nonsensical position and slipped it into a brown envelope. With some unease, he took a last look around the empty room, jammed it in his inside breast pocket and went out.

He had always known he would do this, he had planned it carefully, to take the illicit copy of the report he had helped to compile. He knew it was wrong, but by now he cared more for the laws of humanity than the laws of armies.

So he hot-wired a car from the requisitions workshop and took that. It was a noisy vehicle, for all it had been newly repaired, and open to the elements. The wind in his face seemed to blow all the thoughts from his head. The road spat up dust and grit that lodged painfully in his eyes.

He made his way, unannounced, back to Le Macchie.

The sunset flared in the sky without joy. The remaining heat from the day added oppressively to his sadness. Bright heads of geraniums were crisping to death on the leaf. It seemed no one was interested in pulling them away for renewal.

He found Anna first, in the chapel. He stood for some minutes inside the door before she suddenly looked round at the point he decided to leave without disturbing her. Her face was ghostly in the gloom. He noted vaguely that the Christ figure he had carved for her birthday was hanging on the wall in front of her. Emilio, her first child, her only son – what could he say? He was a raw boy again in the presence of her grief.

In the grounds of the farmhouse there was a pervasive quietness; the jolly rumbustiousness that he associated with this place had completely gone. Tom was chilled.

In the lemon grove he found Giuliana. Her face was pinched of all prettiness. Bright spots burned on her cheeks, the rims of her eyes were red. She was thinner. He longed to reach out for her but did not dare. He waited for a sign from her, but it did not come.

They walked up to the terrace together. Giuseppe had finished feeding the pigs and was washing out the swill bucket. It was a familiar scene, but Giuseppe's natural ebullience had deserted him. His familiar features remained, but the life had gone from behind them. He was silent. Then he turned away and carried on towards the outhouses.

'He won't talk about it,' whispered Giuliana. 'He cries

like a baby when he thinks no one can hear. Even Massimo cannot help him.'

'How are the girls?' asked Tom.

A shrug. 'Not so bad, really.'

'And you?' He was conscious of every breath he took. The life within him seemed to be making too much noise.

'My mother stays in the chapel all night; my father is inconsolable. What else can I do? I have to look after the girls. I did come to Pisa that time, I promise I did . . . and the guilt was intolerable. But now . . . this is the turn the story has taken and it is my turn to do my duty.'

His stomach contracted painfully. I wanted to ask you to come with me, he ached to tell her, but he could not. She could not come with him, not now.

'I have to go back to England,' he said uselessly.

Giuliana did not respond. She looked drained, hollow. She had not protested. Nor had she asked him to stay.

'I came to –' He put his hand into his jacket and started to pull out the envelope. Then he stopped. For what was the point, after all? Why add to their grief by handing it over?

The brown envelope was halfway out of its hiding place, no incriminating name on it. 'I was going to give this to Giuseppe, but perhaps – perhaps I was mistaken . . .' Tom was making a hash of it. Now, confronted with his own powerlessness and that of the Parini family, he faltered. Without thinking, he pulled out instead his battered copy of *Paradise Lost* and a pencil. On the first white page inside he wrote his initials and the address of his mother's house.

Shamed by his own inadequacies, he pushed it at her and said, 'I came to say goodbye and to thank you for all you did for me.'

'It was nothing. Thank *you*.'

They stood apart in silence.

'All I can feel is your absence!' he blurted out idiotically and stepped towards her.

Her hesitation was tangible.

Then she moved awkwardly towards him and let him hold her. She was skin and bone, a frail bird under his hands.

'I have learned how to fall,' she whispered, barely audibly.

He smiled, but he had no idea what she meant. There might have been more, but he could not hear it.

She stopped any question with a brush of her lips drily on his.

'Goodbye, then,' she said. 'It has to be.'

'But –'

'Goodbye Tom.' A brave smile trembled on her lips. 'I'll never forget you.'

He had no courage left. He trudged up the pitted white trail to Petriano. In the square a squalling group of young children was playing, running this way and that, chasing and shouting. They looked at him quizzically, then ignored him. Tom waited and watched.

One small girl was familiar. In truth, he only noticed her because she was staring at him, long after the others had lost interest. His mind was elsewhere. He lit a cigarette and inhaled deeply.

The girl was still staring at him. Then he noticed the pink scars on her cheek.

It could have been her. The little girl he had thrown clear of the blast. Nunzia's daughter. It was hard to be sure.

Did she recognise him, or simply the uniform? Pictures of the explosion. He could not bear it. Impossible for him to look the child in the face. He walked away.

Driving back to Pisa, his head was full of plans to return. The certainty that he would lasted for many months. He was determined there would be a way.

13

The key to survival was flexibility. Tom read some-where that there was an old Chinese saying: the tree that lives longest is the willow, because it can bow with the wind. In an uncertain world, the ability to bend with chance was crucial.

He moved back into the same old room at his mother's house and felt too big for it, as if its four walls would not contain him. The feeling eased as the months passed, but never fully went away.

His first occupation was breaking stones in a granite quarry; heavy work which demanded sweat and built up stamina. It was a vent for his anger and his feelings of help-lessness. He threw his muscle at rocks and spent his days in their dusty scent. When he straightened his back in pain he stared around at the rubble of defeat. For a while he was at war with himself.

Then, as the months passed, he got a job with a firm of builders. He took up again his abandoned apprenticeship as a joiner and studied technical drawing.

He considered contacting Frank and Jonno, Vince and

Titch, but did not do so for some time. After that, he saw Frank occasionally. Frank had jumped on the first ship home, had been dug in for a year. He and his fiancée Irene were about to be married. The years of waiting had paid off. Tom felt humbled by them and envious of their happiness.

He began to tread water.

His interlude in Italy seemed more and more foreign as he consigned it to the strange territory of his youth, as if it had happened to another person. He supposed that was only natural.

Snatches of memory, the scent of freshly cut lemons, certain herbs which released their distinctive aroma when cooking, the consistency of fine white sand, all these could provoke an unwelcome rip in the fabric of his mind's compartments and release them to float around dangerously until he got a grip.

He never had a problem meeting other girls. But Tom, hardly knowing that he did it, would make abrupt (yet kind) departure a feature of any relationship that seemed to be leading anywhere. It was a pattern that was tantamount to running away, a form of assurance that he was still free.

Once, brazenly, a girl who was in love with him asked him why he had not married. Was it because there had been so many other women and he had never been able to decide?

Tom laughed. No.

One woman in particular, then? The relationship had ended badly, or she was unattainable?

No.

He was working hard, he said, to build up his business. Some people are lucky and they meet the person they will marry young. Others have to wait.

As simple as that?

Yes.

So he rattled away on trains from his uncertainties, fled guilty scenes on long-distance buses, spending a couple of days alone in cities and towns that were new to him. Then he would return and try to find comfort in the solidity of buildings.

He met Patricia at work. His firm was doing well and one week a young secretary came as a temporary after another woman had left to have a baby.

Patricia intrigued him; her sure confidence in herself and her opinions touched him. He thought at first that it was her youth, her vitality, that gave her this irrepressible certainty. She was twenty-two.

She had red hair, dark and lustrous, which escaped from the contrivances she used to keep it back from her face. And it was a pretty face, when it was not set determinedly, which was much of the time. She wore fashionably tight clothes, but Patricia was altogether more serious than these suggested. Cheeky approaches from the young men in the workforce were firmly rebuffed.

Tom took her for a coffee after a site visit on a day when the wind had swept and eddied around them. She looked beautiful, with the curls whipped untidily round her pale face, but she excused herself straight away after they arrived in the café and emerged from the Ladies with it tamed once again.

The world had moved on since he was her age; its acceptances and customs shockingly changed. She slept with him eagerly, after he had taken her out only three times. It all seemed so simple.

He had been seeing Patricia for almost a year before she discovered his odd passion. 'What are these drawings?' she asked conversationally. She had gone to his house in Uckfield to take measurements; she was to help him choose some material and then make some new curtains for his sitting room. It was a measure, in itself, of how the relationship was progressing that he was comfortable with her alterations of his home.

Tom looked up.

She stood by his desk and was bending over a sheaf of diagrams he had been studying.

He went over and put his arm round her small waist. 'Those are plans to stop a tower tilting,' he said. 'Not current ones, I might add.'

Pat smiled at him indulgently, so he explained a little.

'I've always known that this was a method that worked, so it was a question of finding the exact written specifications and transferring them into diagrammatic form. I've been in correspondence with a rector from Cheshire, you see, and it was he who finally managed to track them down for me. He sent me the mathematical figures and pictures of the church tower, and this . . . is what I've made of it all.' Tom rather shyly flipped over another sheet showing the tilt of the tower at its most precarious. Then he showed her a photograph of the same outline, this time proudly straight.

'This tower was falling and it was pulled back upright?' Pat whistled softly.

'Oh, yes. A considerable time ago. That is the fascinating part. We can see that not only does the theory prove correct, but that in time the work holds good. And it would work again. There's no doubt of that.'

'So . . . is this to do with something you're working on now — a tower?'

'Working on . . . not precisely. But I've been thinking about it for many, many years. It has become . . . I suppose I would say an enduring fascination.'

Pat gave that secret smile of hers again. 'What is this tower?'

'It's the most famous one of all,' said Tom. 'The Leaning Tower of Pisa.'

Patricia could not help it, but she laughed. The answer was so clearly unexpected, so ludicrously presumptuous.

He was taken aback by her reaction.

'Have you ever seen it?' he asked snappily.

'No,' she replied.

'No,' he said, as if that decided the matter. He gathered up the papers with a sharp sigh.

'Sorry,' Patricia said later. She had taken her measurements across the bay window of his room and he had held the tape. She had noted the exact dimensions in a pocket diary, and they had discussed drops and drapes and shades. 'It's just that it seemed so . . .'

'You don't have to say anything.' Tom was stiffly trying to forget the incident.

'It's my fault,' pressed on Pat. 'I was just being silly and clumsy, and now I can see that it means a lot to you.' She put her face up to his and her arms round him.

'Forget it,' said Tom. 'It doesn't matter.'

*

Tom and Patricia were married in April 1962. His mother Alice, and sister Margaret and her husband Larry could barely contain their delight that Tom, at long last, had found the one and was settling down.

The wedding was a small affair: barely thirty guests at the front of the church in Heathfield, where her family lived; then lunch at the pub nearby. At the time Patricia agreed with him that this was adequate celebration, desirable even, in view of their mutual dislike of fuss and nonsense. He liked her pragmatism and her acceptance of him as he was.

She did not wear white. She was arresting in a silky dark-blue dress and coat with a little hat to match, which set off her red hair and creamy skin.

'You look beautiful,' he told her, as she arrived at his side at the altar. 'Perfect.'

She squeezed his hand and smiled.

Frank, as best man, gave him an admiring thumbs-up.

The ceremony proceeded, was over before he knew it. He kissed the bride. There were the obligatory photographs and family groups outside the church, a few fistfuls of confetti and the party adjourned to the Half Moon.

It was a pleasant but unostentatious pub. In the summer flowers cascaded from window boxes and planters, and they had enjoyed balmy evenings there, but in spring it seemed austere, thought Tom, on reflection.

Frank raised a pint glass to him amid the backslapping in the crowded private room.

'Thanks for doing this for me,' said Tom. 'I know we haven't seen much of each other these last years.'

Tom waited, bracing himself to have to justify his neglect. But Frank gave him a resigned smile. 'It's the way it goes. She seems a lovely girl.'

'Yes,' said Tom. 'She does, doesn't she.'

Across the room Patricia was drinking gin and tonic, and showing off her rings.

Did Frank look as if he was about to say something then? He did not have the chance. Irene arrived back at his side, with their three robust children, two boys and a girl. Tom could see nothing of either of them in the round young faces. Jonno roared up with his wife, a plump dark-haired nurse Tom had met only once.

'It's been a while!' breezed Jonno.

'I know. Too long,' said Tom.

'Makes no odds. Not after what we went through together, eh?'

'That's right.'

'Did you know', said Jonno, 'that after the war in Italy more than two thousand British prisoners of war and several hundred ordinary soldiers were missing – missing in the sense, that is, of being officially unaccounted for by the War Office and the military? I read that only the other day. But it was all free choice – no tragedy. They just stayed living happily with their adopted Italian families. More than two thousand of 'em!'

Frank grinned at Irene. 'They can't have had a good reason to get back.'

'Why would they? To this cold, grey place?' Jonno shrugged.

They all considered that for a moment. Jonno shook his head. 'You stayed on for a while, though, didn't you, Tom?'

He hadn't changed, thought Tom. He still had that way of rushing in headlong without too much awareness of other people. A plant machinery salesman now, apparently. Maybe his toughness served him well.

'Hmm.'

'And there was a family — where was it now? — you used to go and see,' he persisted. 'Maybe we'd better not mention young ladies now!'

Tom was wary of the consequences of too much drink and reminiscence. 'So, how's business?' he asked, looking from one to the other. He could not bear to think of the men who had melted away into the plains and lush valleys of Italy. Not on this day.

Frank came to his rescue, a sympathetic light in his eye. 'Going well, very well.'

'How's the market for the new components?' Tom pressed him.

'Frank's built up his own electrical components firm,' explained Jonno to his wife, whose name Tom had failed to remember.

The beer had gone to his head; he felt uncomfortable, sweaty under his collar.

As Frank held the floor for a while, Tom fought off unwelcome thoughts: Le Macchie in the winter; Giuseppe and the family driven by hunger into the fields of gusting cold; the foul spluttering fires of olive branch prunings. How the warmest place to be was the cow stall. At times it seemed as if the entire family had moved in, burrowing into the hay. Where were they all now?

He could not think about that now. He pulled himself together and scanned the room for Patricia. She was surrounded by her women friends. Their laughter was raucous.

'Do you remember how we made do and mended?' said Jonno, shaking his head.

Tom had no escape.

'I always say to Joan' – *that* was her name – 'the contraptions we came up with, welded and tied on ... Heath Robinson had nothing on us! And we were lucky we weren't driving a ruddy great removal van around, because that was what they gave us at first, back at Salerno.'

'That, I remember,' groaned Frank. 'Funny how we just couldn't get the starter motor in that going again! No matter what we tried . . .'

'I remember you whistling innocently,' said Tom. 'With the wire in your pocket.'

'Better a spot of sabotage', explained Jonno to Joan, 'than being made sitting ducks in a great whale of a lorry through the hill passes. How did they think we would ever have made it in a bloody pantechnicon? Now if only one of the officers had thought to consult the contour lines of a map before ordering us on board . . .'

Tom managed to join in the laughter.

'I think perhaps I need to steady myself before I say a few words to the assembled gathering,' he said as evenly as he could and went to the bar.

For whatever reason, the talk of Italy and the memories it evoked had profoundly unsettled him. He avoided his wartime friends for the rest of the party.

'Are you happy?' he whispered to Patricia when they were seated at the top table for the lunch of mushroom vol-au-vents and coronation chicken.

She nodded and kissed him.

He slipped his arm round her waist. The satin of her dress was slippery under his fingers.

They went to Switzerland on their honeymoon, staying for ten days in a grand hotel in Interlaken, in a style to which Patricia had long aspired. Expectations on both sides were high. For Tom's part, he was determined that he had begun the next stage of his life and had put aside any earlier disappointments. He was gentle and considerate. He did not feel passion for Patricia, rather a loving respect and this, he reasoned to himself, could only be a good thing. They were embarking on a venture together that was rooted in realism.

The last night Patricia said, 'I would have liked a big white wedding you know.'

'I thought we agreed we wanted to do things simply. And you looked so lovely in that blue you wore.'

She hesitated, then said, 'It was the wedding you wanted. I didn't. I would have liked a beautiful dress and a dance and fine food at a hotel. It's not as if you couldn't afford a wedding like that.'

'You should have said!'

'You were set on what you wanted.'

'That's not true!' said Tom. 'You could have had whatever you wanted. You only had to say!'

They returned to England charged with hopes and promises, most of them unspoken.

*

His house was their house now, but warmer, lighter and fuller. Patricia was excited and eager to please. He was happy to carry on his routines with the pleasant addition of her presence.

So when Patricia, flushed and a little nervous, told him some four months later that she was expecting a baby, he was thrilled and yet uneasy about some deeper reaction that stirred. He did not know why, exactly, but he was already beginning to suspect that he had made a mistake.

They did what most other couples in their position did: they put their heads down and got on with it. Tom spent more and more time at work, with the double benefit to him of providing ever more successfully for his small family. Patricia shopped and cooked and cleaned and gardened and sewed with exemplary diligence so that, in the same way, she could not be accused of neglecting her duties. While seeming to be pursuing the same goals, they were pulling ever harder in opposite directions.

Already there were ugly scars where the brightest hopes had burned.

'What's wrong?' Patricia would ask.

'Wrong? Nothing. Why should anything be wrong?'

But the question was enough to send him running for cover in his books, or burrowing deeper into a newspaper.

She would stare at him in puzzlement and hurt.

He knew what she was thinking as he avoided her gaze, and forbore to open up the subject. He did not want to give her the opportunity to delve into his most private thoughts. They were not for sharing.

*

Tom was overwhelmed by love when Isabel was born. He saw in Pat's eyes when they met his over the tufty crown of their daughter's head that this could be a new beginning.

It was not to be.

In Patricia's disappointment in him over the next months and years – in his self-containment, his inability to be the attentive, adoring husband she needed – dated the start of the fissure between them. And all the while he was the devoted father to his little girl. What adoration there was went straight to the child.

As she cared so tenderly for the baby, so she was also tending her grudges in the hours of his absences.

Once Pat suggested that she return to work, play more of a part in the business. She would only work part-time while Isabel was at school, but Tom would not hear of it. Indeed, he surprised even himself with the vehemence of his reaction: he did not want her in his office.

'Your job is at home now,' he told her.

'I can do both. Women do, you know.'

'I don't want you to.'

She was still protesting with well-rehearsed arguments as he strode past her and into his study.

What arguments there were never concerned the real issues. They would be about the pathetic minutiae of daily life, the dirty footprints, the forgotten items of shopping, other guests at a dinner party. Anything but the truth.

Most often, Tom and Patricia argued over the garden. She insisted on a neatly mown lawn, trimmed paths, precise cutting round the beds, which should, ideally, be weedless.

She prized tidiness in a garden above all else. Tom, on the other hand, saw exuberance in plants and flowers. He wanted to see them tumble and tangle together, and to bloom as if they were in the wild. He found her insistence on order joyless; she was discomfited by his ability to enjoy a weedy chaos. In everything else, after all, he was a man who valued precision.

'I don't understand how you can just sit there and do nothing about it,' she would say to him, in a voice at once peeved and resigned to the fact of his negligence. She would make sudden swoops down to the soil to pluck out some offending plant life, frowning as she did so.

Tom would say nothing. Perhaps he would settle further into his deckchair, or retreat behind his newspaper.

'Someone has to do it,' would be the next rejoinder, with emphasis on the *someone*.

So, he felt, she never actually enjoyed her garden, never really looked at the plants, always seeing as she did what should not be there rather than what was.

'I prefer it rather wild,' he said once.

Patricia gave an exasperated sigh. 'You have some very funny ideas,' she said.

This was at the beginning. In later years he found himself positively repelled by gardens full of regimented, weed-free beds, where bare soil around the flowers was supposed to indicate dedication and expertise. Park gardens, he thought of them, with their crumbs of picked-over bare brown earth where the beauty should have been.

Meanwhile Patricia would sigh, a sound designed to provoke a reaction, a sign that she was prepared to make some effort to enable him to be happier than she was.

Nothing was said about the mounting frustrations of the marriage, of course. What could have been said? In the end it was an old-fashioned bargain struck for the support of both. Tom provided the economic security, Pat the clean shirts and well-cooked meals that equipped him to go out and get it.

The distance came from him, there was no doubt about that. Oh, he had tried.

Nowadays if he tried to make love to her, she rebuffed him. She took her pleasure, it seemed, in showing him how high she had built her defences and how independent of him she was. If you cannot be with me, talk to me, love me in all the small considerate ways a happy wife has a right to expect, then you shall not have me, she would say with her hands as she pushed his away from her body in bed at night and turned her back.

But after a while he began to understand that Patricia did not actually want another kind of marriage. She was set in her pattern, and that was of being unable to forgive him. There, she knew where she stood. He sometimes wondered if she found a measure of comfort in the certainty of being a wronged wife.

For Tom, it was a little like being in prison, the bars of which were nonetheless of his own making. There were times when he did not understand himself, could not recall just how he had allowed this to happen. Certainly, he did not like himself for it. But with every day that passed, like a prisoner, he could feel himself becoming truculent and devious.

Mostly, though, he dealt with the situation in the way he imagined most ordinary men dealt with such circumstances. He ignored it, largely, carrying on with his work, which was increasingly successful as he spent more and more time there. He spent as much time as possible away from home, even at weekends. In this, he told himself, he was no different from millions of other husbands and fathers who pursued their hobbies or sporting activities.

As far as Tom knew, the earliest successful rescue of an endangered tower was achieved in 1810 by a military captain of the Royal Engineers, one George Whitmore. The Martello tower C at Clacton was found to be out of true, then it was leaning distinctively, and then the situation worsened to a perilous tilt, all in a matter of weeks. Of all the schemes devised to save it, Captain Whitmore's was the one adopted. He commanded a party to excavate soil from around the base on the higher side, and then hung weights from this taller side. Within fifteen months, the records showed, the tilt of the tower had been corrected and to this day it stands true. It was a resounding success story. The captain went on to work his engineering magic on at least two more towers, including the oversize one at Aldeburgh in Suffolk, and he ended a distinguished military career as General Sir George.

Tom went to see these places, to walk around them deep in serious contemplation. Pat came to see that this was no odder than a grown man taking a notebook to spot train engines, or even sitting on a rain-lashed river bank waiting for a fish to tease the end of a piece of string.

For a very long time even Tom himself regarded his pastime in this light. If he had not forgotten what was at its root, then he did not consider it relevant to his life in the present. The years of shouting and raging were over. Mutual antipathy was the order of the day.

One of his favourite places was near Nantwich in Cheshire, and he made the five-hundred-mile round trip several times, after a long and fruitful correspondence with a local historian. It was here that an engineer named James Trubshaw saved a tilting church tower in 1832, using the method known as under-excavation.

The church of St Chad was built on a hill at Wybunbury. Geologically, the hill consisted mostly of sand with patches of clay. When the tower, almost a hundred feet high, was constructed in the fifteenth century, its north side rested on one of these pockets of clay. Gradually it sank into this gluey alluvium until it was leaning away from the main body of the church. In 1758, when the tilt was apparent to all, official measurements were taken of the problem: the overhang of the top of the tower was nearly three feet. By the time Trubshaw had produced detailed plans, won over the sceptics and had been given permission to begin his rescue attempt, the gap had yawned dangerously to five feet seven inches, the height of a man.

Trubshaw dug down to the foundations and used water at high pressure to flush out the extraneous soil. The process took weeks. Critics scratched their heads and Trubshaw himself paced and agonised. But eventually the tower sank back into its correct position. A success, and in the process an ugly split in the bricks of the tower was neatly closed.

Tom leaned on the lych-gate and marvelled. Then he walked round the tower, fondly imagining he was marching in Trubshaw's footprints, stalking his spirit, peering for telltale signs of disturbance at the base. He had come alone with his notebook and his letters from the local historian. He had not asked Pat if she wished to come, knowing that her response would have been negative. She raised no objections when he said that it would be too far for him to drive there and back in a day, and that the most sensible course would be to take a room in a bed-and-breakfast place somewhere nearby and return the next day. She made him a picnic lunch in a plastic box and kissed him goodbye. All she asked was that he telephone her that evening from wherever he found to stay.

Tom sat happily alone the churchyard with a corned beef sandwich and drew sketches, diagrams and details. He took measurements himself, where he could, with a builder's steel tape and logged his findings.

'Is there a point where it seems happier to lean than at others? Will it settle in at one angle and not be happy at another?' Tom asked his ten-year-old daughter Isabel when he returned from Cheshire.

Isabel looked up, puzzled, as he had intended.

Was she siding with his wife already, in her dismissive acceptance of his peculiar passion? He wanted her to understand, to share his enthusiasm, but she was young yet, too young to be able to translate what that really meant, which was that he wanted her to understand *him* more. He pulled himself up short with the knowledge that she was only a child and he wanted too much.

'How can a stone tower be happy or unhappy?'

'I didn't mean it quite like that,' he replied. 'I was thinking of the set of the stones and the damage already done by weight and pressure on the wrong places.'

'I see,' said Isabel, assuring him that she would have understood. 'So why didn't you say that?'

He supposed it was a strange way to put it.

*

In the evenings his thoughts and the scratch of his pencil on paper filled the lengthening silences between him and Patricia.

When he read in a newspaper one year that another commission had been set up in Pisa to address the leaning problem there once more, he sent a copy of his most promising idea. He heard nothing in return.

14

I t was a split-second decision, made on a night when the skies were exploding.

That March evening, as he was driving home, a meteor shower flashed and smoked above southern England. The display could be seen across three counties and the meteors had a name: the Virginids. It was a perfectly clear night; the moon was full. He was on his way back from the Solent coast and he was late already. He had lingered in a teashop on a cobbly side street of Portsmouth after he had spent as long as he possibly could that afternoon inspecting a Martello tower from every angle. It would need radical underpinning and he took several pages of measurements.

On a whim he pulled into a lay-by and stopped his car. He let the engine idle for a moment while he considered what to do, then swung into a car park and switched off the ignition. He got out. He locked the car and began to walk upwards into the black. Tom watched the display from a high hill. When the racing lights in the heavens had finally dispersed he did not move.

He stood still in the silence.

*

The argument with Pat that morning had been unusually vicious. Normally she had no objection to him going out on a Saturday, but this time she was spitting. It caught him off guard, used as he was to the cold war between them. Whatever had prompted the outburst, she had not told him.

Her face contorted as she hissed out her complaints:

You never loved me.

I can't get through to you.

No matter what I do, it's never good enough.

You used at least to talk to Isabel, but now you hardly even do that. You hate us, don't you? Like we loathe and detest you.

We?

The words flung at him had echoed in his head all day.

The loser in this was always going to be Isabel. He had thought, stupidly, that she could be shielded. He was careful never to run down Pat in front of her and convinced himself that so long as they did not indulge in angry exchanges in her presence she could remain ignorant of the worst.

But that was an illusion. All the sadness and imbalance in the relationship between him and Patricia were joined for ever in their child, as much as his tallness and athletic walk, and Pat's thick reddish hair and earnest eyes. Her capacity for staring at him and making judgements, too. Or perhaps he was mistaken in that. That was only in his guilty imagination.

He wanted to apologise to Isabel, his darling girl, but for what exactly? He had tried, he had always been close to her, or so he had thought. And Isabel was seventeen now, wrapped up in a sulky adolescent existence of friends and schoolwork and interminable telephone conversations. Boys, he had decided. That and Pat's stony influence. Probably Pat was confiding in her, letting slip all sorts of unhappinesses over the years with him. The thought made Tom's guts clench.

Not for the first time he wondered whether it might not have been easier for him if Isabel had been born a boy. More often than not these days she was dismissively rude to him, in a way that was intended to distance him from what was happening in her life. The atmosphere at mealtimes was often oppressive, silent apart from the scrape of cutlery on china, and intolerable.

So why don't you just go? Go and don't come back? There's obviously nothing here for you, you spend so little time at home!

So he had. He had gone to Portsmouth to see a Martello tower. Walked round it and measured as long as he could bear, then sat and looked at the sea, for as far as it stretched.

He reached into the inside pocket of his coat to tuck away his notebook and felt a wad of paper. Puzzled, he brought it out and saw that it was the morning's post. He had only the haziest recollection of picking it up with the intention of placing it on the hall table. But with Pat screaming at him as he stood near the front door, his coat on, his hands must have gone to his pocket instead.

He shuffled the envelopes without interest and replaced the gas bill and a postcard to Patricia from a friend visiting America. The others were a round robin letter from the British Legion and a bulkier packet, which he ripped open wondering what it contained. It was his new passport. He had applied to renew his old one a month or so ago and forgotten all about it, having no urgent plans to travel abroad. He repacked the envelope carefully and slid it into the breast pocket of his jacket.

Then he walked back into the centre of the town and had a pot of tea. He was in no hurry to return home.

It was cold; he remembered that later. He was standing on a hill, miles out of his way home, and all he could think of was the stars, which he could see clearly after the pyrotechnics of the meteor shower had died away, and his conversations, so long ago, with Giuseppe Parini. A logical connection, he assumed. Strangely enough, he had been thinking of Pisa.

It was the oddest feeling, but Tom was aware that his imagination had become extraordinarily vivid. He found he was able to react physically to an imaginary conversation with Giuseppe, then to an imaginary caress from Giuliana's hand. And what was the difference, then, between imagination and memory of a genuine event? Could he make himself happy now by improving on the events of the past? Or was he not yet mad enough to detect the fallacy of this proposal?

He returned to his car and crouched behind the steering wheel. For some hours he remained there, as his odd thoughts chased their tails across his brain.

First – prompted by the starry display, no doubt – was Giuseppe telling him about Galileo. He could recall the story in astonishing detail, as though he had been hypnotised into doing so.

How Galileo Galilei ascended the bell tower, which had always leaned so alarmingly, and dropped, simultaneously, two objects of different weights before the assembled university professors and students. And how it brought him nothing but trouble in Pisa. Giuseppe loved that bit.

According to Giuseppe's book, Galileo was tall for his time, powerfully built with reddish hair and a notoriously quick temper. He craved recognition from his academic peers, yet he would refuse to wear the university gown that denoted his status because he did not wish to draw attention to himself on his frequent visits to the local brothels. When he moved to Padua he took as his mistress a twenty-one-year-old from the backstreets of Venice called Marina Gamba.

This was a facet of the man that had given Giuseppe huge amusement. Tom could hear that gurgling laugh now. He could see Giuseppe stabbing the page of the old book with a stubby finger, looking up gleefully from their reading.

'*Una Donna di Facili Costumi!*'

Tom was puzzled for a moment. The Italian pulled a leery face and pantomimed pulling off his clothes.

'Ah,' said Tom, translating now. 'A woman whose clothes come off easily!'

'*Sì! sì!*'

'Fine way to put it, I must say.' Tom grinned.

In the here and now, Tom sat for a while, hands resting on the steering wheel, then his head too. He thought back to his young, idealistic self at Le Macchie. He closed his eyes; he was tired. The darkness outside, even the bonnet of his car, seemed remote.

In his mind he was still in Italy but he was walking out of a barn into a farm courtyard. 'They've been sleeping in here.' Frank grimaced. 'You can smell 'em.'

Neither had they all gone.

There was a rustle behind a wall. Frank pulled him down. With a second's notice they were involved in close fighting with the Germans. They opened fire: they were shooting from a stone outbuilding in which onions were being stored. Burning tears blurred their vision. Their eyes were weeping from crushed onions as they loosed off their Bren guns. 'I'm crying like a bloody baby,' said Tom and yet he felt remarkably cheerful. Their caked boots were sliding on the floor of shiny wet skins. When there was no more fire in return, they had a boys' game of skidding on onions before they emerged.

There were times when soldiers didn't take their clothes off for weeks on end. The smell of onions lingered unmistakably.

At other times, German and British soldiers fired face to face from twenty yards and not a single bullet hit. Both sides were too frightened in the suddenness of the encounter. By then they all knew the waxy look of corpses, faintly green and muddied. What upset them most was seeing a personal detail, like a letter escaping from a pocket, or a badge, boots exactly like the ones they were wearing.

In the chill black present Tom fell asleep in his car.

When cold morning light filtered into the car, the odd thing was that he did not feel disorientated. He felt nothing. Out of curiosity, he stared at the letter-box view of his own eyes in the rear-view mirror. It was as if he was looking into the face of a stranger. The skin was roughened and lined. The whites of the eyes were bloodshot; there were also worrying knots of creamy white congestion. He tipped his head back a little, then felt a mild disgust at the hair growing thickly from his nostrils.

He could not think what to do next, so he sat where he was for some time.

He was empty; that was all he could think.

At the sound of voices he opened his eyelids. He no longer had this place to himself. A few more cars had drawn up. Standing by one were two young mothers, unloading pushchairs and toddlers. A child began to cry.

With the intrusion of other people he started to panic suddenly. He had no idea where he was. All he could see was green grass ascending all around him. Clearly he was in a car park, but he was not sure he recognised it. He pulled his coat round him in a self-protective gesture and put a leg out of the car. He was perturbed to discover that he was a little shaky. He took a deep breath and shuffled off towards a large sign. Would that be a map? It was. It welcomed him to a place of outstanding natural beauty. He was on Box Hill, it informed him.

What he should have done then was to have found a telephone and called . . . someone. He should have explained that he . . .

And there it was again, the nothingness. Explained what? What could he explain?

So he began to walk away and he did not stop.

There was only one point when his step faltered and that was when he thought he heard a small girl calling out to him. But it must have been to someone else.

After a while the walking became easier. The shakiness subsided. His joints were stiff after spending the night folded up inside the car in the cold. He took one of the paths that snaked like rivulets down the lower part of the great hill. Soon there was concrete under his soles. He continued on pavements, across roads, through knots of people going about their morning business. But he was not a part of it. He was separate and invulnerable. He tried to pin down precisely what it was – and came back to the same again. He was nothing, weightless.

He stopped in a small café for a cup of searingly hot tea. His feet and hands were numb. He felt his fingers thawing on thick white china: they were stuck to the cup.

In the corner, on the way to the lavatories, there was a payphone on the wall. With the life that had returned to his fingers, Tom felt in a pocket for change. He pulled out some coins, saw what he had would do and walked heavily over to the telephone. Leaning as far as he could away from the room of men eating breakfast, he called home.

'Hello.' The strain was evident in Pat's voice.

'It's me,' he said.

There was a charged silence.

'I'm on my way home.'

'Have you been in an accident?'

'No.'

'Then don't bother.'

'Sorry?'

'Have you any idea of what we've been through, last night and this morning? You just disappear off – what are we supposed to do? Sit up all night waiting for the phone to ring with bad news?'

'I'm sorry.' He had no excuses.

'No, you've gone now. I was right. If that's all you think of me after all these years, then I don't want you back. I meant what I said, Tom. I don't want you to come back.'

'What? I know we had an argument, but –'

'I mean it. It's about more than that. It's about years of –' Pat's voice faltered. 'You obviously think nothing of us, you don't want to be with us – so don't be.'

Tom slumped further into the wall. 'Can I speak to Isabel?'

'You've really upset her.'

'Could you put her on, please?'

'She's not here.'

'Where is she?'

'She has gone on the geography field trip – went this morning, as you would have known had you been bothering to listen to a word we say.'

Tom exhaled deeply.

On the wall where he was standing was a poster showing a picture of a bowl of lemons. It began again, the sensation that his imagination was so strong that it could surmount everything. He could touch lemons, feel the knobbled waxiness under the tips of his fingers, pierce their bright yellow skin with a thumbnail and smell the distinctive sharp scent. It was the scent of loss and regret.

He felt himself slipping away again from the indistinct hum and clatter of the present. It swirled all around him in the café.

Pat was howling recriminations again, getting into her stride. He pulled the receiver away from his ear and said 'Bye' to the air.

He realised he was hunched over, straightened up – too fast – and his head spun. He was in a hurry now. He left as if he had been struck by the sudden knowledge that he had forgotten something.

He put his head down and headed back outside.

By the time he reached the railway station he had recovered his composure. Calmly he surveyed the timetables. He was feeling detached now. He could almost stand outside himself and observe this man in late middle age, hunkered down in a dark overcoat, as he deliberated over which train to catch.

Surely he was on the brink of recovering his equilibrium. Perhaps he was not well. The shakes – possibly the beginning of influenza. He had sat for too long the day before on the dank moist stones of the wall near the tower. The cold had seeped into him, and into his spirit.

Or perhaps it was excitement at the discovery he had made about his own imaginative powers. He could make his own vivid world. He would imagine he was home, and warm and secure. The scent of lemons grew irresistible.

He felt inside the breast pocket of his jacket. His new passport was there.

That evening his car was stolen from the car park. It was exactly the type of crime the police habitually warned the public to be on the alert against. Tom's two-year-old family saloon was taken opportunistically by a couple of youths, who drove it around for several hours, then abandoned it near a run-down garage in a back street of Dorking. From there, it was quickly appropriated by the brother of one of them. Within a matter of days it had been resprayed a different colour and fitted with false number plates. It was given a new history, sold on and into obscurity.

But Tom was a man who had been given an unexpected freedom. He took a train and caught the night ferry from Portsmouth to Dieppe.

There was no problem getting on. The boat was three-quarters empty. He did not want a cabin. A banquette would do, where he could stretch out, fully clothed. He did not register the oddness of the looks a few of the other passengers gave him, a man of his age acting like a student. He was beyond that.

During the night Tom woke with a throbbing head. The juddering deep underneath where he slept denoted that he was in motion. He turned awkwardly, moving his watch to what light there was: 3.20 a.m. He had been dreaming he was picking fruit, tearing flesh from his own body as he wrenched persimmons and peaches and berries from branches covered in thorns. He put his head back on the seat and took deep breaths. He remembered now. He was on the boat.

At this stage he was still not certain where he was going. He felt, alternately, a sense of freedom and great apprehension. He had addressed no practical questions. He had a British chequebook but little money with him. He had no luggage, no maps, no intent.

When he got to France he wandered around Dieppe for a morning – then came back. He needed to take stock of this episode, this going off the rails. If he decided to do it properly, he would have to plan properly, at least to organise his finances.

He felt in control now. He could look out of himself at other travellers, could even venture a few private observations and opinions about their probable itineraries. Nearby, a man and a woman of around his own age had clearly made a day of buying cheap drink and having a slap-up lunch the other side of the Channel. Other retired couples seemed to be on board for the ride. A selection of beefy types who called to each other familiarly and raucously across the bar-lounge must have been long-distance lorry drivers.

He stayed in Portsmouth for two days. The bed-and-breakfast place was down at heel. The fraying carpet on the stairs, taps leaking rust from their bases, solid globules of slime round the neck of the HP sauce bottle on the breakfast table, all suited his desire for anonymity, the seediness with which he knew he was behaving. He made calls to several banks, then walked the streets not knowing or caring in which direction, ending always at the edge of the country looking south over choppy grey seas.

Then one cloudy morning he paid his bill at the B & B, put his head down against the whippy chill of the rain and walked on to the ferry. This time he did not return.

If Tom had been asked at this time what he was doing, dependent on who was doing the asking, he would have said that he was taking a little trip away, yes, a kind of sabbatical after long years of hard work; he was treating himself to a short break, going to see some places of interest that he had long wanted to see again; towers, especially flawed ones, held a special fascination for him. He would not have told anyone – least of all himself – that this was anything but a short holiday. In fact, at this stage he was giving serious thought to the volume of music that would have to be faced on his return to Pat.

The idea that he had gone for good was simply not addressed, because that was absolutely not what he had intended.

But then, he did not really believe that he might find Giuliana again. He was fifty-eight years old, with an aching back and a strange obsession, and the idea was madness.

He took a train from Dieppe to Paris, across the fast flat fields studded with ugly villages. He found a room for the night near the Gare du Nord, and set off at dawn the next day for Lyon and the South. He ate dry baguettes with ham and fuelled his escape with strong coffee. He could not read, could not concentrate; yet he stared out of the window with a stillness and intensity that occasionally prompted a fellow traveller to check on his well-being with the offer of a drink or a biscuit. He allowed the rhythmic clatter of the wheels to lull his misgivings and become an accompaniment to adventure.

He was on a quest, a hunt, the mystery of a possessed man. The disconnected beads, which he had guarded and polished for so long, would at last become a necklace.

He changed trains and haunted grand stations until he caught the coastal train to La Spezia. Rattled the final miles on the slow holiday line through Viareggio, sharing his carriage with families and excited children, allowing their exuberance to graft on to him. And then at last he was in Pisa.

The city had changed out of recognition. That was his first thought. It had been so clear in his mind, but here, the reality was blurred and rushing with cars, both smaller and larger than he remembered. His heart sank. His mission was a crass futility. He too was both smaller and larger than he had thought – smaller in stature and ability than he had imagined; larger in misguidedness. It was not the home-coming he had envisaged.

It was early evening. Tom did what had to be done, but he was crushed by his own hubris. He took a room near the centre, dumped his bags and slept at once, in a bed for the first time in three days.

The next morning he woke to diamond droplets on a spider's filigree in the corner of the pane of glass. After the damp cloudiness of too long in England, he saw clear separateness in brightness and dark. It had happened again, just as it had when he arrived at Taranto in 1944, the clarity with which he saw all around him shook him awake after a limbo of existence. And so he embraced the present. He did not want to break the spell of the spider's web and the magic was all about him.

He went to the Piazza dei Miracoli.

The tower.

He retraced his steps of so long past and found the street where the woman had so tragically fallen. Strangely, it was not quite in the place where it had been in his memory. But he recognised the shrine high in the wall of the corner house. There were no flowers now on the shelf before the Virgin Mary. He gave a moment's thought to the old woman and her ladder — what happened to her? — then pressed on. He could not differentiate Luisa Olvari's house and its fatal balcony from any of the other houses.

15

The bus to Petriano smelled of hot plastic and diesel, and warm garlicky food. It was a clattering, whining, mobile stink in which Tom waited for some essence of memory to stir. But it did not. As the bus found its pace, warm air rushed in through open windows and he closed his eyes to be cooled. He was pulled past fields of sunflower saplings. Through green hills and tall straight trees. He was getting closer.

Bastia was a town on a road, amid lifeless fields. He felt it was as unreal as a film running past the wide windows. The bus groaned as it wound up through wooded valleys, squeezed down the narrow gullies of village streets, villages that clung to the sides of hillocks. The most recently built dwellings dripped down the hillsides away far past the church, the bar, the shuttered shops.

He was searching all the time for some point of reference. He could find none. The map, open on his knees, was familiar only in its red-veined greenness and speckling of black place names. Outside the window where he sat was a world that was quite different and separate.

At his first sighting of a road sign to Petriano his heart lurched. But the bus was roaring up a wide new road, flagged with various other signs, most prominently a ring of stars on a blue background, notification that money and co-operation – money mostly – had been diverted here from the coffers of a united Europe. Its surface soothed the rumbling of the wheels beneath him and took away the fear that he might have been on a familiar route but was failing to remember any part of it.

Where there had been few other vehicles on the road, there were suddenly little entanglements with gasping farm engines and tiny battered cars to be swerved past. Tom clutched the map. He was aware he was staring too hard all around him, that he was seeing nothing properly. The bus swung to the left into the outskirts of a small town. This was not his village! His back was cold and wet under his shirt. This was not the place!

There was a sprinkling of houses he could see over to the right, on another small hill – perhaps they had let his place be and built this over here, to allow the real village to continue its existence undisturbed, like a kind of bypass. But no, there were newish-looking houses all along this road where before had only been fields and the dusty road. Like everywhere it was almost unrecognisably built up since the war.

So his thoughts were somersaulting in this way as the bus dived down and round an incline framed with brown stone houses, and drew up at a calm, palmed square. And only then could he see it.

His heart was pounding as he pulled down his bag from the luggage rack. He steadied himself with the backs of the seats as he teetered down the gangway. '*Grazie*,' he said to the driver.

Tom stepped down.

He scanned around him, trying to make sense of it. While he had been away, his mind had transposed the square into more than this scrubby three-sided lay-by. The fountain had been grander, the lines more gracious. Mercifully there were no cars parked up against it to litter what elegance remained with their rusty metal. Across the road was a small car park, spaces marked in white grids, and a run-down café. Was it *the* café? He could not be sure. Everything about this place was wrong: the configuration, the angles of the road, the blue above the low roofs. It would not coalesce with the pictures he had carried in his mind for so long.

There were still benches in the disappointing square and after a moment's thought he made his way over to one of them. He needed to get his bearings. If the stones and bricks and vistas of the village had grown strange in his absence, then what of the people? They would be complete strangers, surely? Was it possible that anyone would remember him, even if he could latch on to some faint clue in another person's face?

The problem was twofold. One, the village and its inhabitants had developed and changed during the years that had passed; and two, he had tinkered with its reality so often in his imagination that what he saw before him bore no relation to the golden citadel he had created for his memories to live in.

Two elderly women shuffled by. They were strangers to him, but the shock lingered when he realised that he might well have known them, once, when they were completely different.

The panic stole up his arms again. He pulled the wet shirt

away from his skin. He had not known it would be so hard. He calmed himself. He was a silly old man. Old? It was the first time he had seen himself as old, rather than middle-aged. But here was the confirmation. Here in the place where he had grown up in a matter of weeks, he had, in a few minutes, taken the next step onwards. So he sat down edgily in the square and wondered whether he would recognise anyone, or be recognised himself. But I have changed so much, ran his thoughts, this is nearly forty years on. At the bar he asked for a telephone directory. He raked through it, a glass of beer at his hand. Surely his fingers would alight on names he once knew.

It did not take long.

There – Sarna. Coia. He wondered if Annunziata's mother was dead – but no, she might have looked old and careworn, but she can only have been a few years older than him. Perhaps she was still waiting with her recriminatory tears. He did not care to dwell on that notion.

It was hot and his muscles sagged gratefully in the sun. Under the disguise of age, he was the same person. Disconcertingly the same person he had been when he was young and crazy. He shivered for a second when he wondered if he was crazy enough to see Giuseppe draw up at the square on his bone-shattering tractor, unaltered from a former time, open shirt badged with olive juice and shouting loud his greetings.

He could not find the name in the directory.

Now the question was should he walk up to Le Macchie and present himself unannounced? He sighed a short laugh to himself. That was his approach once upon a time. But could he even find his way to the lane there from this unfamiliar location? He swiftly abandoned the notion that he could find the river and the site of the camp, and then the snaking path up to the farm. His map was not large enough to show footpaths. He studied it intently for a long time. When he looked up from the papers, his concentration had been so complete that the ground and the houses and the sky were a dark blurry blue. He set off on foot, wondering with every step if he could hear echoes of his original footfalls.

The first time, long ago when he was that other person, that adventurous boy soldier, he had been led up a steep hill by snatches of laughter and giggles by the younger sisters Maddalena and Natalina. The path was silvered on either side of the track with olive groves. He could see them now, scampering ahead and in the trees as he ambled, glad to be away from the camp, so happy to be lost in the warm country-side. Then, as now, the afternoon sun pierced into the pink skin of his bare forearms.

A couple of times he stopped to consult the map, then strode on up the road. He passed the church and strained to regain some sense of familiarity. It was almost there, barely out of touch. He had expected the houses to have altered, but there seemed nothing here on which to graft his recol-lections. He covered the best part of two kilometres before he felt his senses springing to meet his expectations. He walked down an avenue of cypresses and there, like a photo-graph, was the Villa Belvedere. It was unchanged. Further along was a discreet polished wood sign on the roadside that pointed up a dusty path. Le Macchie. He was here – or rather, *it* was here.

The path was still the same – a rough rutted trail. On either side the scrubby bushes and pines were just as he remembered.

Maybe the pines were taller, the trail rather darker, the tantalising path through to a place which had been once. Then he saw the end of it: smaller, narrower than he had revisited in his imagination. The end of the building was covered by scrambling creepers, but the shape – at last! – concurred with his recollection.

The long farmhouse of terracotta plaster. A house with no grand design, doors and windows and outside staircases seeming to grow organically along its length according to need. It pointed down a spur of the hill.

Tom walked faster, craning his neck to look along its length – yes! There was the chapel, the rusty bell still swinging from its arch. In front, the terrace where he had once sat. The pergola was different and there was no pitted table standing there ready for dining under the stars.

In the terraces of the kitchen garden the planting had run to seed. There was something else wrong: it was too quiet. Where were the shuffling of chickens, the cries of the pigs in the land which tumbled away to the east and in the steep woodland to the west?

A gravel path led along the sunny side, until, and at the end of the house there was an arched loggia and an area of gravel.

There was no one in sight.

In his mind he could see them, though: a man and woman were sitting outside the meanest part of the house, shelling beans; the man gnarled by the wind and hard toil; the woman intent. Giuseppe and Anna, casting poor beans into a bowl.

'*Buon giorno?*' the voice cut in sharply from behind him. It was an interrogation. '*Chi sei e che vuoi?*' Who was he and what did he want?

Tom turned to see a stout middle-aged woman, well dressed. She narrowed her gaze as if better to assess the plausibility of his excuse for trespass.

'*Buon giorno, signora*,' he managed.

She was staring at his bag. He put it down and extended his hand. '*Scusi, signora. Mi chiamo Tom Wainwright.*' Words from the forgotten language unfurled awkwardly from his tongue. '*Cerco la famiglia Parini?*'

'*Sì* – but . . .'

'Do they still live here?' If not, then they would be remembered, surely?

He was searching her face – she was becoming uncomfortable under his relentless scrutiny. Could this be Maddalena – or Natalina? He did not want to make the suggestion. He did not think so, but then how could he trust any of what he seemed to see in this place. His memories had been proved false a hundred times already.

'I am looking after the house now,' she said fiercely.

'And the family?'

She was assessing him again, weighing up what to tell him. 'You should ask someone else.' She sighed.

'Who?'

'The doctor . . . the notary . . .' She shrugged. Here was another change: the friendliness and openness of the locals was no longer the natural way of the world.

He had nothing to lose by laying his own cards on the table. 'I knew them all, once: Giuseppe and Anna, Maddalena and Natalina . . . and Giuliana and . . . poor Emilio.'

Her expression changed. She continued to look at him, however, and he could not make out what she was thinking. He noticed now that she had a large bunch of keys in her hand, as if he had been lucky – their visits had coincided.

'During the war,' he went on.

Her frown hardened.

He had to make it clear. 'When the Germans were going . . . retreating. I was at the camp by the river . . .'

'You are British?'

'Yes.'

'This is Maddalena's house now.'

'Is she here?'

A shake of the head. 'She has been gone to America these past two months.'

Two months? He could hardly bear it – he had missed her so narrowly. Still, this was a link. 'And . . . the other sisters?'

'Natalina in Rome, and Giuliana . . . I don't know. She is often away, travelling.'

She *is*. She was not some torture of his imagination. Giuliana existed. She could be found.

'You don't know?' he demanded impatiently, then regretted it. Had his eagerness given him away? Then he thought: what does it matter now?

'She always moved around so often. It's hard to keep up.'

'Could I . . . could I get in touch . . . with Maddalena?'

'Perhaps. I . . . don't know.'

'I remember this house well.'

She nodded her head and weighed up his appearance. He saw the decision made as if it were a cloud shadow across her face. 'You can look around if you like. I am going inside to check on the water tanks. The plumbing has a few odd quirks – always best to check.'

'Giuseppe,' said Tom.

'Yes,' said the woman. 'Old Giuseppe and his grand ideas of plumbing.'

They exchanged wry smiles.

'Maria Galletti,' she told him. 'I live up the road. I act as caretaker.' She pursed her lips and made a play of seeming to assess his likely character and honesty.

Then she left him to his business as she attended to hers.

Tom walked the length of the farmhouse. This was his mythical place, the seat of his sentimental obsession, and he had returned. He was self-aware enough to know that. All the history he had built his life on was contained in this plot. But once again, he was straining too hard to recapture the past and it was as if he was grabbing in a frenzy, achieving only wild fistfuls of nothingness. He had to force himself not to think but to absorb.

Lizards scurried here and there. Beyond, where the land slipped away into wilderness, there were the tall pines and limes and ilexes. Down below were the scrubby olive trees and above, between the outlines of the sentry pines, the cloudy blue of distant hills. The sunlight was intensifying behind them now. The afternoon was dying.

Nostalgia, sentimentality, call it what he would. It was the memory of emotions deep inside him that had never been released. He had to find her. No, he should not try to find her. To see her again would be a terrible disappointment. He must never do so.

He sat down on a wooden terrace under the pines, dizzied by his mind's uncontrollable swings. The terrace was new to him, decking not the stone he remembered, but not alien. Signora Galletti allowed him to sit there for a long time. Was his presence in this place gross arrogance, or humility? A couple of times he felt himself being watched from the house, but still he sat, and she, intrigued perhaps, allowed him this indulgence. At last he went to look for her.

He knocked at a couple of locked doors, then called up the outside staircases at the rear of the farmhouse. The machinery of a small estate could be seen here: the empty animal hutches, drums and barrels, spare parts, rusting engines, pipes stowed away. A motorcycle was inside an open barn.

Tom knocked at various doors this side and gently pulled open one or two of them, but he could not find Signora Galletti.

So, as he had done that time so long ago, he prised open the door of the chapel and stepped into its mothy, musty cool. The door of the confession box was hanging off and there was no holy water in the stone basin to his left. There was mud and dried grass on the red matting on the floor. But the smell was unmistakably the same: the scent of devotion. And there, above the altar, was the carving of Christ on the cross, commissioned by Maddalena. Anna's wartime birthday present, still here! He was amazed. He stood for a while, fortifying himself with that thought.

Outside once more he was surprised to find a darkening in the sky. The heavy warmth of the afternoon had gone. How long had he been there? How late was it? He did not care. He made his way further into the gardens, as far as the small orchard of apple and plum trees. This he remembered; and the memories were unstoppable now. The wind had an unexpected chill on it. That was right; Italy was never as hot as you thought it was going to be and the rain – dear Lord, how it could rain at the worst possible times! He came to the end of the high spit of land. The hill he stood on tumbled away beyond a wire fence, exactly as it had always done. The stars were out, brighter than he had seen them for years.

There was a car in the drive when he walked back down.

'*Signor?*' It was Maria Galletti calling. A man was standing by the open driver's seat.

'Yes,' he called, hurrying now.

'This is my husband Alberto.'

Tom offered his hand. Was the man looking at him suspiciously?

'It is late. We were worried that you might have left,' said Maria.

'Wainwright,' he said, 'Tom Wainwright.'

'Do you have a place to stay here?' Alberto asked.

Tom hung his head, ashamed at last of his impetuosity, his unthinking cruelty to his own family. 'No,' he said.

'Come,' said Signora Galletti softly. 'You can come with us.'

She spoke as though to a child, or a dangerously retarded adult. It was only then that he realised that in his present-day form he was a haunted figure.

She reached out a hand and he took it. He felt shame shrink his entire body as he allowed himself to be led wherever they were going.

In the car the distance to the Galletti house was covered in minutes. There was a heavy clanging noise followed by the sharp ring of metal on metal from the back as they bounced over every rut in the dust path. It sounded like tools in the boot.

At the house, a square narrow windowed dwelling, another couple was waiting. Tom wanted to run now, but was grounded by a sudden weariness that turned his legs to sodden sponges and his heart to lead. This other man and woman assessed him carefully. He stood there sweating and immobile, forced to submit to this unsettling scrutiny. This was not what he had imagined, not at all.

'Wainwright?' asked the man. Did he look familiar? Under an unforgiving light which gave him black holes under the eyes and ghoulish folds from the cheeks, it was hard to tell.

Tom nodded.

The man clapped him on the back. 'You don't remember me? Massimo?'

'Massimo? Massimo Criachi? Is it you?' It was almost a wail. Tom could not believe it came out of his own mouth.

'This is Massimo!' The man spread his arms wide. 'And here is Nina, my wife.'

The woman smiled openly.

Was she one of the village girls who had hovered around him? Surely not, she was too young – by a good twenty years. But maybe not. She was an ample, voluptuous woman, and might have aged well. Tom could hardly tell: the dim light, the exhaustion, the long days of travel, the long years which had passed, had eroded his capacity for rational judgement.

They stared at each other. Then there was an awkward greeting – a handshake, a clasp.

'Giuseppe and Anna – are they still in the village, are they still alive?'

Massimo shook his head. 'No, my friend. Both are dead. For many years now.' Massimo coughed with a wracking sound. It was painful to hear.

'He has been ill,' said Nina.

'And Giuliana?' cried Tom, unable to stop himself. 'Is Giuliana not here?'

A long silence.

'Not for many many years,' said Nina gently.

'Do you know where she is?' He could make no attempt to keep the desperation out of his voice.

The others exchanged looks.

'It is difficult to say,' ventured Massimo at last, after a fit of coughing.

Tom ignored the warning implication. 'Tell me something – tell me something that will help!'

How could he say, at his age, that he had come back for her, that he had abandoned everything in his own country for her? It was just another fantasy, he could see that now; the shame dug deeper under his ribcage and burned through his chest.

'When did you last see her?' he persisted.

'About fifteen years ago,' said Nina.

'Was that here?'

'Yes.' Nina took a pained breath. 'She had come to take her . . . furniture and so on . . . from Le Macchie. She was getting married at last.' It sounded as if the two of them had been good friends.

'And where? Where was she going to live?' Tom could not stop now. After so long imagining, he had to wring every last known fact from them.

'Ah . . . Tom . . . it was so long ago.' Nina looked worried, as if she was unsure whether their visitor was completely in control of himself. 'Giuliana, she wanted to leave here so much and we were sad for her. She made it clear that –'

There was an uncomfortable shuffling of glances.

'She wanted to start from the beginning again. A fresh start,' said Nina.

Had Massimo himself had an affair with her in the end? Tom would not have put it past the old devil.

They gave him food. He could not remember being so hungry, not even when he must have been, during the war. And he was back in the same familiar setting, a cavernous kitchen lined with white tiles, pots hanging from hooks and scents exuded from the enormous black range.

'Tell me how you've been,' Tom asked Massimo between mouthfuls of food and wine. He was much calmer now. It was not so hard to find the long-forgotten words of his second language. 'Did you ever become a famous racehorse owner?'

'Ha!' retorted Massimo. 'Cars, though – that was my bag. And I made a good living eventually. I became a car dealer.'

The others grinned affectionately and nodded proudly.

'A very good one,' said Alberto, 'especially to his friends.'

Massimo shrugged in acceptance of the way of the world. 'And I married Pia,' he added, also with pride.

'Pia!' exclaimed Tom. 'Not my mate Jonno's . . . friend?'

A nod and a grin.

'Ah – and is she – ?'

'I am sorry to say that she died. Many years ago now. I was sad for a long time, then I became myself again –'

'Once more no woman in the village was safe!' Maria Galletti ribbed him.

He winked at her. 'Not only in this village, woman!'

Maria raised an eyebrow at Nina.

'Oh, don't encourage him,' responded Nina.

'And I have a son and a beautiful daughter, Fabrizia. I who know the ways of young men, I keep a careful watch, eh?' Massimo gave a cackle of laughter that disintegrated into more chest heaving.

Then he remembered the rescue of Annunziata Coia. 'No one will ever forget that,' he assured Tom.

'Is she – all right?' His voice petered out. He hardly dared ask.

'Oh, she is still here. She is a teacher. You did a good thing there, my friend.'

'I'm glad,' said Tom. He was glad, of course he was. Glad for the little girl who had grown up to live a full life, but not for himself. He found he was embarrassed and unwilling to dwell on the subject. For that too exacerbated his guilt. If he had not been with Giuliana at the *festa*, if Annunziata's mother had not been fleeing to avoid him, then her son and daughter might not have been driven into the bomb blast. All he had done was to make some small amends. He was no hero.

'And her mother?' He was compelled to ask.

Maria pulled the corners of her mouth down and nodded sadly. 'It would never have been easy for Nunzia. Her husband was killed in North Africa. She had a brother who was missing in action and neither she nor anyone else in the family knew where he was, or if he was still alive. And then the bomb . . . '

Yes, thought Tom grimly, then, on one terrible afternoon, she pushes her own son towards his death because she is running away from a man who has, she believes, snatched the prospect of happiness from her brother. And this same man saves her daughter and, arguably, her life as well. Is Corporal Tom Wainwright saviour or agent of the disaster?

At the time, Tom was praised fulsomely by all, but it was still a tragedy. The boy had died.

'Nunzia had a breakdown,' continued Maria. 'She died when Annunziata was six. Her brother Arturo never returned to Petriano. In the end, I think her heart was as battered as her legs. She never walked without crutches again. Annunziata was brought up with her cousins.'

'She is much loved in the village,' said Nina. 'She is a special person, with a sunny disposition.'

'Annunziata knows first hand that life is transient and the best must be made of every new day,' interjected Maria.

'She has been the village schoolteacher since the age of nineteen,' said Nina fondly. 'She was my teacher. She's one of the loveliest people I know.'

Tom felt no better.

None of the old friends had an address for her, they said. Giuliana had promised to let them know when she was settled, but the letter never arrived.

They had an idea that she had gone to Volterra, a mysterious walled citadel high above the plains to the west. Although what had planted that notion was difficult to say. Perhaps that was where her husband-to-be came from. That might have been it, concurred Nina. Yes, she was pretty sure that was it.

They concluded that Giuliana had cut herself adrift deliberately and they had been too proud to search for her where she did not want to be found.

'Who was the husband-to-be?' asked Tom. His voice was hoarse, unrecognisable to himself.

'He was quite a bit older than her, I remember that,' said Massimo.

'A curator of a museum?' wondered Nina. 'We never met him. We only heard what she wanted to tell us at the time.'

It was a long time ago, they kept reminding him. For Tom, fifteen years was nothing. He did not say this, but he felt the undercurrent of their surmising: why was he so interested after all this time; was there something not quite right about his interest?

'I can ask Maddalena next time she is in touch, but that might be not be very soon,' said Maria.

Who would know? they wondered. It was difficult. The Criachis were old friends of the family, but even they should not intrude on family affairs.

'But Volterra,' said Tom one last time. 'You are sure about that?'

As much as they could be, they assured him.

Massimo began to cough again.

'He has not been well,' said Nina.

'I'm all right, don't fuss so.'

But she bore him off to his bed, despite his protestations. Tom shook his hand as he left.

Tom stayed the night at the Galletti house. Swaddled in Maria's stiff white linen, he slept.

The next morning Alberto insisted on driving him back to Arezzo to catch the train. He wanted to look at a shop there, he said. The ironmongery business was booming, he had gone into partnership with Vittorio Rossi and they were in the mood for expansion. They went past Massimo's house and Petriano receded once more.

Tom was lucky. He did not have to wait long for the first

train to Pisa. Once there he walked to the hotel where he had left his paltry possessions, a bag half full of items he had bought on the hoof since he walked away from his real life.

He was back at the station within the hour, engulfed in the noise, watching intently at the centre of the heart which pumped the trains on to Rome and Naples, and Florence and Venice, then sucked them back and sent them on their way to Nice and Paris and Boulogne. He stood in front of the roar of the Rome Express and the Naples Express, then found his way to the metal artery to take him south to Cecina. The train he would take was not an express; it was a rumbling black monster with worn tartan upholstery, permanently indented in the seat – which was a step up from the narrow wooden benches in the lower-class carriages.

He found it soothing to ride the fixed track, absolved of responsibility for his own motion forward. The brief journey lulled his consciousness and his eyelids fell gratefully into an imitation of sleep. At Cecina he alighted, dazed. After an hour there he found another bus, which took him across the seascape of alluvial fields to Volterra.

V

16

There is nothing to report of Tom's whereabouts in Italy. Isabel's enquiries have reached an impasse. No information has been forthcoming from the British consulate in Florence. Another telephone call to the acting vice-consul, Ms Annette Barclay, has reiterated the fact that she has found no record of Tom Wainwright. The news is either good (no Tom Wainwright has ever registered with the consulate or been in any adverse contact with the authorities due to recklessness or death); or it is bad (there is no indication that Isabel's intuition is right and Tom Wainwright has ever returned for any length of time to Italy).

The trail has gone cold.

But when she telephones her mother to tell her, Isabel senses relief at the other end of the line and is hurt by it.

'Are you coming back now, then?' asks Patricia.

'No. I'm still hoping something will turn up.'

'But why? Why put yourself through this – and me?' Her mother's voice has a shrill edge.

Isabel forces herself to remain calm. 'Don't you understand why?'

'But what good will it do now? Leave it, Isabel. Leave *him* to rot where he deserves.'

'You don't mean that.'

'Oh, I do, believe me.'

'I don't understand why you're so angry,' says Isabel.

'I didn't want you to do this!' shouts Patricia.

The words ring in Isabel's head long after she has put down the telephone. Her mother's reaction is so odd. For all that she has made her long-lost husband the focus of her discontent, Patricia has never played these unpleasant emotional games.

Then she remembers the tang of burned paper hanging in the English twilight.

'I thought she would be pleased to hear from me,' Isabel tells Matteo. 'I wanted her to know I was happy – and in the end I didn't even tell her.'

'She lost a husband, and now her daughter has gone away,' says Matteo. 'It's understandable.'

'We're both hurt,' says Isabel. 'The difference is what we're doing about it.'

'Maybe you're the brave one.' Matteo strokes her cheek gently.

'I love you,' she says. 'Especially when I see you.'

For weeks she has been living in his apartment. But Matteo is preoccupied with the tower and his work is, at times, all consuming. For any other woman – one with a less obsessive father, perhaps – his devotion to a tube of white marble might well be grounds to abandon the relationship.

But there is a kind of balance between their twin

obsessions. He has his tower; she the search for her father. They are happy, she tells herself, and she will not give up on her quest to find Tom – or at least to find out what happened to him. She has her own preoccupations. And so far she has not regretted for a second her decision to be here.

'It won't always be like this,' says Matteo. 'It's a critical time.'

'So long as you still want me here.'

'You know I do. Don't ever go.'

'I may have to go back to England to sort things out. My mother – my job. My boss thinks I'm coming back after a couple of months. I'll have to tell him I'm not. My flat . . . I own it so if I rent it out I can live on the income.' She smiles. 'Dad did that for me – I bought the flat outright with the money from his company when it was sold eventually.'

'You don't need to do that.'

Isabel nods. 'I do.'

'It's very rash!' He is teasing.

'I've never done anything reckless in my life,' says Isabel. 'Until I met you!'

Before her father left, Isabel had been difficult. She knew it. The relationship between them was flawed, strained now that she was no longer a sweet biddable little girl but this large excitable teenager. Her father, too, had begun to detach from her. He seemed to find it difficult to know exactly how to treat her now that she was visibly becoming a woman. She was argumentative. She took refuge with her mother. They would both set themselves against him.

He would talk about the war and Pat would refuse to listen.

His misadventures in Italy, she would say dismissively. What did he have to complain about, she would shout at him, he came back, didn't he?

The atmosphere of suppressed anger haunts her even now. She cannot allow it to seep into her life with Matteo. Whatever happens, she has sworn she would never repeat the pattern.

She and Matteo have had arguments. Of course they have. She has missed him while he has been spending so much time in his office and on site.

'Do you have to go out with the men again?' It's a reasonable question. When he does not reply, she says, 'It's just that . . . you only saw them yesterday evening – and then several you'll see tomorrow at work, and –'

He is looking at her as if he cannot believe what she is asking.

'It's football. I like to go,' he says.

And she is learning to let it be.

This is, as he says, a crucial time for the tower and for the engineers. They are almost ready to begin extracting the soil underneath; a delicate operation is about to be launched, an intricate pattern of calculation and probability and chance.

In the morning he leaves without breakfast, giving her a fleeting kiss. She sees him pass the half-open door, as part of a person in the narrow slit of space. Then he is gone.

Isabel spends days alone in Pisa, just as she did when she first arrived.

She goes again to see Mauro Arinci at the Opera – but he is not there. He does not work on Thursdays. She must also accept that there may be nothing remotely connected with Tom Wainwright there. She is beginning to accept that she may be able to find nothing further.

Sauntering through the streets and alleyways she is seized by a sense of how lucky she is, to be here in this place, to have the leisure to enjoy a walk like this, the smell of white peaches as she passes an *alimentari*, to feel the sun on her face and arms, to have the thrill of a new love. In private celebration she goes into a boutique on the glitzy Via Oberdan and buys a white linen dress, long and cool. It is expensive and she is glad. The brush of the skirt against her bare legs is sensuous.

This is the change she has yearned for, she tells herself, for years without knowing exactly what it was that she needed.

When Isabel sits on the grass in front of the tower, which groans silently under the pressure of lead weights and cables, she thinks of the past, the long-ago past: the windblown silted-up Pisa that had seen better days in the time of Shelley and his wife Mary – Mary who saw monsters under the skin of men.

Shelley wrote of the dark Italian air and shapeless terror, the dust and straws blown along the streets. The shadows of life and death hung heavily over their days – the loss of children, the threat of illness and then the accident at sea. A melancholy time of romance and hope subsiding.

Following her map, Isabel walks the twisting side streets in search of Byron's house. The alleys are medieval, vaguely unsettling. Her footsteps echo on the stones. When she finds the Palazzo Lanfranchi, the vast building Byron boasted could house a whole garrison, it is tatty, streaked with dirt and pollutants. It seems currently to be used as some kind of administrative offices.

Night falls, and still he is not back.

Time stands still as Isabel lies immobile in her bath. Hot water covers most of her body and laps at her breasts. The water is too hot, and sweat has begun to trickle from her hairline and her throat. Patterns of steam swirl and dance in the air above.

As she lies back and allows her thoughts their freedom, she finds they surge back inwards with small revelations.

A thought experiment. How can she construct the logical contradiction?

She tries: If Father were alive, he would surely have tried to contact her in twenty years.

If Father were dead, mother and daughter would surely have been notified.

Therefore . . . (Isabel tries to hold on to slipping thoughts) . . . as there has been no contact or notification, Father cannot be alive or dead.

Cannot be alive or dead – in Britain, she amends. So either she is right and he is, or has been, abroad. Or one of the above statements is false.

What is the conclusion from the logical contradiction? It eludes her.

Isabel goes to bed and cannot sleep. Rain has been lashing the window for hours. It comes in waves, drumming then fading but never stopping.

The clock by the bed, on his empty side, reads two twenty. Where is Matteo? Is he not coming back?

And she is also thinking now: I have missed something. There is another possibility concerning her father. He might have used another name. That is the element that is false. That is what people do when they want to disappear, is it not? Why did she not think of that before?

Hours later the telephone shrills. It is Matteo, his voice barely audible for the noise all around him. There is a crisis at the Campo dei Miracoli. The tower is shifting. She is breaking up, they fear. The fragile shell of marble might shatter at any time. She must be stabilised now, the tension eased, or all will be lost.

She. They all call the tower she. They see her as an obstinate beauty they must save at all costs from a bad end. She speaks to them, they say. When the tension is too tight, she shivers, she sinks into herself under unremitting rain and she has shuddered now, encased in her steel girdle.

Isabel rubs her eyes, then sits bolt upright. Then, hardly before the idea has formed in her brain, she is standing. She dresses roughly, pulls a coat round her, one of his. Then she runs down the central stairs and outside into the howling night. The door is wrenched from her hand by the wind and dashed back against the building. Her hair is full of water already, tails of it are whipping her face. She reaches the car and guns it. She can hardly hear the engine at full throttle above the roar of the deluge. She pulls out into the street on a white crest of drain water.

The corner of the Campo dei Miracoli is lit brightly. As she approaches there are no shouts and hoarse instructions and clamour, as she had imagined. A loaded hush has settled on the place. This is a famous patient on the operating table whose life is about to slip away. Then the sound of the bore equipment begins, slowly, slowly to suck out the clogged soil. Isabel cannot see Matteo, but she can see the expression that concentration will be furrowing on his face.

How apt, thinks Isabel, that she will be here when the tower falls. It is, after all, what she has wanted since she was a child. It would be the resolution to the problem which would satisfy all known laws of nature. And yet, and yet . . .

She is drenched now, but feeling nothing on the outside of her skin. She is merely an intricate pattern of thoughts, each one leaping on to the next so quickly and so instinctively that she finds she has no idea how this one or that one took hold, and cannot retrace the steps they made to get to this point; she knows only that she was thinking of something important and it is there hanging over all this, if only she could get back to examine it in more depth. She was making connections but she cannot see what they meant.

Groups of engineers stand around in clumps. There are others, like her, who have been watching, drawn here for whatever reason. Lights are on at the windows overlooking the site. The President of the Opera is probably praying in the cathedral that he will not be the one to preside over the fall, to have to hang his head over a pile of rubble.

They are quiet again, waiting.

Perhaps the seismologists are taking readings? Has some brave soul risked his life to go inside the doomed cylinder to gather the results? Surely there is an alternative to going inside the tower to collect the data. She does not know. A stab of black humour: man has to go inside and is killed by empirical proof.

She sees a figure walking towards the main group. Is it Matteo? She screws up her eyes. No, it is someone else.

Then there are frenzied shouts and the throb of the extractor bore dies. She waits to hear something from the tower, some terrible cracking, the clap of thunder in which the marble will explode. The hiss of the rain intensifies. Against the darkness it makes heavy bead curtains in the arc lights.

Isabel stands and stares, on and on.

The first glimmerings of dawn appear on the mountain horizon like a night light in a corridor. The tower is pink. A rosiness creeps over the pale stone like health returning to an invalid's cheeks. She is settling again, for a deep sleep after a bad night. This is meretricious, of course. The prettiness of the picture has never signified safety. Isabel is deathly cold, shivering.

'It is all right,' Matteo is saying. 'It is all right.'

He is astonished to find her here.

'You're soaked through!' he says.

'So are you.'

'She is steady again,' whispers Matteo.

The engineers are now watching over their patient and are prey to superstition; they do not want to leave.

The streets are drying already. Cold grey stones glisten.

They drink sludgy dark coffee with milk at a café at first light, with other members of the team. Conversation is unleashed now. Tensions must be vented. Matteo's arm lies across the back of her chair. Isabel sits calmly in the whirl of shouts and gesticulations and laughter.

'I understand now,' she says so that only he can hear.

He gives her an exultant kiss.

She understands other things too. She can focus now on what she has, not what she has lost. After all, in his leaving Tom has led her here, to this man.

B ut still there is no certainty.
Getting ready one morning with Matteo in the flat, he seems distracted. The light is lemon clear in early morning, against the mountain ridges of indigo.

She makes coffee, thick and strong for him, milky for herself. Earlier she went to get fresh bread. She likes the cool and crispness of these mornings, which feel like working mornings far removed from the clammy heat which still signifies holidays to her. People walk briskly up and down the streets, certain of their errands and destinations.

'What are you up to today?' she asks.

'Thursday . . . Thursday lecture at the faculty, then a department meeting.'

She knows him well enough now to know he loathes departmental meetings, all the differing agendas, the rivalry and subtle put-downs, the way hours pass with so little resolved. Professor Cavelli is a particular irritant. Perhaps this is what has dampened his mood.

'Would you like to eat here tonight?'

'I suppose so.' He has picked up a newspaper and begun to read.

'I thought I might go to the archive again this morning – to see whether they've found anything,' she says.

There is no answer, but he looks up. It seems he is about to say something, then decides against it.

'You don't think that's a good idea?'

'No – I don't know. You should do what you want.'

'So you think that if the archivist had anything to tell me, he would have called you?'

Matteo shrugs.

Isabel's buoyancy has evaporated. She bites on her lip to stop herself saying anything that could damage their fragile new understanding. In other circumstances she might have been demanding, 'What do you mean? What is wrong with you this morning?' But she cannot. She lets it go.

He is preoccupied. Measurements of the tower are vindicating the project. The tower has been pulled fractionally back – but the work in progress might, in the long run, worsen the tilt. No one can be certain.

'Look,' he says. 'A miracle has occurred on the Field of Miracles' it says in the newspaper. It trumpets the turning point in black and white, paying particular attention to the – currently discredited – insistence of Professor Cavelli and his rival experts that the project would end in disaster. A British professor has played a prominent role.

'He might read this,' says Matteo. He means Tom. Several pages carry pictures of the tower taken from the same angle; they show the blocks of lead weights and the taut steel cables screaming up and out of the frame.

Isabel nods.

'Do you think . . . if he . . . were able to – he might come to see it?' asks Matteo.

Isabel does not lift her eyes. 'If he is alive. If he is here. If he can still see to read.' She says this crisply.

There is a pause, then Matteo covers her hand with his. She lets it stay there, feeling the warmth and wondering if there is, in the end, such a thing as the protectiveness it seems to offer.

Then she smiles at him, for he only meant well.

Matteo opens his mouth to say something, but clearly changes his mind.

He is holding something back, she knows it.

At times she wonders at her own arrogance in believing that she can understand this man, make this relationship with a foreign man work where she has never been able to succeed with a man who shared a similar background. The longer she knows him, the more that is apparent.

Before he goes he bends over the table and kisses her gently on the lips. '*Ciao, bella,*' he says. And he is gone. The front door has clicked shut behind him.

She clears away the breakfast plates and cups feeling undermined. But by the time she is ready to go out, she has shaken off her misgivings. This is part of getting to know – really know – someone new. The uncertainty is part of the excitement, she tells herself.

A nother morning.

The sheets on Matteo's bed are starchy white and cool. Even where the crumples undulate there is firm body to the cotton, a strength to the soft smoothness. Isabel is alone in the bed. She reaches out to touch the indentations where her lover's body lay next to her. Is it her imagination, or is there some residual warmth from his buttocks and hips and back? She lies still, one hand in the hollow, and imagines she is floating in a space that is filled with contentment. Faint, reassuring smells reach her as they play around the air she

breathes: of coffee from the kitchen, of the droplets of a
tangy aftershave he spritzed into the atmosphere; of pockets
of biscuity-scented natural skin smells in the depths of the
bed. Isabel is awake now and alive to the day's possibilities,
but her limbs are deliciously heavy. She remembers now:
Matteo kissed her and left. She must have closed her eyes
again and gone back to sleep. She could find out the time if
she allowed her arm to droop to the floor and picked up her
watch, but for the moment the effort is too much.

All is quiet. How do you measure peace of mind? All the
tests and indicators are geared to interpret distress. In the
here and now, Isabel feels rooted; she does not want to move
by a fraction. She wants to wallow, like a large animal, in the
warm mud of a satiated present.

The telephone rings.

She will leave it.

The caller does not give up. On and on goes the sound,
vibrating her cocoon. Isabel becomes aware of the distant
hum of traffic. A fly buzzes past.

Reluctantly Isabel lets her feet down to the floor and stands.
Then she realises: it is Matteo calling. He knows she is still
there. She patters into the sitting room, bare feet on polished
wood. She picks up the receiver and says, '*Buon giorno!*'

There is silence, then a click. She was too late after all. Or
was she cut off? She puts the receiver down and waits for a
moment. Perhaps Matteo will try again.

As she waits, she fiddles with a drawer handle on the table.
Then, idly, she opens it. There is a mishmash of papers. Some
are letters. There are receipts. It is the same, small-scale, kind
of muddle he works in. It is only a brief curiosity. She is
about to close the drawer again. Then she feels the hard edge

of a picture frame and slides it out. She is holding a photograph of a woman with a small child, a girl. The two are grinning conspiratorially, aware of the camera.

And Isabel's blood runs cooler. For she knows, somehow – and the longer she stares at the face the more certain she is – that the child is Matteo's. He has not said a word about this woman and this child, and that is how she knows how important they are to him.

Still holding the picture, Isabel walks to a seat and drops down into it. In the morning light and shade of the white apartment, all she can see is the relief of black. The fly is in here now, swooping and humming. Isabel's hands are trembling. She knows; she simply knows. It has all been too good to be true.

He is married, then. Or if not married, exactly, then he has a partner. He is still, or he has been, the husband figure to this woman and the father of this child. They are beautiful, both of them. How could he leave them?

Fool. She knew; she always knew. She sensed the strangeness of this white apartment, where he has lived for a year or two, its impermanence, its pragmatism. And she also felt in it the existence of a framed photograph stuffed in a drawer. She was a fool, she had not trusted her instincts.

Isabel rips a sheet of paper from a pad on the table under the bookshelves. She pulls at other drawers until she finds what she is looking for, a book of addresses and telephone numbers. What is the woman's name? What is the child's? She feels she will know it, by the same instinct that is now awakened and tearing at her heart.

Of course it is a hopeless task. She is disgusted by herself, but she has started now and cannot stop.

Perhaps she will find the name at the end of a letter. Is she to stoop so low as to search through his letters?

She is trembling, allowing the same old anger to swirl around in her, giving in to it. It keys in so neatly to something fundamental that she has learned: that men are not to be trusted, that they let you down, hurt you, no matter how much they are supposed to love you.

Then she pulls it from the drawer where Matteo has saved it so carefully. It is a postcard – a cartoon picture of a princess and a castle – written in a childish script. Luna, it is signed. And at the top is an address.

17

Matteo is going away for three days, he says.
It is a conference in Venice. He has been invited to speak, on new methods of measuring the slip caused by alluvial silt beneath ancient sites. It is a great honour to be asked to give this address to a gathering of his fellow professionals.

'And a chance to catch up with some old friends,' says Isabel.

Something in her tone has made him look up quickly.

'Old colleagues, I meant,' she adds. She is measuring his response. What is he really thinking? She is in that gnawing limbo where she knows nothing, yet suspects everything.

She makes up her mind before he has even kissed her goodbye.

When he has gone, she checks her map is in her bag – and the address she has found – and lets herself out of the apartment. She almost runs to the small white car that she is beginning to treat as her own. The route south, the

SS206, is a fast road of wide bends twisting into the hillocky plains of western Tuscany.

To her left are the shady woodland mysteries of Crespina and its locality; to the right are stark open cornfields. The heat is intense and there is no escape from it. On the map, Gabbro is no distance. She will be there and back in less than the day she has given herself.

As the road cuts past, she can still see wild flowers, thousands of purple daisies growing in olive groves. Now she is looking south over a wide plain where hills of sunblasted wheat roll across hills like waves at sea. A warm rush of wind keeps up its pressure on her and clumps of bamboo are bending like pharaohs' fans. From the small group of houses cradled on the shallow hilltop she can see stately cypresses across a field which remain still as topiary against the long gusts of wind that are whistling through the car.

The harvest has begun; in far-off fields are silent tractors snatching and scraping at the corn. Each patch of the wave landscape is claimed and cultivated.

The village of Gabbro clings to a hill. In the gardens she can see passion flowers and canna and convolvulus in addition to the usual geraniums and oleander. There are cacti, too, which are thriving. Sunflowers, on their last gasp, are drooping – crisp brown showerheads, ready to give up their seeds.

It is a large village. Outside several of the houses there is washing strung out on steel horses. Older women and young children sit and play by open doors, in front of the yawning darkness behind.

The wind has not abated. It seems to be intensifying. When she gets out of the car it is howling a gale of hot breath.

Large trees nearby are doubled over, but still the cypresses across the valley appear immobile. Men have come out of the shops and cafés to take down the awnings and umbrellas. They are stacking outside chairs and tables, lashing them down with rope. They must expect the wind to continue.

'What is it called, this wind? Does it have a name?' Isabel asks one of the waiters who have been giving her coffees at the bar.

He does not seem to understand.

'Like a . . . sirocco, or the mistral?' she prompts.

'Ah, no . . . just a big wind from the west. It could have a name, but I don't know it.' He is very young. Why should he waste his time on knowing the proper names for useless changes in the weather? For him it is the wind that keeps the girls at home instead of parading past his post at the bar on their Vespas.

Isabel is not comfortable. Her weaknesses seem exposed. She is constantly on the alert for sharp rogue pains which jab into a temple, then reappear as an ache in the chest, the manifestations of nervous strain. The old intimations of vertigo come and go. But – and this is a recently discovered phenomenon in herself – she finds that she can turn it to good use. For it points towards those places where she has been too frightened to go, to feel the sadnesses she has convinced herself – wrongly – that she does not feel. The slight disturbance in her vision and sense of the earth falling beneath her feet is not a physical truth after all, she rationalises, but a moment of inner truth that her psyche has recognised.

Now she is walking into the wind. It scrapes the hair back from her scalp and whips it into frayed ropes. Now she is pushing, forehead down, into the hill road. She has memorised the address on Luna's postcard and here is the house.

It is a smooth-fronted house attached to its neighbours on either side although they are all of different designs. It is painted pale yellow and is surrounded by pots of bright geraniums. It is a family house, there is no doubt about that. There are children's toys left carelessly in the small grass yard in front. The wheels of an upturned tricycle are spinning, ridden by the elements.

The woman who answers the door does not fail to let her in. She is petite, dark-haired, full-lipped. She is the woman in the photograph. How could she not be?

Inside, out of the roaring gale, Isabel feels curiously weightless, in a comparative vacuum. She is not herself; she is an actress, moving faultily across a strange stage.

All is clean, white with wooden floors. It is modern and fresh, with antique pieces displayed like prizes against its austerity. She recognises Matteo's style. Perhaps this hall and sitting room are missing some of the artefacts he has taken to Pisa.

'Yes?' asks the woman hesitantly, for Isabel has introduced herself in English.

'I will have to explain,' Isabel says, even as the greater part of her own consciousness clamours for a plausible explanation. What is she doing? What is she going to say? Her sensible rational self has been taken over by this new impetuosity.

Isabel hears her voice say, 'My father fought in the war in Italy and when it was over he came here.' It seems the woman is in for the whole story.

She is willing to let her go on.

'He did go back to England, but he never forgot.' Isabel

is looking around, wildly, it seems to her, looking for some kind of proof that will allow her to rush back to Pisa and pack her bags. Then she will wait for him, for the confrontation, in the flat. Unless, that is, Matteo suddenly walks through the door here –

'He was here?' The woman points, dubious and frowning, at the floor.

Isabel's mind races. They are talking about her father – or some false version of his story. 'Near here . . . he would speak of a big house, the big villa, the village and the people he met here . . .'

'Here, in this place?' the woman asks again.

'No . . . not here, but –'

The woman is suspicious. She wants to know why exactly Isabel has come to her house. She has every right to. Isabel, her appearance wrecked, feels the helplessness of the shopkeeper whose windows have been smashed, his precious wares, his livelihood open on display for anyone to become a thief.

'My husband will be home soon,' says the woman. The door to the sitting room opens and a small girl who must be Luna runs in, hesitates for a moment at the sight of a stranger, then reacts by flinging her little arms round her mother's legs. She must be about five years old: Matteo's daughter, the child in the photograph, a moppet with wild dark curls and extraordinary eyelashes.

Isabel is expecting to see Matteo here. What should she say to him? Why should she ruin his life with this woman who is more than likely blameless?

The vertigo.

And then she sees. She is acting out of spite, in revenge

for Tom. But this will not do. And she cannot go on with whatever it was she was intending.

'I'm sorry. I shouldn't have bothered you,' says Isabel. She makes to leave.

Then there is a moment of madness. At the sound of a car drawing up outside, Isabel panics. She clasps her bag tightly to her body and runs from the house.

It is only after she has pushed past the man and hurled herself the length of his car, that she realises it was not Matteo and not his car.

She runs, head down, into the wind and she is ashamed of herself, deeply ashamed.

I sabel cannot face going back to Matteo's flat yet. Without thinking, she has driven up the Via Roma. She can see the bamboo growing in the botanical garden over the walls and remembers the night Matteo first kissed her in their shadows.

What has she been doing, losing sight like that of why she is here, allowing her purpose in this place to be overtaken by present paranoia?

Parking the car in the Via Trento – see how familiar the street names are becoming, she thinks, trying to calm herself – she walks round to the entrance of the botanical garden.

A path leads to two immense palms labelled *Jubaea spectabilis* and a prominent notice in addition to the announcement of their species: *Do not stand under the palm tree – leaves may fall down.* This warning, with its statement of the magnificently obvious, is repeated as the lane winds round to the rear of a palatial faculty building: *With wind, don't stop under the trees.*

Isabel walks on. Above the tree line of the arboretum are the upper three tiers of the leaning tower. It peeks in cheekily – even here! – inclining into a space between a spruce and a fig tree, a sudden view of the familiar in unexpected surroundings.

In this sanctum, noise from the excitable traffic has receded to a dull hum, fainter than the rustle of leaves. The quiet is intoxicating. She wanders into the southern half of the garden. This is composed of a formal grid of rectangular beds devoted to indigenous flora. Serried ranks of terracotta pots hold precious sprouts. Here and there a puddle of water catches the light, the trail leading to an abandoned metal watering can, but there are no busy botanists or student weeders.

Past the house of shells, past the statue of Paolo Savi, she makes her way to an arbour where she can sit and salvage some dignity.

Then she hears a voice call. She is startled, but does not connect the outburst to herself. She continues on her path. But the cry is stronger than before and she stops to look round. It is the gardener she spoke to with Matteo that first night. He is waving at her as he scuttles through the grid of specimen beds.

'*Signora!*' he pants.

She waits for him to draw up. '*Signor Olvari.*'

'I have been waiting for you to come back! I have something for you!' He is at her side, his close-wrinkled skin dark with physical exertion. He is holding out something. 'I have been waiting for you or Dottore di Castagno to come.'

Isabel, unaccountably, feels tears pricking at her eyes. She is not sure that she deserves his kindness. She cannot say anything.

But Signor Olvari is rushing on with his news, speaking slowly so she can understand each word. 'I told my father about your visit,' he begins.

Perhaps she looks blank for a moment. He suggests that they take a seat in a shady spot and she agrees gratefully.

'He was gardener here before me and even though he is very old now he still comes almost every day. I asked him. An Englishman, I said. Tom Wainwright.'

Isabel nods, willing him on.

'He knew the name immediately.'

'What?' Isabel is jolted from her mood of other-worldliness.

'He knew the name. So I said, "How do you know him?" and my father could barely speak. When he did, and he told me how it was, I could hardly believe it!'

Isabel urges him on.

'It was in terrible circumstances, the worst, as you can imagine. And it was a long time ago.'

Her heart is hammering. 'Tell me.'

Salvatore Olvari puts a hand on her arm. 'No – no, don't think that. Not your father – my mother. It was my mother . . .'

Isabel shakes her head. She is lost.

'My mother was killed,' he says. 'Just after the end of the war in 1945. It was a terrible accident. She fell from the balcony of the house we were living in. The iron was rotten. Perhaps the bombardments during the war had shaken it loose. No one knows. I was only a boy. I was eight years old.'

'I'm sorry,' she says automatically.

'There was an English soldier who saw it happen. He

stayed with her and shouted to the neighbours to call an ambulance and run to find my father. It was no good, of course, but he did all that he could.'

'Yes?' She does not yet understand where this is leading for she has never heard the story.

'The English soldier. When my father thanked him and asked, he said his name was Tom Wainwright.'

'I see.' She does not. It is an awful story, a horrible coincidence and worse, it is no use to her.

'It is a pity my father is not here today. I'm sure he would like to meet you.'

'Yes.' Isabel is in a daze.

Neither speaks for a while.

Then Isabel pulls herself together. 'Did you say you had something for me?'

'Ah, yes.' He fumbles in a pocket and pushes some handwritten paper at her – a letter. He says nothing but prods the postmark on the envelope. It is clear. Volterra. There is a date visible too – ten years ago. And on the left-hand side of the envelope there is a tiny scrawled address.

The note inside is short, one side of the paper only, and it is signed Giuliana. There is a drawing, too, the most beautiful and delicate sketch of a flower.

Giuliana? 'This is from the woman who came with the Englishman asking about the tower?'

'Sì, signora.'

'You are certain?'

'I knew her. The first time I met her I was asked to show her a tree I had been working on. She was the Italian woman who introduced me to the man. We talked about the tower, like I told you before.'

Isabel smiles. Then she says, looking at the note, 'But you know the woman?'

'I got to know her a little. She is a botanical artist. For a while she often came, making drawings for some project or other. After that she would come back occasionally. We talked about some special flowers one afternoon – it had been a while but we recognised each other. Afterwards she sent me this.'

'The man was not with her?'

'No. She was alone.'

Isabel feels that she cannot be certain they are making themselves properly understood. But the most important communication is there, written down. Giuliana. The name of one of the girls who lived at Le Macchie. A botanical artist. Surely it could not be coincidence.

Signor Olvari has kept this one pretty drawing safe, he manages to communicate to her. So safe that he only found it when he was looking for another lost item. And then he remembered her and what his young friend Matteo was asking about the man.

'*Grazie, grazie!*' she is saying. Fingers and thumbs, she finds her diary in her bag and copies the address into it.

Salvatore Olvari is delighted. His smile is full of cracked and broken teeth.

Isabel has a lead at last. It distracts her from the heaviness which descends again after she has thanked him and hurried back to her car.

She has an address, but Giuliana could have moved. But that first evening at Le Macchie – Isabel strains to remember what she had not thought so vital at the time – Bruno told her that Giuliana was the eldest, that she was an artist who specialised in botanical drawings.

What was the surname of the girls? In her panic to remember, she knows only that it is not Sarna, forgets that Giuliana has more than likely changed her name on marriage.

She goes to a bar and pores over the telephone directories in the dark passageway to the kitchens and lavatories.

In the end, sense prevails, a cold beer calms her – and she telephones Elsa.

'Elsa – it's Isabel.'

'Hi! How are you?'

'I'm fine, I'm still in Pisa and I need to ask you something. What was the family name of Bruno's relatives, the girls who lived at Le Macchie during the war?'

Elsa laughs. It is not until later that Isabel understands how crazed, desperate even, she must have sounded, bursting into the languor of early evening in Petriano.

'You told me! I just can't remember!' persists Isabel. 'I think it's important.' She is close to breaking, is holding it all in.

'Parini,' says Elsa and spells it. 'Isabel – are you all right?'

'Thank you, Elsa. I'll – I'll be in touch soon.' She wants to get off the telephone, to rip through the directories she is leaning on.

'Come and see us – come on Sunday for lunch. Will you – and Matteo? He's been calling us.'

'I will, I will. I'd love to. And thank you.'

'*Ciao*,' says Elsa.

'*Ciao*.'

Her fingers are thick and useless until she forces herself

to calm down. She finds the page and scrapes the columns with a nail down to Parini. There is no listing for a 'PARINI Giuliana' that she can see in Volterra.

Back in the car, she sits for a while, trying to gather her thoughts. Then she starts up the engine with a new determination. When she arrives back at Matteo's apartment it is past nine and he is there. He seems agitated.

'I thought you were at the conference in Venice. Is everything all right?' she says.

'I gave my lecture but I decided not to stay,' he says brusquely.

'Oh.' Isabel cannot meet his eyes. Does he know what she has done? Is there some way he could have found out where she has been today?

'You seemed unhappy I was going away. But I called and called on the telephone, and there was never any answer. I thought you had gone back to Petriano – but Gianni, Elsa, Bruno – none of them have heard from you!'

Where shall she say that she was?

Her blood runs cold with shame as she sees the little girl Luna in her mind.

'I was walking – it was later than I thought. I went into the botanical garden.'

'Something's happened. What is it? You look so worried.'

'I met Salvatore Olvari again. Pure luck.'

He listens intently as she tells him.

'It's thanks to you,' she says, aware that she must make up to him for something that he knows nothing and must know nothing about.

'I was worried about you,' he says tersely.

'There was no need.'

He is pouring them both a drink, a bitter-sweet aperitif. The ice hits the sides of the glasses with a hollow ring.

'I didn't mind you going to the conference,' says Isabel brightly, hearing the false tone in her own words.

He hands her a glass. 'You have to trust me, Isabel.'

What does that mean? It is all she can do not to come straight out with it and ask him what he means. Does he know? Is there some way he has found out where she has been today?

'I can tell,' he goes on. 'Your face has that same look as when I go out in the evening, when I say that I have to go away. I won't go away, not in that way. I am not your father.'

She is dumbfounded. Is she such an open book? She cannot meet his eyes. 'I'm sorry,' she says. 'I had no idea.'

He moves towards her and wraps his arms round her. 'Ask me and I will tell you what it is that you do not trust. You never ask me, about now, or about the past. Maybe it is obvious why you do not, but you will never find what it is you are looking for if you do not find the courage to trust.' It is a brutal speech, delivered impatiently.

For what seems like a long time Isabel sits in silence, not wanting to look at him. But he will not let it rest. 'I found a photograph – of a mother and child. I just knew . . . '

Matteo sighs deeply. 'Yes,' he says. 'We lived together for three years. The child is my child, but I did not leave them. She left me, two years ago. She left me for someone else. They are married now.' He is entirely matter-of-fact.

'You and she were never married?'

'No, I told you I was never married.'

'And your little girl – how often do you see her?'

His expression softens. 'Luna. I try to see Luna some weekends. It is hard, but she is happy with Elena's new husband – they both are. I don't want to change that, to make a disruption – but she is my child and I want to see her, and hold her and play with her. Nothing can change that.'

'Does it make you very unhappy?'

'Yes. Sometimes.'

'It must do.'

'You understand now?'

'I do.' For even as Isabel says it, she knows it is true.

'Gianni has asked us to go to Petriano for lunch on Sunday,' says Matteo the next day.

Isabel is sure that her conversation with Elsa has led to this invitation. She must have sounded mad when she spoke to Elsa. The families in Petriano are rallying round her again.

'I'd love to,' says Isabel. She means it. She is infinitely touched. Also, she is desperate to know more about Giuliana Parini and here is her chance.

A telephone call to Margaret has yielded nothing new. Her aunt's attempts to trace her father's old comrades in arms from the army associations have drawn a blank. She has one address, of a former sergeant who has organised reunions in the past, and she has written to him but has heard nothing so far.

More than ever, Isabel feels, the answers must lie in the place where she was first summoned.

*

Sunday is a searingly hot day. A long wooden table is laid with a yellow checked tablecloth on the terrace of the Criachis' house. A pergola above is densely interwoven with vine leaves and tendrils and fruit. It is shady and as cool as anywhere can be on a day such as this. By two o'clock all the guests are assembled: Elsa and Bruno have arrived, with their boys who run into the kitchen immediately and come out gnawing hunks of salami. And Annunziata Coia has come. After the previous gatherings this feels intimate, family. Massimo insists on sitting next to Isabel, which pleases her. She will be able, at some stage, to ask him what she needs to know.

They sit down to a feast. First Fabrizia brings piquant bruschetta, warm tomatoes and basil on crunchy bread thick with olive oil and garlic. The wine tastes deceptively light. By the time she has drunk two glasses Isabel is gently floating above her tensions.

'Tell me what you remember about my father and Giuliana,' she asks Massimo.

Massimo lets out a great roar of mirth. 'He liked her, very much. That is sure – and she liked him too. Always meeting by chance' – another belly laugh – 'walking in the orchard, by the outhouse. Ah, Giuseppe had to keep his eyes on that one!'

'Pappi!' scolds Fabrizia.

'No, I want to hear this. Please tell me some more,' she implores Massimo.

Massimo throws back a tumbler of red wine, needing no such encouragement. He is in his element, an old man jiggling his feet with the fun of it.

'They would sit at the table outside in the nights, holding hands under the cloth, thinking no one had noticed, wanting to be alone. And Giuseppe' – Massimo has to wipe his eyes as his amusement bubbles up – 'he would never leave the table. He would talk and talk, about whatever came into his head, about the stars, the moon, then he started getting books so he would be like the teacher giving lessons, and home-work, and still Tom would sit there, not wanting to leave. Giuseppe would be tired, but still he would not go.

'He would carry on, whatever he could remember, until everyone's eyes were like lead! It was not like today – young girls could not be left with young men, especially when they looked at each other like Tom and Giuliana did. But you know, he liked him very much. I think, in the end, Giuseppe was disappointed that nothing ever came of it.'

'So nothing did come of it?'

'Noooo!' Massimo leans back in his seat. 'The end of the war, you know. Young men go back to their own countries. Everything here was devastated, ruined. Giuliana was a good daughter. She stayed at Le Macchie to look after her parents; and then, of course, Emilio never came back. So he never took over the estate, as he was supposed to, and she had to stay.'

'And you don't think she saw him again?'

'No, not that I ever knew. I never saw him there with her again and I –' he looks around for good-humoured con-firmation – 'I was quite often at Le Macchie.'

'But that doesn't mean . . .' Isabel starts, then thinks better of it. Pure instinct tells her not to play her hand yet. She needs to find out more. 'What became of Giuliana when her parents died?'

'She was very beautiful,' says Massimo. He raises an eyebrow suggestively.

Cries of approbation puncture his swagger.

'I was only saying . . .' he protests.

'She is an artist – a special artist who makes drawings of plants,' interrupts Annunziata. 'She always drew pictures and she began to do that while she was still here.'

'A botanical illustrator?' asks Isabel, feeling excitement surge into her throat. She can see the delicate painted line drawing of the passiflora folded into Salvatore Olvari's letter.

'Yes,' says Elsa. 'Many of her pictures are published in books, popular books as well as academic ones. She is very successful.'

They have all joined in the conversation now. Matteo is quietly watching her. She feels his gaze, and is uncertain what he is thinking. Surely he can understand why she must do this?

She catches his eye and he smiles.

'And does she come back here to see you?' asks Isabel.

'No, not very often,' says Bruno.

'The past decade or so hardly at all,' concurs Elsa. 'There was that time at Christmas, you remember? Several years ago now. But apart from that, no, she seems happy enough to stay where she is. She was always quite spirited, independent.'

Massimo is cupping his hand over Isabel's bare forearm. 'Just like your father,' he says. He screws up his eyes until they are berries in the folds of his wrinkled skin. 'Always questions about Giuliana.'

Isabel drops her gaze and says nothing.

'That was how I knew it really was him, when the face had so changed. It was 1980.'

Isabel feels herself lurch. '1980? It was definitely that year? You can remember now?'

Massimo nods. 'I've been thinking hard. It must have been in 1980.'

The year Tom left. 'You can be sure? How are you sure?'

'There was a terrorist bomb at Bologna station. The Fascists again! More than eighty people were killed. He said he was getting a train.'

This is too much. Isabel's rational thoughts have disintegrated. She is pulling apart in all directions. Tears are filling her eyes.

There is a charged pause.

Massimo is a very old man, much older than he seems, she reminds herself. It is all too believable that he becomes confused sometimes, amazing that his conversation is normally so sparky.

Then she says softly, compacting her napkin into a tight ball, 'Tell me again what you can remember.'

Her father could not have been involved, she tries to calm herself. The letter from Giuliana was only sent ten years ago, not that long after Salvatore Olvari had seen them both in the botanical garden. Logically, it cannot be.

Then Massimo is explaining again – telling the entire gathering, for there is no other conversation now, of the night that Maria and Alberto Galletti, who were acting as caretakers for Le Macchie, brought Tom Wainwright to their house, where he and Nina happened to be visiting in the hope of dinner. And how this barely recognisable Tom Wainwright stayed for one night and then was gone, having found out that Giuliana was no longer in Petriano.

Isabel sits very still, allowing the information to sink deeper into her consciousness.

'And you think he might have been at Bologna, when –'

'I cannot remember where he was going – north, that's all I knew. But that was the time, I am certain of that.'

Annunziata sees Isabel's expression. 'He can't have been involved in the explosion. There were lists of the dead printed in the newspapers. I would have known if I had seen his name,' she says quickly.

At last Massimo seems to realise what he has implied. 'Oh, no, *bella* – that is not what I meant.'

He seems very old now, a man who has seen much and cannot be expected to recall every last detail. There is no reason why, when he saw Tom that time, he would not have imagined Tom had come to Italy for a brief trip before returning home to his wife and daughter.

Isabel takes a deep breath. 'Do you think he might have been trying to get to Volterra?' she asks.

They are all still sitting at the lunch table. It is early evening. The light is white and the air cooler. The sun has finished searing the undulating fields. 'I am going to put roses in the shrine,' says Annunziata. 'Would you like to come with me?'

Isabel would.

They go off at a leisurely pace. Annunziata has brought Peace roses for the job, wrapped in a piece of newspaper.

'Tell me some more about Giuliana,' says Isabel, for she is certain that this is the reason for the invitation. 'I'd like to know about her.'

'I liked her very much. She was much older than me – or it seemed that way when I was a child, but she was always very kind to me.'

'Go on.'

'She is an unusual person – she likes to keep herself a little bit private. She is a person who knows how to keep secrets,' says Annunziata.

'I have a feeling that she is not the only one, Annunziata.' What makes her say that? Some tiny instinct, nothing more than that.

Annunziata stares at her without giving anything away. She waits unperturbed for Isabel to elucidate.

'Have you ever seen my father since the end of the war?'

A long silence ensues. Isabel has the feeling that long-held loyalties are being weighed up.

'Once,' says Annunziata. 'But it was very soon after the end of the war.' They are side by side, picking their way along the stony path. 'He came back to Petriano, and he stood and stared at me. I was with the other children. But he said nothing to me. Then he went away again and Giuliana stayed with her parents and sisters at Le Macchie.'

Annunziata sighs.

'What is it?' asks Isabel.

'It is awkward. You may as well know. I was told long after that Giuliana had once been expected to marry my uncle – my mother's brother. My mother had not forgiven her for breaking the engagement while he was away fighting. And then she and I are both saved by the man Giuliana is in love with . . .'

'So, this was a serious relationship between them, my father and Giuliana?' Isabel is finding a clearer definition to her intuition by the second.

'It must have been. Of course.' Annunziata seems surprised that Isabel should doubt it. From her perspective it is unassailable fact.

'And then, that it should be my father, of all people who was there when the bomb came down . . .'

'Yes, that is strange fate.'

'And you have never seen my father since that time he came back to Petriano?'

'No. I have not seen him, but' – she holds up a hand to stay the inevitable interruption, shaking her head – 'I know that Giuliana has.'

'What?' Isabel is astounded. 'But – I don't understand! Why did everyone go to such trouble to find us then – his family in England? If one of you knew where he was?'

Again Annunziata is shaking her head. 'I didn't know – not until very recently. I am not often in contact with Giuliana. But I did write to tell her what had been decided about the piazza, and that we were trying to trace Tom Wainwright and his family, but I heard nothing. I thought perhaps that she was abroad – she travels a great deal, or she used to – so she had not received my letter.'

'But you knew then that she could have told you where my father is?'

'No. At that time I knew nothing.'

'So you did get in touch with her then, after that?'

'Oh, yes. But it was after you had been here, after the ceremony. I sent her some photographs. The piece in the newspaper about it. You must believe that I knew nothing of this – nothing! – when you were here earlier.' Annunziata is in need of reassurance. 'If I had it would have been a sort of lie and what kind of person would I have been to do that to you?'

Isabel nods. She is desperate to hear what Giuliana told her, what she has discovered. 'So tell me –'

'I wrote and told her about the ceremony and about you. What you were like . . .'

'And Giuliana replied then?'

'Yes.'

'She told me that she would have liked to have been there, but that it would have been very . . . difficult for her. That she had very loving memories of your father.'

'And that was all?'

'Well, no. I was intrigued and I telephoned her. I hardly ever do that. When we get in touch it is usually by letter. She was surprised to hear from me! But I told her that I couldn't let it rest there and why had she ignored the invitation? Was there something more to it? I asked. I thought that she might have had some problem with coming back to the village, that she had had an argument with someone here, I don't know, these things happen . . . And then she told me it was nothing like that.'

Isabel feels tightness round her head. She is clenching her fists, she notices.

'Giuliana said that there was a time when she and your father had been in contact.' It is clear that Annunziata is choosing her words with care.

'And – ?'

'And she said that – and these are her words, all that she would say – a circle had been closed.'

Isabel nods, assimilating this.

'I should tell you, Giuliana lives alone in Volterra,' says Annunziata. She is looking very serious.

It would have been too easy, to discover Tom with her there. Nevertheless Isabel feels a sudden draining of hope. It is the intimation that there was no happy ending for him and

Giuliana that sears her. Then she pulls herself up: she does not know, she does not *know* anything yet.

Isabel has to wait a moment before she can find her voice to ask. She takes the address book out of her bag and flips to the page where she wrote it down. 'Is this still Giuliana's address?'

Annunziata is taken aback. She takes a look and nods. 'How did you find that?' she asks.

'Thanks to someone in Pisa.'

'I see.'

'Do you think she might agree to meet me?' says Isabel.

VI

18

He took a room in a good hotel tucked inside one of the gates to the city. The next day when he woke within the walls of Volterra his spirits had lifted. It was early. A gauzy sunlight seeped through the gaps in the curtains. The rest had replaced his confusion with a kind of manic optimism. He was not himself – or perhaps he was more truly himself than he had ever been. It was impossible to tell.

But the fact was this: he was here in the place Giuliana had made her home; he would walk her streets and see the day as she might see it. If it was in his power, he would find her here.

Tom was all but dancing with the knowledge as he launched himself on the morning outside after an excellent breakfast. His proximity to her lightened his feet and loosened his stride. First he set out along Via San Lino, past the elegant church of San Francesco, making for the massive gateway through which he had entered the previous evening. There, on the other side of the road, he found that the shop he had noticed then was now open. He went in and bought a tourist map of the labyrinth of narrow streets. 'Volterra – "City of the Evening Shadow"' announced the cover.

A city, he could see after a short stroll down the sunny street, which seemed to fall away beyond the forbidding walls. He stood on the narrow road, as if he would pitch forward into the blue and golden haze of fields and sky below. He turned back towards the fortress. This was the place he felt would hold the key to finding her – and himself. It turned out to be a city of churches and tiny chapels set into the corners of walls and the points of joining streets. He was reminded at frequent intervals of Anna's chapel at Le Macchie.

The streets were narrow and shady, intersected by sudden shafts of bright sunshine. He arrived in the main square while there was still a faint chill in the air. It had a fine thirteenth-century tower, which was pentagonal.

Stuck into the formidable Prior's Palace were coats of arms made of glazed pottery. But something about the cramped corner where it stood made it oppressive for modern eyes. He made his way quickly through the Piazza dei Priori and on past a dense jumble of shops. All the while he was looking intently at the people he passed, then up and around him into the stones, lest anyone get the idea he was staring with disconcerting intensity.

He went on to the tiny Via dei Marchesi. Here there was a grand house with a bust set above the door. There was a café specialising in ice creams opposite. He sat at a table outside and gazed up at the eroding stone balcony on the front of the house; already he was exhausted and sore-eyed.

On the side of the building that housed the café, on the way signposted to the archaeological park, he discovered a tap of drinking water, the tap a brass griffin's head. His mouth was dry again already and he was glad of the draught it offered. There was another view of the tower from the park, but useless as a vantage point in his search. It was empty but for a few tourists like himself. He came back down and took a long wide street to an airy square. Here, in the Piazza XX Settembre, there was a statue of an angel holding up a man. The engraved legend beneath on the plinth: AI SUOI PRODI FIGLI CADUTI IN TUTTE LE GUERRE.

All along, under the race of his heart there was a counter-beat. It drummed: if he were to find her, how would she judge him, his state of mind, in being here? Would his presence be construed as another act of aggression, another uninvited arrival with the aim of possession?

No, he would find her. That was all he needed to do.

Tom followed Volterra's Etruscan walls, where the hundred-metre fall of the cliffs known as the *balze* fell away beneath. His guidebook told him that the church of St Just was rebuilt in the seventeenth century to replace the old church of San Giusto al Borgo, which had tumbled stone by stone into the abyss.

Here too the land was unstable. Rainwater erosion had caused subsidence of the clay and coarse sandy soil. Whole churches and necropolises had disappeared into the maw of the *balze*.

The fight was still on to save the Badia, which had once been a convent and cultural centre. Abandoned in the nineteenth century, the foundations were hanging on. Engineers sponsored by the Soprintendenza alle Belle Arti were shoring them up.

Below the town, far below, the undulating fields were shot through with peach and apricot tones.

Tom pushed all thoughts of Patricia and Isabel out of his mind. Patricia had thrown at him that he was never there, that she wanted him to stay away. That being the case, he might as well be distant physically as well as mentally.

On another side of the hilltop, below another wall where he leaned, staring for a long time, was the Roman theatre. The fan of its auditorium was clear through a riot of grass and mosses; the spindles of slim broken columns showed a graceful regimentation. The foundation plan was laid out before him.

He worked out the building plan, while deep in another part of his brain he was lost in the flawed blueprint of his own life and the choices he had made in the construction of his past.

Over the next days he criss-crossed the town, becoming familiar with its twists and double turns, memorising and resolving its confusions. He was in a life-size puzzle high in the sky. He had never been in a place like it, but he could sense his happiness was around the next corner, or the next. He liked that. He liked the ancient rusting lanterns hanging from so many doorways. He liked the precipitous drops on all sides.

He saw her for the first time in thirty-five years late on the third day.

The sight affected him like an electrical jolt. Three days only it had taken him: it was a negligible length of time, nothing in terms of the years of indecision. But it should not have been surprising. On each of the three days he had risen at six thirty and walked the narrow streets and alleys until eight or nine in the evening. He had been covering most of the territory of this enclosed hilltop five, maybe six times in a day. It would have been almost unbelievably bad luck were he *not* to have managed to see her if she was here, which she was.

At first he kept his distance. How could he be so sure that it was her?

The thought occurred to him that he was capable of deluding himself. That he was a mad and desperate man who was about to start following a stranger.

The woman's hair was streaked with grey, but pulled back at the nape of the neck in that same old way with the twist. She had the same dear nose, but cheekbones more prominent than he remembered. She was slighter in life than in his golden dreams, her clothes smarter. He stepped quickly into a shop to avoid her. She moved past him, oblivious. Then he gathered himself and began to follow her. He did not know what else to do. All he could think logically was that on no account must he let her out of his sight.

He was doing nothing wrong, although part of him felt like a criminal.

She made her way up to the streets above the amphitheatre. She had a shopping bag with her, a sleek black one with a gilt detail in place of the rough basket of her youth. In his mind, as he stepped this way and that, unnoticed behind her in the shifting patterns of other pedestrians, he tried to formulate some kind of plan.

He would wait to see whether she would lead him back to her house, perhaps. Then he would know exactly where she was. But what if she was going to visit a friend – or a member of the family, a family that would be completely new to him?

Hastily, he revised that notion. No, he had to act quickly while she was alone. This was his moment.

He had no sooner concluded this when she turned into a doorway some way ahead of him. He hurried on, feeling short of breath, staring wildly at the buildings to his right. It was all right. He slowed down. She had gone into a small bakery. He took some deep breaths. Involuntarily he smoothed down his jacket. His hands felt cold and clammy.

When she came out, he was waiting for her in the middle of the street, smack in front of the entrance, his heart beating to rival a teenager's.

Then they were face to face.

He never had any doubt. It was Giuliana.

He was staring at her face from two feet away. She frowned at first. Then opened her mouth as if to ask him coolly to move out of her way, a stranger who was deliberately block-'ing her path.

It is all over now, he thought sadly. I have come here and found her and I am strangely proud and complete in myself. I could walk away now with dignity and grace, and there will be no tarnish on this golden episode.

But she was not castigating him. She was simply staring back, her expression unreadable.

So he said, 'Giuliana?'

She was nodding. She was not smiling. One hand had moved up to her mouth. But then she spoke: 'I thought I saw you the other day!' It was almost a cry. 'I could not imagine why I should be thinking that after all these years. But then I could not stop thinking that you were here. I thought I saw you on every corner! And now . . .'

They made to fall at each other, then stopped, each seeming

to remember that they were their present selves, not the people they had been in another time so long past.

There was a silence. The seconds swelled. They held too much; decades were compacted into their ordinary span.

'What an extraordinary coincidence!' said Giuliana carefully.

For three days he had walked every street in this town, looking for her. He had decided he would not leave until he found her. 'A wonderful coincidence,' he said. 'What amazing luck – that I should be here now – today, at just this time . . . !'

Giuliana's forehead was just as he recalled, despite the lines. He wanted to cover those lines in tiny kisses and moisten them with his tears. He held back.

'What are you doing here?'

He shrugged. 'Just . . . visiting.'

But then her cheeks were wet too. She brushed the tears away with the back of a hand.

Tentatively he touched her shoulders with shaking hands. She did not back away. He leaned closer. Then he buried his face in the old fragrance of her hair and closed his eyes. She was saying something to him. Her voice was barely above a whisper. 'I'm so happy to see you!' she said, over and over.

And then he remembered with a breath-stopping jolt. He was still not thinking straight. She was married. Back in Petriano they had told him she was married.

She led him back down the Via San Lino, past the church of San Francesco and out of the city walls.

They took the Borgo San Stefano, where the road of small houses and suburban flats ditched away from the town, and

DEBORAH LAWRENSON

the immensity of the vista took his breath away. It was like living in the sky.

Her home was a relatively modern house. She led him inside and closed the door softly behind them. He was waiting for her to call out to someone who was expecting her return, but she remained silent. She took off her coat, and made to take his jacket. He was still waiting expectantly for another person, wary in the white-painted hall.

She sensed his unease and smiled.

There was no doubt. She was still his Giuliana, older but just as beautiful to him. Only –

Not his. That was the pain of it. She never had been.

He had to speak his thoughts directly, before he foolishly went too far. He blurted it out, feeling foolish anyhow. 'Is – is your husband here?'

Her reaction was as calm as ever. She continued her task of hanging up their outdoor clothes, smoothed the shoulders of his jacket on the hanger, then turned, unmoved by the rasp of his breath in his chest. 'I have no husband,' she said at last. 'Would you like to come into the sitting room?'

And once again he was in this country of bright light and warm shade, a place indistinguishable in his mind from make-believe.

She brought him a small glass of wine.

There was no husband. He looked at her hand as she handed him a bowl of olives. There was no gold band on the third finger. He turned over the information like a precious stone in his palm.

'But I thought . . . they said . . .' He stopped himself before he could give himself away. 'Somehow I always imagined you would be married.'

'I could have been, once.'

'Oh?'

'I could not do it,' she said. 'I thought I could, but I could not. I had come here to be with him. The day was set, the church was booked but . . . no. It would not have been the right thing to do.'

'What happened?' His blood was fizzing with joy. He was jittery as a boy.

'The funny thing was that when I got here to Volterra it turned out that I liked it much more than he had ever done. He wanted a bigger city; he yearned for Florence. He was a scholar and curator of museums – and ambitious then. In the end he got a job there and left, while I stayed on. We had always been friends. We even see one another now and again.'

There was a sudden awkwardness after her burst of exuberant patter. They nodded at each other across the small low table, but the pause stretched into silence.

'And you?' she asked eventually. 'Are you married?'

It came like a punch while he was unprepared. In all his obsessive notions about her it seemed he had forgotten the facts of his own situation. It was a measure of his madness, he was able to rationalise later, that at the time he had been able to put it so completely out of his mind. He did not know what to say. He had no right to ask her that question and be disappointed or otherwise with the reply.

She was watching him intently.

Tom felt his elation drain. Patricia and Isabel. Isabel! He could hardly bear to think about Isabel. What had he done to her? What kind of man was he? It was over a month since he had left, without a word, and the longer he was silent the harder it would be to make contact.

'No . . . yes. That is . . . I have been.'

'I see.'

Did she? It was no answer. Was it possible that he caught a hint of disappointment in her eyes? If so, then it was quickly extinguished. No, he was being stupid. Stupid and naive, once again. What was he trying to do – persuade himself that she too had made more of their sometime liaison than anyone in their right mind would have done?

Suddenly he felt his age. He was all stiffness and fury with himself. He should not have come, should have left her alone and his obsession in the past where it belonged. Perhaps he was ill, really ill. And yet, and yet . . . he was here, with her. He had longed for this. He wanted to take her hand and reached out instead for his glass to raise to his lips. It was trembling as he tasted the wine.

He would drink it and go.

'You did well when you went back to England?' she asked conversationally, astutely sensing the need to head off introspection.

He gathered himself. 'Yes, pretty well. I have my own company. A building company, mostly new houses – good quality new houses.'

'I always thought you would do well. Always everything the best you could make it, even if it was out of nothing.' She laughed gently, as if to encourage him to tell her more.

So he obliged, as he struggled to find his balance. 'The others did well, too. A lot of them built up their own businesses. Frank makes electrical components – jolly good they are too. Had a big family with his Irene, so that worked out in the end. Jonno was last heard of buying and selling plant machinery . . .' He tailed off. The sound of some large vehicle outside broke the fragile atmosphere. 'Tell me about your family. After the war – '

'It was hard. Emilio – after he died it was many years before they would accept what had happened.' She sighed. 'Along with millions of other men and women. The boys who went to the Russian front . . . nothing was ever heard again of so many of them.' Giuliana shook her head as if to say that she could not talk about it any further. Then she gathered herself. 'It doesn't get any easier to understand with time, no matter what they say.'

'No.'

There were volumes of understanding in the silence.

'My parents, they carried on running the farm and I lived there too. My mother was sick first. She died in 1968. She was only sixty-two, not a great age. It was cancer. And then my father passed away not six months after. You know, they had been together since she was sixteen.'

'I'm so sorry.'

'He always talked fondly of you. How the British were not really soldiers, not like the Nazis with their war machines and their drills and their terror of each other. How you were always mending things, taking a little bit from here and a little bit from there, and welding it together until it looked like a monster – but it would go.'

'What a shambles it was, in other words.'

'A shambles, yes, but a friendly shambles,' she agreed. 'And you know the village has never forgotten you – for saving Annunziata Coia's life when the bomb struck.'

He still did not want to think about this.

His felt his throat constrict as he prepared to ask. 'And you – did you ever think of me?'

'There was not a day went by when I did not think of you.' Her eyes filled.

'Then why – ?'

She was shaking her head. 'You had gone back to your country. You had done enough for us. What right had I?'

They were talking of the customs of half a century ago.

At last they were talking, having the conversation he had had with himself all these years. There was so much to ask. The veils between him and the world had miraculously lifted. He was free to live in the glorious present.

'I still remember it all so well,' mused Tom, 'that first afternoon when I walked up the dust track and came across the house. And later on, I asked your mother what Le Macchie meant. The shrubs, she told me, and then she added that the name could also mean dark stains.'

'That's right.'

'In the years afterwards, I always remembered that. The stains – for everyone who had been there – on what had once been a place of happiness.'

There was a long pause.

'I try not to think about that too much now,' said Giuliana.

'Yes,' said Tom. 'That's what I tried to do, for a very long time.'

The problem with that, he thought, was that the thoughts do not go away, they go deeper.

'Until one day, when a person believes he has cleared his mind of them and is free at last, nothing could be further from the truth. He is disarmed, then suddenly gripped and undermined. It is the most dreadful feeling – as if the mind and the body cannot continue to function while they are so at odds, as if there is a separation inside the body.' He stopped abruptly, dismayed. He became conscious that his breathing was rapid and shallow, his heart knocking uncomfortably.

'Is that what happened?'

He nodded.

'When?'

'A month or so ago.'

'While you were still in England?'

Another nod.

'You didn't get help?'

Tom shook his head. 'I just . . . needed to think – to allow myself to think.'

'And' – she hesitated – 'you decided to come here on a holiday to do that?'

'In a way, yes.'

'That you should come here – of all places!'

'Yes.'

She shook her head as she stared at him, but he was unable to decipher her meaning.

'Tell me about you, and the family,' he urged her again.

There had been good times, but bad times too, she told him. In the years before Giuseppe died he had become increasingly angry and resentful.

'The Italian government, yet again they had let down the people who had suffered so much. You know, after all the work you did, and others like you, they closed all the files on the massacres of women and children in the villages. They did not want to hear their cries for justice. He would talk of you, Tom, about what you did, what you tried to do for us – and then what happened? That men like Emilio had gone to fight and disappeared into nothing. That our own country was denied its true history.

'There were no murderers facing trial for this, only the stories of what has gone on, stories that soon become village legends with not a word to support them in the court records. Whatever happened to all the work you did that year after the war had ended, the information you were gathering? Did anyone ever make it into a report? If they did, no one ever saw it, or read it out in any court to condemn the guilty men. All we got was nothing.'

Tom hung his head. He remembered the papers he had hidden, the plain envelope he had slipped into his pocket, the words he had judged too hurtful to hand over in that place of sorrow. He had imagined he was doing the right thing but he had made a mistake. Another misjudgement it was too late to undo.

He opened his mouth to explain, then thought better of it.

'Stay – stay and eat with me,' she said.

'If you're sure . . .'

'I would like nothing more.'

Over a supper of melon and ham, pasta and salad, he listened intently as she told him of her work as an illustrator for botanical books. Her pictures, more technical than those of her girlhood at Le Macchie, were packed into card folders and artists' portfolios. There were copies of published books to which she had contributed.

'Still surrounded by flowers,' he said.

He reached out without thinking and took her hand. He turned it over and ran a finger down the palm.

'They are such old woman's hands!' she chided him.

He wanted to keep holding her hand, just as he used to.

'Where are you staying?'

He told her.

'It's not far,' she said.

'No, hardly any distance.'

'Perhaps you could come back here tomorrow.'

'I would like that very much,' said Tom. He got up to leave. 'This has been wonderful.'

'Yes.'

She gave him his jacket and stood close by as he shrugged it on. 'Not so very much changed,' she ventured playfully.

He shook his head in contradiction.

Giuliana opened the front door. 'Goodnight, then.'

Tom was on the threshold. Now his thoughts were straight. He wanted no more pretence, no more secrets to undermine the present. He hesitated, heart hammering. 'I have something to tell you. I have a child in England.'

She did not answer for the longest time.

He was as guilty and wretched as he should have been.

'A child?'

'A girl. Isabel. I say a child – she is seventeen, as old as you when –'

'And you think a girl of seventeen does not feel?'

He was caught, trapped in a vice of logic.

'What have I done?' he murmured.

'Only you know that,' said Giuliana.

The one who makes the pretty speech is the one who is not in love. Tom was familiar with that aphorism and felt it bearing out as he tried to find the words to stitch together. He was stutteringly incoherent. His explanation – the truth, even – of how he came to be standing on her doorstep seemed an old frayed tale.

Giuliana was impassive. No expression registered in her features to give him hope.

'Would it ever be possible . . . that we could begin again?' he asked at last.

She reacted then. She laughed. Then she realised he was serious. 'How? How would that be possible?'

He looked away.

'No. You're right.' After a while he said, 'Would you do one thing for me?' He hesitated, knowing how foolish he sounded. He played for time. 'You're right. I should go home. But before I do, would you . . . would you come to Pisa with me?'

She did at least smile at that. Then she said, 'We are both too old for all that.'

'But I don't feel old now!' Tom burst out. 'I feel younger than I have done for decades! I spent my forties feeling sixty and now I have those years back, in my mind.'

'You were always a dreamer,' said Giuliana, but fondly.

'Is that so wrong? To want to make up some lost time and be happy?'

'No.'

'Well, then.'

She was shaking her head. 'Go back to your hotel, Tom.'

She let him out and closed the door as soon as he was through it.

So that was it, then.

He woke too early the next morning and lay stunned on the bed unable to summon the strength to move. His energy was gone; now that there was no focus, his body had begun to exact the price for the previous weeks of frenetic activity. His back ached badly, as did the joints in his legs. He felt his age and his weaknesses magnified.

He supposed vaguely that he should throw his few possessions back into the bag and take himself away from this place, away from the crushing disappointment.

Hours passed in blankness.

The telephone by the bed rang twice and he ignored it. The next time he pulled it off the cradle and took his time bringing the receiver up to his ear. He mumbled into it, uncaring what he was being troubled for.

'Tom? Is that you?'

Involuntarily he was bolt upright. 'Giuliana?'

'Yes, it's me.'

He did not know what to say.

'Are you still there?' she asked.

'Yes.'

He was waiting for her to continue.

A pause seemed to indicate that she was as uncertain as he. Then, a deep breath before she said, 'I am driving to Pisa this morning. Do you want to come with me?'

And so Tom and Giuliana retraced his steps of that day when he had followed his instincts so blindly. This time they were in her small car, a Fiat or some such, which she drove with a casual aggression that caught him by surprise. He had the sensation that he was burrowing into his own past, the very recent past and the long-buried past, and understanding it for the first time. He was coming full circle.

He and Giuliana did not talk much.

She pushed a cassette into the player and they were enveloped in a symphony, he did not know which. He let the lush sounds lull him and at times felt inexplicably close to tears.

They arrived some two hours later.

Still in silence, they left the car in a side road north of the river.

'What are you thinking?' asked Giuliana.

Uncharacteristic of her, to ask such a question, he thought. 'That this has not been a lucky place for us. I have no happy memories here, only the memory of happy hopes,' he said, as honestly as he could.

She did not respond immediately.

'I have to meet someone at the university,' she said. 'After that, we can have our time.'

She was here on some professional pretext. This surprised him, but only in the sense that he had been so wrapped up in his own thoughts and motives that he had somehow formed the notion that she had invited him on a romantic whim. He was instantly deflated by the knowledge.

She led him swiftly to the botanical garden. She spoke to the official at the gate office, greeting him as an old friend. A call was patched through to a person deeper in the university faculty and they waited, Tom looking around at the displays on the walls, until the official told them to proceed.

She had to go into the main building to see a professor who had engaged her to illustrate a volume of botanical history he had written, she explained. 'Why don't you have a walk around, while I'm in with the professor? I will see you . . . let us see. By the shell house. I won't be very long.'

He had no trouble in locating what she had called the shell

house. It was a fantastical façade on the mid section of a building by the cedar garden — embellished not only with shells, but fossils and corals too. He sat down to wait.

After a while he closed his eyes and jutted his face up to the sun. The heat soothed him, penetrated the layers of tension which had built up like armour in his muscles. He was here; it was now. He remembered her necklace of shells.

When Giuliana returned she was with another man.

Tom stirred awkwardly, as if he had been roused from a deep sleep.

'Allow me to introduce Tom Wainwright — an old friend of mine,' she said. Was there an edge to her voice as she said it? There was certainly an awkwardness. 'Tom, this is Salvatore Olvari.'

The man was considerably younger than either of them. He was wearing old, muddied clothes. He had a startled, bony face and quick, darting eyes. He stared at Tom, appraising him.

Tom stared back, a little affronted. Guilt again, he supposed. But he was doing no wrong in allowing himself to be called an old friend.

'Salvatore is one of the gardeners here,' went on Giuliana. 'He has been showing me the cinnamon camphora which the professor wants me to draw in detail.'

'Hello,' said Salvatore, smiling although his glare bored into Tom. Then he repeated, 'Tom Wainwright.'

Tom was standing by now, smoothing his jacket, feeling at a distinct disadvantage.

Salvatore said, 'I know your name, but I can't think why.'

Tom shook his head. 'I'm sorry, I don't think –'

'No matter,' said Salvatore. 'Perhaps it will come back to me.' A shrug hoisted his creased suit jacket up to his ears. The gesture released something in Tom's mind. For a moment he could not think what it was. Then he remembered. Massimo Criachi. That was his shrug, too.

'You been here before?' Salvatore asked Tom.

'Long time ago. It's changed a lot.'

'That's still there, at least,' Salvatore nodded to Tom, pointing over the trees. 'The tower.'

'Yes.'

'They keep saying she's going over, but she doesn't. Like this, see' – he pointed to an ancient fig tree – 'skewed as anything, but strong.'

'Might need some help, though.'

Salvatore gave another expressive shrug. 'All those schemes – what a circus! It won't do any good.'

'I'm not sure I agree with you on that,' said Tom. He looked steadily at Giuliana. 'If something is that beautiful, what is wrong with trying to prolong its existence as long as possible?' She did not react. Tom tried to salvage his dignity. 'In England, towers far less important than this one have been successfully brought back into a position of stability.'

And he explained how.

'What would you like to do now?' asked Giuliana as they left the garden. She was determinedly matter-of-fact.

'Where would you like to go?' He was encouraged to think that their visit to Pisa was not over yet.

'The palaeontology museum, perhaps.' She gestured towards the entrance as they made their way up the Via Santa Maria. 'As we seem to be living in the past.'

He stopped abruptly, as if he had been hit. 'What do you mean by that – that you have brought me here as some kind of . . . punishment?'

Giuliana glared at him. 'You were the one who came to find me,' she said.

'That's not –'

'We are not the people we once were, Tom.'

'Do you think I don't know that? . . . Are you angry with me?' he demanded of her.

'I am angry with myself.'

Tom hesitated.

'And I am angry with you,' she admitted. 'You who know everything about machines and buildings, and nothing about people.'

That hit home.

'So what can I do about it?' he asked in despair.

They walked. The air between them was a pleasant temperature. There was no reason not to carry on and none to stop now that they had started. They ambled at a comfortable pace, back down the Via Roma, along the Lung'Arno, across the river, passing in front of the church of Santa Paola a Ripa d'Arno, back on to the embankment drag, right along to the Scotto gardens.

And they talked.

By the time they were back by her car the evening was gathering. They were tired, suddenly, extraordinarily tired.

It was a long drive back to Volterra, one that he would not have wanted to undertake at that moment.

'Are you hungry?' she asked.

He was suddenly ravenous. 'What shall we do?'

'We could eat dinner.'

'I'd like that.'

They ate in a small trattoria away from the tourists. They tried to talk about inconsequential things, to keep the subjects small and impersonal. After a while they gave up. They emerged into darkness and went to the car wordlessly. The silence, alternately companionable and charged with uncertainty on his part, lasted until they arrived back at her house at some time past midnight.

Preposterously, neither wanted to make a mistake.

For years, he wanted to say, I only had to smell the scent of cut lemons, the zest of a lemon when my wife or daughter made a cake . . . The smell of lemons – and it would all come back to me.

'You can stay here,' she suggested shyly. 'If you would like to.' A pause. 'It is one of the greatest regrets of my life that I did not act then as I wanted to.'

'What did you want to do?'

She hesitated, then brushed her lips against his cheek.

VII

19

I sabel has heard nothing from Annunziata Coia since the
lunch that Sunday in Petriano. The waiting in this state
of agitated limbo is almost unbearable. 'You have to let
her do it in her own time,' counsels Fabrizia when Isabel calls
her.

Matteo has been spending time he cannot spare digging
deep into the archives at the Opera. He is winging his teach-
ing commitments at the university; piles of messages and
essential reading material teeter and fall over his desk, while
his own research stands still.

On a hot September evening Isabel is waiting for him at
the flat uneasily. He has been working late, again. The room
where she sits is slowly darkening. High above the Arno and
the plain she is bathed in the same purpling air as the mountains beyond. She knows that her tension is the legacy of a
long-held fear of abandonment. Matteo will come back. It is
one thing to know this and quite another to feel the truth of
it.

She is wondering what to do next, whether she should
simply go to Volterra by herself and find the house where

the elusive Giuliana lives. She should be bold and decisive, take back the quest into her own hands. But she has tried. She renewed her efforts to discover a telephone number for Giuliana, using the address given to her by the old man at the botanical garden, but without success.

There is no listing for Parini, but Matteo explained there was nothing unusual in that. 'It has to do with residency. It means that a person can live in one house in the same town for decades but not be considered officially resident for the purpose of elections and taxes.'

'A very Italian concept,' says Isabel.

Matteo allowed that. 'Telephone numbers are only issued in the name of the official resident of the house, so Giuliana's number could be listed under a different name. It's a rather good system.'

'You're joking.'

'No, it is, in some ways. Anyone in that position will obviously give their number to anyone they want to have it and the telephone directory will let any interested parties look up the number by knowing that the person is living in the former home of whichever family used to be there.'

'As a piece of Italian logic it's hard to beat.'

Like the theory that foreign visitors might have had to register their arrival in the early 1980s due to the terrorist threat – or maybe, in practice, they didn't.

Isabel tucks her legs further underneath her and wills the telephone to ring.

But the next moment Matteo has let himself in with a soft jangle of keys. His expression is triumphant. He waves some paper at her, then lopes towards her, his arms outstretched.

As if the lines of synchronicity have merged, Matteo is

pressing on her some numbers scrawled on office paper. 'It's Giuliana's telephone number – Annunziata has contacted me!' he says.

'When?' asks Isabel stupidly – as if it mattered. And it is not synchronicity, in any case; it is inevitability, for Isabel has been sitting in this chair at the end of the day for weeks since she last spoke to Annunziata, waiting for precisely this to happen, in some form.

'This evening. She says she is sorry it has taken so long.'

'But why didn't she call me?'

Matteo shrugs. 'It is the way she thought it was proper to do it,' he says.

Isabel, about to question that too, does not. But she is mystified – not only by the unexpectedness of the manner her answer has come, but by a sudden sense of the foreignness of these people to whom she is entrusting herself, their ways and their understanding of a situation.

'And does this mean . . . Giuliana will speak to me?'

Matteo bites on his lip. 'Annunziata thinks we must be a little careful.'

'What do you mean?'

'That is why she wanted to speak to me first. Annunziata wants to help you but it will be quite difficult – she does not want Giuliana to know that it was she who gave us the number.'

'But why not?'

'She says that Giuliana seems . . . unwilling. A little frightened, perhaps, to get involved.'

'But –' Isabel's mind is spinning.

Matteo puts a hand over hers. 'Let me do it,' he says. 'I think I know the way.'

It is the easiest thing in the world to pick up the telephone and dial the number. Matteo does it and presses a button that allows Isabel to hear the ensuing exchange as it is broadcast to the room.

A woman's voice has answered. Isabel tenses.

Matteo speaks in friendly, rounded tones. 'Is that Signora Parini?'

'Yes,' the voice replies, a little warily.

Matteo is direct, without apology for any interruption or blather about wondering whether she could help him. 'I am trying to contact Tom Wainwright – I understand that he lived at this address some time ago.'

'Who are you?'

Isabel is sitting on the arm of a chair, clenching the covers in her fists. She and Matteo are looking into each other's eyes as he speaks slowly and clearly. Knowing the subject matter, she can understand almost all he says.

'My name is Matteo di Castagno. I am involved with the commission's latest project concerning the bell tower at Pisa. I have his address from a detailed letter he wrote to us and which is in our archives.'

'You must have had it a long time.'

Isabel's heart is pounding. The woman has not yet denied that she knows Tom Wainwright.

'Well, yes,' agrees Matteo. 'We have been . . . re-evaluating the information in our archives. Is – is it possible to speak to him? Is he there?' Only now is his voice betraying emotions.

Isabel is horrified to find she is shaking.

'I'm sorry – no,' says the voice from the box. 'He is no longer here. He has not been here for some time.'

'Ah. May I ask . . . are you a friend, Signora?' It is an agonising politesse.

'I was his . . . friend. Why do you need to know all this?' She is clearly becoming suspicious, as well she might.

Matteo's idea is ham-fisted, idiotic, thinks Isabel.

'What is all this about?' demands the woman's voice.

'Do . . . do you have any idea where I could contact him, Signora?' persists Matteo.

'I am sorry. What do you want?'

It is hopeless. Perhaps Matteo is not comfortable with duplicity after all.

Isabel leaps to her feet. And then she is shouting, 'Can I speak to her? Let me speak to her!'

Isabel crouches by the speaker, still trembling. 'Signora, I am his daughter, Isabel. Does that mean anything at all to you?'

They will go to Volterra.

'What is it that you want from all this?' asks Matteo. He is holding her tightly in his bed.

It is the simplest question and the hardest to answer. Isabel burrows into the curves of his body and inhales his scent. 'Just to know,' she says at last. 'To have some certainty.'

In the shadows, Isabel can sense the cold place between disappointment and despair. In Volterra, like any of the ancient hilltop towns built as defences, the chill of history lingers in the dark stone crannies and corners despite the unremitting heat of high summer.

They are a mile high above the waves of an undulating plain. It feels remote, horizonless as the distant blue melts into sky. It is a landscape of mud slides, Matteo is telling her. His voice seems distant too, a murmur on another set of sound waves. The heat is a barrier between them, oppressive and full of watery smears on the air.

'They are called *balze*.'

Isabel and Matteo look down over the city wall at the golden rolls and dips of this unstable landscape. They have come up, up, up the winding road to reach this place at last, past the stripped cork trees, past silver of olive groves clinging to precipitous slopes, on past the grey-blue clay of the hummocky ploughed fields littered with boulders and scree, past the shops selling artefacts in alabaster. Now the immense vista is spread out before them.

After a while they turn and walk into the town.

Along the shadowy streets, pierced by sunlight, Isabel is quickening her pace. She screws up her eyes, feels the stretch of her skin across the bridge of her nose in the intermittent dazzle. These are Etruscan stones she is walking over, the streets winding and climbing and doubling back on higher levels. She is inside a giant fossil, tracing the trails of two thousand years. It is an impregnable place, outside and in, with its forbidding walls.

They pass through the Piazza dei Priori, a space full of people, brightly baggy-clothed visitors surrounded by the menacing height of dark thirteenth-century walls. High, high above is the tower of the palazzo. She feels its looming presence over the small square; she hurries along, head down.

Purpose fills her limbs and makes them strong. She is no

longer sitting and thinking, but is sure, with a violent, sick conviction, that her purpose is just. She scents an answer after all.

There are more twists and turns, then a plunge downwards towards the plains far below and they stand at last before the door they have come to find. Matteo nods at her, meaning for her to decide when to announce their arrival, understanding that she will hesitate. She squeezes his hand before reaching out for the bell.

She has been absorbed so deeply in the mesh of the past and what is about to be that she has quite forgotten that he is present, here with her.

The door is opened promptly. They are expected.

Giuliana is a tiny woman. She is in her mid seventies and her eyes gleam brightly. She is limber and greets them with fluid movements, a huge smile. Her hair is still dark – grey but not white. It is drawn back from her face but without severity. Isabel takes her hands and is still surprised to find her so small. There is nothing about her that suggests shrunkenness, the curving into herself with arthritis that her mother has begun to suffer. Giuliana could not be more different, physically, from Pat.

She leads them into a white-walled sitting room. Isabel can smell, very faintly, the strange ashiness of mothballs. It hangs on the coat-tails of more vigorous scents: flowers and furniture polish and roasted meat. For the first anxious minutes conversation is stillborn. Generalities, social pleasantries die on Isabel's tongue. She sits where Giuliana invites her and stares around, uncertain where to go.

Giuliana, it seems, has no small talk for this occasion.

In its own recess in the wall is an icon of the Virgin Mary. It is gilded and shiny. The face is heavenly — but bears a curious suggestion of a smile which defies solemnity.

When Giuliana speaks softly, in English, it is as though she is kissing the words as they fly on their way. And is it Isabel's imagination or do her words bear learned inflections, stresses that she has not heard for so long they have become buried in her subconscious so deep that it had seemed they had never been familiar until now?

'You know it already. He was here once. For a time this was his home with me,' she says simply. The house is dark and mercifully cool. From the open door comes the sharp tangy smell of geranium leaves. 'Sit and look, it's all right. I will go to see to the food for a little while. Then we will talk.' And she walks out of the room, pausing briefly on the way to lay a hand feather-light on Isabel's shoulder.

Isabel and Matteo are left to the heavy ticking of a clock in a wooden case and the complicity of their hostess in their strangers' explorations.

Giuliana returns about ten minutes later. They have heard no noises from the kitchen to indicate that she has been making late preparations for lunch. 'Would you like to eat?' she asks. 'It is all ready if you would like to come.'

Again they follow her in silence, this time to a small dining room. It is set formally. She serves soup and veal and salad, cheese and wine. She has cooked an excellent meal. The silver cutlery has been polished. It feels weighty and cumbersome in Isabel's nervous hands.

'So . . . you found me through the botanical garden?' She smiles incredulously.

'The head gardener Salvatore Olvari,' Matteo says. 'He remembered you.'

'Head gardener now, you say? Good for him.'

'I had a photograph of my father as he would have been at the time and Salvatore thought he might have been the Englishman who once came with you.'

Giuliana nods in acknowledgement of the possibility.

'But have you ever met his father – Paolo?' asks Isabel. 'He was a gardener, too.'

'No,' says Giuliana, 'I don't think so.'

Isabel and Matteo exchange looks.

'When Salvatore told his father, Paolo, about us – and the questions we were asking – Paolo told him the strangest thing. He knew the name Tom Wainwright straight away.'

She pauses to catch any reaction from Giuliana – but there is none.

'The reason he knew the name was because his wife – Salvatore's mother – was killed in a tragic accident just after the war. She fell from a balcony that had gone rotten on to the street below. And there was an English soldier who was passing who stayed to help and sent someone to find him.'

'And his name was Tom Wainwright,' said Giuliana.

There is a startled silence for a second.

'You knew! So it was him!' Isabel cries.

'Yes,' says Giuliana. 'It was your father.'

'It was definitely him?'

'He told me about it.' Giuliana is clasping her own hands nervously. 'But I never knew that the woman who died was Salvatore's mother.'

She does not say that it is a dreadful thing or any other such platitude.

Isabel wonders about the layers of experience and what remains hidden, the tiny moments of history when the unseen structures of one person's world fracture and are re-formed.

'You are like him,' says Giuliana abruptly. 'So very like him when he was a young man.'

Isabel feels tears welling behind her eyes.

So this is how they will begin the story: with an acknowledgement that he was hers. She thinks to herself, as she has thought so many times in recent months, how meekly she accepted the years of uncertainty and bewilderment when, as his child she should have been crying, 'He is mine and I want him here!'

But Giuliana is calm. And she is making no babbled apologies.

They have eaten and there are grains of salt on the table. Giuliana watches them, but she is still. She does not fiddle with them, or sweep them into a small pile, or busy about with a brush and crumb catcher. She remains perfectly still as she speaks and listens and smiles. Perhaps she is waiting for Isabel to tell her that she hated her, that she stole her father and crushed her family.

'I used to think he was obsessed with that tower,' says Isabel. It fails as an attempt to sound light-hearted.

'Only it wasn't really the tower,' says Giuliana.

'No, I'm beginning to understand that now.'

'He loved to visit all the hill towns – and their towers. San Gimignano, that was his favourite by the end.'

'Tell me.'

'There are twelve towers in San Gimignano.' A shy look of recognition passes between them. 'Once there were over seventy, but only a dozen survived. He wanted to go there. He said it looked from a distance like the town was wearing a crown. We would go in the evening, in the summer, when they would be lit up for the tourists. I would tease him that he was always the tourist. Musicians would play in the squares after dark, and we would sit outside and eat ice creams – at our age!'

There is a pause while they consider this.

Despite her rigid self-control, Isabel cannot suppress a smile.

'Siena – he liked Siena at night too,' says Giuliana. 'Always at night – from the time the sun went down, and we could sit outside at a café and watch the shades of blue change in the sky.'

'Why did you come here, to Volterra?' asks Isabel.

Giuliana sighs. 'A long story.'

'But Le Macchie – it's yours . . . it's such a beautiful place.'

'And I was there for a long time.'

'And my father, Giuliana?'

She knows the answer already. She sensed it the second she came into this house: it is too late. It has been too late for years. That is not why she is here now. It is to find him in a different sense altogether.

There are floral arrangements on the tapestry cushions, flowers in the garden have colonised the house, real fresh flowers, not the faded and dusty silk and plastic varieties more often found in such houses. There is softness and gentleness all around, but Tom is not here, can only be placed here in her imagination.

The question must be asked. It takes all her courage. 'What happened to him, Giuliana?'

'I think you know already.'

Isabel nods. 'But I want you to tell me how it was.'

VIII

20

I t takes only six seconds to plunge the five hundred and thirty-five feet on to the rocks below Beachy Head. Once the fall starts, it is too late to pull back. On one side is the dark and sucking sea, on the other a wall of ridged chalk, then oblivion. At least one person a month, on average, takes this route. Some years there are twice as many as expected.

It is always blowy on the cliffs. Near the edge the wind whips up gamely, swirling and buffeting those who resolve to go and those who are simply testing their mettle by peering over. Where the drop is sheer, no one survives. But there are other spots where humpy ledges and brambles intervene and deny this certainty of outcome to those who have not made a study beforehand of the geographical facts. Some people arrive and then run at the edge to give themselves no chance of stopping once they have resolved on their action. These are the ones who are caught out.

Tom knew the cliffs and their pitfalls well. Being a meticulous man, he had planned his day with the aid of maps as well as memory. In the pocket of his overcoat was a half-eaten sandwich. There did not seem much point in finishing it. There was nothing that could identify him. He had carefully disposed of his wallet, his passport, all of his papers. He did not want to be identified.

Here on this coast of crumbling white and high green folds of hills, it was a place of retribution, a place of final cruelties inflicted by the hurt and misunderstood, and the sick. A father would run over the edge with a small child in order to kill some part of his former wife as well as himself. A mentally unstable person would tell her social worker that she would be cheered by a walk in the bracing wind high on the dipping green of the cliffs, then further fortified by a cup of tea from the café, and while the hapless guardian's back was turned, would race to the horizon and hurl herself off.

If he could find the courage he would follow.

Tom Wainwright, who had thought he had waged his battles, had engaged in another. He was a man at war with himself.

As he contemplated ending it, he thought: my life began again that afternoon in Pisa with Giuliana.

That night they returned to Volterra together. They drove through the darkness and barely a word passed between them.

He lay in her bed and held her in his arms. 'Something I always wondered,' he said. 'When I left Petriano, you said you had learned how to fall. What did you mean?'

'Did I say that?'

'Can't you remember?'

'Honestly . . . no. I suppose . . . I meant I had fallen in love with you.'

Tom felt his eyes were wet. 'I never stopped hoping that was what you meant. I used to turn the words round and round for other meanings.'

She stroked his face tenderly.

'I worried that maybe you meant the opposite . . . that you had hardened your feelings, learned how to control yourself so you would never allow yourself to get hurt again.'

'No,' said Giuliana. 'I meant I loved you.'

He swallowed hard. 'I've waited half my life for this moment.'

And after it his life was restored to him.

A week later he telephoned his bank on the Isle of Man. He had held an account there for many years: his rainy day money, beyond the reach of the inland revenue and his wife, for that matter. There was more than £90,000 in it. Not for rainy days now: for sunshine and happiness. If he was careful he could make it last.

He arranged for a sum to be transferred regularly to a bank with a branch in Volterra.

Should he contact Patricia?

He did. It was even worse than the telephone call from the café that morning so long ago. She did not want to speak to him. No, she would not allow him to contact Isabel. Isabel was better off without him, had come to terms with his desertion and should on no account be upset further, Patricia assured him.

So he spoke to his solicitor at length and in confidence. He made over his share of the business to Patricia and Isabel. He wrote a long letter to Isabel, intending to entrust it to the solicitor, but then crumpled it up. It was too trite, too sentimental, too hopeless.

With that it was done. He was hardly leaving his family destitute. Materially he had given them much more than he had kept for himself.

He and Giuliana had not been apart since. Except now.

Perhaps it had been the heat and happiness of Italy that had masked the worsening of his illness.

Deep in himself, Tom had felt so light and free that he floated through the time he had with Giuliana. He took the decision to think only positively, to abstain from all negativity, and he had lived by that.

In the early years of his retirement he had felt so well. The aches, the hollowed-out feeling he would have in his upper body after a day at work seemed to fade. At first, both he and the doctors were convinced it was arthritis.

But no.

Eventually, after an agonising winter, the correct diagnosis was made: a rare disease, a condition that turned muscle and tendon to bone, until it was as though the entire skeleton were seizing up and locking. His torso was rigid from neck to waist. His right arm had fused at all the joints. It hung solid and useless from his stiffened shoulder. There was medical understanding of the disease, which was known as Fibrodysplasia Ossificans Progressiva, or FOP as the doctor would write on his notes, but no way of arresting its progress.

He was a man turning to stone. There was nothing that could be done.

There were periods of inactivity when the bone-growing stopped. But then, just as hope had settled, another episode would begin.

And then, during a period when the pain was so intense that he could hardly speak, he found another consultant who confirmed the source of the agony. He had seen a case once before, had studied the ways the disease began to manifest itself. No, Tom could not rule out the possibility that he had exacerbated his condition by overwork or stress. It might even, suggested the consultant in that emotionally detached way he had of showing he was fascinated by his subject, have been accelerated by the years Tom spent as a young man in the mud and floods of the Abruzzi, then sleeping in sodden slit trenches.

It was only a thought, he said hastily when he saw Tom's expression.

Another doctor explained to him that they could do little beyond monitor his progress, by which they meant his decline. It all came to the same in the end. If he did indeed have the disease he wanted, that he deserved, then any attempt to saw out the offending bone would only make the problem worse by causing more bone to grow in its place, the medical books told him.

He knew what would happen next. With his customary curiosity and attention to detail he had spoken at length to the orthopaedic surgeons and searched out relevant papers under their guidance. By the time he died, his limbs would be welded to the sides of his body. His head would be held vice-like on his immovable neck. Ribbons of bone would have filled in the gaps in his ribcage making it torturous to breathe. He would be trapped and suffocated by his own being.

In life, so in death. It was no less than he deserved.

It was a fine balance. He would soon lose the ability to

walk, and then he would no longer have the choice. To leap or to suffer, which was it to be?

The days he had once spent on this coast were foremost, with his guilt, in his mind. He thought of his daughter Isabel more and more often. He had not seen her for more than nine years. She would not want to see him now.

He had come to East Dean to see the cottage for rent. It was one of a row of four, built a hundred years ago, or more. The wind had streaked the stonework with dashes of grime, and earth and sand. It was pitted, weather-beaten. Two up, two down. There were no curtains at the windows and he wanted none.

The place had the sea and the Downs, and a pleasant pub called the Tiger. He wanted to live as the world turned. Giuliana had not been happy but she seemed to understand.

Nine years they had been together in Italy. The best part of his whole life, without a doubt.

The episodes ran through his mind. He could not stop them, did not want to.

That first summer she had taken him to San Gimignano and Siena in the evenings. At San Gimignano there were a dozen tall thin towers where there once were seventy, according to her. At night they were lit up and they would wander the streets and piazzas until their feet were sore.

The great shell-shaped Piazza del Campo in Siena. He was overwhelmed by its size and beauty. She waited at a café eating ice cream while he climbed the Torre del Mangia.

But best of all were the small domestic places. Giuliana's house in Volterra. Its courtyard garden packed too full of aromatic leaves and vibrant flowers spilling from their pots.

Scents mingling with those from the kitchen. The white bedroom with its cool crisp sheets. Her kisses in the darkness.

Her desk by the window in the south-facing kitchen where she would work.

At other times, when she was travelling for work on commission, he would sit there himself after tending her plants and think about plans for the famous leaning tower, what he might suggest to the authorities. Sometimes he drew diagrams and attempted calculations, but nothing ever came of that. He never sent them to the committees in charge. The compulsion had gone. His obsession was sated.

He travelled with her, too. One commission took them to Peru for a month, another to China in the footsteps of some nineteenth-century botanist and collector. Less exotically, they went to Holland, Austria and Germany.

But always he was pleased to come home – to Volterra. It was as if this was the home that had always awaited him.

He and Giuliana could never marry but they were joined in the strongest of unions, as he had always somehow known they would be. She shrugged off the conventions of her Catholic traditions and her peers with a resoluteness which wrong-footed him at first. He had not imagined there would be so few obstacles to their coupledom.

There must have been times when they had exchanged sharp words, had had periods of irritation with each other, but he could not recall them.

Just the sun on his skin and a lightness inside.

Early retirement had much to recommend it, he told the new friends he made in the cafés of Volterra. He would not be going back to England. Yes, he was simply another of those cultural refugees who came to hide away in the rippling hills, content in the heat and peace and seclusion they found there.

The years passed by so quickly.

H e did not jump.
For the past week she had been calling him, once during the day and once in the evening. On a couple of evenings they had talked for hours on the telephone. Her message was plain: she wanted to come to England to look after him. His response was equally clear: he did not want her to take on the burden of nursing him. Deeper was his pride. This took the form of an overriding wish that she remember him as he was and not as this degenerating, weakening man.

'But can't you see how you are hurting me by this?' she cried at last. 'You are a stubborn, silly man!'

He gave in. He walked up to the Tiger Inn, making more and more strenuous efforts. He went straight up to the bar, bought half a pint of bitter with a ten-pound note and took the change over to the payphone. His fingers locked as he dialled and he had to stop and try again.

When Giuliana answered he said, 'I want you to come, as soon as you can. I'm so sorry.'

'You cannot change what has happened. You can't spoil the rest of your life for it. You can only learn to live with it,' she told him.

'I know that now.'

It was summer, thank God. England would not be too cold and bleak for her. Giuliana arrived and two days later the country was sweltering under a heatwave. She was enchanted by her new surroundings and to be with him.

She came with news of all his old friends. They spoke in Italian – it eased the pain, he told her, although why this should have been he had no rational explanation.

'The biggest story,' said Giuliana, raising her eyebrows as they sat over a glass of the red wine she had brought with her. 'Nina has run off and left Massimo.'

'No!'

'It's true – and for a younger man. Some kind of pen-pusher at a bank, apparently.'

'Poor Massimo.'

'Tuh! Poor Massimo! I don't think so. He is back to his old ways with the ladies. Not, I think, that he ever entirely gave them up in the first place . . . '

'So he's all right?'

'The happiest he's been for years – and the busiest!' Giuliana laughed.

She was constantly occupied, improving their surroundings. She painted the cottage white inside and hung the old carved crucifix, the one he had made so roughly and so long ago for Anna and the chapel at Le Macchie.

Outside in the tiny garden she sketched the English flowers where he could see her doing so. It was perfection of a kind. It is a place of catharsis, she told him and she was right.

'You should get in touch with your wife, find Isabel,' she said one evening. She was sewing a bright patterned cushion cover from some material she had found at a jumble sale. Her hands were as deft as ever, he noted.

He did not answer.

Giuliana had bought lemons. She had arranged them in a deep blue bowl she had bought for pennies at a charity shop in the town and placed them in the middle of the table.

'Hand me one,' he asked her.

She put down her sewing without a word.

He reached out to take it but his grasp failed. The lemon fell and rolled along the floor. She scooped it up, then took a knife and cut into it. Then she scraped back the pitted skin to release the zest and held it up to his nose. He inhaled as deeply as his frail chest allowed.

The scent was still magical to him.

'Is there any reason why a lemon tree would not grow in this country, in a pot?' he asked.

'I can't think why not.'

'Could we get one? – imagine, the white blossom, and then to see the fruits growing in front of my eyes . . .'

'I can try. If I can find a place to buy it.'

'It must be possible.'

'Of course it must be possible.'

There was a pause.

'Until then, I tell you what we will do.' She reached for a saucer from the table. Then she cut the lemon into quarters and flipped out the pips. 'We can make a start right now. I'll put a little water over these. Then, in a few days, I'll plant them in a flowerpot. Let us see if they will grow.'

'It will be a long time until they are big enough to flower and fruit.'

'Yes, it will be.'

'If they flourish at all.'

'That is true.'

'Then –'

'Then maybe you will discover there is a pleasure to be had from a beginning as well as an end,' said Giuliana.

Giuliana persuaded him to call Patricia one still and thundery twilight. She brought the telephone to him, placing it on the small table by his armchair. 'Either you will make the call or I will,' she said.

And so, after nearly a decade of silence, he spoke to Patricia.

It was a brief and hostile exchange.

'I'm selling the business. I suppose that's why you called,' she said tersely.

'I didn't know that. It's yours to do what you want with.'

'I know.'

'How is Isabel?'

'She's fine. What is it that you want?' asked Pat.

'I wanted – was wondering whether Isabel –'

The line went dead.

Neither he nor Giuliana mentioned the conversation again. Some time later she asked him gently, 'Why don't you try to contact your sister?'

Tom sighed. 'How can I, now? I've lost Isabel . . . I don't deserve . . . After all that I've done?'

'Does that matter? Won't she just be glad to hear from you?'

He did not meet her eyes. 'Why bring up old hurts? Best to leave it.'

His condition worsened. His body was seizing up, locked into bent awkwardness. 'Backbone,' he said, still sardonic, 'that's what the troops need.' For it was not physical frailty that was killing Tom Wainwright. It was his own mind, which turned constantly in on him and left him broken, battered with regret and guilt.

'You must not think of this now,' Giuliana would say.

A sigh.

'*Parliamo italiano.*' Let's speak in Italian.

And so they would.

'You remember Natalina's daughter's wedding? That silly boy who was her friend from college? She says in her letter that he is finally getting married himself – and he is a million-aire now!'

'Never.'

'It's true.'

'How?'

'This and that, mainly furniture, I think.'

'Furniture? How do you make that kind of money out of chairs and tables?'

And so he would be eased back into a different language, a different world, where he had been happy. Where they had been happy together.

His bones did not hurt so much when his brain was engaged elsewhere, in retrieving the words in Italian.

'*Hai notizie di Massimo? Il vecchio diavolo!*' What news of the old devil Massimo, he would ask, knowing he would be entertained.

Tom did not want to be in a hospital. The National Health Service trust which ran the local hospital was in turn glad of this and his doctors made no great effort to persuade him to reverse his decision. Home visits by nurses were agreed, by all concerned, to be the best option until such time as his needs grew too great.

Meanwhile Giuliana ministered to him and they talked – to the end – about Italy and Le Macchie, and the lads he had long let slip away from him.

When he died he was a curiously happy man – not wholly happy, but a man at peace. The end came suddenly – more swiftly, too, than the professionals had expected from his assurances to them that he was comfortable and in good heart.

A bowl of cut lemons was at his bedside, a blue sky outside his white room and Giuliana's hand in his.

IX

21

Giuliana takes Isabel into a bedroom. She opens a wardrobe of dark polished wood and the smell of mothballs is released. Inside is a short row of exquisitely pressed dresses. She pulls one out, then another. They are handmade in the style of sixty years ago. 'I could never throw them away,' confides Giuliana. Then she laughs. 'I always managed to persuade myself it was because my generation could not bear waste.'

Isabel stares at the brightness and patterns of these garments, and thinks, 'These are the clothes Dad saw.' His hands – hands younger than hers – must have touched these bright roses and leaves and ribbons.

'I did not ask him to come,' says Giuliana. 'Never.'

Isabel reaches out to her. She cannot help herself.

'I was so dreadfully upset when everything went against us at the end of the war. But I was young. I thought of it as a good lesson; I knew that whatever happened I would get by. He said he would be back, but he didn't come, and he didn't come, and yet still I survived. And I persuaded myself that that was for the best, I could do what I liked with my life.

And in the end, when he did come back, it was by accident.'

It is as though Giuliana is talking to herself, quietly and determinedly facing the truth as she sees it, working out and weighing the evidence even as she puts the words together.

Isabel listens intently.

'When he went again, it was like hearing a sad song on the radio that made me think of the first time I heard it, of the person I was then, and not of the sadness in the present. For I did, I learned my first lesson well: whatever hole you have fallen in, you have to pull yourself up and go forward. There is no other way.

'When you are separated from something you love, when you can no longer see with your eyes the person, or the place or the object, they become more detailed. The absence forces you to think more clearly about them, to envisage every detail. In the end, this is done so effectively, so often, that it has the effect of polishing. You see their fine qualities far more clearly than if they had grown stale through seeing them daily. And you . . . you know exactly what I am talking about. The danger is, the person or the place can never live up to the imagination's standards. But sometimes . . .

'To find such happiness when you are old . . . When you are older you will see that there is such a sadness in it. When you have wanted something for so long and clung to a belief in its perfection . . . how is it possible to tell what is real and what is imagined?'

The first she knew of Tom's illness was the winter his body began to lock up. 'Some people never stop recounting their aches and pains, but not Tom.'

Isabel nods. This is true enough.

'He kept it to himself,' Giuliana continues. 'When I asked him why, he would say that if he could ignore it hard enough the pain would go. But in the end it was obvious how bad it was.'

Isabel thinks about her father's capacity to suppress his own pain by refusing to acknowledge it. 'What did he do?'

'He said he was going to England, to be treated there, where it was free and he was with his own people.'

'And did he?'

'He did not want me to come,' says Giuliana. 'That was the worst time – worse than before. But I could not tell him what to do; he never would be told what to do by other people.'

'No,' says Isabel, managing a smile, thinking of her mother.

'I thought, at the time . . . I dreaded maybe, that he had gone back to you, to his family . . .' Tears are rolling silently down Giuliana's cheeks.

'No,' says Isabel. 'He didn't come back to us.'

'I know that now. But he did contact your mother.'

'I don't think so.'

'Yes, he did.'

What is Giuliana saying? 'You are absolutely sure of that? Which year would this have been?'

'1989.' It is as definite an answer as could be given.

'You are absolutely certain of that?' Isabel is astounded.

'Yes. I was there with him,' says Giuliana. 'I was there. I watched him dial the telephone number, heard him speak. I could hear . . . the shouting from the other end.'

'But – my mother –' Isabel does not understand. Unless her mother has lied.

'I am sorry.'

Patricia . . . *what has Patricia done?*

'You were there, when he telephoned my mother?' reiterates Isabel, still not able quite to believe this.

'It was I who wanted him to do it. He missed you so much, Isabel. He never stopped missing you. Feeling the same guilt. For a long time, I think, he had persuaded himself that it was for the best he did not try again, that you would not want him after all that had happened. And at the end . . .'

A lump rises in Isabel's throat.

'In the end, we could not be apart. I would not let him go. How could I just let him go like that, when he needed –' she hesitates – 'me the most?'

Isabel nods.

Giuliana continues, 'So I packed up the house here and went to England to be with him as long as necessary. I wanted to bring him back here. But it was not possible. I was with him when he died.'

Isabel's eyes are blocked with tears. 'I'm glad,' she says. 'I'm glad that he wasn't alone.'

'No, not alone. In his way he was happy – as happy as a man who held so much guilt could be.'

'But why did we not know that he had died? Surely we would have been told?'

'I wrote to your mother. I looked in his notebook for the address and I wrote to her. I told her about the funeral. But there was no response. I was the only person there.'

'Where was this?'

'Eastbourne. He died in East Dean.'

This is unbearable. The bitterness of deception, its cold sick edge.

Isabel feels her body filling with the old rage. But this time it is directed at Patricia. She cannot believe this: Patricia has known the truth for a decade and has never said a word. How could she do that? Isabel thinks back to her mother's shock and reluctance to act when the letter about the piazza first arrived. What lies of omission have been uncovered? She is making sense now of certain reactions she had attributed to more compassionate impulses.

'I am so sorry,' says Giuliana, again and again.

'I want to show you something that my father showed me and my sisters, a long time ago,' says Giuliana. 'And we showed your father.'

Giuliana looks around her — and in her swift turns are the first signs of impatience Isabel has detected in her. She alights on a magazine, opens a glossy page at an advertisement, folds it about two inches in, presses the crease with a horny thumb-nail and rips off the strip of paper. Then she holds it up like a magician and ties it carefully in a simple knot. Then she places it on the table and flattens it slowly and precisely.

In the centre of the strip is the perfect pentagon.

Giuliana is scrabbling in a drawer in the table. She produces a tape measure, such as she has probably used for her dress-making. 'You see . . .' she is saying, as she lays it along the length of one side of the shape and then another. 'Exactly the same.'

Isabel is nodding. 'He showed me how to do that.'

'Then you'll understand when I show you,' says Giuliana.

She leads Isabel back into the sitting room where Matteo is waiting patiently.

'We have to go outside,' says Giuliana unexpectedly. 'We can walk. And I can show you where I was when suddenly he came back to me.'

And so once more they are out in the jagged brightness and dankness. But the sun is lower in the vast horizon now and the shadows slant further across the streets. Where they have dropped, down the narrow alleyways, is a mysterious deep gauzy indigo. Again, Isabel has the sense of being led through a maze. The spell is strong and pulls her on. Isabel does not – and cannot – resent or resist this woman. She is captivated by her.

And then they are back in the oppressive Piazza dei Priori. The tower still looms, expressionless. She will still not take it in properly; she is too wrapped up in herself and the unsettling sensations of vertigo it induces. She keeps her eyes at human level.

'Look!' says Giuliana. She points upwards. 'Do you see?'

Reluctantly, Isabel tips her head back. And at last she does see. The tower is pentagonal.

'I was here, on this corner, when I stopped because I thought I saw him. I remember it so clearly. A man fiddling with a strip of paper. Not even looking at what he was doing. He was staring up at this. But I knew that I must be mistaken and I hurried on. The next day I felt as if I was being hunted. I could not stop thinking that he was here. I thought I saw him on every corner. And then, one evening . . .'

Giuliana breaks off to lead them further onwards, down into more intricacies of the stone puzzle, into the entrance of a shop selling elaborate pastries. 'I was coming out of *here* and we were face to face. There was no doubt. It was Tom. He had been here for three days, in this town, walking every street, looking for me. He said he had decided he would not leave until he found me.' Giuliana's plump cheeks are wet now. She brushes them roughly with a back of a hand. Her voice is barely above a whisper again. 'He knew only that I might be here, after all these years. I was so filled with joy, I would break!'

A youngish woman pushes by, irritated they are blocking the door to the bakery. As a body, they move into the middle of the alley.

'It was the week after Easter. The shop still had special cakes – they were selling them more cheaply. And all I could think, at first, was that it was a kind of Easter miracle. Then, that it was a strange coincidence, as old friends meet in un-expected places, and that he was a tourist here – the English always come in spring – and that he would have an English wife with him. But no. It was not quite like that.'

Isabel cannot speak. All the years of not wanting to know have hardened into a globe in her throat. There is so much she wants – she needs – to ask.

It is late. The shadows are all around. As she and Matteo are about to leave, Isabel reaches into her bag. 'I have some-thing which you should see,' she tells Giuliana. 'I think you are the person it will mean the most to.' And she slides the plain brown envelope from its secure pocket and holds it out. 'It is one of the few things my Aunt Margaret – Tom's sister – was able to find when I asked her to search for anything of my father's from the wartime.'

Isabel's heart is pounding. Is she doing the right thing? In the months it has been in her possession it has weighed on her conscience. Perhaps her father was right to have kept it hidden away. Perhaps he knew better than she did that there are instances when knowledge can be oppressive as well as liberating.

Giuliana peers at the document, then has to delve into her handbag to find some reading glasses. She opens the envelope and gives the document inside a cursory look.

'No, don't read it now.'

But Giuliana is reading it. She stiffens visibly and pales.

'Take it home, where you can read it properly,' Isabel urges her.

'I think I can see what this is,' says Giuliana. Then, as if to herself, 'There *was* a report! All these years . . . and he never said.'

'I'm sorry if it – perhaps I shouldn't have –'

'Yes, you should,' says Giuliana curtly. 'The Italian government betrayed its duties to its citizens – its own victims – and all for what? For more politics. They didn't want to embarrass Germany. Can you believe that! In the fifties, they thought it was more important that Germany should be allowed to join NATO than that their murderers should be brought to justice. Governments! Don't ever speak to me of governments . . .'

Isabel is taken aback by the vehemence of this unexpected diatribe.

But Giuliana has not finished. She does not seem to care who might hear her in this public place. 'That is why we have a Piazza Wainwright. We do not forget what the ordinary people have done. My father Giuseppe would have approved with all his heart.'

'But now', says Matteo more quietly, rationally, 'the truth

is coming out. Only last year an Italian military tribunal acknowledged that thousands – thousands! – of investigations into wartime atrocities were blocked forty years ago.'

'The answers we needed were all hidden away as not wanted,' says Giuliana stubbornly. 'All the work done by men like Tom – the British and the Americans – it ended up so much yellow paper in the files that no one ever saw. All that justice, locked up in a military vault until most of the guilty men had lived their lives and died to rest in peace.'

She waves the papers, now restored to their innocuous envelope. 'This is why he stayed – for my father and mother, for us. To find out what happened to Emilio.'

And, for the first time, Isabel understands completely the full human consequences of what the papers hold. Shattered pieces of the picture have been painstakingly assembled, to show their lives, and thousands like them, interwoven in a heart-rending tapestry.

'May we meet again?' asks Isabel.

'Yes,' says Giuliana. 'If you would like to.'

'I would,' says Isabel. 'Do you go back often to Petriano?'

'Hardly ever. Not now Maddalena and Natalina have moved away. Only sometimes . . . The crucifix in the chapel – he made it for our mother. I put it back when he died. So there is a part of him there. I hear the news from the village. I heard about the dedication ceremony. I should have gone. But . . . I could not go back. I did not think I could meet you, but I was wrong.'

'Thank you,' says Isabel. 'Thank you . . . for everything.'

*

There are reminders everywhere. Isabel is in a state of rawness, oversensitive to the slightest change in the light, to the recognition of conflict she feels as a terrible empathy which arrives uninvited to gnaw at her spirit. She hurries past building sites, not daring to look where before she would have been fascinated to see into the dark holes and patterns of steel.

'Nothing is safe. The only safety you have is within yourself,' says Giuliana on the telephone when Isabel calls to talk to her because she feels there is no one else who can understand this need. 'Make peace with yourself and you will find it.'

Giuliana has read the document. She knows what she is talking about.

'You know, I may be wrong but I think your father did bring the envelope to Le Macchie the last time he came, but for some reason he did not hand it over.'

'What do you mean?'

Giuliana sighs. 'He said he had something for Giuseppe, my father. I remember he put his hand inside his jacket as if to bring it out and then he stopped. I don't know. Perhaps he was going to give it to me, then decided to give it to my father himself. At the time, it seemed unimportant in the circumstances. Perhaps I imagined it all. It is so long ago I can't be certain.'

'You never talked about it with my father in later years?' asks Isabel.

'Yes – that is, he let me talk. He never contradicted me when I told him we knew that Emilio had died in the north.'

'Did he talk much about the war crimes investigations?'

'All those years afterwards? No. We did not talk about it

much. By then, we had all devised our own ways of living with sadness.'

'But how?' blurts out Isabel, childlike.

'All I can say is that you must find the safety inside yourself,' she repeats.

But for Isabel that does not seem possible yet. 'I have to go back to England, to see my mother,' she tells Matteo. 'I can't put this away until I have spoken to her and heard what she has to say.'

Matteo is not happy about this. 'You may not like what you hear,' he says.

'I'm sure that I won't.'

She is tired, utterly exhausted. It is the cumulation of months of strain, she tells herself. It will pass.

'Would you like me to come with you?' he asks.

She shakes her head.

She and Matteo drink a last brandy in a tawdry bar at Pisa, somewhere near the airport before her departure.

Her flight back to England leaves at eight forty. She does not want to go, but she must. There must be a confrontation, an acknowledgement of the truth between her and Patricia. And she wants to see Margaret, to tell her in person what she has discovered. There is no other way.

Outside the open door where she sits with Matteo there is a snarl of small motorcycles. Out there it is still light, the sun bright, in contrast to the fuggy gloom where they sit. He takes her hand across the table and says, 'It has been lovely, Isabel.'

There is a note of finality in his voice. Her stomach gives a lurch in response and she braces herself for the inevitable 'but' to follow, the prelude to letting her down gently. Instinctively she looks away, as she feels her eyes fill. A sense of shame steals up on her; shame that she could ever have hoped for more than this. It makes her realise how much she wants him.

'Hey!' Matteo lifts her chin with his hand. His eyes are infinitely soft and he is a kind man. 'What's the matter?'

She shakes her head, feeling childish, not wanting to betray herself.

'I know. I hate that you're going too.'

A tear is trickling and he wipes it away. 'I wish you could stay – stay for always! I know . . . shall I come with you? I could just come now, be with you and help you!'

Isabel stares stupidly. 'I thought you were telling me it was over!'

'What?' Now it is Matteo's turn to be dumbfounded.

She is trembling, hardly able to frame the words. 'I thought . . . you were about to say that . . . this was the end for us. Now I've found what I came for and now that I'm going back to England . . .'

'No!' He can barely take in what she is saying. 'Is that what you want?'

'No. No!' She has never been more certain.

Matteo clasps both her hands tightly. 'In the beginning, you said "No promises". Is that what this is about? Have we not come further than that now?'

'I thought –'

Somehow he manages to make his sigh of exasperation an expression of tenderness. 'Too much thinking. Not enough telling. I love you, my Isabella. I want you to stay here. But you tell me that you cannot, that you have to go. I know you must. So all I can say is – when can you come back? Back to me?'

Isabel sees herself with absolute clarity in that moment. How, by living in the past, she has been able to be certain of what comes next. How she has held herself in check – like Patricia – for fear of change, clinging to damaging certainties and the false security of leaning back.

'Soon,' she says. 'As soon as I can.'

Lost in his kiss, she feels extraordinary. As if she has been released somehow.

She tells him then what she has been holding back: 'I love you so much. These past few months I've been so happy. Happy in a way I've never been before and perhaps I thought I never would be. I don't want that to end.'

He understands; she knows he does.

Back in England after so many weeks away, she interprets the familiar with a mind subtly altered. The pace of the crowds under cloudy skies is faster. They consist of so many individuals going about their own business. She has no sense of constant interaction as she does in Italy, the sociable knots in the *passeggiata* as its groups of participants tie up for conversation and move on.

In the evening, she notices there are no children out and about, grubby and tired but happy, with their parents in cafés and restaurants, no squares where they can run around as the adults finish dinner.

The air has a chill after nine o'clock at night.

Even the flat which has been Isabel's home for eight years feels slightly alien. Under these circumstances she does not mind, in the end, when its last dusty traces of her occupancy are removed by the firm of professional cleaners she hires to make it ready for its first tenant.

She is pleased by this, in fact. It shows that she has made the right decision.

Isabel is moving through her duties as if in a dream world. A gauzy, detached place in which she often feels so tired that she could sink down somewhere soft and sleep for a week.

The meeting with her mother does not go well. Ostensibly Isabel has come to the old family house to collect the inconsequential remnants of her life that have been boxed in cardboard for years. She finds them in the lumber room. Books mainly. Geography texts. Some files of coursework. An odd collection of old clothes now smelling quite musty.

They are standing in the hall, looking at them.

Pat pulls a face. 'So what are you going to do with those now?'

This is a good question. There was never any room for them at her flat. For the time being, the three boxes will have to stay in her car. Their removal is symbolic, in any case. It is a way of showing Pat that she is absolutely serious about moving on.

'I'm sure you don't want them,' says Isabel.

Pat has to agree. 'Just like your father,' she says. 'You can't let anything go.'

That is it. Isabel has her cue. It was only a matter of waiting.

But Pat has her own agenda and is already letting rip. 'And Italy!' she cries. 'Of all places! I knew no good would come of ceremonies and such. I knew it!'

'What do you want me to say, Mum?' Isabel sounds harsh, even to herself. 'That I won't go because of all that you have done for me?'

'And what is that supposed to mean?'

Isabel takes a deep breath. 'I know what happened to Dad.'

Her mother does not reply immediately. Then she says, 'He goes off, just walks out of here one day, and I'm left to do my best for you for years. Have you any idea how hard it was for me?'

Or for me, Isabel wants to say, but she does not.

'Mum, just – just . . . tell me one thing. Tell me what you think happened to him.' That is all right, not too accusatory.

Pat smoothes her hair with a fluttering hand. 'I don't know,' she says at last.

'You don't know what happened, or you don't know whether you want to tell me?'

A loaded pause.

'He went to Italy to be with another woman. There. It's said.' Pat crosses her arms defiantly.

'And?' cries Isabel, losing control now. 'And?'

Pat blinks, closing her eyelids a fraction too long. Isabel wants to shake her, shake the truth out of her carefully lipsticked mouth.

Isabel is trembling. 'And you never heard from him again?'

'Well . . . not –'

'Because that's what I've always assumed, Mum. That you knew as little as I did. But that's not true, is it?'

'Isabel, darling – let's not quarrel.'

Isabel shucks off the consoling hand her mother has put on her arm.

'I only did what was best for you,' says Pat.

'No,' says Isabel. 'Best for you. And you haven't answered my question. Did you hear from him after he went?'

It is a long time – they can hear the clock ticking in the sitting room – before Pat says, 'Yes.'

Isabel exhales. 'And you didn't tell me.'

'No.'

'But you knew he had come back to England and you knew some months later that he had died.'

Pat nods. Her eyes have filled but Isabel is sure she is crying for herself.

'Why didn't you tell me? Didn't I have a right to know?'

There is no answer. Perhaps Pat is ashamed. Perhaps she is about to apologise, to plead for Isabel to forgive her for her misjudgement. Her hands hang limp by her sides. Her face no longer looks healthy against the beige of her dress.

'You are doing exactly what your father did,' she counter-punches. 'No matter what I did, it was never enough.'

Isabel feels weak suddenly. She is overwhelmed by the notion that time is not linear after all, but in strata. In one place, like in this house, the episodes of her life and her father's are overlaid in archaeological layers, each one affect-ing the level above and below.

But much more makes sense. Pat's reluctance for either of them to get involved with the naming of the Piazza Wainwright. Her disinclination ever to discuss Tom. Her lack of emotion – eagerness, even – when it came to selling the building firm.

There is something else. Isabel is positive her instinct is

correct. 'But you had heard from him long before that, hadn't you?'

Pat is a strong, capable woman. If she is taken aback she will not show it. Although perhaps there is a hint of panic in the set of her shoulders, a glitter in her eyes. But she squares up even as Isabel thinks this. 'Yes,' she says. 'I did. Maybe I should have told you. In retrospect, that's what I should have done. But as I say, at the time I thought I was doing the right thing.' There is an ugly edge to her voice.

'I'm listening now,' says Isabel.

'We hadn't been getting along. We had a terrible argument that morning, the day he went off. He . . . he was never a good husband. It wasn't easy for me, you know.'

'Did he tell you he was going?'

Pat does not respond.

'Or did you tell him to go?'

Silence stretches, agonisingly.

'And that . . . that would explain' – Isabel is thinking aloud, still controlling herself with false calm – 'I always wondered why the police didn't seem to do more, why the missing persons bureaux were so unhelpful. You didn't even contact them, did you?

'All these questions I've asked myself so many times with hindsight – why didn't we do more at the time? I actually thought it was because you were too upset, it was too hard for you to keep on talking to the authorities, and I was too young, too scared, to do it myself.

'But now . . . this makes sense. I'd always assumed that Dad must have had some money to live on. He must have got something out of the firm. And the accountant would have known about that . . . so there was someone else who knew more than he was letting on.' Isabel is speaking louder and louder. 'More than me – and more than Margaret! What about Margaret? Could you not have thought she might want to know the truth about her only brother?'

Pat lets her rant until she stops, breathless.

'Well, anyway,' says Pat coolly, 'as it turned out I was right to be suspicious – he did have another woman in Italy.'

'It wasn't quite like that.'

'And?' Pat spits. 'Go on. Tell me all about her, this marvellous Italian woman!'

Isabel can hold back no longer. 'Why couldn't you have told me? I was old enough to understand. But you let me go on thinking that he had simply walked away from us without a backward glance!'

'Because I wanted you to hate him as much as I did.'

There, it was said.

Isabel turns on her mother, no longer able to contain herself. 'And now I know why he left! Because you are so devious and such a liar. And you couldn't bear that I might find him and the two of us might have a good relationship. That's it, isn't it! You were jealous!'

Isabel makes a move. She bends over to pick up one of the boxes from the floor, her head swimming.

'Isabel!'

'I find it hard to believe that anyone could act so selfishly – and maliciously!'

'What are you doing? You can't leave, not like this!'

Isabel stands up with the box, fireflies exploding across her vision. She says nothing as she takes it out to her car and returns to collect the other two.

Pat has sunk down on the hall chair, watching her.

'Isabel?'

'Goodbye, Mum. I'll be in touch.'

People hold on to mistaken notions, thinks Isabel, and chief among them is that the way they see things is the only possible way. They are so sure they are right, when in fact it is their own thinking which is askew.

And of course the thought experiment was flawed. But the logical contradiction was there all along. If there has been no contact during life, or no notification of death, then father cannot be alive or dead. If there was no contact. There is the crux, the answer.

Isabel ponders this insight as she drives her car into the garage she is borrowing from a friend. It will stay there, the useless boxes still in the boot, until she is certain she will not need it again.

She is exhausted by the infinity of possibilities before her, the subtleties, the variations of understanding, her own and other people's. She cannot be certain she is right in what she has decided to do; she can only hope she is.

Her Aunt Margaret's house is sprucer than ever outside, but alive inside with mementoes. Margaret, gaudy in a home-knitted emerald-green cardigan and sparkling paste brooch, is in vivid contrast to most Italian widows of her age in their fluttering crow-black.

'You look well, dear,' she says. 'Happy.'

Isabel accepts tea served in a proper thin porcelain cup and saucer, and smiles. 'I am.'

Everything has changed in the months since she was here last. She is happy, about the here and the now. Let there be no qualification of that. She thinks of the burned and unstable landscape where Matteo waits for her; his fierce declarations every night on the telephone begging her to return soon.

'It's love,' she says and the word hangs a little awkwardly between them. This has never been a family used to such discussions over tea and custard creams.

Margaret beams delightedly. 'I'm so glad.' Touchingly, she shoots a glance at a framed picture of her late husband which stands on the sideboard. His photographer-shy gaze seems to hold hers for a moment. 'Will you tell me about him?'

'I met him in Italy. He's involved with the leaning tower.'

They both laugh. Isabel relaxes, thankful that her aunt is the kind of woman who wants to rejoice in the good news before considering the sad.

'I know! It's bizarre. He's nothing like Dad, if that's what you're thinking. It's his job – he's a soil mechanics engineer at the university. How can I describe him? His name's Matteo di Castagno. He's strong, in all senses, and passionate about what he believes in, and clever . . . and gentle and thought-ful. Even though he's an Italian man and when he wants to drink coffee with his friends or play football, that's what he's going to do . . .'

'And handsome?'

'Attractive – *very*.' Isabel can feel her face flushing. 'I've never been with anyone like him. I feel . . . that when I'm with him I've come home. Wherever we are. I feel protected and precious, even if I don't see him for days on end.'

How to find the words to convey how she went to Italy knowing only absence and returned with such fullness?

'He was amazing, really. The way he took on the search for Dad. He wouldn't always discuss what he was doing, just got on with it and never gave up.'

'It's serious, then?'

'It is.'

'I'm so pleased for you. It's wonderful.'

There is a pause before Margaret puts her cup and saucer down and finally asks, holding her back straight in her chair, 'And your dad . . . ?'

When Isabel has finished telling her, Margaret dabs her eyes with a handkerchief. 'Silly beggar,' she says. It is the worst she will allow herself. 'Such a lot of secrets.'

Isabel recognises the judgement for what it is: a lament for all the waste and the hurt.

'There were plenty like him, too,' says Margaret. 'They got back from the war and they just closed the book on it. Never spoke about it, didn't want to think about it. The more I think about it now, the braver they seem: not only the fighting, but the closing down and living with it afterwards. They didn't want to upset people, least of all themselves.'

'But the awfulness didn't go away.'

'Of course it didn't. But you dug in, and got on with it.'

'It's taken until now for the Italians to want to open up about what happened during the last year of the war, the terrible atrocities and destruction,' says Isabel. Then she remembers. 'He never showed Giuliana's family the document, you know, the one you gave me from the biscuit tin. She knew nothing about it till I gave it to her. I think he couldn't bring himself to hurt them with the truth of what happened to the son of the family.'

'He must have thought it was for the best.'

'I'm sure he did,' says Isabel. 'And who's to say he wasn't right?'

A pause.

'Whatever he did, he always thought it through,' says Margaret. 'He had a good heart and he always tried to do the right thing. It's just that, sometimes . . . these men . . .'

'Yes. I understand that now.'

'Once he had made the decision, he couldn't go back on it. But he wouldn't have wanted to do any damage. That's the stupid thing.'

They are no longer talking about the document and the Italian family.

'I know,' says Isabel.

'So you're going back to Italy?'

Isabel nods.

'I couldn't be happier for you, love.' Margaret smiles.

'But you'll come and see us? You'll love him too, I promise. And Giuliana as well. You and she . . . I think you'd like each other.'

'I'd like that. Very much.'

22

I n the cathedral in Volterra Isabel and Matteo light a candle. When they emerge from its echoing cavern the flicker of votive flames is imprinted on their vision like dark flares on the bright day.

Isabel is happy but tired again, unaccountably weary.

Hers is a tiny history, she thinks. Her concerns are small ones now. Beneath her feet, beneath the stones of the road, are shifting layers of history. This land has been inhabited and dug and cultivated and passed over for millennia. It is an ancient place, and she and her tiny history barely touch its surface. She is a skimming stone cutting across its expanse.

But for the first time in decades she feels secure inside herself, no matter how the world turns and shifts around her. Her perspective has altered this summer and new knowledge has brought a kind of calm at last. It is only now, in this blissful release, that she realises how tightly she has been holding herself in check; how fruitlessly she has been striving against herself.

Matteo's hand holding hers is dry and strong. In the shadow of a tall stone wall he pulls her to him. His beautiful angular face seems darker than ever, his lips softer. She closes her eyes as they kiss. She believes now what she had never dared before: this is more than a passionate interlude; he is steadfast and together they are stable.

'I lit a candle every day for you while you were away,' he whispers. 'That one was to say thank you.'

And at last she is beginning to admit to herself in words what her body has known for some weeks. The absence of blood, these last months. The slight feeling of sickness. The sporadic moments of all-consuming tiredness that she has forced herself through, wading through the waves of heaviness and lethargy. Deep inside her a minute speck of the same continuum of history has formed, and it will grow and grow, God willing. It was not too late after all.

She turns to Matteo, squeezing his hand.

'I have something to tell you,' says Isabel. 'I'm going to have a baby.'

The earth is moving again. This time, across the Arno in the south of the city, it is giving up a treasure it has held suspended in sticky alluvium for two millennia. At the San Rossore railway station workmen have been digging the foundations for a new control centre for the renovated high-speed link between Genoa and Rome.

Amid the noise and judder of progress against the clock – an unrealistic deadline set by the rail company, the elasticity of time required for different constructions in different circumstances, the EC directive on working hours permitted – all has fallen silent in one part of the site.

The workmen have happened upon another shift in the

thin surface of the earth: they have found that this was once water: the harbour at Pisa. The first hulking shape eighteen feet down in the umber silt, which halted the excavator's claw, has proved to be the first of many. Beneath and all around there are perfectly preserved timbers, masts and broken hulls, which are uncovered in the following weeks by the tracks on which modern passengers are sent like bullets to their destinations. They are the trading ships of Ancient Rome. And there is a warship. Eight ships have been found, but the archaeologists and academics who have gathered are certain there will be more. The wood is as fresh as the day the ships sank, preserved by the glutinous mud. There are oars as well as masts. There are even remains of the ropes used to tie up the boats in their lagoon harbour. Scholars have rushed to witness the event and are astounded; it is only the design of the boats that gives away their great age, for the wood is as pristine as that of a present-day sailing craft which has been hauled back to the surface.

'The ancient port of Pisa has come to life before our eyes,' marvels the Minister of Culture in *La Stampa*. The Superintendent of Archaeology at Pisa has ventured his opinion that all the ships had fallen victim to a sudden catastrophe such as a flash flood, which overwhelmed them; other factions dismiss this in favour of the theory that all would have suffered different fates at different times. At this time there is only the fact of their discovery, and all else is speculation until a history wrought from science and geography can be agreed for them.

More and more finds are being brought up: amphorae that once contained cherries and plums, chestnuts and walnuts, olives and oil and wine. The jaw of a wild boar with tusks has been salvaged. These must be the smaller vessels that were loaded with goods from larger cargo ships on the open sea and which then made their way up some kind of canal right into the city.

Meanwhile other, more pressing present-day arguments have broken out. The reconstruction of the railway station is being held up, deadlines are being missed, the money men are becoming nervous, other projects are having to be postponed. The builders and engineers are under pressure to resume work on the control centre. The possibility of more historic finds does nothing to sway their bosses in the here and now. San Rossore is needed to funnel through the high-speed link and will also be essential for the tourists who come to marvel at the city's more famous landmarks.

Matteo is certain. 'The engineers will win,' he says. 'Eventually.'

He has been to see it for himself. Matteo has little interest in ships, it is the soil which transfixes his imagination, the way it has moulded itself to the wood and held it safe, safer than any place outside in the air, which would have dried them to dust centuries ago.

He is happier than he has ever been, he tells her.

It is Matteo who is organising the wedding.

It takes place in Petriano in late afternoon. The civil ceremony is conducted in the mayor's office and Isabel emerges married, wearing a filmy cream dress which skims the swell of her stomach, into the Piazza Tom Wainwright surrounded by friends old and new. The party walks to the wedding feast at Le Macchie.

Patricia has not come, but Margaret has. She is talking to Giuliana.

Isabel has left them to their own conversation, two elderly ladies, heads together, on a bench under a canopy of vines. After a decent time, wrapped in happiness, she slips from Matteo's side and wanders over.

'It's the best thing', she says to both of them, a touch nervously, 'that sometimes I can ask, "What was happening in 1985 when I was starting my first job and I wondered what Dad would have thought of that?" – or some other question that occurs to me. And Giuliana can tell me.'

Giuliana considers a minute and takes her cue. 'Let me see, 1985 . . . that was the year I had been asked to do the artwork for a book about a botanist who brought rare Asian specimens back to this country. We went to China! We stayed in Shanghai for a week – the museums and colleges there are extraordinary. It was the most marvellous trip. Tom adored it. While I was working he walked around the city, fascinated and appalled at once by all the new building. And he bought the funniest hat!'

'You see?' Isabel smiles at her aunt.

And so they talk on, filling the gaps.

Giuliana's sisters Maddalena and Natalina have come for the party too. Chic married ladies in their sixties, they are nevertheless in the thick of the excitement. They congratulate Isabel and Matteo heartily, and tell her they have plenty of tales to tell her about her father. Maddalena, especially, sunglasses worn on the top of her head all the better to produce a startling wink, still has plenty of dash.

Matteo's ageing parents embrace her fondly. His brother and sister and their families make the customary jokes about what she is taking on. They have brought Matteo's daughter Luna. In between hugs and shrieks for her father, the little girl has given Isabel a buttercup and a shy damp kiss on the cheek. Formalities over, she and her cousins are running around wildly through the woods and the olive groves with the younger Sarna boys. 'This is as it should be,' says Matteo proudly. Isabel agrees.

Close friends have arrived from England. Isabel has neglected them this year, but they are pleased to be here and know there is nothing to forgive. Isabel introduces them to their hosts Elsa and Bruno, to Fabrizia and Gianni, and of course to Massimo, who is already making a humorous play for one of her former colleagues, an attractive blonde quantity surveyor.

Gianni has brought his latest girlfriend: a sleek, confident career woman with a mobile phone which rings constantly.

'You should settle down . . . !' Annunziata tells him, not caring who hears it. She smiles wickedly. 'The trouble is . . . would *she* want to?'

The mayor Vittorio Rossi is giving Matteo his opinion – highly sentimental – of the local characteristics. Isabel, swollen with happiness, sits in the shade and lets her mind wander a little.

'Creation and destruction have long been able to coexist in this country without contradiction,' intones Vittorio. 'The treasures of the Renaissance have all survived from an age of violence, when the quest for domination set city against city. The people here are the descendants of that fury and that fruitfulness.'

'Sometimes it is war,' says Matteo, 'sometimes it is the force of nature. Look at the earthquakes a while back. But gradually now out of the dust, what was lost is being reclaimed.'

Isabel agrees with a passion. He is right. She has seen, inside the subterranean medieval stables beneath the monastery in nearby Assisi, the shattered face of St Francis staring up from a table, reassembled piece by piece from fragments of plaster blown from Giotto's frescos in the aftershock of the earthquake. Now they are back on the walls.

'The twelve saints had looked down from the upper church for seven hundred years,' goes on Vittorio, 'and in seconds they were sucked into a roaring cloud of debris. But the engineers have restored the fabric of the basilica. They have made it stronger now than it has ever been.'

It is a time of hope and regeneration.

According to a professor of sociology at the university – who is making short work of the festive champagne – the cathedral and the circular baptistry in Pisa are built on a perfect east–west axis, while the tower is aligned twenty-three and a half degrees off the axis, the lean notwithstanding. 'The rays of the sun strike the centre of the tower on the days of winter solstice' he says. 'In midsummer, the bright sunlight floods through a south-facing window of the baptistry on the *festa* of St John the Baptist, who is the patron saint of Pisa. The rays strike the statue of St John which stands at the font with perfect precision. It is quite beautiful.'

Other scholars, of mathematics and computing, have pointed out that the baptistry's four entrances are lined up to face the four points of the compass, he goes on. Now musicologists have joined with the computer experts to map the patterns of the sound waves with its cupola and curved inner walls. There is to be a concert during the solstice in June.

The organisers plan to draw on Renaissance compositions by Vincenzo Galilei, the father of Galileo, which will be given sound and tone by electronic synthesisers.

Tom would have loved this conversation, thinks Isabel. Perhaps part of him is still here.

It was he, after all, who led her to Italy.

She has come to a civilised country where the demands of the outside world stop for three hours in the middle of the day while the earth bakes and the roads dissolve into heat patterns. A place where the past and the present coexist seamlessly.

It is a misty dawn when Isabel climbs the two hundred and ninety-four steps to the top of the Leaning Tower of Pisa. Matteo has finally gained permission for her to accompany him.

They stand at the top for a long time, hardly daring to touch the wrought-iron rail to steady themselves. But Isabel is sanguine about that. For all her professional indoctrination, she has come to believe in the possibility of magic, the Pisan tower and its dance with the dynamics of falling.

Nothing unsettles her; her balance is true. No vertigo tugs at her senses.

To the south and west the horizon is flat. Closer in, as they look out over the intricate roofs from this rare angle, there are distortions of the bridges in the moving water of the Arno. Behind them and away beneath the blue hills the countryside unfolds.

Isabel and Matteo stay until there is a golden light across the landscape of stone carvings and the sculptures of men and beasts are casting their shadows back on to other walls of stone.

The bells are ringing. The curious ting ting of this country's church bells connects across this state of happiness and flux.

The contents of a plain brown envelope

The envelope, which came to be in Isabel Wainwright's possession, contained copies of two documents. It was taken covertly to Petriano in August 1945 but never handed over. The original documents lay undisturbed in a closed military archive for fifty years due to political expediency.

Document 1

Copy of Field Marshal Kesselring's order, 20 June 1944

In my appeal to the Italians I announced that severe measures are to be taken against the partisans. This announcement must not represent an empty threat. It is the duty of all troops and police in my command to adopt the severest measures. Every act of violence committed by partisans must be punished immediately. Reports submitted must also give details of countermeasures taken. Whenever there is evidence of considerable numbers of partisan groups a proportion of the male population of the area will be arrested, and in the event of an act of violence these men will be shot. The population must be informed of this. Should troops etc. be fired at from any village the village will be burned down. Perpetrators or ringleaders will be hanged in public.

[Signed] Kesselring

Document 2

Affidavit

I, Tom Wainwright, a Sergeant in the Corps of Military Police, serving with 78 Section, Special Investigation Branch, Central Mediterranean Forces, with a permanent home address at 56 Meadow Road, Uckfield in the County of Sussex, make oath and say as follows:

1. On 16 August 1945, acting on instructions, I commenced investigations in the area of BARDINE SAN TERENZO, Italy. In the course of my investigations I questioned a large number of Italian civilians and as a result of the statements made by 47 of these civilians, I concluded that between 17 and 27 August 1944, German troops killed 369 Italian civilians, mostly women and children, in reprisal for partisan activities.

2. The area of Bardine San Terenzo is in hilly terrain to the north of Pisa and east of La Spezia. During July and August 1944 there was a considerable amount of partisan activity in the region. The 16 SS Reichsführer Division was deployed to counteract this activity.

3. On 17 August partisans attacked a party of SS troops returning from a requisitioning raid, with the result that

17 German troops were killed and their vehicle set on fire. On the same day in a different part of the region, partisans attacked a German staff car, killing a colonel of the German army and a passenger.

4. In immediate retaliation for these actions, SS troops searched villages in the area, looted houses and killed 24 civilians. Next, 53 men from a nearby SS detention centre were marched to the burned-out German vehicle. These men were then either tied to the remains of the vehicle, or to fence posts nearby, and shot. A total of 49 were killed. Their bodies were not removed.

5. At the same time, civilians in San Terenzo were rounded up by SS troops. These civilians were mainly old men and women and children. The German troops took them to the village of VALLA and shot them indiscriminately. The reprisal continued until 19 August and resulted in 175 persons killed, 104 of whom were women and children.

6. Another more extensive reprisal was planned at the Officers' Club at CARRARA, at a meeting on 23 August attended by 23 SS officers and a Colonel LUDOVICI of the 'MAI MORTE' Bn (Italian). It was agreed that a further reprisal should take place in the area of the APUANIA ALPS and should commence early the next morning. The Italian colonel promised 100 Fascist soldiers to operate with the SS troops.

7. A band of Italian partisans led by Emilio PARINI was captured and executed at VALLA. Partisan PARINI was taken away. He was publicly tortured. Before his death he betrayed the whereabouts of a larger group of his compatriots. This group of at least 40 men, including one

American liaison officer, was hunted down and shot by SS troops.

8. The next morning large numbers of SS and Italian troops entered villages across the region and carried out an organised massacre. They also looted and burned houses and farm buildings. The operation was continued for four days.

9. Between the 17 and 27 August 1944, altogether 369 civilians, chiefly women and children, were massacred. Damage included 454 houses totally destroyed.

arrow books